A Murder of Crows

Books of Aerie II

Jeanette Battista

Also by Jeanette Battista

The Moon Series
Leopard Moon
Jackal Moon
Hyena Moon
Hunter Moon
Fox Hunt (short story)

Long Black Veil

The Demon's Gate Series
The Iron Bells
The Stone Golem
The Demon's Gate

Played

Books of Aerie
An Unkindness of Ravens

A Murder of Crows

ISBN-13: 978-0-9973197-3-6

DEDICATION

To you, the tall one with the hair. Yes, *you..*

CONTENTS

ACKNOWLEDGMENTS

House Aves thanks go to Ian for your invaluable help with poisonous plants, both real and imaginary. I imagine the garden Denevah sits in to look a bit like what you helped to create at Vizcaya.
House Dauricus thanks to my editor, Bev, who polished this manuscript until is was diamond bright. Thanks to my critique readers, especially Tracey whose helpful notes of "I want to kill everyone, they're all horrible people" told me I was on the right track.
House Accipitus thanks go to the readers and fans who continue to support me and to those new readers who will find this book and—hopefully!—enjoy it. An army of readers is a pretty cool thing.
House Corvus thanks go to my family, for putting up with the voices in my head that talk to me at all hours, and to my dear friends who understand when I want to be social and when I don't. I couldn't do this without you all.

CHAPTER ONE

"That was just sad." Benedetto shook his head in mock disappointment.

Denevah muttered a blistering curse under her breath and heaved herself to her feet. The apprentice assassin she'd been fighting backed off, allowing her room to recover. Benedetto sat on the floor, back against the wall, watching to gauge the progress she'd made since beginning her training at House Corvus. He was very vocal with his opinions.

She'd been sparring for over an hour. Her body ached, her clothes heavy with sweat, and her lungs felt like they were ready to leap from her body in protest. Denevah wiped her sleeve across her forehead to mop up some of the sweat there, praying for a real break.

"You're missing opportunities." Benedetto gestured for the trainee to continue. Denevah grimaced in disappointment.

Blowing out a tense breath, Denevah took up her stance once more. She was rubbish at hand-to-hand. She tried not to feel inferior—she'd only been training for less than a season, while all of the others of House Corvus had been training their entire lives. The Crows—the nickname for all those born into Corvus—were Aerie's finest assassins and spies. She couldn't expect her skills to match theirs, but that didn't stop Denevah's inner voice from pricking her at every opportunity.

She'd never expected to wind up here. She'd been born to House Aves—or, more accurately, been adopted into it. Denevah had never known her birth parents; Lord Rodolfi, the man who'd adopted and raised her, had been the most respected alchemist among the Ravens. She was from the House of scholars and knowledge seekers, of magicians and alchemists. When she Matched with a young man from House Dauricus, she'd expected to live out her days there. Denevah had been instructed in the skills needed to be a politico's lady, hosting dinners and parties as the power brokers of the Great Houses vied for supremacy.

Things hadn't turned out as she'd thought.

"If there's any kind of sand or mud, pick it up and throw it in your opponent's eyes," Benedetto instructed, pulling her thoughts back to training.

"That doesn't seem fair," Denevah gasped, jumping back to avoid a leg sweep.

"Neither is the fact that all of this," here he gestured to his body, "magnificence is still unattached. But there we are." Benedetto smirked. "And you're in a fight, not a council meeting with the Doge. Nothing's fair about it. Your job is to win and to survive. To do so, you use every advantage at your disposal. Even cheaty ones."

Denevah frowned, but said nothing. It didn't sit right with her, but she understood Benedetto's point. Crows were assassins, killers available to those willing to pay the high price for their singular expertise. To get their fee, they had to finish the job. The Crows were given a certain amount of respect and more than a hefty dose of suspicion because of their calling. Fairness never entered into their negotiations.

What good did fairness do anyway? Was it fair that she could never touch another living thing skin to skin without killing them in a painful, horrible way? Was it fair that her entire being was a weapon that could go off on anyone, whether she wanted it or not?

She could control herself of course, but she couldn't control every single person in the world. Pietro, the young man who'd stolen a kiss from her at the Match Ball, had taught her that—a lesson that he'd died to teach her.

Fair didn't even factor into it.

Her opponent got too close so she kicked him lightly in the chest in warning. They circled for a few moments before he came at her again, this time going for a grappling hold on her leg. He tried to bring her to the ground. She slipped away, but didn't see the padded knife he flung at her until it hit her in the ribs.

She grunted an expletive and put her hand over the sore area. She'd have a gorgeous bruise there tomorrow. Benedetto gestured for the other Crow to leave and took his place. He'd wrapped his hands in rags so his flesh was completely covered.

"What are you doing?" Denevah asked as she gulped air into her aching lungs. Fresh sweat sheened her body and her legs were trembling with exertion.

She watched Benedetto warily, pushing the stray hairs that had escaped her hood away from her face. Her face was the only part of her left uncovered whenever she left her room. She had to take precautions when she sparred—the gear she wore mitigated the risk of skin on skin contact. Benedetto wore sleeves and wrapped his hands, but those were his only concessions.

Benedetto stood across from her, limbs long and loose. He gave her a cheeky grin. Denevah felt her lips twitch in an answering smile and just barely bit it back. Benedetto was one of the few Crows willing to voluntarily practice with her—or be friendly to her.

"Knitting. What does it look like?"

"But you're fresh. You've just been sitting there watching!"

"Your stamina is shit," Benedetto said, lip curling as he took stock of her red face and heaving chest. The trainee she'd been sparring with snorted his amusement as he took his leave. She wanted to throw something at his head in response.

Denevah stared at Benedetto, unable to find words to express how wrong she thought the situation was. She couldn't beat him, and not just because he was relatively fresh and she'd been working for hours. He had years of experience on her. Then again, as he said before, she couldn't expect fairness in this life. She was a Crow now.

He tsked. "The proper response to a jibe like that is 'So's your mother.' Do I have to teach you everything?"

"I was taught that it was rude to add insult to injury," Denevah replied, checking her own rag and light leather wraps to make sure no flesh peeked through. Finding them acceptable, she glanced up at Benedetto and finished, "It's bad enough she had you for a son."

A blinding grin that split his face. "Oh, that was a good one. You'll learn proper taunting yet, I tell you."

"Are you going to talk or fight?" But inside, she preened a little at his praise.

"Punches and kicks only. Knees are okay too. Got it?" And then he attacked.

Benedetto fought like he talked, light and taunting. He always looked for a way to subvert what she was doing—be it blocking or attacking—into something that worked in his favor. He didn't seem to be holding back, although logically Denevah knew he had to be, otherwise the fight would have been over too quickly to be a useful lesson. He was ridiculously fast; Denevah could barely keep up with him, let alone try to surpass him.

She managed three more rounds before her knee gave out and she couldn't pick herself back up any more. She felt like she'd failed.

Denevah lay flat on her back on the cold stone, trying to soak some of the chill into her overheated skin. Sweat plastered her braid to her neck and the stray hairs that had escaped her hood stuck to the sides of her face. She felt like she'd been dumped in the canal; she could probably wring water out of her clothes. She lifted her head on a neck that shook with the effort so she could look around the room.

It was a mess. Practice dummies lay on the floor, spilling their hay innards everywhere. Pieces of armor littered the room, flung about like toys during a toddler's tantrum. A bench lay on its side. Benedetto sat with his back against a wall, taking slow deep breaths.

"Not bad," he said as she dropped her head back to the stone floor.

She snorted. He gave a wry chuckle and continued. "But you missed a lot of things."

Denevah rolled onto her side, propping her head on her hand so she could watch him. "Such as?"

He pointed at a freestanding rack of weapons. "You could have knocked that over. It would have forced me to get out of its way and impeded my progress. Anything that can make footing more difficult for your opponent is to be used." His golden brown eyes scanned the room. "You missed a few benches to kick in my way. And you could have yanked on that rope," here he pointed to a shelf containing padded training vests and gauntlets, "to release that shelf's contents on my head. You could have flung any of those," he pointed around the room at various objects, "at me. Put me on the defensive, make me keep my distance."

"But I don't want you to keep your distance." Denevah flushed, realizing how that sounded. Benedetto cleared his throat, looking anywhere but at her. "I mean," she began again, "I can't kill someone if I can't touch them somehow. And for that, I need to be close."

"If someone knows what you can do, they aren't going to let you get close," Benedetto countered, stretching one long leg out in front of him and resting his wrists on his upraised knee. "If you're dealing with a larger or more skilled opponent in that situation, you don't want them to close on you anyway. It only takes an instant for them to slide a knife between your ribs or snap your neck."

He stared at her, gaze picking apart every part of her. "You're not complete garbage in hand-to-hand. I think with more training, you'll end up pretty good. But your poisons aren't an active weapon. You have to lure someone in, get them to touch you. It's going to make things hard for you in a straight-up fight."

Denevah swallowed at his comparison, feeling guilt rise like thick tar in the back of her throat. Benedetto's words were too much like what her fath—like what Lord Rodolfi had said to her. The most beautiful flower in a garden full of them, designed to draw all the bees to her. Pretty and deadly. She began to unwrap the rags and leather strips from her hands.

"Lord Trapinze is right," he sniffed, as if it caused him irritation to admit this. "You rely too much on your poisons and that limits you. Yes, you are deadly at close range. Your primary offense is subterfuge. But relying on only one weapon is a good way to get killed. Quickly."

"So how do I deal with the limitations?" The question came out more of a challenge than she'd meant it to.

Benedetto didn't seem to mind. He rubbed at the back of his head thoughtfully. "I know Trapinze mentioned coating your blades. We don't know how effective your poisons are outside of your body and for how long—you might want to check and see."

Denevah went pale, sick to her stomach. "I'm not going to kill things just to take notes on how fast they die."

"You're a Crow now. Time to get comfortable with killing." Benedetto had the grace to look embarrassed when she glared at him. "It was just a suggestion," he added, holding up his hands in surrender.

He began to strip off the rags covering his hands. "We could experiment a little. Blow guns and the like. Arrows. Those give you range and distance attacks you didn't have before. Throwing daggers maybe." He raised a heavy eyebrow. "Any of those sound good to you?"

She shrugged, then flopped down on her back again. Her breathing and heartbeat had returned to normal. The sweat had dried on her skin, but her hair was still soaked and so were her clothes. She felt disgusting. She wanted a bath desperately. At least that was one indulgence allowed her in Trapinze's enormous palazzo: a private bath. None of the others wanted to risk sharing with her, not that she could blame them.

She felt a kick at her booted foot. Denevah glanced up to find Benedetto holding out his gloved hand to her. "Come on, it's not that bad. We'll figure it all out."

She accepted his help, feeling the twinge in her muscles. Her shins and knees would be nothing but bruises tomorrow, her forearms too. She'd done her best to block Benedetto's strikes but stopping or deflecting them didn't mean she got away free. He pulled her up and she groaned.

"Good job today."

Biting her lip to keep from smiling, Denevah studied the floor at her feet. She heard the practice room door open and looked up. Lord Trapinze, the leader of House Corvus and the deadliest of all assassins stood in the doorway, hooded eyes watching them.

"Leaving so soon?" the man asked, his presence casting a pall over the room.

Denevah bit back a groan. She wasn't sure she had enough energy for another round, but she knew better than to say no to the man who held her life in his hands.

Denevah hit the floor hard, and took her time getting back to her feet. She pushed herself up with arms that shook with exhaustion. She could barely climb to her knees. All she wanted to do was sit back down and rest for the next several days. She couldn't feel her feet anymore.

Benedetto backed off, giving her room to stand and recover. Lord Trapinze watched their practice from one end of the room. His face was an impassive mask; he could have been watching a particularly uninteresting dance rather than trained killers from his lack of expression.

"Sloppy," he commented, though he didn't specify to whom he referred.

Benedetto stared at her, waiting. Denevah set her jaw. He usually waited her out, stretching out the moments until she attacked first just for something to do. She vowed she wasn't going to fall for that ploy again. She kept her gaze on his upper chest like Lord Trapinze had instructed. It allowed her to see her opponent's arms and feet all at once.

Denevah didn't have to wait long this time. Benedetto struck first, clearly trying to keep her off balance, forcing her to react. She raised her leg to block his kick with her shin. He followed with a flurry of punches. Denevah threw her body backwards at the waist before snapping forward to launch her own series of punches with the added momentum.

Benedetto skipped backwards, moving out of harm's way easily. Denevah didn't pursue. Instead, she circled him, watching for an opening. He didn't leave her much. A few feints were easily blocked. He moved lazily, as if he could barely be bothered to parry her strikes.

It was really irritating.

Still, Denevah managed to keep her temper. Another lesson courtesy of Lord Trapinze. Her rage had served her well against her father, but it would be a detriment on any other assignment. She shunted her irritation and insult into a blank space at the back of her mind and focused. No emotions. Just the target in front of her.

Benedetto dove at her legs. His arms hit her shins, forcing her to fall forward. Denevah caught herself on her hands, throwing herself into a forward roll. She spun around as soon as she gained her feet.

He grabbed her shoulder. Denevah countered with a hold Trapinze had demonstrated: one hand on his wrist and the other just above his elbow. Benedetto twisted, breaking the hold and tossing her to the ground over his hip. Denevah landed hard, the breath in her lungs all but bursting out of her in a rush.

Denevah kicked out at Benedetto's knee, but he dodged. She was on the ground—he wasn't. He rushed her. Denevah pulled her knees up to her chest, ready to catch his midsection, but he flew over her head in a graceful parabola. His hands hit the floor, pushing him up, and he flipped to his feet.

Denevah scrambled to stand with considerably less grace. "Now you're just showing off," she said disgustedly, folding her arms over her chest.

"That's enough," Lord Trapinze said, leaving his spot against the wall to join them.

"You're getting better, Bella Muerta," Benedetto told her for Trapinze's ears, a smirk on his pleasant, dark face.

Denevah made an acknowledging noise through gritted teeth. Diluvians, she hated that pretentious name. "Nowhere near as good as you, Milord Crow," she managed to tease back, despite the words feeling like ash in her mouth.

"Only because you're hobbled," Benedetto said, sketching her a loose bow. "If you fought with all of your attributes—"

"I'd be down one rather foolish assassin," Lord Trapinze finished. "If she fought bare-armed or handed, one mistake could kill you."

"All she has to do is spit on me, if she really wanted me dead," Benedetto answered, a gleam in his eyes.

Sometimes Denevah suspected Benedetto wanted to test her— to pit his skill against her poison. He had a sort of leashed manic power in him that made her wonder about his stability. He wasn't mad, that wasn't it. Denevah couldn't quite put her finger on it, but Benedetto seemed to enjoy taking things to the edge and then sticking a toe over it just because he could.

"A lady does not spit," Denevah chided. "Although it is awfully tempting when you start tossing me about like a cat toying with a feather."

"I let you down easier that time," he protested.

"Tell that to my tailbone," she returned, rubbing at the bruise.

"Bend over and I will." His dark face split wide in a wicked grin.

"Spitting sounds more appealing by the moment."

"Children." Trapinze interrupted their banter with the tone of a man whose patience was being sorely tested. "That's all for today, Benedetto. Thank you."

The younger assassin bowed to the Lord of House Corvus, threw Denevah another devious grin, and disappeared through the door to parts elsewhere in the palazzo. Denevah watched him go with envy. She still had weapons training and distillation. Learning to be a paid killer turned out to be more complicated than just sticking her knife in people. She was grateful for all of the lessons—it kept the time when she'd have to earn her keep in Corvus away that much longer.

"You're friendly with him," Trapinze observed.

From anyone else, Denevah would have thought such an obvious statement was simply small talk designed to fill an uncomfortable silence. But this was Lord Trapinze—a man who was uncomfortable silence made flesh. He never stated the obvious unless he could gain something by doing so.

He waited for her to say something, to defend the relationship perhaps. But Denevah had learned her lesson quite well with Cyngare. Relationships were for people who didn't kill with a single touch. Denevah didn't have friends; she had a body count.

She pulled off the hood that covered her pale hair and shook out her braid. "He's one of the few here who's willing to train with me," she told him mildly. "I don't want to drive him away."

"A new sparring partner might not be such a bad thing," Trapinze mused. "Offer up a fresh perspective. Shake things up a bit."

She searched his expression for clues on how best to respond. The man was unreadable. Sometimes she wondered if he really was as cunning as everyone supposed or if he let the rumors of him do his work for him and lived off of people's assumptions. And uncharitable way to think of the man who'd accepted her into his

House and offered her his protection, but it helped her maintain her calm. If she really believed he was as shrewd as the stories about him said, she'd be terrified.

"Is there a problem with my training?" she asked, carefully choosing her words. It felt like having a conversation with her father all over again—navigating the pitfalls that suddenly yawned open in front of her at the first hint of a conversational misstep. She did not even want to hint that there might be a reason to be concerned with her or her skills, not when Trapinze and his Crows were the only people keeping her from the grasp of the three other Great Houses calling for her blood.

Of course Aves would want her dead for killing Lord Rodolfi, no matter that he broke every rule they had when he'd created her. House Accipitus howled in outrage for her blood over the accidental death of Pietro, the son of the head of that House. The Hawks, as those in Accipitus were called, were warriors all, and they badly wanted their chance at justice. And the most powerful House in Aerie, House Dauricus, wanted retribution for the death of her Match. Skilled politicians, they brokered the alliances with rival nations, and they made sure the city itself ran, if not smoothly, then with no obvious interruptions. They would not come at her with swords, but she would fall to their machinations all the same.

Trapinze crossed to a rack of sparring swords, their edges and points blunted for practice. "On the contrary, I am pleased with your progress considering your absolute lack of useful fighting skills."

Denevah frowned, unsure whether to take that as compliment or insult. "That's . . . comforting."

A quirk of his lips passed for a smile with no feeling, just there and gone in a blink. "Isn't it just." He busied himself by setting up a series of straw man-shaped targets for knife practice.

"It is easy to become complacent with a talent such as yours. You are deadly, there is no denying that. But your poisons do not work instantaneously. In those few moments you are vulnerable."

He stepped back, eyeing the dummies critically. "A blade between the ribs," he continued, adjusting one of the practice forms, "is just as deadly to you as anyone else, my dear."

He crossed the room and took her chin in his gloved hand. "It would not do to forget that."

Something pricked the cloth beneath her left breast. When she looked down, she saw the glint of a knife's blade pressed against the fabric of her shirt.

Trapinze reversed his hold, passing Denevah the handle of the knife. His blue eyes watched her with all of the warmth of his House's namesake. She managed to keep hold of the throwing dagger, shaking fingers closing around the hilt, stupid in their clumsiness.

He took a few steps behind her. Denevah flinched when his hands dropped to her shoulders, fingers holding her in an iron grip. He leaned in close, breath loud in her ear. "Now, let's see how you've progressed with your other skills."

Denevah waited until his hands fell from her body to take aim at one of the targets. She felt proud when her hand shook only slightly on her first throw.

CHAPTER TWO

Ettoni pushed the journal he'd been reading away in disgust. Going through his former master's notes on how he'd managed to create Denevah's . . . abilities . . . made him want to take a bath in hot lye. He felt like he'd barely scratched the surface of the man's careful planning, even after weeks of research. He was no closer to reversing his master's life's work than when he'd started.

Rodolfi had been a master alchemist without peer in a House full of them. House Aves—the Ravens—specialized in magical and alchemical studies, in potions and knowledge. Ettoni's master had been obsessed with transmuting a woman into a weapon, and finally he'd succeeded. He'd managed to create Bella Muerta.

Now Ettoni labored to unmake what his master had done, but everything he tried failed.

He knew he shouldn't be surprised. Lord Rodolfi had had seventeen years to work on Denevah, plus however many years he'd labored before that. Toni was trying to overturn everything the man had worked toward in a fraction of that time.

It didn't help his guilt that he felt complicit in some of what had been done to Denevah. As Rodolfi's alchemical apprentice, Ettoni had been aware of what the man did to his adopted daughter. He'd even brewed a number of the poisonous supplements Rodolfi slipped her, and he'd mixed the herbal concoctions she took with every meal. He'd hated himself every moment, but that didn't keep him from following his master's instructions.

He'd wanted to tell her. Every moment he'd spent with Denevah, the words sat heavy on his tongue, like crystallized honey that refused to dissolve. But he couldn't push the words out—the spell that bound him as Rodolfi's apprentice ensured he would keep his master's secrets with his silence upon pain of death. Ettoni had only been able to watch and wish things were different.

He turned his gaze to the plants he had brought to his master's—now his—workroom. These weren't from the garden below. These plants were from physiks' gardens throughout Aerie: healing plants and herbs, some with astonishing properties. He didn't need to wear a mask or gloves around these cuttings. It was a welcome change.

A servant knocked at the door, pulling Ettoni from his dark thoughts. "Yes?" he asked the young woman.

"Lady Grimauldi is here to see you, sir," she said, indicating the brightly dressed figure waiting behind her like a less-grim spectre of Death. "She wouldn't wait," the servant whispered.

"Quite all right," Ettoni assured her, waving her off with a smile. He refused to make the girl feel like she'd failed when Grimauldi wouldn't have taken no for an answer. "Thank you. That will be all for today."

Lady Grimauldi waited until the girl disappeared down the winding stairs before entering Ettoni's workroom. He stood. "To what do I owe this honor?" Lady Grimauldi did not come to the palazzos of other Aves; other Aves came to her. He felt his shoulders tense with trepidation at her unexpected visit.

She turned a slow circle, taking in the tables and the burners, the distillations and glassware, the books on shelves and the diagrams on the walls. When she'd finished her perusal, she turned her measuring gaze on him, her dark eyes narrow and thoughtful.

"My Lady?" he prompted, growing uncomfortable with the silence and her intent stare. "Was there something you needed?"

She stepped around Ettoni, walking to the center of the workroom with the presence of one completely comfortable in her own skin and thus in any environment. He could almost imagine her standing before the Diluvians, sporting a bored expression and asking when the entertainment would be starting.

"You were cleared of wrongdoing in the case of your master's death." When she looked at him, he knew she held her own suspicions about what had really happened the night of Lord Rodolfi death, but she kept those suspicions to herself. For now.

It did not put Ettoni at ease.

Instead he said, "I was," even though she hadn't asked a question.

"It was a near thing, you know," she said conversationally, as if his life hadn't hung in the balance as the elders of House Aves determined his future after the events of Rodolfi's experiments came to light. "Most wanted you disciplined quite harshly. The only thing that kept you from being made an example was the apprentice bond you were under." She ran an idle hand along the top of a table. "Although there were several who wanted to overlook that in favor of making an example of you."

"I-I did not know that," he answered, sweat breaking out along his spine beneath his stiff protective clothing.

"Oh yes," she continued, not bothering to look at him, as if he were beneath her notice. "A good number thought that allowing you to continue drawing breath was still too lenient considering what happened on the night of his death. Rodolfi did have a number of supporters, even after it came to light what he'd been up to all of these years."

Now she did turn to Ettoni. "Quite a feat, wasn't it?" She gave him a bright smile.

"Yes," Ettoni said, swallowing down the sour taste of the lie on his tongue. "He was a remarkable man. The loss of his knowledge is a tragedy." That, at least, came close to the truth.

"How close are you to understanding his work?" she asked, stepping so close to him that Ettoni could feel her breath on his cheek.

Holding back a shudder, he answered honestly. "It is going slowly, my Lady. His notes are dense and at times make little sense."

She nodded, but her eyes burned with a strange light. It took all the will he possessed not to back away from the most powerful woman of House Aves. "And the girl? Have you seen her?" The light in her eyes kindled to a blaze at her mention of Denevah.

Ettoni knew he could not speak the truth. Part of the strictures placed on him as punishment for assisting his master—although there was no way he'd have been able to resist Rodolfi's orders due to the magics placed on him as the man's apprentice—were that he have no contact with Denevah. If she tried to see him, he had to inform Aves immediately on pain of death. They wanted her dead for killing her father and for the danger she represented to House Aves and Aerie.

Bella Muerta. They could not risk her existing uncontrolled. If Aves couldn't control her, no one else would be given the chance.

He'd agreed to their rules—Ettoni would have agreed to anything if it meant he could keep working on a cure for Denevah. "I have not had contact with her, no," he answered, praying to whatever gods might hear that she believed him.

Lady Grimauldi smiled, lips pulling taut across even teeth. The expression held no joy, only a fierce hunger. "She is quite unique, is she not?"

"Denevah?" He sniffed, as if he couldn't be bothered to consider her. "I suppose."

"You seemed fond of her at the Match Ball, what with the way you watched after her." The woman's smile deepened, red lips parted and lush.

Ettoni stiffened. Keeping his voice steady took effort, but he did his best. "Lord Rodolfi ordered me to keep an eye on her throughout the festivities," he told her coldly. "There was nothing else between us."

"Of course," she said, lowering her gaze back to the table covered in journals and notes. "I think it quite wasteful to just kill her before we find out how she works," Grimauldi said reprovingly, resting her fingertips on the pages of a book filled with herb lore. "Think of all of things we could learn if she were allowed to live, at least for a little while."

Ettoni took a step closer to her, torn between hope and fear. Was she really willing to deny the will of House Aves just for a look at Denevah? Or was this a test of his loyalty? "My Lady?"

"Should she seek you out, I would be most appreciative if you would tell me before you speak to the others," she said, her gaze spearing him like a pin holding a rare butterfly specimen. "I think I would find some time with your Denevah quite . . . edifying."

Ettoni drew back, feeling sick. Whatever Grimauldi had in mind for Denevah, the girl would not enjoy it. But he had to tread carefully. Aves already mistrusted him after what Rodolfi had done. He couldn't afford to further alienate the powerful people within his House.

"Should she seek me out, I will contact you straightaway," he told her with a strained smile.

"You do that," she said, patting his cheek as she passed by him on her way out of the room. "I have taken up enough of your time. Good evening, Lord Ettoni."

"Always a pleasure, Lady Grimauldi." He inclined his head to her in deference.

"Of course it is," she retorted as she sailed out of the room.

Ettoni followed her at a safe distance, locking the front door of the palazzo once she had boarded her barcariol to make her way down the canal. The lingering scent of her perfume clung to his nostrils as he climbed back up to his workroom, dread a tight ball in his gut. Lady Grimauldi had come to deliver a warning and offer a deal. He wanted neither, but he'd be foolish to ignore them both.

He walked to the workroom window that overlooked the canal and closed it. He wouldn't be able to concentrate on any of his experiments with Grimauldi's conversation still running wild in his brain. Best if he took a break. He sat, idly flipping through a book on restorative plants and their properties, and tried to make sense of the mess he found himself in.

A bell rang above his workroom door. Ettoni pushed himself up from the long table, kicking the stool out of his path, and made his way down the circular staircase to greet his visitor.

Dusk settled over Aerie. The sky glowed with the dying crimsons, virulent oranges, and poisonous yellows of the setting sun while the blues and purples of encroaching night bled down from above. The sunset coated the canals in vivid hues that Ettoni supposed some would find beautiful. He found his beauty in other places.

He stopped by the kitchen to check in with Cook. Her name was Beatrice, but Denevah had always called her Cook and so the name had stuck.

"She's in the garden," Cook told him when he popped his head in. She folded up her apron, setting it aside for the washer woman. Her florid face was a study in grief.

She pointed to a plate of almond cakes dusted in coarse sugar. "She didn't stay for these," Cook said, turning away to hide her face from him. "If you'd bring them with you, I think she'd like them." Those cakes had always been one of Denevah's favorite treats.

"I'll do that," he assured her, taking the plate in one hand. "Thank you, Cook."

She paused in her folding. When she turned to face him, her eyes were sad. "Just see to her," the older woman begged, her voice breaking. "She's hasn't got anybody else."

Ettoni swallowed roughly around the sudden tightness in his throat. "I will," he promised.

He waited until she shut the outer door that led to the canal behind her, shoulders hitched as if expecting a blow. Then he bolted it before making his way to the garden.

Ettoni loathed the garden. It smelled of rot, of sickly-sweet dying things. He'd avoided it as much as possible, only walking its paths when he needed a cutting. The rest of the time, he let it grow wild.

When Rodolfi lived, the garden had always been Denevah's demesne. Ettoni couldn't bear to change that, no matter how much he would have liked to burn the plants to the ground and sow the ashes with salt so that nothing else could grow in that poisoned earth.

He walked the overgrown paths, boots sinking into rich soil. Ettoni could hear her voice—she spoke to the plants. He followed the sound of her hushed tones, navigating by memory as dusk fell to night, the sky lit by a half moon.

She stood with her back to him, and Ettoni felt her presence hit him like a blow to the chest. He allowed himself a moment to collect his thoughts and slow his racing heartbeat, to get used to the physical nearness of her before stepping forward once more.

His gaze traced the slim line of her back. She sat on a bench, spine straight as the shaft of an arrow. She wore her pale hair in a complicated braid wound around her head, the color contrasting starkly with the crow-black clothes she wore. She turned her head and Ettoni caught a glimpse of her profile: high, sharp cheekbones, stubborn chin, angled jaw. Her face held little softness anymore.

But she would always be his Denevah.

Clearing his throat, Ettoni stepped forward. She slewed about on the bench, allowing him to see that she held a serpent lily. It moved beneath her hands, reminding him of a kitten imperiously demanding a pet. Denevah smiled absently, stroking its petals.

"Cook made these for you," he said in lieu of a greeting. He held the plate out to her.

Denevah's gaze dipped down to the contents of the platter, before returning to rest on his face. Her smile vanished.

"I saw them," she said listlessly. "I wasn't hungry." She coaxed the serpent lily back up so that it stood tall on its stalk without her.

Ettoni rubbed his eyes, which had already begun to redden and tear from the garden's array of virulent pollens and perfumes. He set the plate on the bench beside her, but remained on his feet some distance away. He didn't want to crowd Denevah.

For her part, she stared down at her palms. Her eyes were a deep blue, almost purple, the color of twilight. Ettoni swallowed, turning his face to the riotous tangle of plants surrounding him rather than stare at his adopted cousin.

"Did anyone see you?" he asked, not wanting to look at her. It hurt him to ask her that. This palazzo had been her home just as House Aves had been hers before her Match into House Dauricus. All of this should have been hers by right. But after what happened on her Match Night, she belonged nowhere.

The elders of House Aves had ordered her caught. The Ravens were scholars and pursued knowledge relentlessly. Denevah represented an amazing opportunity to learn. It didn't matter to them if she died in agony during the process of their study. Ettoni would not let that happen, House loyalty or no.

"No, I don't think so." A pause, and the sound of shifting on the bench. "I've become quite the prodigy at skulking."

With Houses Aves and Dauricus as enemies, Lord Trapinze's reputation and status as head of the most feared and reviled Great House in Aerie could only protect her from obvious threats. The Great Houses of Aerie tended to dismiss the obvious in favor of subterfuge and ambush. Denevah might be safe in the confines of House Corvus, but as soon as she stepped foot outside of its walls, she was just as vulnerable to an 'accident' as anyone else. She had to be cautious.

His mouth twitched in an aborted smile. He'd missed her humor. The garden fell quiet.

"I heard what Lady Grimauldi said to you."

Ettoni started. "How?"

"I was on the roof above the window. Doing the aforementioned skulking." He heard her shift on the bench. "Are you going to contact her?"

"Of course not," he snapped. "How could you even ask me that?"

She said nothing. The only sound in the garden was the heavy drone of bees and the odd birdsong. Denevah had gone still on her bench.

"How are you feeling?" he asked after a few minutes, just to have something to fill the silence.

Her trill of darkly amused laughter set his teeth on edge. "Like a plague given legs, Toni. How are you?"

He held himself from a flinch at the sarcasm in her tone. She was a far cry from the happy girl he'd grown up with; but that girl hadn't known her power. The girl before him now knew her capabilities. He felt deeply sad and utterly useless.

"I see the Crows have taught you sarcasm as well as murder." The jibe came out before he could stop his angry words.

And he felt angry—very angry. At Denevah, at Lord Rodolfi, at Lord Poullo, at Cyngare, at himself, at the Diluvians who'd refused to undo their magic. He wanted to lash out, to inflict some of the pain he held on someone—anyone—else. Denevah was the only one there.

She didn't even try to fight what she was. She'd given up, deciding to use her innate skills as a weapon rather than searching for any other way to live. Rather than give him time to find and brew an antidote, she'd chosen to use her power to kill people. She didn't trust in him.

In fairness, he hadn't proven particularly trustworthy. He pushed that thought from his mind and waited.

"I learned those from my father, Ettoni. As you well know." Denevah gave him a small, chilly smile. "It is hardly my fault that I am turning out to be such an apt pupil."

Ettoni felt like he might be sick, ready to lean over and spew his supper all over the henbane. "Why do you keep coming back here then?" He gritted his teeth against all the other words he wanted to shout out.

"I have nowhere else," she said simply, head bowed over a bed of wormwood. "This is home for me. Much as I might wish it otherwise." Her gaze captured all of the unspoken words between them. "And sometimes I find that I miss it."

Ettoni clenched his hands into fists at his side. He wouldn't let his emotions ruin one of the rare visits he got with her. "I'm sorry," he said, moving forward until he stood beside her. "I'm not cross with you." He didn't want to argue with her, not like this.

She glanced up at him through pale lashes. Ettoni felt his heart stutter in his chest. "But you are cross," she countered.

"Den, you're a member of the house of assassins. The other Houses are calling for your blood. And I helped make it happen and I can't figure out a way to fix it! Of course I'm cross."

She dug her fingers into the earth of the wormwood bed. Ettoni couldn't tell if she was angry or drawing strength from the plants. He shivered when he thought of her strangely symbiotic relationship to the garden—something he still didn't understand fully. One more mystery Rodolfi had taken with him to his grave.

"It's not your fault," she told him, but Ettoni thought she sounded like she needed to convince herself as much as him.

"Then why didn't you stay?" The words were out before he could stop them, a whisper from the heart.

Logically he knew the reasons why Denevah chose to remain at House Corvus. Trapinze would be her patron for as long as she proved herself of use to him. Houses Dauricus and Accipitus—the Rooks and the Hawks—wanted to execute her in punishment for the deaths of Cyngare and Pietro. House Aves had a standing order to capture her so she could be vivisected to figure out how Rodolfi had managed to create her in the hopes of creating others like her. And this palazzo was her father's, the man who had created her— there were far too many painful memories for her to stay here. Yet it still stung that Denevah would not stay here. With him.

He could protect her . . .

Because you did such a stellar job of that, didn't you? Ettoni's inner voice sounded suspiciously like Lord Rodolfi. He ignored it.

"This isn't where I belong anymore, Toni." She stood, brushing her dirty hands on her dark breeches.

"And a house of murderers is?" There he went again. He couldn't seem to control his mouth.

"When you're the murderer that all of the other murderers fear, yes." Denevah watched him with her sad eyes.

"You can trust me," he whispered, wanting to cross the space between them. Instead he held himself still.

"I know," she said, but her face went blank, like a curtain drawing across a window. "But I'm not letting you throw away your future on me, Toni. You can be a great alchemist for House Aves. My future is fixed. Yours is not."

"Helping you is not thro—"

"Do you need any cuttings?" she asked, cutting him off as she stepped further away from him. "I can do it while I'm here. I know how much the air in this place bothers you."

Ettoni swallowed his sigh of frustration and let the subject drop. His nose had already begun to run and his eyes had nearly swollen into slits. "That would be helpful. A sampling of honey would be good too."

Denevah nodded as he rattled off his list of ingredients from memory. She went to gather the shears and basket and glass jars to collect the items he listed. Ettoni could get the honey and comb himself, but that would mean donning the heavy robes, gloves, and protective headwear to ensure he wasn't stung. Denevah could just walk into the apiary and gather what he needed barehanded. The bees had never bothered her.

Sensing that she wanted to be alone, Ettoni thought it best for him to return to his laboratory. "I have more of your supplements," he told her as he walked away. "Come up before you leave so I can give them to you."

He hurried up the stairs, needing the solitude to clear his head. Seeing Denevah hurt him, reminded him of his failures. Stalking to the bank of shelves along one wall, he rummaged through the precariously stacked books until he found the one he wanted. The leather cover was cracked and weathered with age. The page edges were torn and ragged, the embossed lettering on the cover worn smooth. It read A History of Diluvians in Aerie: A Compendium.

Setting the tome on the worktable, he flipped through the pages. It had been well-thumbed, some of the older pages as thin as onion skin, the ink fading but still legible.

This book collected everything known and observed about the Diluvians, the water dragons that were bound to the fabric of the land. It went back hundreds of years, to the first alchemist of House Aves and had been added to by every alchemist since. The notes held some history, some theory, some fact, and some wild conjecture.

Rodolfi's had been the last entries, his strong hand going on for pages and pages. Ettoni had found the details of his first meeting with the Diluvians years before, his introduction to the mystically bound water dragons that held the safety of Aerie in their powerful coils. He'd read of his former master's dreams of revenge, of his research into poison plants, and eventually how to transmute poisons into flesh and blood. He'd even found the notes detailing the deal made with the Diluvians for their help in creating Denevah's affliction.

And none of it brought him any closer to curing her.

A knock at the open door of the workroom pulled him from his bitter musings. The object of his research stood on the threshold, reluctant to enter. He couldn't blame her; the last time she was here, she'd realized the full scope of her father's betrayal and killed two men. She peered at him now, holding out a basket full of plant clippings and honey jars.

The large pouch of herbs sat beside his elbow where it rested on a work table. It should last her a season. He didn't want to wait that long to see her again, but with the rest of House Aves hunting for signs of her, it wasn't safe for either of them to continue their visits. He knew the palazzo would be watched, if it wasn't already.

After Grimauldi's visit, he couldn't afford to endanger Denevah just because he longed to see her.

"I can pick more when I come again," she said, setting the basket down on the floor just inside the doorway.

Though his heart beat faster in his chest at the thought of seeing her again, Ettoni forced his face to show none of his emotions. He took the bag and walked over to her, keeping on his side of the doorway. Holding it out to her, he said, "That should be enough to last a while."

Denevah looked at him curiously, hefting the weight of it in her hand. Ettoni kept his eyes on the bag clutched in her fist rather than looking at her face.

"Toni?"

He almost couldn't bear the question in her voice, but he hardened his resolve. She would be safer at a distance from him, at least while he worked to find something that could help her.

"Send word and I'll make sure to have more ready when you need it. Perhaps through Benedetto." Ettoni knew the Crow well enough, and while he did not trust him, he thought he could be relied upon to ferry simple herbal remedies back and forth.

"It almost sounds like you're telling me not to come back."

She tried desperately for humor; Ettoni could hear it in her voice. But beneath the surface ran the dark current of her fear, tempered by a glimmer of hope. She'd lost so much, but Denevah refused to believe she'd lose this too.

"I am." He kept his words short and harsh. There could be no mistaking their intent if he wanted her to survive.

He'd expected a fight, like the one they'd had in the garden. She caught him by surprise with her soft, "Oh." Her hand clenched around the neck of the bag of herbs that would allow her to digest food.

Ettoni watched as Denevah busied her hands by tucking the pouch inside of her jacket. He couldn't stand the shuttered emptiness of her expression.

"House Aves wants you dead," he blurted.

"The line forms to the left," she snapped. "Behind Accipitus and Dauricus."

"Denevah, this is serious," he insisted, needing to make her understand. "I've made them believe you'll never come back here, but if they see you, they won't be stopped, and my research will be for nothing." He crossed the threshold of the room, wanting to take her hands in his gloved ones.

She stepped back. "They'll never stop," she told him, eyes downcast. "Not until I'm dead. Or they are."

Taking a deep breath, Denevah squared her shoulders, the black jacket with the sigil of House Corvus stitched on the shoulder pulling tight around the laces. She turned to go.

Ettoni dropped his hands to his sides, defeat welling inside of him. "They might," he breathed.

"Only if I can change the past," she scoffed, not turning around. "Is there a potion for that in fa-Rodolfi's notes, do you think?"

"If I can reverse what he did, it may be enough," he called after her.

A sharp intake of breath. She went still, tension quivering in the lines of her body. Ettoni admired the line of her jaw, the flare of her cheekbone beneath the fine, pale skin, a bit freckled now from time spent unprotected in the sun. The delicate line of her nose and the canted pink lips were as familiar to him as his own face, but as distant and untouchable as the stars wheeling in the sky above. He clenched his fist.

Denevah held herself there, caught between staying and going. "Have you found something?"

Ettoni closed his eyes, needing space to think. Her face shimmered behind his closed eyelids. He nodded once. "I'm not sure it will work for you," he hedged. "But I'm going to try."

A pause. Denevah's chest rose and fell shallowly, as if she feared to breathe too deeply and break the spell of Ettoni's words. "House Aves won't allow it," she whispered, voice strangely choked.

"Aves will not know," Ettoni assured her, putting all of his confidence into his voice.

He stared at the rigid line of her spine clothed in Crow colors. She looked ink-stained and too hard for her years, weighed down by the deaths she'd caused before she knew what she could do.

He would fix what Rodolfi had done to her. For her.

"Let me try," he pleaded.

Her head bobbed, once. Then she stalked down the stairs, away from him, her words floating in the air separating them. "As if I could stop you."

CHAPTER THREE

Savino's eyes blurred. He'd been up early for bladework, followed by meetings and study with his tutors. Now he'd been reading for hours—treatises on political theory, old trade agreements with the Imperium, histories of past Doges and their relationships with Aerie's allies—and his retention of the information suffered. He loved to puzzle out what hadn't been included in the texts just as much as he loved reading what had, but it was past time for a break. He stuck a piece of scrap leather between the pages and shut the book. Resting his arms on the table, Savino pillowed his head on them and closed his eyes. He just wanted to rest for a moment.

The sound of the library door opening and closing again roused him. Savino sat up, rubbing at gritty, tired eyes, to find his mother at the corner of his table, a bemused expression on her face. A tray holding a bowl of soup, half a loaf of bread, a few wedges of different cheeses, and a plate of various fruits sat atop some of his scattered notes. A pitcher of watered wine and a pot of steeping tea were also on it.

Savino poured himself a cup of tea, foregoing the wine. He didn't need to be fuzzy headed or sleepy with everything he still had left to do. He wanted to be well prepared when he went before the Doge's council. "I missed dinner again, did I?" he asked with a rueful smile.

His mother nodded, brushing her hand through his hair fondly. He held still for it, even as his body tensed at the contact. "I had the kitchen prepare you something. You need to remember to eat." She set a letter on the tray, wearing an expression of concern. "This came for you."

Drawing a tired hand down his face, Savino eyed his mother, draped in mourning black for his half-brother Cyngare's death. "How displeased was Father?"

His father wouldn't have ordered a servant to come and fetch his errant son for the meal, nor would he allow his mother to do it either. But he would be angry about Savino's absence at the table, despite the fact that it had been an avoidable offense had he just summoned him.

Savino sighed. He'd grown tired of playing this game with Poullo. At least when Cyngare was alive, the man's attention had been almost exclusively on him. Savino didn't exist, a fact he hadn't minded in the slightest. To have his father's attention was akin to being a bug trapped in a bell jar. And Poullo enjoyed nothing so much as watching his youngest—now only—son flounder and fail.

His mother gave him a bracing look. "He was not pleased," she managed, hesitating before the last word.

Savino could imagine how not pleased his father was. He grabbed the bread and tore himself off a chunk as his stomach grumbled at its emptiness. Around a mouthful, he asked, "Anyone important at table?"

House Dauricus—or the Rooks as they were known—handled the political business of Aerie, usually over polite dinners and state functions. Unlike the Hawks of House Accipitus, the Rooks liked to keep their battles bloodless. They fought with words and ideas rather than swords and spears, but Rooks were no less deadly for it. House Dauricus had controlled the Doge's power and that of his council for generations, and they had no interest in letting that slip away from them now.

Savino knew the likelihood of getting into a row with his father was less if there was no one of consequence at dinner. Cyngare used to handle all of the dinners and social functions anyway, whereas Savino had little practice with it because Poullo hadn't ever wanted him there. As he grew older, Savino took it for the gift his preferred absence actually was. He wanted to be Doge, of course he did—what good member of House Dauricus didn't?—but the political maneuvering it took to get and remain there was exhausting, especially when under constant scrutiny. He preferred to read the policies enacted and bide his time rather than making a run at the spotlight before he was ready.

"Just a few minor players from Accipitus and Aves. No one of any real note." Her heavily lined eyes turned sad. "I wish you'd make more of an effort, Amate," she chided, using the affectionate term from his childhood. "It would mean so much to your father."

Savino bit back on his disbelieving snort, not wanting to upset his mother. He doubted anything he did would matter to Poullo. Dutifully, he said, "Yes, Mother. I'll try."

He finally glanced down at the letter, stiffening when he caught sight of the seal. The sigil of House Accipitus—a hunting hawk in full stoop—stood out in detail in the black wax. His mother's old House, before she'd married Poullo. She still had friends there, which meant he did too. Savino turned the letter over to hide the seal and tried to pay attention to what his mother's words.

The library's door opened again. Savino watched as his mother deflated, sinking deeper into herself, and he knew without looking who had entered.

"Hello, Father," he greeted without turning around.

"Leave us!" Lord Poullo barked at his wife. She threw a worried glance at Savino before hurrying out the door, closing it behind her.

Savino rose to his feet and inclined his head. "I apologize for missing dinner."

His father slashed his hand through the air, cutting through Savino's words. He paced, moving gracefully despite his bulk. He appeared to be arguing with himself. Savino waited, leaning one hip against the table, ready to dodge in case his father threw one of the many small objets d'art that filled the room at him.

Finally the man stopped, breathing heavily. His eyes were red-rimmed and bloodshot, his face flushed. Savino saw the marks of grief on the man—he had lost weight, his complexion bordered on sallow, his clothing more rumpled than the man ever allowed, even if he stayed home. If Savino had been a better son, he would have offered comfort.

If Poullo had been a better father, he would be deserving of it.

"I'm left with you," he said with withering scorn.

Savino raised his eyebrows. "If you'll remember, I didn't ask for any of this." He'd grown well used to his father's dismissive tone.

"If I thought you did, I'd beat you bloody." Poullo rounded on Savino with a near-feral rage.

Savino kept his *but you already have* to himself. No need to antagonize his father past the bounds of reason. There would be time enough for that later.

The storm of Savino's grief for his half-brother had passed, but a hole still gaped inside of him. He and Cyngare hadn't been friends, hadn't even really had the closeness of brothers for years, yet Savino still missed him. On the rare occasions Cyngare had acknowledged him, Savino had felt seen in a way he never experienced with Poullo. It had been hard to let his hopes of a real bond with his brother die, but he'd learned that such a friendship would never be allowed by their father.

As much as he despised Poullo, Savino would never use Cyngare as a means to hurt him. He was not that cruel.

Leaning against the table in a pose designed to appear distant and uncaring, he also blocked Poullo from seeing the letter on the tray. If his father saw who sent it, the hold on his anger would snap. Savino swept his father with an appraising glance. It took everything he had not to glance at the letter sitting in plain view.

"Am I to assume you've come to find me for some reason?" he asked in a bored drawl. "Perhaps to tell me that you plan to play kingmaker with me like you did my brother?"

Poullo struck him backhanded. Savino's teeth bit into the tender inside of his cheek as his head flew to the side. He swallowed the blood as he always did, just as he had learned to swallow his outcry. He took a moment to straighten his head, before grinning wolfishly at his father.

"Not if you were the last man in all of Aerie," Poullo said, so angry he practically spat in Savino's face.

Savino shrugged as if it didn't matter, an insouciant movement designed to irritate his father and keep his attention. Part of him warned this wasn't wise, that he should wait until Poullo calmed to have this discussion, but he set aside those warnings. He wanted— needed—to have this out now, to strip away the lies between them. He could wait, but then he wouldn't be able to manipulate Poullo as easily into making a mistake later. A few bruises were worth it. Diluvians knew he'd suffered worse.

"There's the father I've come to know," he said, mouth pulled up in a lazy smirk.

Lord Poullo glared at him, as if Savino's very presence insulted his sensibilities. "You're not worth half of Cyngare. You never will be. You should have been the one Matched to that witch and rotting from the inside out."

Savino's nostrils flared around his indrawn breath, the only outward sign of his anger. He imagined himself a still pond, rippling outward from the rock that had been thrown into it. The water accepted the intrusion without emotion, the ripples dying away to nothing. He could do that too, accept the rock that was his father and drown the man in his depths.

"Then why are you here?" Savino tilted his head, like a bird inspecting a curious piece of bread before deciding to eat it.

"We'll be throwing our influence behind Matsino for the next Doge." Taking a few steps back, Poullo adjusted his jacket. "I expect you to talk him up at the next dinner we have—which you are required to attend," he said in a tone that warned Savino he should be grateful for the honor.

Savino pushed away from the desk to face his father, keeping his body in front of the tray. He wanted to grab the letter, but feared his gesture would be too noticeable. He stood taller than Lord Poullo, but he kept enough distance between them so the height difference wasn't noticeable. His father hated to be reminded of his short stature, especially by his worthless son. "I'd have to be invited in order to attend," Savino said lightly. "And somehow I never seem to be notified when you're having guests to dinner. Ashamed of me, Father?"

When Poullo set his jaw and refused to answer, Savino continued. "As for supporting Matsino, that is all well and good for *you*. I am afraid I can't, in good conscience, do the same."

Savino watched as his father froze in place, confused, as if he hadn't understood the words coming from his son's mouth. Meaning finally registered and Poullo's face darkened like a thundercloud. In a quiet voice, he asked, "What did you just say?"

"I won't be supporting Matsino for Doge," Savino repeated, just slow enough for insult.

Poullo's hands clenched into fists at his sides. "Why not?"

Savino blinked slowly, waiting a beat. "I think the present Doge will be ruling for quite some time. And because I plan to put myself forward as a candidate for the position."

The silence that followed was charged with violence. Savino held himself very still as his father teetered on the knife's edge of explosive rage. Poullo's face went red, the veins in his neck bulging. Savino longed to step away from his father's anger with every part of his being, but he locked his muscles and forced himself to face it. He could not run from this. He *would not* run from this.

Poullo's meaty hand closed around Savino's throat. Savino held still, gazing back at his father calmly even as the man started to squeeze. "You. Will. Not." He punctuated each word with a shake.

"Matsino is an idiot," Savino rasped out, glaring at his father. "You know that."

"I know that you'll never be Doge!" his father roared in his face.

"Why not?" Savino shouted back, despite the hold Poullo had on his throat. "I'm your son, aren't I? What about me is so repellent to you?"

"You're not him," came the rough answer.

Cyngare. He would never be Cyngare, never be the son of Poullo's beloved first wife, dead all these years. Cyngare had been the only bit of her that remained and now, he too, was gone. Instead, the man had a wife and son he didn't want from a House he didn't respect. Savino's gaze flicked to the letter lying on the tray for a brief moment before sliding back to meet Poullo's. He hoped that his father hadn't noticed the look.

Poullo had. He released his grasp on Savino's throat and reached out for the piece of parchment. Savino reacted. He grabbed his father's thumb and yanked it all the way back. The man howled in pain as his son nearly dislocated the digit just as his hand closed around the letter. It crumpled in his fist.

Savino tore at Poullo's hand, forcing his father to give up the letter. He pried open his father's fist, finger by finger, until he'd freed the letter from his father's grasp. The parchment tore, the seal cracked, but at least it was back in his possession with his father none the wiser to what the letter contained and who sent it.

"That's not for you," Savino warned Poullo, letting him go. He tucked the letter inside the pocket of his jacket. He refrained from rubbing his bruised throat even though it ached. "It's private."

The two men stared at each other in silence for a long moment. Savino could feel the ever-present gulf between them widening further. "Is there nothing you find admirable about me?" he asked his father, cursing inwardly as he did so. He'd stopped offering his father opportunities to hurt him long ago. Why had he weakened now?

Poullo's eyes widened, and for a moment, just a moment, Savino thought his father might give him the kind of answer he been waiting to hear. His breath got caught up in his chest—the simple motions of breathing forgotten as he waited for his father's response.

The jaw tightened. The eyes narrowed. Brows knit together. The generous mouth turned down in a fierce frown.

In those minute expressions, Savino had the answer he'd needed. He tucked away his disappointment where all of the rest of it lived inside of him, and gave his father a hard grin. Poullo's frown deepened.

"Nothing admirable," Poullo asserted, eyes as cold and dead as scorched earth. He gestured to Savino's jacket with his good hand. "Keep your whore's letter." He rubbed his thumb to ease the strained muscles.

Savino wanted so badly to throw the letter in his father's face, but he held himself still. He let the anger wash him clean. "I shall." He stared down at his father, using his height like a hammer.

Poullo gazed up at him, wearing an expression of disbelief. "Are you telling me that you want power?" His father mastered his fury and continued on in a more reasonable manner. He gestured at their surroundings, the books on the walls. "All you've ever shown a talent for is reading. You'd be better placed in House Aves!" He spat the last word like an epithet.

If you wanted that, you should have offered me to them as an orphan tithe. Savino almost wished Poullo had taken advantage of the now-defunct practice the Houses had for dealing with unwanted children generations ago.

Savino laughed. It came out colder than he would have liked, the edge of bitterness to it sharp as a blade's edge. "Of course I want power. I'm your son, much as you might wish to deny it."

Ignoring the look of disgust on his father's face, he turned to the tray of food his mother had brought him, remembering all the times she'd assured him that his father did love him, that all it took was time. His three year old, five year old, and eight year old selves had never understood those words. How long could it take to love your own son? At thirteen he'd stopped waiting. At fifteen he'd stopped needing it. At sixteen, he no longer cared. Now at seventeen, how the man felt about him no longer interested him.

He cut his gaze back to his father, seeing Poullo standing there, finally at a loss for words. He didn't deny what Savino had said. "But I'll be damned if I'll accept it from you as if it was yours alone to bestow on me."

Poullo began to bluster. "I'd like to see you try it without me!"

Savino spun so that he again faced his father, and this time he did step closer, close enough to throw the man in his shadow. "You do not get to dictate terms to me, not anymore. I know what you and Cyngare made me out to be in public, to the other Houses. I am well aware of what you think of my abilities."

His voice was silk-wrapped steel, the soft volume a counterpoint to its hard edge as he continued. "Did you think I did nothing while you took Cyngare around to the High Houses of Aerie? Did you think I'd be happy to wait for you to acknowledge my existence only when you saw fit to?"

Savino shook his head in disbelief. "I made friends and allies of my own, Father. I know how worthless a spare heir becomes when the firstborn takes the place meant for him." He gave Poullo a chilly smile. He'd read all of his father's correspondence, had listened in on endless private conversations, and catalogued the promises made between his father and countless other nobles in Aerie. He wasn't an idiot.

"You think you can dictate terms to me, boy?" his father shouted.

Savino walked to the door, but stopped with his hand on the handle. He twisted around to face his father, a frigid smile on his lips. "I do," he answered pleasantly, happy to have familial loyalty dispensed with. Savino refused to entertain the lie any longer. He'd been expendable until he suddenly wasn't, and he knew it would be that way again. "You want to play at being a kingmaker, then I suggest you bring your best game."

He paused, letting his words sink in before continuing. "Because I certainly will." Then Savino walked out the door, leaving his father alone in the vast, empty library.

A few days passed. Savino avoided his father—business as usual for him—and Poullo did likewise. Savino felt grateful for the solitude, although he did feel bad that he'd inadvertently lied to his mother. He couldn't try to make more of an effort to have a relationship with his father if the man refused to work on it with him. He knew their strained dynamic hurt his mother, but he doubted he'd be able to fix it, even if he bent all of his considerable talents to the task.

In order to make her feel better, Savino made sure to spend as much time with her as his studies and meetings allowed. She was lonely, living in almost cloistered isolation in Poullo's palazzo. He saw it as a very fine gilded cage, but a cage nonetheless. Savino did not know why she didn't go out and meet with some of the wives of other House Dauricus families, or even matrons from one of the other Houses; he assumed Poullo had ordered her not to do so.

She sat reading in her sunroom at the topmost flight of the palazzo when he found her. The midmorning light seeped in like melted butter, gilding the room a burnished gold. His mother rested in an elegant green velvet armchair, a book held loosely in her hand. She was not reading it, but rather stared out the mullioned panes of glass. Her mind must be very far away, thinking of happier times.

"Good morning, Mother," he said as he closed the door to the sunroom behind him.

He carried a bouquet of water roses—he had them delivered to the palazzo every few days to make his mother feel better. Placing these on the table beside the remnants of her breakfast, Savino leaned in to kiss the air beside her cheek

"Amate," she greeted fondly, eyes focusing on his face. She cupped his cheeks in her hands, gazing at him.

Savino held himself still, position hunched over and awkward. There were dark circles under her eyes, stark against the sickly pallor of her face. The dark, high-necked gown she wore didn't help either, the color making her look even paler. She still dressed in mourning for Cyngare.

His half-brother's murder had cast a pall over the entire family. Impotent rage simmered inside Savino's chest at the thought that Cyngare's killer would face no consequences. With Rodolfi dead and Denevah ensconced in House Corvus, only the alchemist's apprentice was left to answer for his master's crimes. He dismissed such unhappy thoughts with effort.

"Are you feeling ill, Maman?" he asked, using his childhood name for her.

"I didn't sleep well," she said, giving him a wan smile. "I will feel much more myself after a rest."

"Do you want me to fetch Father?" Savino kept his voice and expression neutral. He did not wish to upset her further.

"No, my dear." Her hands still rested on his cheeks, her eyes filled with a sad resignation. "Don't bother Poullo on my account."

"Maman?" Savino heard something brittle in her voice, a hitch that hinted at a serious wrongness. "What is it?"

Her hazel eyes sheened over with tears. Savino wanted to pull out of her grip, but managed to arrest his movement through hard effort. Instead, he placed his hands over hers, offering her his wordless support. Worry bubbled inside his chest. His mother was always sunny and blithe, though there had always been a tender sadness rooted through the foundation of her happiness like weeds in a garden.

"You look so much like your father," she whispered, a tear spilling over her lower lash line, a bright jewel against the dusky skin of her cheek. "I am so very proud of what you've become, my Savino. Never doubt my love for you."

He wanted to protest, confused. He didn't look anything like Poullo, neither in build or in aspect. But his mother stared at him expectantly, waiting for his answer. He pushed aside the strangeness to answer.

"I never will, Mother." Dread filled him, the bitter dregs of black wine poured from a poisoned skin. "Is there something you're not telling me? Do you need a physik?" It was the wrong season for marsh fever, but there were other illnesses to worry about this close to water.

"No," his mother said quickly, pulling her hands from his face. "I'm not sick."

She turned her head to glance at the flowers he'd brought. As she did so, the collar of her dress shifted, revealing a dark bruise on the side of her neck. Before he could stop himself, Savino had stepped forward, index finger pulling the fabric farther down so he could get a better look at the mark on his mother's flesh.

Fingers. The imprint of fingers bruised and blackened her soft skin. His mother pushed his hands away with a gasp, eyes sweeping up to meet his. "Did he—?" he began, then trailed off, unable to get the words out.

"No," she said firmly, implacable. "It is nothing."

"Mother," Savino tried again, but she cut him off.

"It is *nothing*." She stood, spine straight, head held high. She met his gaze with a fierceness that startled him. An abiding strength simmered in her eyes, the power of water to wear away the stone. "Understand me, Savino. This is not your business."

He threw his hands up in frustration, in impotence. "You're my mother!"

"And you are my son!" She rarely raised her voice, but she did so now. "And you will abide by my wishes, yes?"

Setting his jaw mulishly, Savino stared at his mother, unwilling to agree to such a thing. "It was Father."

"Will you abide?" She did not shy from him, just stood there with a simple pride. When still he said nothing, she stepped closer. She reached out to grip his chin in her hand. "Savino? I need you to agree."

Something inside of him broke, reformed, and hardened in that instant. He remembered all of the times his mother had done her best to please Poullo, only to have him ignore her efforts. She'd endured his slights, his absence, his coldness, and she'd done it all with a smile on her face. She'd endured his casual cruelty with a patience that seemed limitless.

Seeing her now, he realized the strength it took to do as she had done. His love for her stretched to fill his empty spaces, and he wondered why he deserved her care. He didn't know if he could have done as she had, her quiet endurance well beyond him.

He could only do as she asked. It wasn't much and she deserved all that she bade of him and more.

"I will abide. But only for you, Maman."

Her smile shone like the brilliance of the stars overhead. "Amate," she breathed, releasing his chin.

Savino's face turned serious. "I will abide," he repeated, before adding, "but if he lays a hand on you again . . ."

His mother walked to the mullioned windows to stare down into the canal. The light threw the shadows of the leading in bars across her face. "He will not. I will take care of this." She smiled at him, wistful. "You must trust me."

Savino bowed and took his leave, needing to work out his stymied anger on the dummies in the practice room.

CHAPTER FOUR

Denevah stared at a deck of cards spread across the table in front of her. It was a Futures deck, like the one Malina had used to read her fortune only a few moons ago. The backs of the cards held the sunburst symbol in the center with the four dragons anchoring each corner. Long, spindly fingers shuffled the cards, the painted cardboard making a strange hissing sound against the wood of the table. Denevah couldn't see the person the hands belonged to.

The cards began to move about the table of their own accord. As she watched, Denevah saw a few flip over, revealing their faces. She saw some she recognized from her previous reading—The Flood, The Reaper, and The Fool—followed by cards she had never seen before. She saw The Realm, which had two dragons twined in a figure eight, eating their own tails, and one called Fate, which held an hourglass filled with blood. Denevah didn't like that one, a shudder slithering through her at the sight of it.

More cards turned over, too fast for her to catch them all. Then they all swept themselves neatly back into a stack, coming to rest between the hands that lay flat and white on the table.

Lifting her gaze slowly from the cards to the person who sat opposite her, Denevah peered into the darkness. She could make out a seated figure, but nothing else. Then the person shifted and leaned forward, coming into the circle of light that illuminated the table.

Denevah gasped, drawing away. She stared into her own face. Light hair, purple-blue eyes, the familiar shape of her face, the slightly crooked nose. There were differences, but they were small: the face was much thinner, more starved looking, the lips bloodless, the expression harder, crueler. But it was still her.

"I don't understand," Denevah whispered.

"**I am your future**." The voice sounded like the Diluvians had when Denevah had thrown herself off the Bridge of Heartbreak.

"No." Denevah said it firmly, rejecting what she saw before her.

"**Yesssss**." The s dragged out in a hiss. "**I am what you will become**." Violet eyes glittered with cold amusement.

"The future is not set. I am what I choose to be." Denevah pushed herself up, palms flat and braced against the top of the table as she faced off against this *other* her.

The other laughed, a strange sound caught between a squawk and a hiss. "**You are poison. You are death. And you will always be alone**."

She tried not to tremble at those words, her deepest fear. Denevah had been alone much of her life, but hadn't realized she'd been lonely until recently. Her fear that she would never get to feel another person's bare hand on her flesh, never get to touch another living being was too great an idea to process. It clawed at her insides, a constant gnawing at the back of her mind. She tried to shut it away, but it was always there. How could it not be?

"No," she said in a small voice, a mouse's squeak before a cat's gaping maw.

The other hummed, pale lips tilted up in an icy smile. "**With us you would never be alone again. We would make you whole. You would complete us**."

"What do you mean?" Denevah whispered, unable to look away from her double's night-dark gaze.

"**This**."

The other Denevah lunged forward, fast as a serpent's strike. As she did so, her face morphed, changing into the blue and white scaled and feathered head of a Diluvian. It opened its jaws impossibly wide, its fangs white blades in its mouth. Denevah felt the air of its breath slide across her face. Lifting her arm, she brought it up as a barrier between the Diluvian's sharp teeth and her neck.

Pain exploded into her consciousness, dragging Denevah from her dreams. She came to full waking with a startled cry, as a knife slashed across her forearm. Denevah didn't hesitate as the lessons Lord Trapinze drilled into her for surviving a sneak attack rose automatically to mind. She rolled away from her attacker, sweeping her sliced arm in the man's direction. Droplets of blood flew all around her, but she wasn't concerned. Cutting her had been his fatal mistake.

She gained her feet, eyes searching for the man in her room. He crouched near the head of her bed, a long dagger in his hand. Denevah didn't recognize him though she assumed he had to be a Crow to have made it this far inside House Corvus. None of the other Houses possessed the skills needed to bypass the guards and traps that the Crows used to hide their secrets. Yet he wore no sigil on his black clothes.

Her blood had caught him across one cheek. Garnet drops dripped down the side of his jaw. Otherwise his skin was covered from neck to feet.

He was a dead man who just hadn't fallen down yet. But he would.

She gestured to her face, in the same area where the blood dripped crimson from him. "Got you," she murmured.

Denevah watched him put his gloved fingers to his cheek, smearing red across his skin. He blanched, face going white as he realized what she'd done.

He rushed at her, blade arcing toward her body. Denevah stumbled backwards, flinging her bleeding arm up to block. Trapinze's warnings came back to her. She may have poisoned him, but she still needed to stay alive while it took time to work.

And with this man's skill, that was going to be difficult.

Denevah grabbed whatever she had to hand and flung it at him with all her might. It didn't matter if the object hit him, although she thought it excellent when it did; she had to slow him down so she could keep away from that knife. A wash basin flew through the air, followed by the porcelain water pitcher. He swept the basin to the side, but the pitcher crashed into his chest, shattering upon impact and soaking him down to his waist.

"Oops," Denevah said, already reaching for the next item. She wished she could reach the dagger and sword she kept under her bed, but he stood between them and her.

The man lunged. Denevah flung herself back, the blade nicking her elbow. More of her blood flowed, and the man took a wary step back. She kept moving to her left, where the door waited. She would only have a moment to risk yanking it open, but first she had to make it there. She heaved a small paperweight at his head.

The sound of a cough drew her up short. The man had his free hand pressed to his mouth, his eyes wide and horrified. Denevah hoped this would be enough to end the fight. She watched him nervously.

The man launched himself at her. She managed to catch the wrist of his knife hand in both of hers. They fell to the floor in a graceless tumble, the man landing on top of her. He pressed his advantage, bearing down with all of his strength. Denevah felt the muscles in her shoulders and arms quiver with the strain of keeping that blade out of her body.

His knees were on either side of her waist, so she felt it when the first tremor worked through him. Denevah thought his grip wavered the slightest bit, but the man recovered and bore down harder. She shoved back with all of her strength, bare hands still on his covered wrists. This close, she could see the wildness and desperation in his eyes. He moved his free hand over the hand holding the knife and pushed down.

His desperation gave him a frenzied strength. The knife moved closer to her, bit by bit. Their harsh breathing filled the room. Denevah panted, unable to even scream, only focused on not letting that dagger get any closer to her neck. She gritted her teeth and pushed back with all she had, bare feet scrabbling against the stone floor as she tried to gain some kind of leverage. The slash on her forearm throbbed with pain, but she ignored it as best she could. His weight pressed her into the cold floor, smothering her attempts to get out from under him.

His cough took them both by surprise. Blood sprayed out, hitting Denevah's face. She flinched, closing her eyes, but didn't loosen her grip on the assassin's wrists. More coughing, and more warm wetness splashed her. Denevah pushed back, feeling his resistance slacken as more shudders shook him.

With a heave, she shoved him off. He fell in a heap, too busy coughing up blood to give her much of a fight. He lay on his side, curled up around the pain of his insides. He groaned in between fits, shivers ripping through his body. After wiping away some of the blood from her face with the sleeve of her nightshirt, she plucked the dagger from his weakening grasp.

Denevah dropped onto her bed, knees shaking and weak. She put her hands on her thighs and felt them tremble as she did her best to catch her breath. Her lungs felt bruised and tight, but she knew that it was only a passing feeling. Her gaze kept sliding back to the man on the floor; he convulsed, moans of pain escaping from between gritted teeth. His wet-sounding coughs came less frequently, but a red stain spread beneath his head where it lay against the cold stone.

She couldn't look and she couldn't not. Seeing him this way reminded Denevah of her Match Night with Cyngare. The panic of that night gripped her once more in its claws. Denevah's breath came out in shallow pants, her heart tumbling unmoored in her chest. Sweat broke out all over her body, sliding down her face and back. She felt a hair's breadth away from passing out.

Her hands clenched on her thighs. She felt sick. Hand clamped over her mouth, Denevah closed her eyes as she waited for the man's death. Deprived of sight, her other senses made up for the lack. Her hands felt tacky from the drying blood on them, a heavy stickiness. Her forearm burned, but the blood that still slipped from the cut felt cold on her skin now. The air held the heavy scent of iron, the smell that of slaughter. But worse yet were the sounds she couldn't block out: the faint hitches in the man's breathing, the choked off whimpers of pain. Far too much like Cyngare. She opened her eyes again, panting out panicked breaths through her open mouth.

He fought against the inevitable. Locked jaw and cries held silent behind a dam of teeth didn't stop death. Denevah hung her head, a bone-deep weariness settling inside of her. How many more would die because someone wanted to test her?

"Who sent you?" she asked, opening her eyes. She stood, crossing to the man's side in a stride. Then she knelt down beside him, heedless of her bare legs and billowing shirt. She'd done her worst to him already.

She got a ragged moan in response. Instead, she grabbed his chin, forcing him to look at her face. His chin gleamed, wet with blood. "Who. Sent. You?"

His eyelids fluttered and he coughed again, a dribble of blood sliding down his face. Denevah ignored the unsettled roiling of her stomach and the pangs of her conscience, scowling down at him. "Tell me!"

"I failed," the man gasped out.

A hard hand gripped her arm, right where her wound still bled. Fingers dug into the gash painfully. Gritting her teeth, Denevah yanked her arm free of him, falling on her backside as she did so.

Surprisingly, the dying man followed her up, hatred gleaming in his fevered eyes. "More are coming, Abomination. You won't last through the new moon."

He fell back, a rictus grin on his face, teeth stained red. Heart beating wildly in her chest, Denevah scrambled as far away from the man as she could get. When her back hit the opposite wall, she stilled, watching him until he breathed his last.

It took her several minutes to make herself move. She knew she needed to get someone's help to remove the body, she knew she needed to dress her wound, she knew she needed to report this assassination attempt to Lord Trapinze. But each time she tried to climb to her feet, her body shook so badly she had to sit down again with her arms wrapped around her middle as if she could keep herself from flying apart. She refused to look at the dead man on her floor; instead her gaze roved around the room to the window opposite her bed. The pane had been pushed open just slightly. It had been closed and latched when she'd gone to sleep.

Now that she had something else to focus on, she could get up. Crossing to the casement, Denevah looked closer. The latch hadn't been broken or even lifted out of its hook, it had been cleanly cut through. She opened the windows wide and peered at the wall. She leaned over the sill, feeling around for handholds or holes in the brick that might tell her how he got up to her room. She found nothing.

She knew she should search the body, but she didn't want to go near it. Shrugging off her ruined nightshirt, she wrapped it around her bleeding arm and got dressed. Once in her clothes, she felt armored and better able to face the dark work ahead.

She went straight to Lord Trapinze's room. Rapping loudly at the door, Denevah sagged against the wall to wait.

The door opened almost immediately, surprising her. It was late, well past midnight. She expected the head of House Corvus to have been asleep hours ago. His white shirt lay open at the neck and unlaced at the sleeves and he stood in bare feet, but otherwise he looked as awake as he did at midday. Did the man never rest?

His sharp eyes swept her from head to foot, pausing only briefly at her wrapped and bleeding arm. "What happened?" he asked, words clipped and curt.

Denevah didn't waste time on pleasantries. "Someone attacked me in my room. I killed him, but he's still lying in there. I thought you'd wish to know."

She sounded braver and less affected than she truly was, but Trapinze didn't need to know how much she wished she could throw up, how much she wanted to curl up in a ball and cry. It frightened her how good she'd become at parceling out her feelings, shutting them up behind mental doors because she had neither the time nor desire to deal with them. If she didn't do it, she didn't think she'd survive.

Lord Trapinze's mouth twitched in a barely perceptible frown when she mentioned the attack in his own house, but he said nothing. "Does anyone else know?" he asked.

"No. I came to you first." She crossed her arms over her chest and did her best not to glare at him. She wanted to go back to sleep, but she couldn't go back into that room alone while the body lay in a still heap on her floor.

He glanced at her arm. "You should have that seen to."

"I'll be fine. It's nothing." She refused to let anyone risk skin-to-skin contact with her for the rest of the night.

He frowned, imposing. Denevah fought the urge to swallow like a guilty child. It was late, she was tired and in pain, and all she really wanted was her bed and pillow and a good night's rest.

"Fetch Benedetto," he ordered. "I'll meet you in your room after I've changed." He turned and, not waiting for her reply, disappeared back inside, shutting the door in her face.

Denevah hurried away, until she came to the corridor that led to the main floor of the palazzo. From there she took the stairs up to the second flight, found Benedetto's door easily, and knocked.

And knocked again.

And waited.

Then knocked once more. Louder.

Eventually she heard a muffled groan after her last assault on door. She tried not to switch her weight from foot to foot as she waited. The door opened a crack to reveal one dark, bleary eye, and a sliver of the tall assassin's naked, muscled chest.

"Do you know what time it is?" She suspected the huge yawn was only for effect.

"Should it matter?" Denevah tried to peer around him, hoping to see something embarrassing. "Why? Do you have someone in there with you?"

"Psh," he blew out between pursed lips. "If I had, I wouldn't have answered the door." His eyes raked over her in her hastily thrown together clothes, lingering on her wrapped arm. "Are you offering?"

Denevah gave him a flat stare, his careless words lighting such a fire of longing inside of her she thought she'd be sick from it. "Do you ever think about the words coming out of your mouth before you speak?"

"I try not to," Benedetto said with a shrug. "Keeps life interesting that way." He stretched his arms above his head, shoulders cracking like nuts roasting in a hearth fire. "So since you're obviously not here for my physical charms, what do you want?"

"Lord Trapinze ordered me to get you."

Benedetto's easy manner vanished, tension roosting in his neck and shoulders. "Give me a moment." He closed the door without inviting her inside.

Denevah leaned back, one foot flat against the wall. Benedetto's flirtatious words were simply that and nothing more—he joked like that with everyone—but they still rubbed her raw. What if she had been of the inclination to join him? She would never be able to, and to be reminded of that so offhandedly made her chest throb and ache in response. She pushed thoughts of her kisses with Cyngare out of her mind.

It only took Benedetto a few minutes to dress. When he opened the door, Denevah jumped, not expecting him so quickly. His jacket was unlaced, and she could see the white shirt he wore beneath it. He had a small pack slung across his back, and he gestured for her to lead the way.

"What happened?" he asked her as they walked through the empty halls of the palazzo.

She didn't bother denying anything had happened—there was no other reason for why he'd be roused in the middle of the night. "Someone tried to kill me."

Benedetto looked pointedly at her wrapped arm. "Unsuccessfully," he responded, a statement and not a question. "You know why?"

"No, but he said more would be coming." Denevah felt proud that her voice sounded level and calm. She'd worked hard to stifle her fear.

Lord Trapinze had just arrived when they returned, and they met him in front Denevah's closed door. He was tightly laced into his black jacket and pants, his boots shining even in the dim glow of candles. He had stubble on his chin, the only indication it wasn't daytime. The Lord of Crows alwaysappeared impeccably clean-shaven.

Pushing open the door, she let the two Crows go inside before following after them. She did not look at the body on the floor. Instead, she sat on the edge of her bed, back to it, her wounded arm resting in her lap.

"Let me take a look," Benedetto said, pulling the pack off of his back. He tugged on a pair of thin leather gloves. He knelt down in front of her, placing items on the bed beside her: a small water skin, a pack of needles and thread, alcohol, and a series of salves in small pots. He began with the smaller cuts, treating them gently.

When he finished with those, he carefully unwound the cloth from her arm. The cut was messy, still leaking blood, but the flow of it had slowed. He wiped away what he could with the ruined shirt, then poured out water from the skin over the cut to clean it. Denevah looked away, feeling queasy at the sight of all of her blood. She braced her free hand on the bed, swallowing thickly.

"This is going to sting," he warned, before pouring alcohol over the wound. Denevah hissed in pain, holding herself stiffly and breathing deeply through her nose.

Benedetto peered at the cut. "It's going to need some stitches."

"Of course it is," she sighed, resigned.

She distracted herself by watching Lord Trapinze in his examination of the body as Benedetto made his preparations to sew her up. The man went about searching the dead man carefully but completely, his gaze distant and almost clinical. He turned the failed assassin's chin this way and that, he patted him down to check for hidden pockets, he rolled him over and searched his back. He even pried his bloody mouth open and fished around with this gloved fingers.

"Did you search the body?" he asked in a neutral tone.

"I did a quick once over, yes," Denevah told him, sparing a glance at Benedetto and his work. "I didn't find anything odd."

He made a humming noise, his gaze assessing. Denevah kept her expression open and her gaze on him. She could tell he doubted her, but he had nothing else to press her with and she had nothing to hide.

"Find anything useful?" she asked finally, flinching when Benedetto threaded the needle into her flesh.

"He's one of ours," Trapinze said, sitting back on his heels a thoughtful look on his face.

"Corvus?" Benedetto asked.

Lord Trapinze frowned deeply, as if the thought of one of his own taking a job without his permission rankled. Denevah thought that was the closest she'd ever seen the man come to outright anger. "Yes."

"How can you—OW!—be certain?" The first stitch had gone in. Denevah gritted her teeth, making a sound like an annoyed tea kettle.

She swallowed hard at the look Trapinze leveled at her. "Because I know every Crow in this House," he said, voice frosty with disapproval at her questioning. "He is one of ours." He pointed at the dead man's chest. "He wears no sigil, has no identifying marks, and his weapon," here he hefted the knife so both she and Benedetto could get a closer look, "is of a type we do not use. But I know him."

Denevah hadn't noticed the dagger before, other than to note its sharpness and proximity. Now she took a close look at it and realized that the shape and make of it were most peculiar. She had never seen a blade like that in her life. The curved blade had strange etchings set into the metal. And the hilt and grip were different than the stilettos she'd seen and used.

"But you've seen something like it before?" she asked, wincing as Benedetto tied off the stitches and cut off the extra thread.

"Yes, I have. I've even practiced with a blade similar to it on occasion just to keep my hand in. But it is typically used in the interior of the Ostvian Imperium. I know of perhaps two others beside myself who would be proficient enough with this blade to wield it. He's neither." Trapinze's tone said that he was not mistaken.

"He didn't use it well," Denevah said, doing her best to remember the fight. Everything had happened so fast. She took her time remembering, slowing every movement down in her head. "He was awkward with it."

"Hmmmm," Lord Trapinze unhelpfully offered.

"Could be he thought it would throw everyone off his trail, using a different knife like that," Benedetto said. "We find you dead with a foreign dagger in your chest and he gets away clean."

Denevah opened and closed her mouth, trying to think of something to refute his theory. She couldn't. "That's actually . . . a really good plan."

Benedetto opened a pot of something sweet smelling and held it out to her. "You're going to want to spread some of this over the wound," he told her. "You can see a physik in the morning—well, later in the morning—and he'll clean you up proper. Until then, this will do."

Denevah sniffed the contents of the pot. "It's honey," she said. Benedetto nodded. With a shrug, Denevah dipped her fingers in the jar. The honey felt cool and sticky against her hand. She rubbed it carefully over her injury, and then waited while Benedetto wrapped her arm in a clean cloth bandage.

"Helps prevent infection and keeps the wound clean. Also helps it stay closed. My stitching isn't all that great." He stripped off his gloves and threw them on the heap of dressings and Denevah's ruined shirt.

Trapinze stood and made his way to the window. "He got in through here?" he asked, peering through just as she had done.

"Yes." She nodded at Benedetto in thanks, cradling her sore arm in her other one, keeping it pressed close to her body. Now that the adrenaline rush had faded, all she wanted to do was fall back into her bed and sleep for hours whether the dead man was removed or not. She forced her eyes and mind to focus. She could sleep later.

Sticking his head farther out the window, Lord Trapinze looked up instead of down. Whatever he saw satisfied him. "He came from the roof."

Denevah hadn't thought of that. She'd look out later, after they all had gone to see what she'd missed. "The latch didn't appear to be broken or picked," she told Trapinze as he performed his own examination of the locking mechanism. "It looks almost like something sliced through it."

Benedetto said, "At least we know how he bypassed the guards and traps. He came from inside."

Lord Trapinze took out a cloth from his coat pocket and rubbed something on the outside of the window casing near the latch. Denevah watched his expression as he studied it closely. He nodded to himself, folded the silk cloth, and then turned back to Denevah and Benedetto. "He used some kind of acid solution. It helped shear away the metal latch."

"House Aves makes a concoction that does something similar," she said. Realizing she was jiggling her knee up and down, Denevah tamped down on her nervousness. She wanted to move, to be doing something, or to drop into dreamless sleep. This sitting around did not help her. "Could Aves have hired him?"

"Possibly." Trapinze frowned, clearly bothered by something. "Or someone is paying to make it look as though House Aves is behind the contract on your life. They aren't the only potion makers in the world." He paused, thinking. "Did you notice anything different about him, Denevah?" Trapinze asked her, ignoring Benedetto for the moment.

She thought back. "I had a nightmare and I jerked awake. That's what saved my life—I put my hand up in the dream and I must have done it in real life too. Instead of slashing my throat, he just got my arm." Denevah chewed the inside of her lip, casting her mind back to the fight. "He knew about my, um, skill," she said finally.

"Again, not surprising. He was a Crow."

"He said, 'I failed.' Before he died."

Lord Trapinze's eyes flickered, his expression stony. Denevah shivered with unease.

Benedetto tapped one long finger against his generous lips. "How'd they get him to agree to turn on his own House?" he asked. "All contracts are approved and assigned by you, my Lord."

Trapinze looked murderous for a brief moment before stifling all emotion. "With proper leverage anything is possible," he said calmly, even as his eyes promised painful retribution. "But with Corvus compromised, I want no chances taken. This stays quiet until I can find out who is responsible. Understood?"

They both nodded. Denevah felt dread pooling in her stomach. She was supposed to be safe here.

Denevah began to slump, and then caught herself. She straightened up as Lord Trapinze spoke. "I cannot let this challenge go unanswered. Whoever sent him, they took one of my House to kill one under my protection. A message must be sent."

Silence met his words. Trapinze walked over to the body. "Benedetto get some men to dispose of this. Quietly." He poked at the body with the toe of his immaculate boot.

The other assassin nodded and left. Denevah stared at the master assassin. "You did well," he told her.

"I did?" She raised her injured arm.

"He was a Crow. You're the one still alive. That's doing well." He glanced at the pile of bloody cloth.

She understood his meaning. "I'll dispose of those myself." Anything she bled on, she burned.

"Good." The sound of Benedetto returning with several Crows caused him to step aside.

They got to work, wrapping the body and cleaning up the blood. A stain still marred the stone floor—Denevah vowed to scrub it away in the morning—but the worst was gone, carried through the door in a shroud. Lord Trapinze followed the column of men out of her room, closing the door behind him.

Denevah sat on her bed, back against the wall, gaze shifting between the bloodstained stones on the floor and the broken window casement. Lord Trapinze had not offered a new room, and she knew better than to ask. It wasn't until dawn broke the sky that she fell into a fitful sleep.

CHAPTER FIVE

Benedetto studied the woman who sat in the chair opposite Lord Trapinze's desk. He watched from the murder hole in the wall behind the Lord of House Corvus, listening to the conversation at Trapinze's request. He crouched further, pressing his forehead against the timber struts so that he wouldn't miss anything.

She was older, probably about Benedetto's mother's age—had the woman lived that long. She was a handsome lady, but no great beauty, although her good nature seemed to shine through her otherwise bland appearance, her sweetness making her more attractive somehow. Dark auburn hair fell about her face, grey streaks cutting through the tawny like ribbons of silver. Her face was lined, especially around the eyes and mouth—smile lines, no doubt. Soft of face and of body, the lines of her had rounded with middle-age.

What could a woman like her want with the Crows? Many people passed through these doors, willing to pay for the services of the premiere assassins of the realm. But all of them had been angry or frightened or cold—hurt in some fundamental way. This woman exuded none of that.

Benedetto shook his head, trying to figure out what this woman could want with them. Her dress spoke of money, but anyone who hired the services of House Corvus had that—their skills did not come cheap. He focused on the embroidery on the sleeves of her gown, picking the symbols of her House out of the threads that wound around the silk. He saw the scepter and rook of House Dauricus, but there were other, more subtle symbols among them. A sword, a crown, a hawk. So House Accipitus too? Few people wore the symbols of more than one House.

She shifted at something Trapinze said. Benedetto froze in place, listening to her answer. Her voice rang low and musical. She spoke like someone born to privilege, but she didn't sound dismissive or haughty like some of the other Great House folk did. When she moved Benedetto caught a glimpse of her neck, and of the bruises ringing it.

He settled back on his stool. Ah, so that was why. Her husband acted a heavy handed brute toward his sweet wife, and she'd finally had enough of it. Nothing too surprising then; a lot of wealthy wives arranged for their husbands to shuffle off this mortal coil a bit early when they started misbehaving. Crossing his arms over his chest, he listened closely to what she and Trapinze were discussing.

"My Lady Castiza, surely you can find someone else to entrust with this endeavor," Lord Trapinze said. Benedetto raised his eyebrows in surprise. Lord Crow trying to pass off a job? That wasn't something a man heard about every day, let alone got to witness.

"There is no one else." Lady Castiza spoke low, her words urgent. "My son does not know the enemy he has made in my husband. He needs protecting."

"You'll forgive me," Lord Trapinze's voice sounded indulgent, perhaps a touch condescending, "but protecting isn't something we Crows are known for."

A rustle of silk. Castiza slid forward in her chair, forearm braced against the edge of Trapinze's desk. Her voice changed, grew harder, when next she spoke. "I won't. Forgive you that is."

Benedetto pressed his face against the spy hole. The sweet-faced woman had vanished like a ghost with the morning light. In her place sat someone implacable, immoveable. Here sat a woman who should have been ruling kingdoms, commanding men. Her eyes held no pity or mercy. Again Benedetto had to wonder just who was this woman.

"Castiza," Lord Trapinze said, rising from his seat and blocking Benedetto's view. The lord of assassins shifted and he could see again. "Let's not be hasty."

Benedetto cocked his head. Trapinze sounded like he knew this woman; his voice held a familiarity his assassin rarely heard. The fact that the Lord of Corvus hadn't thrown her out for her boldness in speaking to him like he was a boy to be scolded also spoke to some kind of special relationship.

Castiza drew herself up to her full height—she barely came up to Trapinze's broad shoulder. "Have I ever been a hasty woman?" she asked.

"Once," he answered, but not unfondly.

"And I paid for it," she returned tartly. "But since then?"

"No," Trapinze admitted. Benedetto would swear he heard a smile in the man's voice. "You have been the very portrait of restraint."

Castiza smiled. It lit up her face, crinkled her eyes into happy slits. "Sarcasm is terribly unattractive."

Trapinze actually leaned forward, inserting himself in her space. "Says you."

She laughed, a bright trill, like birdsong. Then she took a step back, interposing distance between them. Benedetto would have given his left arm—well somebody's left arm, he still had use for his—to see what Trapinze's face looked like. He'd never heard his master be so openly relaxed, so. . .flirtatious? Benedetto didn't even think the man knew what that word meant.

"Why don't you just ask me to kill your husband? I'd do it for free."

Benedetto nearly choked. Free? Lord Trapinze, the man who only took the highest paying jobs for himself, was offering his services as an assassin for free? Who *was* this woman?

Castiza sighed, some of the light going out of her face. "If he died now, who do you think would take the blame for it?" She waved her hand as if cutting off some verbal protest from Trapinze. "I know how careful you'd be and I know you'd leave no trace. But he'd still be dead and suspicion would fall on my son."

She shook her head. "No, he must remain blameless. He's going to be Doge one day. I'll not have him sullied by rumors that are not of his own making."

"And if they find out who his father truly is?" Trapinze came out from behind his desk and stood beside her.

Benedetto stiffened. Did Trapinze mean what Benedetto thought he meant? Had the man fathered a child with this woman? Is that who she was?

"I think some in Accipitus already suspect," she murmured, so low that Benedetto had to strain to hear her.

Trapinze took her hand in his. Castiza allowed it, a small smile playing about her full lips. "He could have been ours, you know." Trapinze stared at her fondly. "You would have been a formidable Lady of Corvus."

Okay, so whoever this mystery son was, he wasn't Trapinze's. Benedetto felt an inexplicable surge of relief at that.

Castiza raised her other hand to Trapinze's cheek, her fingers resting against his jaw. Her eyes warmed when she looked at him. Benedetto wondered what it felt like to have someone look at you in that way. How did it happen? And once you had it, how did you manage to survive without seeing it every day?

She looked up at Trapinze sadly. "Would that my father had accepted your Match offer. I would have liked that." Then she smiled, trying to lighten the mood. "It would have saved us all a great deal of trouble."

Trapinze gently took Castiza's hand from his face, bringing her fingers to his lips. He kissed each fingertip before releasing her.

They stood there for a few moments, still holding each other's hand, locked in comfortable silence.

"Will two be enough?" Trapinze asked, letting go of her other hand. "For protection?"

Castiza smoothed out her silk skirts. "If you've trained them, I trust they will be more than adequate." Her polite mask was back when she looked up. "I'll send payment along."

"Don't bother. It's my gift to you." Trapinze settled back behind his desk once more, his own mask firmly in place.

"Nonsense. Payment will be sent," Castiza said in a tone that brooked no arguments. She turned and walked to the door, only stopping once she reached it to face the Lord of Corvus. "Thank you."

"Always," Trapinze returned and in his voice, Benedetto heard the promise that he gave to her.

Castiza nodded, opened the door, and glided out.

Benedetto hurried out of the hidden corridors that honeycombed the palazzo and knocked on his master's office door. When he received permission to enter, he found Lord Trapinze still sitting behind his desk, fingers steepled against his chin, a thoughtful expression on his face.

"Take a seat," Trapinze said, gesturing to the one recently vacated by Castiza. He tapped his steepled index fingers against his lips. "I trust you were paying attention."

Benedetto nodded. He felt awkward at having witnessed something so private, but Trapinze didn't look like he minded. Then again, before today Benedetto would have laid money on the Lord of Crows never having an honest expression if he could help it. He wished Trapinze hadn't asked him to observe the meeting; Benedetto didn't know how to handle this strange and new incarnation of the man. To know that he had a heart, that he cared about someone—it made Trapinze human in a way he'd never been before. Benedetto realized what a huge amount of trust his master offered him by allowing him to witness it.

"So we're protecting people now?" Benedetto asked as he pulled out one of his throwing daggers and began to clean it, needing something to do with his hands. He always had at least three secreted about his body at all times. In addition to his stilettos, darts, garrote wire, poison powder, and his very obvious sheathed sword, of course. He liked to be prepared.

"So it would seem." An amused rumble came from Trapinze as he leaned back in his chair.

"Just two of us?" At Trapinze's nod, Benedetto asked, "Me and who else?"

"I thought this would be a good job for Denevah." Trapinze's gaze caught his and Benedetto felt like a fly trapped in honey, just left waiting for the spider. "I've already sent for her."

Benedetto felt his guts tighten with suspicion. Trapinze was shrewd. If he assigned Denevah to this job, he had a very compelling reason and none of them were likely to be beneficial to the girl. Benedetto grimaced. Just because he'd gotten a glimpse of Trapinze's secret heart didn't make the man any less of a bastard. It just meant the man could compartmentalize very, very well.

"Who's the job?" he asked, already debating if he really wanted to know.

"I'll share everything as soon as she arr—" A knock at his door cut him off. "Come in!" he called.

Denevah let herself in, coming to stand to the right of Benedetto's chair. She stood, straight and easy, the lines of her body already changing under the harsh training regimen she was under. Gone was the soft girl from some moons ago.

"Denevah, thank you for coming so quickly."

Benedetto looked up from cleaning his throwing dagger. As if she had a choice. When Lord Trapinze sent word, you dropped what you were doing to attend to his wishes—a perk of being the man in charge.

Denevah waited, stiff and formal in her tightly laced jacket and black gloves. The jacket's neckline laced up to chin. The whole thing looked remarkably uncomfortable to him, though he knew his fellow assassins appreciated her precautions. Benedetto himself didn't much care. He trusted in her fear of killing another person unintentionally to keep him safe.

"What can I help you with?" Denevah asked, her gaze locked somewhere over Lord Trapinze's shoulder. Benedetto noticed she avoided meeting the man's eyes as much as she could. He wondered what had brought that about. Of course, the Lord of the Crows was a deeply unsettling man to most, with eyes as cold as a stooping hunting bird's. Few people could meet his gaze steadily; most found it easier to just avoid the issue altogether, for fear of winding up on some kill list somewhere. Benedetto always snorted at the thought. The rumors that the Crows accrued enemies like other Houses did baubles or gold were downright laughable sometimes.

The list didn't exist. People simply didn't stay alive long enough after offending Trapinze for him to need one.

"I have accepted a job," Trapinze began. Benedetto thought Denevah went a shade paler at his words. "It's not our usual assignment. I need a two person team to protect someone."

Denevah took a step back in surprise, shaking her head as if she'd heard wrong. "I'm sorry, but did you just say protect someone?"

"Yes."

"But we're—"

"I realize it's a first," Trapinze said, cutting off her protests. "In this case, I made an exception."

Denevah practically vibrated in place with tension. Benedetto glanced between Denevah, who did her best imitation of a piece of statuary, and Trapinze, who looked like the cat who had swallowed all of the cream in the larder.

"Who will we be protecting?" Denevah looked like she might pass out any moment.

Trapinze sighed in a close approximation to concern. Benedetto didn't buy it for a second and neither did Denevah from the way she watched the man. "That's where things become delicate."

Benedetto leaned forward, curious. He'd finally get his questions answered about who Castiza was. Trapinze coughed behind an upraised fist, but Benedetto caught his smile even if Denevah didn't. The sight chilled him.

The Lord of Assassins spoke in the silence. "Your former brother-by-Match."

Denevah reared back, white to the lips. "No." Benedetto barely heard her shocked refusal.

Trapinze was adamant. "Yes."

She shook her head, eyes wide and haunted. "You can't expect me to–"

"I expect you to do as I say." Trapinze's voice held warning and threat.

Plucking at his bottom lip, Benedetto eyed Lord Trapinze thoughtfully. So the woman was House Dauricus—Benedetto had gleaned that much from her clothes. Denevah had been Matched to Cyngare, which meant that his brother and their charge was . . .

"Savino? Lord Poullo's other son? That's who we're guarding?"

Trapinze didn't look at Benedetto, but he nodded in answer. Denevah shook her head, lips still forming silent 'no's' as she took another step back. Benedetto put a hand on her wrist to stop her, feeling her whole body flinch at his touch.

"I don't understand," she managed to whisper finally. Benedetto could feel the tremble of her frame beneath his fingers. He let her go. "How do you think I can protect anybody?"

A good question, and one that Benedetto hadn't thought of himself. But as he watched Lord Trapinze's face, he thought he might understand what the man was thinking in handing out this assignment. Denevah felt incredible, impossible guilt for what she'd done to Cyngare—no matter that she hadn't meant to kill him. Trapinze wanted to use that guilt; she would make an excellent bodyguard for Savino because she wouldn't want anything to happen to him if she could help it. She'd kill herself to protect him as a way of making things right.

It was very neat in its execution. It also made Benedetto a little sick to think of the manipulation behind it.

"Are you certain this is wise? After what happened?" Denevah's hand had clenched so tightly into a fist behind her back, the leather of her gloves creaked. Trapinze couldn't hear it, but Benedetto could.

"My dear," Trapinze began, and Benedetto resisted the sudden urge to flee the room and possibly the entire palazzo. Whenever the Lord of Assassins spoke in that dulcet tone, it meant that something you wouldn't like was going to happen very soon, most likely involving your spleen and a fish fork. "You're the perfect candidate."

Benedetto felt more than a little ill now.

"He's Cyngare's brother. There's no way he'll accept my protection," she argued, words and gaze blunt as practice weapons.

Trapinze's pleasant mask slipped for just an instant, but long enough for Benedetto to catch the barest glimpse of his lord's displeasure at being interrupted. Apprentices had been flogged for far less serious offenses. Denevah courted trouble with the same fervor as a young man vying for his first Match.

Benedetto stood, grabbing her around the upper arm and jerking her to the door. "For that display of insolence, you'll be cleaning the practice room," he growled, shoving her through the door. "His Lordship doesn't have time for your whining."

He bowed to Trapinze, still seated implacably behind his desk, so solid it looked as though the room had taken root around him. Lord Crow inclined his head with a faint smile. Benedetto had no illusions—his master knew what he was up to with the distraction. He could only hope that Trapinze didn't think it worth punishing them both to make a proper example.

"I'll send along instructions with dinner. I suspect the young lady will be quite exhausted after a day spent cleaning the room and its contents."

Benedetto inclined his head in understanding and deference, then hurried after Denevah, who was in the process of marching away in a huff. He easily caught up with her, his long-legged strides eating up the ground separating them. He tried to touch her, to pull her to a halt, but she yanked her arm from his grip, practically spitting at him.

"Will you relax?" he hissed. There were a small number of apprentices in the halls, having been dismissed from their lessons to practice forms or climbing. He didn't want their fight to be overheard. There were too many damned eyes and ears in this House. And Denevah was spoiling for a fight.

"You came insanely close to getting us both horsewhipped, you know that?" Benedetto continued in calmer tones.

"Trapinze wouldn't do something like that. He *needs* me." The insistence in her voice surprised him; he wondered who she hoped to convince with her words—him or herself.

She threw her hood back with a haughty little toss of her head, and Benedetto debated just turning around and telling Trapinze to do whatever he wanted with Denevah's spleen. She'd forfeited it by being a brat. He locked up his irritation. Denevah didn't understand what it meant to be Corvus, what it cost. She only barely understood the rewards that came with it. But ignorance was no longer an option.

"Not alive, he doesn't," Benedetto muttered, loud enough for only her to hear his words.

Her head turned. Denevah's violet eyes were wide in her suddenly too pale face, but otherwise she didn't appear overly shocked by his warning. She licked her dry lips, gaze fluttering over his face and around the room, coming to rest on a low table and chairs. Beckoning him over, she took a seat on one of the low slung chairs, nearly sliding out of it. With a grunt, she caught herself and managed to remain upright in her seat. He bit back a laugh when she looked as offended as a wet cat.

"What do you mean by that?" she murmured.

Benedetto decided it past time to remove some of Denevah's naïve illusions of how much power she actually had before she gambled the little she held away and lost everything. "Right now, you're useful to Lord Crow because he thinks he controls you. All of the other Houses hate you and want you dead. You've got nowhere else to go and no one else to run to." Benedetto saw her gaze shift to the side before coming back to rest on his face. She gave a nod. So she'd had these thoughts as well.

He moved on quickly, not wanting to drag this out. "That means you've got no choice but to stay here and do as he says."

"But," she prompted quietly, waiting for the rest.

"But," he continued, hitting the 't' hard, "the moment you become too much trouble is the moment he starts thinking of a way to be rid of you. He'd rather have no blade at all rather than a sword in the wrong hands." He stared hard at her, hoping she'd heed his warning. "You understand?"

Denevah nodded slowly, clearly mulling over his words. "He needs to think he can control me."

"He needs to think he *does* control you," Benedetto corrected softly. Lowering his voice further, he leaned in close. "Everything about you is poison, right?" When she nodded again, he whispered, "It doesn't take much effort to steal from a corpse. And they're a lot simpler to control." He smiled darkly. "They stay where you put them."

He watched her eyes go wide as understanding dawned. "He wouldn't be able to kill me," she protested in a hoarse voice.

Benedetto pushed up from his chair. "I wouldn't be in a hurry to test that, if I were you."

She stared up at him, fear finally bleeding into her expression. Good. "So if he says he's sending me somewhere . . .,"

"You say 'when do I leave?'"

"And if he orders me to kill someone?"

Benedetto met her frightened gaze with an unflinching one of his own. "You ask in how many pieces he wants them."

CHAPTER SIX

Ettoni settled in the council room of the Doge's palace, doing his best to appear as the self-assured master alchemist he was supposed to be, and not like the utter fraud he knew he was. He had traded in his workroom robes for a black-on-black embroidered jacket with the symbol of House Aves stitched over his heart in silver and gold threads. His pants were tucked into black boots and he had even put on the heavy Master's ring that Rodolfi had left behind. He, like his master before him, only wore it for rare formal occasions. It was the only sign of his rank, but it would be recognized by others in the room.

He had taken a chair well away from the almost-throne at the head of the council chamber, a spot where he could watch the proceedings without being drawn directly into them. He was only here to observe as this was his first time in council. His invitation had come from Lady Grimauldi.

Arriving relatively early, Ettoni enjoyed the opportunity to watch his peers as they entered. The room filled quickly, and he found he recognized most everyone in the room. Lord Trigeste, head of House Accipitus, presented himself in his perfectly polished naval uniform, surrounded by admirals and generals of the military. Lady Grimauldi and others of House Aves, trickled in singly or in intimate groups, most locked in deep discussions. They sat nearby and he lifted his chin in greeting before subsiding back into his chair, eyes seeking out the new arrivals.

He nearly gasped as Lord Trapinze and a contingent from House Corvus strode into the chamber, the grace and power of a stalking tiger carrying him into the midst of the council. He and his group sat uncomfortably close to Trigeste and the rest of his warhawks, but the Accipitus did not seem to mind. He greeted Trapinze, while not with overt warmth, then at least with a generous helping of respect.

Corvus was present and in numbers. From what Ettoni understood, Trapinze rarely attended council meetings; he usually sent a single representative. To see him here, now, made Ettoni very uneasy.

It didn't stop him from searching the faces of everyone in the Corvus contingent, in case one of them might be Denevah. He knew he was being foolish—it was suicide for her to show her face in the Doge's council chambers in the presence of three Houses that wanted her dead—but he couldn't help himself. Any glimpse of her would have been welcome.

A small commotion by the entrance interrupted conversations and then the Dauricus councilors walked into the room. Ettoni saw Lord Poullo at the front of the group, speaking to a thin-faced woman wearing a thoughtful expression. She seemed to be paying careful attention to his words, even as they selected seats closest to the almost-throne where the Doge would sit.

A young man that Ettoni vaguely recognized wearing House Dauricus' sigil came in with them, but veered away to sit with the Accipitus group, in a seat that had been held for him. Ettoni saw Poullo give the young man a furious glare, before going back to his conversation. The young man didn't give Poullo a backward glance.

He knew that young man from somewhere, but Ettoni couldn't place him. He settled back in his chair to wait. Another Aves sat beside him, a man only about ten years older than he. "Lord Ludovic," he greeted with a nod.

"Lord Ettoni." He clasped his hands over his stomach, elbows on the carved armrests of his chair. "First council meeting?" At Ettoni's nod, he smiled slightly. "They really are quite boring. All of the terribly interesting things happen out of the chamber."

"I'm quite happy staying out of those negotiations," Ettoni told the other Aves. He didn't want to be dragged into politics any more than he had to be, not when he already had enough on his mind.

Ludovic glanced down at the ring on Ettoni's hand. "Yes, well, I suppose you have other pursuits to keep you occupied." The thread of censure in his voice made Ettoni's guts knot up. All of Aves knew what Rodolfi had done. Most disapproved.

"I do indeed," he managed to say, casting about for a new subject. He heard a nearby Accipitus whisper the name Navolio and latched onto it with the intensity of a drowning man. "Which means I don't get out very often. What is this I hear about a street preacher with strange Diluvian theories?"

Ludovic leaned toward Ettoni in commiseration, his gaze searching the room before he spoke. "The Doge's patrols haven't been able to catch the man yet. It has Accipitus whispering that perhaps his men aren't up to the task of finding one lone rabble-rouser." His voice lowered further. "Or that it stems from the Dauricus's own incompetence."

"They speak openly against the Doge?" Ettoni whispered back, knowing the answer but wishing to keep the man talking. He remembered Denevah asking about something she'd overheard concerning Navolio during the Match Ball that seemed so long ago.

Ludovic scoffed. "No one is quite that foolish yet, but there are rumblings of disquiet if you listen in the right corners."

"And what do those corners say?"

"That perhaps a change is in order."

Ettoni leaned back in his chair to consider what his fellow Aves had told him. Lord Ludovic opened his mouth to speak again, but a flurry from the back of the room stilled his tongue.

The Doge entered, trailed by his secretary, a priest from Temple Mark, several guards in Dauricus livery, and a few servants who arrayed themselves about the room at his word. The man, a Dauricus by the name of Adriano, had held the position for nearly a dozen years, and seemed in no danger of losing his grip on the office any time soon despite what Ludovico had said. He was a short, slight man, but Ettoni had heard that the mind housed in that body was the Doge's true weapon. Ettoni couldn't help leaning forward to watch.

Sliding into his seat, the Doge held out his hand to his secretary, who placed a scrolled piece of parchment into it. "Gentlemen, ladies, I am going to make this meeting brief and get to the meat of it. We have a growing problem." He raised the scroll clutched in his fist. Ettoni looked around at the others in the room to gauge reaction. Most looked unconcerned or mildly curious. The familiar looking young man had leaned forward slightly, gaze on the parchment. Most everyone else appeared content to wait rather than seem interested. It was gauche to look like you cared.

"You've all heard of this street preacher—Navolio, I believe he's called."

Ettoni watched heads nod around the room. A few people from Accipitus leaned close together to commiserate in whispers. Ettoni glanced at Ludovico, who looked just as surprised as he felt. Apparently no one had expected the Doge to bring up the problem of the street preacher so quickly.

"This man is fomenting rebellion among the common people, dragging them back into the dark ages of mysticism and mummery." The Doge leaned his fists on the table, body canted forward. "He must be found and silenced before he drags the city into chaos."

The priest from Temple Mark stood stiffly behind the Doge's chair, his face set in hard lines. Ettoni wondered how the man felt at having his faith in the Diluvians dismissed as mysticism and superstition. He bit back a smile, imagining the Doge's shock if he came face to face with the Diluvians as Ettoni himself had.

"I'm creating a new position on my council. This posting will specifically deal with hunting down information about this preacher's whereabouts and the councilor will be tasked with bringing him to stand before me in judgment." The Doge's gaze swept the room as if daring anyone to speak.

The silence stretched into something uncomfortable. People fidgeted in their seats; small movements, nothing that would call attention to them, but the room became loud with the slide of cloth over bodies and the minute shifting of furniture.

"I would like to put my name forward for consideration for the position, Your Excellency."

Ettoni turned toward the voice.

It belonged to the young man who had entered with Lord Poullo, the one who now sat with the Hawks. He'd stood, the sigil of House Dauricus gleaming on the chest of his jacket. A murmur filled the chamber as people turned to look at him. The young man possessed an innate grace, a quiet confidence easily overlooked unless he didn't want you to. Ettoni cocked his head, still puzzling over where he'd seen this Dauricus before.

"Absolutely not!" came Lord Poullo's objection.

"It speaks well of your concern for your remaining son, Lord Poullo," the Doge answered, and at his words Ettoni realized who the young man was. He'd seen him at Denevah's Match ceremony to Cyngare, seated with Lord Poullo. He'd only seen him that one time, and Ettoni had tried to forget everything about that day.

He was Cyngare's brother. Savino.

Lord Poullo sucked in a breath at the Doge's subtle dig. Even Ettoni murmured in surprise. He recognized that hidden currents were at play here, a power struggle between several players for control of the board—at least temporarily. Perhaps he should pay more attention to Aerie politics rather than just focusing on House Aves.

Savino spoke up. "My father's concern for me is well known by most everyone in this room." He paused a beat, as though letting his words sink in before continuing. A few titters of laughter punctuated his remark. "And while I appreciate the sentiment, I feel it is my duty to serve the Doge and Aerie in this capacity."

"What makes you more qualified than others?" Lord Trigeste challenged.

Savino inclined his head graciously, as if he'd been expecting such a question. "Part of the problem with catching this street preacher has been an inability to track his movements. This speaks to something more than an unwashed mystic seeking attention for his crackpot theories." Savino began to pace as he warmed to his subject.

"No, this speaks of organization, of planning. The street preacher is not working alone. How else to explain your guards being unable to ferret him out? He's somewhere in the city, yes. But that only means that he has someone helping to hide him."

"Are you implying one of the Houses?" Lady Grimauldi asked, offended.

Turning to her, Savino bowed an apology. "Not at all, my Lady. I am simply saying that there is another player in the game of whom we are not aware. I would make finding out who is helping this Navolio my first priority. Cut off his legs, and the man has nowhere left to run."

"I presume you have a plan for how to go about this?" the Doge asked, head tilted in question.

Savino smiled. "Does that mean I have the position?"

The Hawk sitting beside Savino stood. "I support Lord Savino's nomination." Others from Accipitus and Dauricus noddeed.

An angry noise spilled from his father, but Savino paid it no heed. His gaze stayed on the Doge's face. The Doge regarded the young man thoughtfully. Ettoni found himself leaning forward for a better view of the drama playing out before him.

With a slight smile playing around his lips, the Doge responded, "Yes, Lord Savino, let's see what you can do with the position."

"I will need additional help, if Your Grace will permit," Savino said.

The Doge waved a hand. "Whatever you like. But for all of this, I expect results young man." The threat in his words had not been lost on anyone in the room.

Ettoni realized why no one else had bothered petitioning for the position or fought the young Dauricus for it. No one wanted to take the risk of failure. Even the Doge hadn't been successful at ferreting out where Navolio holed up when he wasn't preaching about rebellion and sea monsters. The odds of success were limited at best and nonexistent at worst. No one in their right mind would take on those odds.

And yet, Savino did.

If he failed, Savino would lose any hope he had of a political future in Aerie. He'd be disgraced. But if he succeeded . . .

He'd be feted throughout the city and be a shoe-in as a nominee for the next Doge. Ettoni's gaze drifted to Lord Poullo. The man glared at his son as Savino took his seat. Poullo's eyes followed Savino with poisonous hatred; he didn't even attempt to hide it. This man would do everything in his power to ensure that his son met only with failure. As Ettoni surveyed the room, he saw a small number of other faces who thought similarly. The young man was practically doomed before he started.

Until Lord Trapinze cleared his throat.

"Your Grace," Trapinze began, "I thought perhaps Corvus could be of assistance to Lord Savino."

"Are you offering your Crows for this endeavor, Lord Trapinze?" The Doge sounded amused.

"It would appear that I am," the man returned, his own voice dry with humor.

Absolute silence. The Crows never offered their assistance in political matters. They were contracted quietly, never publicly, to remove certain impediments to Aerie's continued ascendency. For Trapinze to want to associate so openly spoke of a radical change in behavior. Savino's chances just became even more precarious.

"And I presume you have candidates in mind for this particular endeavor?" The Doge eyed the Lord of the Crows with bright-eyed curiosity.

Trapinze inclined his head sharply. "Yes, Your Grace. I have the perfect candidates at hand for a mission of such delicacy. If Lord Savino approves, of course."

Ettoni sucked in a breath. He couldn't be referring to Denevah, could he? He would not endanger her like that, nor would she agree to work with the brother of the man she'd killed. It was madness! Ettoni clenched his hands around the arms of his chair so tightly his knuckles cracked and tried to calm his racing heart. There were plenty of Crows Lord Trapinze could have in mind for such a project, all far more skilled than Denevah. He concentrated on keeping his breathing even, shunting his worry to the back of his mind.

Savino wore the smallest smile for a moment before it vanished as if it had never been. "Of course, Lord Trapinze. I am happy to accept any help on offer." He sat in his chair, the picture of relaxation, legs crossed at the knee and wrist balanced on the intricately carved armrest. The Rook was the picture of gracious unconcern. Even Lady Grimauldi stared at the young man thoughtfully, mentally reevaluating his power ranking among the Houses.

"Excellent," said the Doge, rapping the tabletop with his knuckles. "Our second order of business deals with a request from the Ostvian Imperium. They'd like to send an emissary to discuss our trade agreements. They would like to renegotiate."

"Who are they proposing to send?" Lady Grimauldi asked.

The Doge tilted his head, the picture of thoughtful introspection. "Their chosen emissary is Prince Abhishek."

"The Asp?" Lady Grimauldi chuckled. "Are we sure negotiation is what they're after and not assassination?"

Laughter echoed around the room. The Doge allowed the amusement to die down before continuing. Ettoni looked to Ludovic who leaned over to explain.

"Abhishek is second in line for the throne of the Imperium, after his brother Ashvaq." Ettoni nodded; he knew that much. "Abhishek is called the Asp because he's been waging a campaign of rumor and slander to discredit his brother, trying to prove that he is unfit for the throne. Ashvaq has the support of the military, but word is that Abhishek has bought the support of the viziers on the royal council."

"Why would he come here then?" Ettoni asked. "It would seem a mistake to leave the country when his brother could easily work to unseat him."

"Unless Abhishek's own plans hinge on something here in Aerie."

Ettoni leaned back in his seat, exhausted by the implications of everything he'd heard. He just wanted to go back to his workroom and deal with poisonous plants. That sounded much less complicated and a good deal safer than navigating the dangerous waters of politics. He was out of his depth in these discussions.

The Doge spoke. "Regardless of the prince's actual motives, he plans to depart in several weeks." He turned to Savino. "You have until then to seek out this preacher's refuge and destroy it utterly. Do you understand, Lord Savino?"

The young Rook met the man's gaze with a steady one of his own. "Perfectly, Your Grace."

Savino inclined his head as the Doge moved on to the next piece of business. Ettoni didn't pay attention, far too interested in the hateful glances Lord Poullo sent his second son. Savino ignored his father, keeping his face a studious blank. The Accipitus he sat with leaned over to say something in his ear. Savino listened and nodded. Ettoni would have given a lot to know what they were saying.

Then Savino raised his head and looked squarely at Ettoni. The alchemist drew back in shock at the anger simmering in the young man's gaze, noticing the way his jaw tightened as if holding in his rage. Ettoni didn't remember him well enough to know if he'd ever done something to offend the Dauricus, but he didn't think he had.

As Ettoni stared, Savino mouthed one word. It took Ettoni a moment to understand, but when he did, fear washed over him.

He'd mouthed *Apprentice*. His eyes spoke of revenge.

Ettoni was going to need to be very careful indeed.

CHAPTER SEVEN

Finding a place to meet with the Crows that comprised his new team turned out to be more difficult than Savino originally anticipated. He refused to meet in his father's palazzo, and meeting in House Corvus was not something he could even consider. There were too many unwelcome eyes and ears in both places for him to feel comfortable speaking of his plans, especially when he knew people wanted him to fail. He'd thought briefly of asking the Doge for a room in his palace to use, but he didn't want the man knowing what he had planned either. Those in power had a way of protecting what was theirs. If Savino successfully tracked down and nullified this street preacher's threat, the power shake-up would be tremendous. He would make enemies.

That wasn't even counting his father who hated him on general principles. Poullo would love to see him fail. The man had already tried to have him removed as leader of this engagement, and Savino had used his contacts in Accipitus—his mother's House— to outmaneuver his father's machinations. His few allies in Aves had been helpful in securing council support, and Poullo's continued campaign to fight Savino's appointment before he'd even begun began to raise eyebrows. His father had been forced to give up. For now. Still, Savino would never trust anything said inside Poullo's palazzo to remain secret.

Savino had come up with a simple solution: he hired a barcariol. It was large enough that they would be able to speak without being overheard by the pilot, and there was no chance of someone being able to spy on them. He sent word that he would pick up the two Crows outside of their palazzo.

When the time for the meeting came, the barcariol pulled smoothly against the front landing at the palazzo of House Corvus. It was a massive structure, nearly a city block long. Most of the other Houses had multiple dwellings for all of their important members; Corvus all stayed in the same building. Savino appreciated the wisdom of this. As the House with the least number of members, it made sense to share the burden of security with each other. No one in their right mind would dare attack a house full of the deadliest assassins in the country, but they might seriously consider sending a force after a lone Crow.

As the pilot pushed his pole against the dock to control the barge and keep it from banging into the pylons, Savino signaled for a servant to retrieve the two Crows. Moments later, they both appeared at the door and made their way to where the boat waited.

He caught sight of Denevah's tell-tale light hair, the end of a bright braid peeking out of her hood. Savino felt his breath catch in his throat. She was here. Denevah terrified him and drew him in equal measure. She'd killed his brother, but he didn't blame her for it. He believed her when she'd told him she hadn't known what she could do, just as he'd believed that her grief over his brother's death was real. That she chose to be with the Crows confused him. She wasn't a killer by choice. She was a study in opposites, a conundrum that he desperately wanted to figure out while knowing at the same time he should stay far, far away from her.

Beside her walked a tall man, a few years older than Savino. He did not wear a hood, so Savino got a good look at him. Dark skin, nearly shorn dark hair, a flashy smile. The man loped along, but the way his gaze always moved reminded Savino of a creature on the hunt. This man was a predator and everyone else was prey.

Savino moved back, allowing them room to board the barcariol. The young man stepped in without hesitation, but Denevah drew up short at the very edge, eyeing Savino cautiously. He waited a heartbeat, then addressed the woman who'd killed his brother.

"Lady Denevah," he greeted coolly. He gestured for her to come aboard.

Her gaze flicked from Savino's face and then back to the door of the palazzo, as if she wanted to run inside and hide. From the corner of his eye, Savino saw the young man gesture impatiently for her to climb in. Savino simply waited for her to make up her own mind. With one last look at the door, she stepped down and moved to stand beside her companion.

He turned his gaze the young man at her side. "And?"

"Benedetto," he answered, snapping a stiff bow at the waist. "We're here to keep you out of trouble." He grinned.

Savino inclined his head to Benedetto, unable to keep from smiling back. The man's good cheer felt infectious. Or maybe it stemmed from the promise of this endeavor, out from his father's ire and the memory of his brother, on his own at last with the world stretched out before him.

He led them to the seats at the front of the boat, signaling the pilot to push off. Gesturing for them to sit, Savino poured them each a goblet of watered wine before settling himself in the seat across from them. He drew the light curtains almost completely closed, so that they would not be easily seen from the banks of the canals. The fabric roof covered them from prying eyes on the bridges.

When he looked back at his companions, Benedetto stared at him, one eyebrow raised in a wordless question. "What?" Savino asked him, then took a small sip of his wine.

"Seems a bit much for a short trip, don't you think?" the Crow asked.

"Where are we going?" Denevah asked in a low voice, refusing to meet Savino's eyes.

"Nowhere." Savino allowed himself a small smile at the surprise on their faces. Leaning forward, he rested his elbows on his knees, rolling the cool metal goblet between his palms. He cast about for where to begin, finally deciding that simple was best. "May I be honest for a moment?"

Benedetto snorted. "A Rook preferring honesty?" He made a show of leaning out to look up. "Just checking to make sure the sky is still blue." He drank deeply. "It is, in case you were wondering."

Grinning, Savino looked down at his boots. He wished he could take exception to Benedetto's words, but the Crow spoke truth. Those that made up the powerful core of House Dauricus loved playing political games that relied on deception and subterfuge. Sometimes Savino wondered how people like his father and the Doge hadn't been strangled by their own insides, so twisted up were they.

"I know that many think—or hope, rather—that this plan of mine fails. I can only assume that unfriendly eyes and ears are everywhere and that no place with four walls will be safe to meet and maintain the secrecy this assignment requires. So we'll be meeting on boats like these when we have need. I trust that I can rely on your discretion that everything said here remains between the three of us." Savino looked at each of them in turn, waiting for their nods.

"It's a smart move," Benedetto said, sharing a glance with Denevah. "But if you're going to be under that much, ah, scrutiny, I think it best that one of us stay with you at all times."

"What?" Savino exploded, and then poked his head out of the curtains to check on the pilot. The man poled the barcariol along the Capitol Canal, unaware of the outburst. He pulled the curtains closed once more and in a lower voice, asked, "As in a bodyguard?" Savino glanced at Denevah who still stared somewhere over his shoulder rather than looking at his face. "Or guards in this case," he amended.

"Makes sense," Benedetto said with a shrug. "If we're supposed to help you with finding this preacher, we might as well go in all the way."

"And it gives you a way to report back to your master on all of my movements," Savino countered sourly.

"Ah, now there's the Rook I was expecting." Benedetto said it with that wide smile of his, but this time it didn't reach his eyes.

Savino frowned, opening his mouth to speak when the Crow held up a hand. "Since you were honest with us, I'll do you the same courtesy. We've got orders to see that nothing happens to you. So we're with you whether you want us to be or not. But it would be much easier if we don't have to deal with you trying to duck out on us all of the time."

Leaning back against the padded seat, Savino set his goblet on the bench beside him. "I'm going to assume you've got other priorities than that of my safety," he said drily, glancing at Denevah. She looked a bit pale, making Savino wonder if Trapinze had told her who exactly she'd be working with.

"Assume whatever you want," Benedetto said in an indifferent sort of way. "But we're with you, like it or not. You can make it easy on us and have the benefit of all of our combined skills or make it difficult and run the risk of getting a knife in the back. Or the front. Possibly the side." Benedetto shrugged again as if to emphasize his point.

Savino rubbed at his eyes, pinching the bridge of his nose. This conversation hadn't taken the turn he'd expected. Putting it aside for the time being, he focused on why they had gathered. Biting back his irritation, Savino said, "All of that can wait until later. We've got a job to do now. What do you two know about Navolio?"

Benedetto opened his mouth, but it was Denevah who answered first. "He kills young girls and throws them in the canals.

Says they're a sacrifice to the Diluvians." Her hands were clenched into tight fists, and her violet eyes were bright with fury.

"He does what now?" Benedetto blurted out, shock and disgust twisting his features.

"How did you find this out?" Savino asked, turning in his seat to look at Denevah. She was just as lovely as the first time he'd seen her at the Match ceremony to his brother, though now that beauty seemed shadowed by something else. Grief? Regret? He couldn't begin to say.

Her gaze locked with his, snapping with anger. "I saw it." She turned to Benedetto. "It was that same day you helped me find a skiff to take me home when I wasn't feeling well." She bit her lip and stared down at her hands.

"That's more than I have," the other Crow said, watching Denevah like she would stab him in the leg. "Far as I know, he's just some crazy guy who talks about the Diluvians coming back while he tries to get people to riot at some undetermined point."

Draping his arm across the top of the seat, Savino tapped his index finger as he considered. "I wasn't aware of the sacrifices," he told Denevah, "but that matches with what information I have."

Savino had been busy in the days before and since the Doge's council meeting. He'd collected everything he could on Navolio's movements from the Doge's guards, informants, and his own forays into the streets. He'd worked hard on separating the wheat from the chaff, on weeding out what was rumor and what truth and what held enough of both to be interesting.

"He hasn't met in the same place twice yet, but he manages to let his followers know when he'll be speaking and where without getting the attention of the Doge's guards."

"In fairness, it's not like that's hard," Benedetto muttered. "Let's just say the Night Watch is not renowned for its intelligence or motivation."

"True," Savino agreed, giving Denevah a surreptitious glance, "but even the Doge's own elite men couldn't track him down."

Benedetto snorted at that one. "They couldn't blend in if their lives depended on it. Of course they came back with nothing."

"Are you planning on interrupting me every time I speak?" Savino snapped, giving the Crow an exasperated look.

"I don't know, are you ever going to say something interesting?" the assassin shot back.

"Navolio always preaches in a public square after an earthquake."

Savino watched, silently gleeful, as Benedetto opened his mouth once, twice, and then kept it shut. A smothered snort came from Denevah's direction, but Savino didn't turn to look at her. Raising an eyebrow, he waited, but the Crow gestured for him to continue.

"Someone must be helping him move around the city and making sure he gets away when the guards get too close. We find out who they are and we can find out where Navolio stays, who he is, and what he's after."

Benedetto nodded his head, absently plucking at his bottom lip. "Think one of the Houses is behind hiding him?" he asked.

"I don't know. I have my doubts though." Savino shook his head. "From everything I've observed, Accipitus is the House most disappointed by and vocal over the Doge's failure to bring this man to heel. But that doesn't equal them being willing to have some mangy peasant running around telling them what to do. The Houses will capitalize on this situation and any weaknesses it might expose, but I doubt they're the ones protecting him."

Benedetto nodded thoughtfully. Pleased, Savino turned to Denevah who quickly looked away. "Denevah? Anything to add?"

She shook her head, stubbornly silent. Savino pressed his lips together, irritation rising. He understood this was difficult for her, but he didn't have the time or energy to coddle her. He signaled to the pilot to turn them around. He'd hoped for better from this meeting.

Marshalling his patience, he outlined his plans to the two Crows. Benedetto added a few suggestions. They lapsed into silence. Savino absently rubbed his knee, feeling the change in the nap of the fabric between his fingers. He needed Benedetto and Denevah's help to get his idea to work, and so far the meeting hadn't filled him with confidence. Savino heard Benedetto speak to Denevah, but she wasn't speaking to him either.

"I may have an idea of where we can meet that doesn't involve a boat," Benedetto offered thoughtfully. "Let me look into it."

They docked. Savino pulled back the curtains, watching as Denevah's gaze swept the streets around the palazzo. He thought he saw her stiffen in her seat. He peered in the same direction, but saw nothing out of the ordinary. People, nobles, and common folk alike bustled along the narrow streets, all of them giving the palazzo of House Corvus a wide berth.

Denevah was the first out of the boat, stepping onto the dock with easy grace. She didn't look back, nor did she wait for Benedetto. House Corvus swallowed her up as if she'd never been.

Savino watched Benedetto watch her leave, noting the way his mouth pressed down in a disapproving line. "She's probably a little uncomfortable around me because she killed my brother on their Match Night," he told the Crow, leaning one hip against the side of the ship.

Benedetto made a choked noise of surprise at his bluntness. Savino smirked. Benedetto passed a hand over his eyes and said, "That could make things awkward."

"I'll take care of it."

Benedetto raised an eyebrow at his confident tone. "I'm hoping you mean that in a conversational way and not in a stabby business kind of way because, boy, will you be in for a surprise."

The noise of the canal traffic drowned out Savino's quiet laughter. "No, I meant that I'll talk to her. I know what she is."

Benedetto turned to him, expression serious. "And what is she?" His voice held a warning.

Savino tilted his head to better study the Crow. Benedetto watched him warily, suspicion in his topaz eyes. "What her father made her," Savino answered. "It remains to be seen if she can become more than that."

Benedetto folded his arms across his chest, eyes noting who came and went on the street. "Fair enough," he acknowledged quietly. After a few moments of silence, he added, "I don't think you were the reason she left so quickly anyway." He lifted his chin to indicate a niche between two buildings that gave a good view of the front door of the palazzo.

Savino glanced over and registered someone dressed in dark clothes standing half-hidden in a nearby doorway. He squinted trying to get a better look at the man watching their boat. Denevah had been looking in that direction when she'd stiffened beside him. Could this man be the reason she left?

The man turned his head and Savino recognized him. Rodolfi's apprentice. Heat filled him, starting in his guts and moving through his legs and down to his feet, circling back up until he felt the flush spread up his shoulders and neck to his face. This man had helped Rodolfi craft Denevah; he'd surely known what she was. He was just as complicit as her father was in Cyngare's death.

"That's Ettoni," Benedetto murmured. "Her adopted cousin."

"Yes," Savino said, mastering the anger inside of him with effort. "I know exactly who he is." Benedetto looked at him strangely but Savino said nothing more.

CHAPTER EIGHT

"Where are we going?" Denevah asked him for what must have been the fourth time in nearly as many minutes.

Benedetto sighed, but didn't answer her. They were on the rooftops. Dusk fell over the city like a waterfall. His pack bumped against his back as he jumped across the edge of one roof to another, mindful of his footing in the fading light. Denevah followed him, landed clumsily, and staggered a few steps before righting herself once more.

"We need to work on that," he told her, grabbing her by her pack to help her regain her footing.

"You aren't going to answer my question?" Her lungs worked like a bellows, her breathing raspy.

"We're almost there," Benedetto said, setting off again, but at a slower pace. "You need to get over whatever it is with Savino."

Denevah went still. It was only for a moment, a brief stutter in her steps, her whole body locking up. Then she shook the shock of his words off, like a duck shedding water, and continued on as if he hadn't spoken.

"I'm serious, Denevah."

"I'm fine, Benedetto." She mocked him by mimicking his tone.

The Crow pulled her to a stop. "You're not fine." When she opened her mouth to protest, he stopped her by talking over her. "And it's fine that you're not fine. But you can't be not fine when we have a job to do. Fair enough? We can't do the job if you refuse to look at the man we're supposed to be protecting."

"I know," she said, staring down at the top of her boots. "It's just," she lifted her hands, and then dropped them in frustration.

"That he's your dead Match's brother? Yeah, I imagine that makes things difficult."

He smirked when she gaped at him. Benedetto was a 'yank the arrow out quickly' kind of person; he didn't believe in wasting time making things sound better than they were. Lying was only used on those who couldn't bear the truth. He knew that Denevah, despite her own insecurities, could handle it.

"That was simple," she said when she'd found her voice.

"I'm not babying you," he warned. "You're a Crow now. You logged your first kill as one. Play time is over."

Her throat worked on a swallow as she turned her face away from him for a moment. Benedetto imagined that this wasn't where Denevah saw herself ending up when she went to the Match Ball all those moons past. He wanted to feel pity for her, but it wasn't in him. He too hadn't always been a Crow, but being one had opened up paths he never would have been allowed to walk in his old life.

He'd come to the Crows at eight or nine springs old, though he didn't remember most of those first weeks. His mother had died, he didn't know who or where his father was. He'd spent days alone with his mother's body slowly going to rot on her bed before any of the neighbors had noticed their absence. His friend Luc had been the one who'd knocked, noticed the smell—worse than what wafted from the canal—and brought help. He'd been orphan tithed to the Crows since that day.

Denevah leaned forward, squinting. "Is that one of ours?" she asked, pointing to a figure moving over the rooftops several blocks away.

Benedetto peered at where she indicated. They were too far away and the light too dim to determine much about the person traversing the rooftops; all he could tell for sure was that the person moved quickly and easily over the uneven terrain. He stared for a few more minutes before replying.

"I don't think so." They weren't wearing Crow black, that much he could see. "Maybe a thief scouting out a job." Benedetto chewed on his lower lip thoughtfully. The roofs weren't solely the path of the assassin, but Crows held right of way just by reputation.

Denevah kept her eyes on the retreating would-be thief as she asked, "What should I do about Savino then?"

Benedetto leaned against a low wall of crumbling brick. He had a feeling he was in for a long conversation. "Maybe it's time you accept who you are. And what you can do."

He drummed his fingers against the rough surface of the wall as he waited for her reply. She stared down at her gloved hands, expression lost. "I don't know who I am," she whispered. "This wasn't who I was supposed to be."

"Do you want to live?" Benedetto kept his voice soft, but he put steel in his tone. She'd just flung herself off the Bridge of Heartbreak when he'd fished her out of the canal and brought her to Corvus. She'd told him she'd meant to drown herself, but for someone who claimed they wanted to die, Denevah spent a lot of time figuring out how to survive.

She turned to him, eyes wide with shock and confusion. Shaking his head, Benedetto said, "It's a simple question." When she didn't answer right away, he told her, "I think you do. I think that if you wanted to die, you would have let that man in your room kill you. I think you would have found a way to do it yourself by now if that's what you really wanted. You could turn yourself over to Accipitus or Aves or Dauricus."

He folded his arms over his chest, staring at her down the length of his nose. "You need to stop fighting who you are and what you can do. We've been tasked with keeping Lord Savino alive." He shrugged. "So use what you are to balance the scales."

Pushing himself off the wall, he dusted off his hands. "Now let's move or we'll be late."

Denevah followed quietly after him, lost in her own thoughts. Benedetto didn't worry about her distraction too much; the rooftops were like a second home to him and he stayed alert for trouble. The city of Aerie stretched out at his feet, the world open all around him. He could see anything that came at him from this high up.

More concerning to him were the threats that might come from within House Corvus. They'd been breached—the attack on Denevah proved that. Someone had gotten inside, had turned one of their own. Benedetto knew that where there was one, there were likely more. Corvus was no longer a safe haven for Denevah.

Trapinze had approved Benedetto's suggestion that they remove her from the palazzo until the Lord of Corvus could find out just who had betrayed his House. Benedetto suspected that Trapinze would be his usual ruthless self in ferreting out the disloyal and that he and Denevah would be back in only a matter of days. In the meantime, he had arranged a place for the two of them to stay as well as somewhere they could meet with Savino without having to worry about the usual prying eyes.

"Down here," Benedetto said, pointing toward an open balcony window several flights above the canal. He hoisted himself over the edge of the roof and found the spikes he'd driven into the palazzo's wall the day before to help Denevah navigate the brick façade. He didn't need them, but he used them now since it made things easier.

"Put your hands and feet where I do," he called up to her. Her face was a pale moon above him, the only color in the unrelenting black of her clothes. He swung onto the balcony with ease, crouching down to watch Denevah's descent.

She moved carefully, sliding over the lip of the roof with cautious grace. Reaching down, she found the first set of spikes and dropped down. She climbed slowly, lowering herself to the next set and then the next. Benedetto reached out his hand to steady her as she shifted her body and stretched toward the balcony. He caught her arm and hauled her in, only releasing her when she had her feet back on solid ground.

"Not bad," he complimented, white grin flashing in his dark face. He gestured for her to go inside. As she investigated the elegant sitting room they found themselves in, he told her, "Wait here. I'll be right back." Then he slipped out the door.

This palazzo exuded elegant refinement. As Benedetto made his way to the stairs, he marveled at the paintings and tapestries along the walls, the hand carved furniture with its wood polished to a burnished sheen, the delicate blown glass vases and marble busts that sat in niches illuminated by witchlight. He'd always been taken by the loveliness of this place, even if it did make him feel coarse and uncomfortable. Benedetto enjoyed nice things, but he wasn't used to this level of luxury. The places he frequented were considerably less opulent.

He found a servant and told her to find Kinendra before hurrying back to Denevah. She had taken off her pack and set it beside on of the chairs that circled a gaming table. He found her against the far wall, perusing a shelf of leather-bound books. She touched their spines reverently, her gloved hands sliding along the gilt-embossed leather.

"Find anything interesting?" he asked, leaning one shoulder against the wall.

"This is quite the varied collection," she said. "There are books on cooking, on geography, some political treatises, mapmaking, etiquette, and, um," here she reddened, "a number of books on how to please a, uh, suitor." Denevah stared at him over her shoulder, one eyebrow raised despite the burning flush on her cheeks. "Where did you bring me exactly?"

The door opened to admit a tall, handsome woman in an elegant dress, and Savino. The woman's bronze face creased in a smile as she glanced from Denevah to Benedetto. He straightened and bowed deeply before giving Savino a grin. The Rook looked wryly amused.

"He brought you to me," the woman answered. "I am Kinendra. Be welcome in the House of White Feathers."

Benedetto lounged on the low chaise, one arm draped lazily over the back of it, his gaze on the ceiling. Occasionally he glanced over at Denevah where she sat ramrod straight in one of the fluffy chairs on the opposite side of the large room, a blank expression on her face.

Savino spoke from his spot at the gaming table. He'd unlaced his dark green jacket and sleeves and now sat comfortably, laces trailing. He wore an amused smile. "This is a brilliant idea, Benedetto."

"It would be more complimentary if you didn't sound so shocked," the Crow said, dropping his head back onto the arm of the chaise. Still, it pleased him that Savino saw the genius of his idea.

The House of White Feathers was the perfect place to meet. Savino could come and go as he wished without suspicion—any number of young nobles from the Great Houses spent their time and coin at the most refined pleasure house in all of Aerie. Savino would just be one more lorded louche looking for a good time and pleasant companionship. It also meant that Denevah could stay in one of the long-term guest rooms. House Corvus wasn't safe for her any longer, and Trapinze approved of Denevah's absence while he cleaned house.

In a terse voice, an echo of the tension in her body, Denevah asked, "How can you be sure we can trust this place?"

Benedetto chuckled. He doubted that was truly what bothered her; the assassin sometimes forgot how sheltered Denevah had been for much of her life. Still, he answered the question she'd asked. "This is hardly the most interesting or important secret these Doves have ever been asked to keep."

Savino nodded, his hazel eyes alight. "This is the most exclusive pleasure house in the city," he explained. "I don't think we're even in their top ten." The Rook took a sip from the tea that a servant had brought. "How did you come to know Kinendra?"

"Trade secret," Benedetto said with a laugh. He saw Denevah's mouth twist, clearly not appreciating his sense of humor.

He lied, but he couldn't help how much he enjoyed annoying her. Trapinze had assigned him a job a few years before. Kinendra had taken out the contract on a customer who liked to get too rough with the Doves of White Feathers. She hadn't been the Nest's right hand like she was now; just a working girl who didn't like seeing her friends and coworkers hurt or being hurt herself. She'd gathered up enough funds from the group and hired a Crow. She'd been surprised that one so young had handled the job with such skill—she'd insisted on thanking him in person, even after she'd sent along payment. Benedetto had looked out for her ever since.

"She's trustworthy," he told the Dauricus.

"I've no doubt, if you vouch for her," Savino replied.

Benedetto raised his eyebrows, sharing a surprised glance with Denevah. The Rook surprised him. He actually sounded sincere when he'd spoken. Most Rooks were so twisted they'd choke on their tongue before giving an honest response, but Savino made him question all of his assumptions.

"What makes this place so exclusive?" Denevah asked. "Aside from the window dressing, they're still selling themselves."

Benedetto huffed and dropped a hand into his lap. "I forget, you haven't seen the way the poorer quarters work." He waved his hand at the walls. "When you're talking about a Dove's Nest, those window dressings are a lot of the appeal. The refinement of the girls, the wealthy trappings of the Nest itself, the location of the palazzo—all of these attract a certain clientele. For the Doves working in places like this, it's a measure of safety and comfort. Men coming here pay for the privilege of such an experience and expect certain, uh, refinement for their money.

"But most prossies don't congregate in places like this. They usually work out of their homes. And they attract customers by cooking."

Denevah gasped, "What?"

That sent Benedetto into gales of laughter. He couldn't help himself. It jarred him, how innocent she could be for all of her deadliness.

Savino explained. "As Benedetto explained, the Doves are the expensive mistresses, prostitutes, and courtesans for hire. They have proper Houses of their own, like this one, which they live in and work out of, but there is a significant cost for such service. This is all fine for those with the coin to pay for the kind of decadent experience these places provide, but that doesn't cut it for the poorer common folk."

Savino continued. "In the poorer quarters, a woman will cook a meal and set it on the window sill. Customers walking by can choose their," here he paused, as though searching for the right word, casting a wary eye at both of them, "um, dalliance based on who has the best smelling food."

"I don't believe you," Denevah gasped, as if unsure whether to be appalled or delighted by the ingenuity.

"Oh, it's true," Benedetto assured her, fighting back a grin. "You didn't get to see the really interesting parts of the city, cooped up as you were."

"Have you ever," Denevah began to ask, then trailed off with a blush.

"I'm hurt that you would even think I had to pay for companionship." Benedetto shook his head in mock disappointment.

"Well then, how else would you know?" she challenged.

Benedetto figured he might as well come clean. He wasn't ashamed of where he came from, and he refused to hide it. "My mother was one."

Both Savino's and Denevah's heads swiveled in his direction. Denevah's eyes had grown as wide as platters, but Savino simply raised one elegant eyebrow thoughtfully.

"And that doesn't bother you?" Denevah asked tentatively.

"Eh, I made my peace with it long ago. She did what she had to do to provide for us," he answered, and then chuckled. "She was possibly the world's least successful whore."

"I don't understand," she said, cocking her head in confusion.

"Most women turn to whoring when they can't make enough cleaning," Benedetto explained. "My mother took in laundry because she couldn't make enough on her back."

Savino chuckled, the sound warm and bright. Denevah still looked at him, her brow furrowed, confusion still evident on her face.

Benedetto rested his ankle over one knee. "My mother only knew how to cook food from her homeland. Most potential customers steered well clear of the strangely spiced smells. She had a few regulars—mostly settlers like herself—but not enough to feed the both of us on the regular. She went hungry so that I had something to eat. I think that's why the swamp fever took her so quickly."

"Wait," Denevah said, holding her hand up. "Were you there when your mother . . . entertained?"

Benedetto's head jerked up. "Well, sure. Where else would I be?" At Denevah's shocked look, he smirked. "I didn't watch! She sent me outside to play if it wasn't too late. I usually got into fights instead or I ran around with my friend, Luc. Women like my mother work from their homes."

"They aren't like the kept women or courtesans or the Doves that work in the pleasure houses." Savino spoke softly, respectfully. "They make do with what they have."

"How do you know about all this?" Denevah asked Savino.

Benedetto watched him. It made sense that a posh Rook would know about Doves and their pleasure houses—he had the money to frequent them. But to know the ways of the streets and how the poor made money—well, Benedetto hadn't expected the young man to ever be familiar with them. Had he been slumming at some point? In his time at House Corvus, he'd heard how sometimes spoiled rich boys went looking for a bit of danger in the poorer sections of the city. It made them easy marks. Savino didn't strike him as the type to engage in such activity. He seemed more interested in intellectual pursuits.

Savino turned his head, his profile backlit by the candlelamp. In that moment, Benedetto felt like he saw Savino for the first time, separate from his family and from Aerie. He was just a young man, sitting with them in the dim parlor.

"I'm not blind to what's happening in the city," the Rook said, his voice soft. His hazel gaze flickered over to the balcony overlooking the canal. "The divide between the Great Houses and the rest of the people only grows. I've spent time in the ghettos. The Doge isn't interested in stopping or fixing it, so long as his own power remains in place."

"What, so you are? You care about the little guy?" Benedetto scoffed.

"I care," Savino enunciated slowly, "about the people who catch and grow our food, who sell our goods, who keep the city running smoothly. The quakes affect the poorer quarters more than most, and the people who live there grow tired of laboring to rebuild without help. Is it any wonder why they listen to Navolio's talk of a watery revolution?"

As if in confirmation of Savino's words, the floor of the room rippled as the palazzo shook on its foundation. Benedetto gripped the back of the chaise tightly as the walls juddered and the sounds of screams and falling masonry carried from the open balcony doors. Books fell from the shelves behind him. He heard the crash of glass breaking as something shattered on the marble floor out in the hallway. Another quake threw Denevah to the ground. Savino grabbed hold of the gaming table, knuckles going white with the force of his grip. Cries filtered up from the lower flights of White Feathers.

After a few long minutes, the tremors stopped. Benedetto rose cautiously to his feet as Denevah pushed herself up from the floor. Savino moved to the balcony for a look outside, his eyes wide and startled. Benedetto followed him, snaking his neck out for a better look over the Rook's head.

All of the palazzos on this block appeared intact. But he could hear screaming and shouts coming from a few blocks over. Clouds of dust were clearing over the rooftops. Another building, or maybe a bridge, had gone down in the quake.

"I should go assess the damage," Savino murmured, eyes on the dispersing cloud.

Benedetto held back a sharp retort. What could the man do now? The building had already collapsed, the lives inside it already lost. Aside from standing at a distance watching everything with a critical eye, Savino would be next to useless there. He'd only be in the way of the people actually equipped to get things done.

Denevah's quiet words saved Benedetto from responding. "Navolio will be preaching tonight. You can bet on that."

"Then we should get some rest," the Crow said, stepping back inside the room to settle himself on the chaise once more.

He could hear the bustle of the girls in the hall as they cleaned up plaster dust and glass and whatever else had fallen during the quake. Denevah began to tidy the room, starting with replacing the books to their places on the shelves. A knock sounded, just before Kinendra opened the door to check if everyone was unhurt.

Benedetto watched as Savino took one last look out the balcony door, something like regret on his face, before his expression returned to its blank, genial mask as he greeted the Dove.

CHAPTER NINE

Ettoni found himself ushered into Lady Grimauldi's parlor with a minimum of fuss. He was glad for that—he already felt on edge at being called to her palazzo with no warning. Worry and guilt had struck him like a spear thrust. Did she and the others of House Aves know of his efforts to find a cure for Denevah? Had they uncovered his lies about what happened on the night of Rodolfi's death?

He forced himself to sit still on the ornately carved brocade couch. The marble tiles on the floor gleamed with mother of pearl and gilt inlays. Ettoni's gaze roved around the room, taking in the fine tapestries, the delicate blown-glass sculptures, the carved wood paneling, and the intricately painted porcelains. Everything in this room displayed her wealth and taste, designed as much to humble a guest emotionally as to please them visually.

He slid his hands down the front of his black jacket, smoothing out the lines. He'd left his working robes at home in favor of his finest clothing. He wore it like armor, and imitated Rodolfi's half-lidded bored stare as best he could. He was an alchemist in his own right now, taught by one of the leaders of his House. He would not be cowed by things. He remembered the scrape of the Diluvians' scales sliding across the marble floor of their temple as he called them forth to strike a bargain for Denevah. That had been terrifying.

Sitting in a parlor with a mortal woman was simple and straightforward when compared to that.

Lady Grimauldi swept into the room, attended by another woman and two men, all of them leaders of the families that made up House Aves. Ettoni stood and inclined his head to each of them. He recognized Lady Raffaella from Rodolfi's description and Lords Mesuline and Orlanto from meetings with them as his master's apprentice. Now he stood before them, while not exactly their equals, then at least within reach.

"I called you together to speak of the problem Rodolfi left us with," Grimauldi began, wasting no time on pleasantries.

Ettoni returned to his seat as the others took various chairs and couches scattered about the room. A servant brought in a tray of refreshments, served each of them, and left again. Ettoni sipped at his wine and waited for the others to begin.

"Have you made any strides into determining how to replicate the process Rodolfi used on his daughter?" Orlanto asked, corpulent body sprawled in a large chair, glass of wine dangling from stubby fingers.

"I have been through his notes and papers." He had, just not in the way they expected. "There is a piece missing though, some kind of handhold that made the girl able to withstand her own toxicity. I have not discovered what that is—my master made no specific mention of it."

Ettoni did not mention the Diluvians to any of them. Rodolfi had broken more laws than they would ever know when he created Denevah. He'd bonded the water dragons with a human girl, something no one had ever tried before. It was unheard of and very dangerous, with consequences none of them could ever fully fathom. If word of it got out, both his and Denevah's life would be forfeit.

Mesuline regarded Ettoni carefully, staring down at him along his aquiline nose. "I still find it odd that your master wouldn't have developed an antidote to his particular poison. Seems rather short-sighted to me."

"Especially in light of what happened to him," Orlanto offered with a derisive chuckle.

Ettoni kept his gaze fixed firmly on Lady Grimauldi's necklace, his face a blank. "I have found no mentions of antidotes—or even the barest development of one—in all of his journals. Although I have begun my own experiments to search for one."

"Purely altruistically, I'm sure," Orlanto said, glaring through his dark, beady eyes. "I would imagine the young lady is none too fond of you."

Ettoni nodded, not trusting himself to speak. He took a sip of his wine, imagining the bored expression Rodolfi would wear if he'd been forced to listen to any of this. When he was certain he had the intonations correct, he drawled, "I think such a thing would be of interest to all of us, should the girl get it into her head to blame all of Aves for her father's madness."

He hid his small smile behind his hand when Orlanto blanched.

"Where is the girl now?" Raffaella asked abruptly. She was older than the others. Her hands wrapped tightly around the head of her cane, skeletal fingers clenched together like a bird's nest of branches.

"Safely ensconced in House Corvus," Lady Grimauldi answered. Her eyes glittered as they watched Ettoni over the rim of her glass. Her lips were stained red by the wine.

The woman set her glass on a lacquered wooden table beside her. "She's become a rather difficult liability to contain," she said, rising to her feet in a rustle of dark blue silks. "We'd hoped to leverage her strange abilities for our own uses, but it seems we will not be given the chance. We can't touch her while she hides out with the assassins of House Corvus, and we haven't found a way to neutralize her so she's no longer a threat to us. The problem she poses is too great to play our usual game of wait and see. We must find a way to strike even if she is under Trapinze's protection."

"You have something in mind?" Mesuline asked, tapping his chin with a long finger.

"We have sent word to operatives loyal to us that should they see an opportunity, they are to secure the girl and bring her to me."

"Forgive my boldness," Ettoni said, struggling to keep his voice even and calm even as his stomach plummeted to his feet at her words. "But are you certain this is our best course of action? If word gets back to Lord Trapinze, he could declare war on our House."

"Then it should behoove everyone here to keep their mouths most assiduously shut," Grimauldi told him, skirts swishing as she paced. "We can either use this opportunity to be rid of a wild card in our deck or squander it and miss out entirely."

"You have faith in this person?" Mesuline asked.

"Diluvians, no!" Grimauldi trilled with a laugh. "What a funny world that would be!" She composed herself, brushing her hands down the midnight silk of her skirt. "But they are ruthless enough—and intelligent enough—to understand that our interests, in this at least, align. They will serve us." She smiled at Ettoni.

He swallowed, fighting down the urge to retch. "It seems a risk," he protested, careful to keep his tone distant and intellectual, "and relies a bit too much on luck for my tastes." His brain already searched for a way to get word to Denevah that she had merely traded one danger for another. Perhaps a coded letter? He had no doubt that his correspondence would be opened and read; Ettoni wasn't fool enough to think that Aves trusted him without strings yet.

"You speak of luck? You who are lucky to still be drawing breath at all?" Lady Raffaella told him, haughty voice laced with threat. "You knew what the man attempted and yet you said nothing to anyone. To create a weapon of such magnitude is madness—as he learned too late. The only reason you're alive is the mitigating circumstance of the apprentice bond he placed upon you."

Ettoni said nothing. Lady Raffaella had been particularly forceful in calling for his punishment and Denevah's destruction, while the others on the council had been more measured in their outrage. The binding spells placed on apprentices ensured that a master's secrets stayed his own; Ettoni couldn't have betrayed Rodolfi's confidence to anyone, even if he'd wanted to. The spell forbade it. The magic stopped his speech and stilled his hands. He'd experienced it firsthand every time he'd tried to warn Denevah.

"While you may question the decision, it has already been made, Raffaella," Lady Grimauldi chided in a tone that brooked no dissent. "I see no point in belaboring the outcome simply because you do not agree with it."

Lady Raffaella made a disgruntled noise as she settled back in her chair, spine still as straight as her cane. Ettoni bit back a satisfied grin; that certainly shut the old biddy up. Grimauldi went up a few steps in his estimation.

Mesuline said, "We can't allow the girl to stay with Corvus—it would shift the balance of power too much. She could be a powerful tool in their hands."

Ettoni clenched his teeth around the words he dare not speak. Denevah was not a tool. She was a person, and an Aves, with all of the rights that came with it. She'd had no say in what Rodolfi had made her, and yet they wanted to punish her for it as if she had. Everyone wanted to use her abilities in some way, or be rid of her to protect themselves and their position. No one wanted to treat her as anything more than a thing.

No one but him.

He re-evaluated Grimauldi's place in his respect when she spoke next, "One does not worry about the tool—it can be broken or destroyed. One's concern should be the hands that wield the tool." Her gaze sought out Ettoni's face, the cunning in it palpable.

"And since those hands are not ours, we simply remove it from play."

Her fingernail tapped against the polished wood arm of her chair. "Isn't that so, Ettoni?" Her dark brown eyes glittered as she watched him, eyes avid for a sign of rebellion.

He had no choice but to bow his head and answer, "You are right as always, my Lady."

CHAPTER TEN

"How do you want this to go?" Benedetto asked Savino as they walked along the dusk-filled streets. Denevah waited for them at the House of White Feathers. He didn't like being the only one left to guard the Rook, and he didn't like that he didn't like it. He didn't want to rely on anyone, let alone a newcomer like Denevah, but he liked having a second person on the job, if only to distract him from his thoughts.

He didn't like to think.

Savino paused to lean against the stone rail of a bridge. He folded his arms along the top of it and stared down into the water below. Benedetto mirrored him a few feet away, back against the stone, elbows propped atop it, and head tipped back to watch the sky.

"I'll go in, see what I can hear. Listen to the sermon," Savino said. "If I'm lucky, I'll be able to follow him when he's finished—see if I can find out where he disappears to afterward."

"What about me?"

Savino tilted his chin up. "The roof. I want you where you have the best vantage point. If Navolio escapes in a boat, I want to know it. If he skips over the rooftops, you're the best bet to catch him."

"I can't protect you from the roof," Benedetto warned.

A mirthless grin crossed Savino's face. "I can protect myself. Navolio is more important."

"Not to me." Benedetto countered. "My job is to keep you alive and I'm in favor of anything that makes it easier," he clarified at Savino's questioning look.

Savino smiled down at the dark water. "I know what you meant."

Benedetto cocked his head so he could study the Rook's face. Savino was a dark profile, one side of his face lost in shadow, the other side washed with light from the lamps. The lantern's glow picked out the burnished bronze waves in his hair. Savino looked too posh to truly blend in with the rabble, even in his borrowed shabby clothes. Benedetto reached over to mess up his hair.

Savino flinched away from the contact. The assassin pulled his hand back, offended. "I was just going to make you look messier. You're too neat right now to blend in with the crowd."

"I don't like people touching me," Savino said, voice low. He reached up and dragged his hands through his hair, pulling it out of its neat style so it hung around his face and in his eyes. "Better?"

Benedetto considered him, then nodded. "Add some dirt on your hands," he advised. "You're still too clean." After a moment, he tilted his head and asked, "Anybody touching you?"

Taking a breath, Savino nodded. "Anyone. I don't like the feeling of hands on me." He shrugged. "I never have. I've learned to tolerate it from certain people—my mother, mostly—but my preference is to not be touched."

Benedetto settled back against the stone, mulling over what Savino had told him. He didn't understand it, being a touchy person himself. He enjoyed physical contact—a lot—be it touching someone or being touched by them. He couldn't wrap his brain around someone not enjoying it. What had happened to make Savino that way?

They stood in silence for a few more minutes. Savino bent down to rub his hands in the dirt that had gathered in the corners of the bridge. The quiet was comfortable, almost pleasant.

When Savino straightened, he said, "You take your work seriously."

Benedetto shrugged, uncomfortable with the statement. "I suppose," he answered.

"Huh," Savino responded, staring at Benedetto now.

Straightening from his slouch, Benedetto snapped, "What do you mean by that?" He waved his hand at the Rook. "What does 'huh' mean?"

Savino looked a hair's breadth away from laughing. He put a hand up to his face, covering his mouth to hide a smile. "Just that you put a lot of effort into seeming to not care about things, but it's pretty obvious you take what you do to heart. It matters to you."

Benedetto's first response was to splutter and deny, but he stopped that impulse, even though this whole conversation made him want to throw himself off the bridge to escape it. He usually called people out, not the other way around.

He tried for a flip response. "When how well you do your work directly affects your ability to keep drawing breath, damn right you care."

Benedetto saw the corner of Savino's mouth quirk up in amusement when the man lowered his hand. "But that's not the only reason," he said, giving the Crow a sly look—a look that seemed to say he knew Benedetto, that he'd ferreted out all of his secrets.

The Crow scowled. "Shouldn't you get going?" He glanced at the rooftops. The Thief's Path—that's what the roofs of Aerie had been called when he was a boy. Now Benedetto knew better; worse than thieves ran the rooftops overhead. He was one of them.

Savino pushed away from the stone rail. "I should," he agreed. "Find me after." He turned and walked away.

Benedetto waited a few minutes before finding his own path. Night had fallen and the lanterns were lit, but there were still plenty of shadows for him to coast through. When he found a crumbling brick building that suited his needs, he scaled the side like a lizard and pulled himself over the roof's edge to settle in and watch the building opposite.

The gathering wasn't obvious, not at first, and not if you weren't looking for it. In ones and twos people gathered along the side street, far from the main arteries of the Capital Canal. Small boats, skiffs, and sandolos full of people began to filter into the alley's waters, packing in tight.

Benedetto shook his head. The Night Watch would get lucky tonight if they stumbled upon this little gathering—although that was a pretty big if. People wouldn't be able to get out of their way unless they felt like taking a dip in the filthy canals. He thought he saw Savino standing among a group of day laborers near the far wall of the alley. At least he wasn't in a boat.

A murmur ran through the crowd, causing the mass of people to lurch forward expectantly. Must be the man of the hour. Benedetto's sharp eyes scanned the darkness of the nearby rooftops, ignoring the crowd's mumbles. He stayed still, not wanting to give away his position through stray movement as he searched for any sign of a lookout.

Nothing. That didn't mean they weren't there though. They could be just like him, hunkered down and waiting for some sign. Benedetto settled in to wait, gaze roaming over the rooftops nearby.

A man's voice rose above the din, quieting the gathered throng almost immediately. Benedetto listened with only half an ear, attention still on the neighboring roofs. He flexed and relaxed his muscles to keep them from stiffening up as he waited for something to happen. Occasionally his eyes would dip down to find Savino in the crowd, the sight of his dark crown of hair or the strong bones of his face in profile an assurance that the Rook hadn't been murdered horribly yet. Savino listened intently to the preacher's words, some nonsense about the Doge not caring for the people of the city and how, when the Diluvians returned, everything would be solved.

Benedetto nearly snorted in his disgust. Of course the Doge didn't care about the populace that comprised much of Aerie. Everyone knew the Doge didn't want to bother with the people he pretended to care about only when it served his purposes—though no one dared announce it so brazenly. Why bother? Might as well say the sky was blue, or water was wet. The power of the Doge and the Great Houses had lasted generations, sunk deep into the foundations of Aerie. It would take more than a simple preacher and his rabble to unseat it.

Instead Benedetto thought about what Savino had said earlier. *You care.* The Rook hit too close to home, Diluvians take him. Benedetto did care—he wanted to do a good job, even if that job sometimes meant killing people. He was a Crow—if not by birth then certainly by effort—and he would not sully House Corvus by doing a job in half-measure.

Navolio had arrived at the meat of his sermon, his voice cresting and ebbing like the waters of the lagoon they all lived on. "The hour for our deliverance is nearly at hand, my friends. She who is the key is coming. We must raise our voices so that she knows where to find us, so that she knows we are ready to help her in her sacred duty. It is time for the Diluvians to rise and cleanse this place of the corruption of the unjust! And she—the key—will bring about their release!"

Smiling bitterly to himself, Benedetto rolled his eyes. Always some poor chosen bastard to do all the saving instead of the people doing it for themselves. Probably just a bunch of made-up nonsense from the man's drink-induced dreams. Benedetto could probably find at least four girls at Lady Aliene's House of White Feathers that would happily bend over backwards to fit the description. Quite literally.

A shrill bird call sounded from the rooftop to his left. Benedetto jerked his head around, gaze darting from rooftop to rooftop as that shrieking call passed each to each. It was a signal, obviously, and the people below began to disperse quickly as men from the Night Watch turned the corner a few blocks away and bore down on the assembly.

He saw movement from the corner of his eye. A slim boy with a limp ran across the roof of the building next to him. Benedetto took off, making a running leap from his roof to the boy's, landing in a roll and coming to his feet without losing much speed, years of training leaving him surefooted on the uneven roof tiles. The boy spun, gaping, then raced away, short arms and legs pumping wildly.

As he closed on the boy, Benedetto dropped a throwing dagger into his hand. He flung it underhanded at the boy's bad leg, intending to wound him enough to slow him down so Benedetto could take him to Savino for questioning.

Something flashed past him, colliding with his thrown knife to send it spinning to the ground. Benedetto's instincts took over. Flinging himself to the side, he ducked into a roll to get out of the path of any more projectiles. He felt the breeze of one pass over where he'd been a moment before.

He gained his feet and spun, hands already full of his next set of daggers.

A slender pointed rod flew through the air at his chest; Benedetto knocked it away with his own blade. Benedetto had never seen a weapon like this one—a cross between an arrow and a throwing dagger, but bigger than a dart. He flung his own dagger in the direction the attack had come from even as he dodged another. It missed.

Benedetto saw a dark shape moving at a good pace, already vaulting over the next section of wall. The boy was long gone by now. But Benedetto could discover who the boy worked for if he caught whoever had helped him escape.

The Crow had to admit this person was good. Only Benedetto's reflexes had saved him from catching at least one of those flying spikes in the chest. He snagged his dagger from the roof as he passed in pursuit. They drew ahead of him steadily, even more familiar with the rooftops of this part of Aerie than he was. Every time he felt like he'd gained, they found a shortcut or cut a corner that Benedetto hadn't known about.

He threw the dagger in his hand again; again, he missed. With a muttered curse, Benedetto put on a burst of speed. He had height on this one, despite the other's speed, and he'd bet he had a longer reach. When he had closed enough, he reached out and caught a fistful of fabric—the back of the person's shirt. As he pulled, he caught sight of a tattoo of two birds, one impaled on a branch of thorns. Benedetto jerked, thinking to pull them off balance, only to receive a booted foot to his stomach as they slammed him with a back kick. He folded over, letting go of the fabric.

Looking up through watering eyes, he saw the spike heading for his throat, so he threw his body backwards enough for it to pass where he'd just been. When he straightened, they were off again.

Benedetto followed after. They were nearing the edge of this section of roof. If he wanted answers, he needed to catch this person quickly, before they were separated.

He flung another dagger. This one arced through the air and would have stuck the person's arm if they hadn't turned and swatted the blade away. Benedetto would have been impressed if he'd wanted the knife to hit home, but he'd only been hoping to slow them down. He kept running and came at them with a long knee.

He noticed two things in rapid succession. The first: that the person was a girl, a bit younger than Denevah. She had huge eyes set beneath a cap of unruly dark curls. The second, which he saw when she crossed her arms to block his knee strike, was that she was missing a hand. Her left arm ended in a stump.

Filing all of this fascinating information away for later, Benedetto unsheathed the two long daggers belted at the small of his back. A spike flew from her fingers. He ducked and came back up with his daggers out.

He expected the fight to be easy. It was anything but. The girl was fast, faster than him. She made up in speed what she lacked in reach, and she was fiercely strong. He found his two blades were practically useless—he couldn't get close to her to stab her. She blocked everything.

In fairness, so did he. They fought to a standstill, neither one of them giving ground. They bled from any number of shallow, superficial wounds. Benedetto realized he might have a few more than she did. He smiled, longing to compare injuries.

They were face to face, the crescent moon giving him a little light to see by. She had dark skin like him. She wore a rag that covered her nose and mouth, hiding half of her face. He couldn't tell anything else about her, except that she might be better than him. He expected that to bother him more than it did.

"Who are you?" he wound up asking, wishing he could wipe the stupid smile from his face.

In response to his distraction, she shoved him. Benedetto fell backwards, unable to catch himself as he tripped over the foot she'd hooked behind his ankle. He landed on his ass with a bump. In the instant he took his eyes off her, she disappeared.

Benedetto ran to the edge of the roof and peered over. Another spike flew at him and he narrowly dodged it before it could sink into his eye socket. The girl slid down a length of rope, a loop of it wrapped around her handless arm. Her feet hit the ground and she ran off down the clogged street, fast as a rabbit. Benedetto debated about following her, then the sounds of a struggle filtered to him from the other side of the street. He hurried over to the opposite side of the roof. Leaning over, he saw Savino and several others from the sermon struggling with guards from the Night Watch.

He quickly sized up the knot of people as he shimmied down to the small balcony directly below him. If he landed right, he could dispatch most of the guards with relative ease; if he didn't, he'd end up in the canal or stabbed. Possibly both.

Eh, it was worth the risk.

He jumped.

Benedetto only had a second to register Savino's eyes widening in shock as he used two guards to soften his landing. He hit them like a meteorite slamming into the earth, knocking one out and one into the canal. Spinning in a circle, Benedetto cleared the immediate area, then grabbed Savino by of the collar of his coat to drag him away from the others still beating on the remaining guards.

"Come on," Benedetto cried, shoving the Rook down the street ahead of him.

More guardsmen poured into the alley from the opposite end. "Not that way," Savino cursed, out of breath.

Benedetto reversed course, dragging Savino along in his wake. He knew he should be tired, but he felt like he could run all night. Shouts to stop split the night behind them, the sounds of fighting echoing off the water of the canals. Benedetto kept them moving.

"More coming from the left," Savino warned, urging them down a street branching to the right. "I heard the guards say they've set up a cordon to catch Navolio."

"He's long gone," Benedetto said, taking a second to get his bearings. Once he knew where they were, he knew where they had to go. "This way."

As Benedetto led Savino through the ever narrowing streets of Aerie, he asked, "Why don't you want them to catch you? Wouldn't getting hauled in with all of them give you an in?"

Savino staggered on, holding his side. At Benedetto's raised eyebrow, he grunted. "One of them got in a lucky punch. And I have a side stitch." He pressed on. "I can't risk being recognized by the guards. How would it look if I were released and the others weren't? They'd never trust me to get close enough to Navolio." He shook his head. "Not a good idea this early. Perhaps if I get desperate."

The sound of booted steps came from the mouth of the street, along with the sounds of a scuffle. "We've reached the end of the cordon," Benedetto said. "In here." He dragged Savino through a rickety doorway and into a shabby tavern that catered to the poorer classes.

Taking a seat at the bar, Benedetto signaled to the bartender. Two pints of ale slammed into the scarred wood of the bar top in front of them. He took his drink in hand and toasted Savino with it, before draining it. Setting the empty pint down, he waved at the barkeep for another. Savino stared at him in astonishment.

"Drink up," Benedetto told him. "We're going to be in here for a while."

"What?" Savino whispered harshly. "We don't have time to get drunk!"

Benedetto turned so he could survey the room, leaning his back against the edge of the bar, elbows resting atop it. The tavern stood perhaps half-full, most of the patrons male and ranging in age. Thank the Diluvians that Savino had changed from his usual Dauricus finery into something rougher and more plainspun; otherwise the Rook would have stood out like a hawk among doves. The men in the tavern were primarily tradesmen, maybe a few clerks of less prosperous merchants. None of them were likely to recognize them.

"Relax," Benedetto said, plastering a smile on his face. He heard the thunk of a full pint hitting the wood of the bar, and he reached over to grab his fresh drink. "You want to waltz over to the Night Watch when they're on alert, just looking for anyone who might have been at that sermon?" When Savino didn't respond, the Crow nudged him.

"Of course you don't because you're not a complete idiot. So we're just going to stay here, enjoy a few drinks and wait for them to get good and tired. Understand?"

Savino nodded, but he didn't look happy about it. He frowned as he took up his mug of ale. He took a deep drink and made a face. "That's horrible."

"Of course it is." Benedetto clinked his mug into Savino's. "Now shut up and drink."

Benedetto estimated at least two—possibly three—hours had passed since they'd entered the tavern. That should be enough time for the Night Watch to have rounded up the more unlucky attendees of Navolio's sermon. They'd been sitting at the cordon doing a lot of nothing, and were probably very bored and wishing they were at a tavern themselves or in their beds.

Savino leaned over and muttered, "I am fairly certain that I've heard cats yowling that was more pleasant to listen to than this fellow." He jerked his head to the minstrel singing a questionable folk song about a fisherman's wife and her encounter with a wish granting fish.

"That's the stupidest thing you've ever said!" Benedetto yelled, shoving Savino's shoulder.

"I wasn't aware you were a fan of subpar tavern singing," the Rook returned in a low voice, wearing a confused expression.

Benedetto pushed away from the bar, staggering slightly. Putting a bit more slur in his words than was probably necessary, he squared off with Savino. "If I wanted your opinion, I'd beat it out of you!"

"Have you lost your wits completely?" Savino's gaze took in the room. All eyes were on them. He reached out and grabbed Benedetto's arm. "We're leaving."

"Not yet," Benedetto whispered, giving Savino a wink.

"What else are we waiting for?" the Rook asked, catching on to Benedetto's plan.

"Well first, I'm going to need you to hit me."

Savino grinned hugely. "I've always wanted to know what it's like to punch a master assassin."

"Really?"

"No."

"Good. You'll live longer. Now try to look offended." The Crow jerked his arm out of Savino's grip.

"Wha--"

Benedetto took up his glass—mostly full—and threw the contents in the Rook's face. Savino fell back, startled, then cursed. He wiped at the wetness on his face with his sleeve, blinking as the alcohol burned his eyes.

"Sunova—" Savino shouted and came around with a thundering hook that caught the assassin in the jaw.

Benedetto staggered, rolling with the punch to lessen the impact. "Nice," he whispered, before taking a swing of his own.

Savino ducked out of the way, but not before grabbing his own drink and flinging it at Benedetto. The Crow had to give it to Savino—the man learned fast and was a natural improviser.

"OUT!" came the shout from the tavern's proprietor, just as Benedetto had expected. Bar fights were expensive and no owner in their right mind wanted to encourage them. It led to broken furniture, lost customers, and injured employees. A waste of money all around—money that the man likely couldn't afford.

"I'll not have you two fools wrecking my place!" The man signaled to a beefy man sitting on a stool in the corner.

Benedetto felt himself being lifted by the collar of his jacket, and turned his head to see Savino receiving similar treatment. The Crow struggled weakly, not concerned with getting away as the man dragged them to the door that the owner held open for him. He and Savino were tossed into the street outside.

"We were done anyway!" Benedetto shouted, climbing unsteadily to his feet. He shook a fist at the now closed door.

"Now what?" Savino asked, still on his hands and knees, alcohol-soaked hair hanging about his face.

"Now," the Crow began, hauling the Rook to his feet and draping a companionable arm over his shoulders, "we act like proper slurring drunkards on our way home to be chastised by our long-suffering wives."

He felt Savino shoulders tense at his proximity. "Sorry," Benedetto told him as he got them underway, heading towards the line of Night Watch guards at the end of the street. "It's just to get us past them."

"I know," Savino said, teeth gritted with the effort of not shrugging off the Crow's arm. Instead, he leaned drunkenly against Benedetto's side and began to sing an absolutely filthy song about a Warhawk's unhealthy attachment to his sword.

Naturally Benedetto joined in.

They stumbled over to the waiting guards, stupid grins wreathing their faces. Pulling them up short when they were nearly upon them, Benedetto blinked slowly. "What's all this then?" he slurred, nudging Savino who'd all but collapsed against him.

Savino, bless him, launched into the next verse of the song, practically falling over his own feet. Benedetto hauled him upright with a raucous laugh as the disgusted guards waved them through with barely a glance. They shuffled away, laughing uproariously until they were well out of earshot.

Savino slid from Benedetto's grasp, straightening his jacket and shoving his mess of hair out of his eyes. Benedetto stretched, suddenly feeling all of his cuts and bruises.

"I hope all of this was worth it," he groaned.

A flash of teeth in the dark as Savino set a quick pace. "Oh, yes."

"Spill it."

"Not until we see Denevah," Savino said with a chuckle, and led them down more dark streets.

CHAPTER ELEVEN

Denevah didn't hate the House of White Feathers as much as she'd been expecting to, and that surprised her. She'd never been inside of a pleasure palazzo before—hadn't even known such a thing existed before Benedetto's suggestion to meet there—but the reality turned out to be far different than whatever nonsense she'd made up in her head. She'd thought it would be all girls in beautiful dresses and heavily made-up faces—a sort of Match Ball fantasy— just sitting around the parlour.

That was not the case at all. The girls who were on, as Lady Aliene called it, did have to wait in their finery and masks and paint for customers. Sometimes regulars booked an appointment to make sure they were paired with a particular Dove, which meant that she worked that day too. But those girls not otherwise engaged didn't lay about; they worked. They cleaned the palazzo, learned sums and letters, took care of the laundry and cooking. They were busy with anything that could improve their life and increase their value. Any number of older men from the noble Houses might look to make his mistress his wife for a second or even a third

Match. Lady Aliene prepared her girls well and took a hefty finder's fee when such a Match happened.

Denevah sat in the solar at the top floor of the palazzo. The room was well away from the entertaining parlors of the lower floors and the guest rooms where the girls met with their clients. She'd flung the glass doors wide to get some much needed night air circulating through the heavily perfumed room, and now she sat with her head bowed over her mending. She'd been told she'd earn her keep here, just like everyone else for as long as she stayed with them.

She'd been good at needlework, even if she didn't necessarily enjoy it. She'd learned embroidery and other things appropriate to a lady of House Aves during her years as Rodolfi's daughter. She'd always preferred drawing and gardening to sitting and sewing, but there wasn't much else to do here that she could do, short of killing someone. The thought of what happened in the lower rooms made her stomach churn. She didn't know if it was in jealousy or disgust.

The door to the solar opened to admit Kinendra, a lovely woman with liquid amber eyes and skin as dark as Benedetto's. She moved with the feral grace and ferocity of a pirate queen, like those that roamed the waters off the coast of Ostvia. Denevah found herself intimidated by the sheer presence Kinendra possessed. It felt like being in a room with the Doge, though probably more dangerous. She'd graduated from being a Dove to helping Lady Ailene run the House of White Feathers.

Tonight Denevah saw a slight hitch to her step, a small limp. Denevah had never noticed it before and wondered what had happened. She set her worries to the side when she saw Benedetto and Savino trooping in behind her, looking much the worse for wear. Savino had one hand pressed against his side, moving gingerly. Benedetto was covered in cuts and slashes and bruises. They both smelled like the floor of a tavern, and their clothes were dirty and torn in places. Kinendra gave them both a sour look.

"Try not to drip on the carpets," she warned as she moved to close the door.

"Wait," Savino called, arresting her exit. "Would you mind staying, my lady? There's something I'd like you to have a look at."

Kinendra arched one dark eyebrow, but nodded. She closed the door and came to sit in a beautifully carved wooden chair beside a bank of windows. The moonlight glinted and splintered off the canal behind her. Savino prowled the room, searching for something, so Denevah called Benedetto over to have a better look at his wounds.

"What happened to you?" she asked as he sat beside her on the low couch.

He grinned, pulling at the scab on his mouth. Blood beaded on his dark lower lip. "I ran into someone."

Denevah tipped his chin up to get a better look. "With your face? Ten times?" She took one of the mending rags and dipped it into the pitcher of water on the low table beside her.

"It's not that bad." Benedetto laughed as Denevah set about cleaning off some of the dried blood from his face. "Savino's responsible for some of it."

"What did you two idiots do?" Kinendra asked dubiously, crossing one leg over the other.

"Listened to Navolio preach, got into a fight with a girl with one hand, took on some guards, went to a tavern for a drink, staged a bar fight, and came here." He spread his hands. "Slow night."

Kinendra scoffed. Denevah gave him a once over with a critical eye. "Do I need to stitch anything?"

Benedetto craned his neck, as if that would help him see all of his injuries. "Nope, don't think so." His delighted laughter filled the room.

Sitting back, Denevah called to Savino. "Just how hard did you hit him?" She'd never seen Benedetto acting so strangely. He'd always been prone to excitability, but this was something else. She'd never heard him sound so completely carefree before.

"Not hard enough, apparently," Savino answered drily, coming over with his hands full of parchment and charcoal. He began to sketch something, the charcoal moving quickly across the page.

Denevah found herself leaning forward to watch. Savino's hair fell across his face, still damp and curling. The reddish highlights of it glimmered in the lamplight. She felt Benedetto bump his shoulder against hers, one of his elbows coming to rest on her knee as he tried for a better view of whatever Savino was doing. Denevah sighed, unsure whether to be pleased or worried. Benedetto didn't treat her like her very presence was poison, one of the few that didn't shy away from coming in contact with her even when she was covered up. She didn't know if that made him a friend or someone with a deathwish. Maybe he was both.

Savino set aside the charcoal, raising his head to look at each of them in turn. "Have any of you ever seen something like this?" He held up the parchment so everyone could see what he'd been working on.

He'd drawn a bird in bold draftsman-like strokes. Not a raven, that much Denevah could tell, but what kind of bird it was, she couldn't say. It sat on a branch of some kind with what looked like thorns. Another bird lay impaled on the points.

Shaking her head, Denevah said, "No. Where did you see that?"

"It was a tattoo on one of the man's arms that was close to Navolio. Once I saw it, I started looking for it on other people in the crowd. A few others had something similar."

"The girl I fought on the roof had something like it," Benedetto said, voice tight with excitement. "On the back of her neck. I saw it when we were fighting."

"A girl, huh?" Denevah gave him an arch look. "Is that why you're in such a good mood?"

"I've never had a fight like that in my life," he said with a grin.

"A knife fight is your preferred method of flirting?" she asked, shaking her head in mock despair. "Are you going to send this girl a bouquet of daggers next?"

"No, but maybe one made of these." Here he pulled a slender pointed rod out of his pocket to show her. The metal spike gleamed in the dark palm of his hand. Denevah had never seen anything like it. Kinendra leaned forward for a better look.

"I would think the last thing you'd want to do is arm her further," Denevah chided, finishing her bandaging.

Kinendra ignored their banter. She walked over to Savino with her eyes fixed on the page in his hands. "It's a shrike," she pronounced after staring at it for a few moments.

"A what?" Denevah asked, watching Kinendra's face.

The Dove's eyes glittered. "A shrike," she repeated, her voice deeper and darker than Denevah had ever heard it. It was like listening to the tides speak, or the moon. "It's a kind of bird—they're known to impale their prey on branches or thorns and leave them there while they pick off the meat. They're sometimes called butcher birds."

"It's no coincidence that several people in the crowd have tattoos of shrikes on them, is it?" Savino dropped the parchment on the table.

Denevah picked it up, studying it closely. A shrike. The lines of the bird were fluid, the outline of the branch stark and black. Savino had drawn it quickly, but it was very good despite that. The Rook had an artist's eye.

"It is not," Kinendra answered, turning to face the open door that led to the balcony. A light breeze blew the damp tendrils of hair from Savino's face. Kinendra smiled and closed her eyes, enjoying the cool wind.

"So the Shrikes are involved." Benedetto said, impatience coloring his voice. At Kinendra's angry glare, he snapped, "The mysterious act isn't exactly helpful, Endra."

Savino looked from one to the other, gaze level. "Who are the Shrikes?"

Kinendra pursed her lips, her expression impossible for Denevah to read, and gestured for Benedetto to handle the explanation. The Crow cleared his throat, shifting in his seat. He rubbed a large hand across the back of his neck. Denevah inhaled deeply, taking in the stale scent of the canals and the refreshing crispness of an impending storm. She hoped it would give the city some relief from the heat.

"They're not important," he began, which he amended when Kinendra shot him a warning look. "They've never been a threat before now. They're just a bunch of petty thieves."

Kinendra snorted. "Hardly," she disagreed, gliding elegantly away from the window, limp gone. Denevah had no idea how she moved like that; if Denevah tried it, she'd probably trip over something and break her nose hitting the floor.

"If you want to tell it so badly, why'd you have me do it?" Benedetto protested, slinking lower in his seat, his face set in a petulant frown.

Kinendra stood before Savino with the haughty bearing of a member of a Great House. Her voice was low and rich when she spoke. "The Shrikes haven't concerned themselves with politics because they haven't needed to. They have an agreement with Corvus of course, who in this city doesn't? It's a sort of non-interference pact. The Shrikes stay to their business and leave everyone else alone. For this to have changed, for them to align themselves with a rogue preacher such as the one you hunt—it means that they have decided to take a more active role in the city's future." She shook her head, worry pinching her brows. "It would do to be wary."

"Where can we find them—these Shrikes?" Savino asked, his hazel eyes distant, almost as if he'd split his focus. Denevah knew that part of him still listened to Kinendra's words, but another part worked on planning out his next move.

Kinendra's slowly smiled, the expression sliding across her face like honey from a dipper. Her hawk's eyes glittered with something close to malice but not quite. "That I cannot tell you. They are not the type of bird to come when called." Her golden gaze swept the room, and Denevah shivered when it passed over her, resting for only a moment before moving back to settle on Savino once more.

"But before you go looking for trouble, you would do well to remember how the shrikes came by their name. They are not called butcher birds because they are amusing party guests."

"That would be one hell of a party," Benedetto quipped.

Kinendra ignored the Crow, all of her considerable attention fixed on Savino. "Be cautious. It would not do to attract their attention."

"And if I want their attention?" Savino said, his mouth a grim line.

"Then be very aware of thorns, my Lord," Kinendra said, making her way out the door which shut with a faint click behind her.

It was silent for a few moments. Benedetto broke it with an exhausted sounding, "That was enlightening."

"What now?" Denevah couldn't keep the nervousness from her voice. They weren't going after just the preacher any more. These Shrikes sounded like they didn't play around.

Savino glanced at her. His smile was bracing, a sign of encouragement. He didn't seem at all worried about facing thieves and killers. Then she looked over at Benedetto, still slouching beside her. Maybe there wasn't a reason to be afraid. Maybe the reputation of House Corvus and the threat of two assassins would be enough to keep them all safe.

She pushed away her unease. When she'd first been given this assignment, she'd been almost relieved that she'd been tasked with protecting someone rather than killing them. Now Denevah realized that things in Aerie were never that simple. If these Shrikes were as dangerous as Kinendra believed, she might just end up earning the name of Crow yet.

Benedetto's hand closed over one of hers and he squeezed. She glanced at him, unable to stop her smile when she saw his excited grin. "Now we find out where this," here he tapped the drawing of the shrike tattoo still in her hands, "leads."

CHAPTER TWELVE

It was late and Ettoni wanted to be back in Rodolfi's palazzo and in his own bed. He couldn't think of the palazzo as his own yet, even though it had been moons since his master's death and he'd inherited it. He'd made the workroom his, but that was all he'd staked a claim to. The master's suite of rooms still looked as though he expected Lord Rodolfi back at any moment.

Still, it was home to him, and had been for more than six years. It felt strange to walk the stairs and no longer have to worry about Denevah slamming out of her bedroom to gallop down the stairs at an ungainly sprint designed, he thought, to break her neck should she make a misstep. It felt even stranger to open the workroom door and not see Lord Rodolfi hunched over a table, dark eyes poring over some obscure text or watching a bubbling alembic.

He'd been at another dinner at Lady Grimauldi's palazzo and needed the walk through the city to clear his head. The Accipitus contingent kept pressuring the Doge to take a harder stand against the local unrest in the city, and pushed Aves to throw in with them. Aves, for their part, focused on the ever increasing earthquakes, their magicians and engineers and alchemists delving into what they felt was the greater threat to their stability. It had been a tense dinner.

Ettoni felt the night air do its work on his tight muscles as he crossed the bridge from one square to another. He pulled the hood of his coat up and enjoyed feeling the tension seep out of his muscles as he walked. The city guards patrolled in pairs; he passed a set as he crossed another bridge. The lanterns spaced at even intervals along the canals had been lit at nightfall, and they gave pockets of illumination as Ettoni traversed the streets. The shadowed alcoves and pools of darkness between still made Ettoni tread carefully.

As he walked, he noticed a number of people moving in the same direction. A steady stream of singles and pairs of the working class moved in tandem, all headed to the same place. Ettoni hesitated, stopping to lean his forearms against the stone railing of a bridge as he watched a man glance around for guards before continuing down a side street.

Ettoni usually reserved his curiosity for alchemical problems, but this furtiveness piqued his interest. He turned his coat inside out, hiding the Aves insignia embroidered on the shoulder, and made his way to the street the man had taken. He kept his hood up to further obscure his features, not that he expected anyone he might run into to recognize him.

He saw more people streaming in from the other end of the street: a surprising mix of women and men, old and young alike. Ettoni made his way to the nearest group, pulled along in their wake, and tried to look like he knew where he was going. Every other lantern along this path had been doused—it wouldn't be enough to arouse too much suspicion with the Doge's Night Watch, but it left a good cover of darkness so the crowds went mostly unnoticed.

A few people nodded at him, giving Ettoni tentative smiles. He nodded back, but kept his gaze abstract, watching the crowd and his surroundings rather than focusing on particular faces. As they neared a decrepit palazzo, the murmurings of the crowd grew in their excitement. Ettoni felt the quality of the crowd shift, like a wave rippling across the waters of Aerie. It sat heavy against his skin. For a moment, he wondered if he'd made a mistake in following his curiosity, but then someone pushed him over the threshold and Ettoni had no more time for second guesses.

The interior of the rotting palazzo was packed and more people shoved in behind him. The building had been abandoned years prior and the elements had taken their toll. The wood of the walls had warped and pulled away from the plaster in the humidity, the stone floors weeping with it. The remaining furniture wouldn't hold weight, the fabric rotting away into mildewed tatters. A crack ran from the base of one wall all the way up to the ceiling and disappeared into the next flight, and Ettoni could feel that the foundation was no longer level. The quakes had damaged this house, and the next one would likely take it down entirely.

The whispers of conversation crested to a dull roar of sound before dying completely. An older man stepped onto a box so he stood head and shoulders above the crowd and held up his hands, though for silence or in benediction, Ettoni couldn't say. Even the shuffles of people shifting their weight stopped. The alchemist took stock of the man: reed-thin, dressed in simple clothes. His unwashed hair—what he had of it—stood up in a cloudy nimbus around his haggard face. But it was his eyes that caught and held Ettoni's interest. They were bird-bright, burning with the fires of conviction. A furnace burned inside of this man, consuming him from the inside out. Looking into those eyes, Ettoni understood the allure of him then—the wild, uncontained pull to do something, anything, to have that intense attention turned on you was infectious.

Navolio. He had to be.

But the timing didn't make sense, and neither did the venue. Everyone knew that Navolio spoke in a public square right after a quake had rocked the city. They'd had a few over the course of the past several days and Navolio had been absent. Now he showed up here, in an empty palazzo that was far more private than the squares. Was Navolio getting word out to his followers some other way in the hopes of avoiding the Doge's Watch—not that the guards were particularly effective? What had Ettoni stumbled into?

The man began to speak. "Friends," he said, his voice a gravelly rasp that carried across the now-silent congregation. "We've had three quakes in the past five days. I know you have felt the earth quiver beneath your feet, I know you have felt the spike of fear in your chests. When will we be swallowed up by the waters? When will we be pulled beneath the waves?"

Ettoni edged his way closer to the wall, where the crowd thinned. A few people pushed against him, reluctant to make way, but he slid past until his back rested against something solid. Murmurs of agreement were interspersed with shouts and a few raised arms as the preacher warmed up.

"And does the Doge listen to the warnings?"

A tepid chorus of No's answered this charge. Navolio repeated, "Does he?"

The answering reply grew louder. The energy in the room turned darker, more dangerous, with a harder edge. Navolio played the people's emotions like an instrument. "The Diluvians are returning—the tides tell us that! And still the Doge refuses to acknowledge their power!"

Ettoni watched the man's eyes glitter with manic glee as his followers began to cry out for action. Navolio held up his hands to quiet the crowd. It took a few moments but when the hubbub subsided, he continued. "The Diluvians are angry and they show their anger in the quakes that rock our city. While the Doge and the great Houses pretend that there is nothing wrong, who suffers?"

"WE DO!" came the roar from the congregation.

"Yessss," Navolio hissed, and his eyes met Ettoni's as the young man started. In Navolio's voice, Ettoni would swear he heard the echoing sibilance of the Diluvians.

Ettoni froze, caught in the preacher's dark gaze. He saw Navolio grin and fear slithered down his spine. He looked like a man who knew all of Ettoni's secrets, like he wished to rip him open and examine all of his hidden pieces for his own amusement. Ettoni waited for Navolio to point at him, to send his followers, already primed for violence, at him. How the man knew who he was, Ettoni didn't know. He wanted nothing more than to fade into the darkness and leave this gathering behind, but he didn't dare move while the preacher's gaze speared him like a fish. He seemed to take pleasure in watching Ettoni wriggle.

Finally Navolio turned back to his audience and began to preach once more. "Are you ready to fight?" he asked them. "When you are called up, will you fight?"

Ettoni slipped away as quickly as he could under cover of the roar of the crowd. Arms waved in the air, fists pumped high. He could hear Navolio's voice grow more and more strident as he urged the people gathered in this place to be ready for the coming change, to be on watch for the signs of the key.

Ettoni stopped, head tilted to listen. "She is coming," warned Navolio, his voice rising to a crescendo. Ettoni heard the Diluvians' voices winding about his words, the scrape of their scales along the stones of their prison in his shouts. "She is death, but she will bring us life. She is light but carries darkness inside of her! She is a slave who doesn't know her true power. But when she discovers it, she will break the chains holding the Diluvians. She will free all of us!" His last words were practically drowned out by the excited shouts of the crowd, but Ettoni caught them. "She is the key. Find her!"

Ettoni's blood chilled, his body too heavy to move for a moment. Mind reeling, he staggered at the implication in the street preacher's words. Denevah. But it couldn't be her. It was simply because she'd been on his mind of late—the only reason why his thoughts went immediately to her at Navolio's prophecy. It couldn't possibly have anything to do with her. The preacher didn't even know about her!

He took a step forward, knowing he had to get out of there. He stumbled as a man in rough homespun clothing crashed into him. His hood fell back as he collided with still another stranger, who grabbed him by his jacket to keep them both on their feet. As Ettoni straightened up, the man's fist yanked his jacket open, revealing the Aves raven embroidered on the fabric.

A lightning bolt of fear blasted through him. The man's eyes narrowed, his hands fisting harder in the cloth of Ettoni's jacket. "What is someone like you doing here?" he snarled.

His heart beat a heavy tattoo inside of his chest. Ettoni didn't answer, didn't think twice. He ripped away from the man's hands and took off, sprinting for the door to the palazzo. He heard shouts and cries behind him, but he didn't slow or risk turning his head to look back. Keeping his eyes straight ahead, Ettoni burst through the doors, slamming into the humid night air.

Skidding on the wet stone of the street, his momentum nearly sent him into the canal. He regained his balance, but it cost him; he heard pursuit right behind him. Ettoni took off the way he'd come, determined to outrun whoever chased him. He carried a knife in his boot for protection, but it would be useless against more than one opponent.

He saw the lighted section of the next street bobbing ahead of him. It was a main thoroughfare and would likely be better traveled. Ettoni knew that he could easily flag a sandolo to carry him home, or catch a patrol to send after the gathering, though Navolio and his listeners would be well away by the time anyone investigated.

Rounding the corner of the street, Ettoni kept his feet better and put on a burst of speed. He passed beneath a lantern post, and risked a look behind him. Three men still pursued him, but they were slowing down . . .

Ettoni collided with someone and bounced off with a loud exhalation as his breath burst out of him. A strong hand wrapped around his elbow, keeping him upright. Looking up through sweat-damp curls, he saw a black coat, stitched with the sign of House Corvus. His gaze continued its path until they took in the stubbled jaw and dark blond hair of the man who ruled the Crows: Lord Trapinze.

He heard the men behind him mutter, "Damn murderers," as they hurried in the opposite direction of the master assassin.

"Lord Ettoni?" Trapinze asked, dark amusement coloring his voice. "Isn't it a bit late to be running an errand?"

Ha, running, very amusing. More important, how did Lord Crow know his name? He'd only been by House Corvus once to see Denevah and he'd only spoken to lesser Crows. "Lord Trapinze, my sincerest apologies for bumping into you like that. I wasn't looking where I was going."

"Yes, I saw," he answered wryly

Ettoni straightened his jacket, tugging at the bottom hem ruthlessly. "It's a lovely night to be out. Enjoying the weather?"

Trapinze's smile grew wider. It wasn't mocking, but it didn't make Ettoni comfortable either. Ettoni wished he had his master's skills with bindings; he'd spell his tongue never to speak such stupid words again. He'd just asked the most powerful assassin in all of Aerie what brought him out on the streets at night! As if he didn't know!

Clearly, he had a death wish. Perhaps the Diluvians could be prevailed upon to appear just so they could swallow him whole and save him from future embarrassments.

"Something like that," came Trapinze's dry reply.

Ettoni nodded just for something to do. He wanted to be out of this man's presence desperately; he'd run from one danger into something far worse. "I don't want to keep you from your," Ettoni made a vague gesture to the street and bordering canal since he couldn't think of a polite way to say murders. He moved to the side so he could pass by the Crow without coming in reach of him again.

"Hold a moment." Trapinze held up his hand.

Ettoni froze, the muscles in his neck tightening sharply. He had to force his shoulders down so he didn't cringe in response to the man's request. Instead, he glanced up and said in his best bored voice, "Yes, Lord Trapinze?"

"You were at the council meeting." The man rested his hands on his hips. Ettoni watched the long fingers where they sat perilously close to the hilts of the daggers sheathed there.

"I was." Ettoni did his best to sound respectful, but to also close off any avenues of further conversation. He wanted to get away from him, not prolong their talk.

"What did you think of it?" Trapinze threw his question out with a casual nonchalance that immediately put Ettoni's hackles up. Lord Crow was not a casual man, nor was this conversation.

"It was enlightening."

Trapinze sighed, glancing away from Ettoni to stare across the canal at the street opposite. "I thought it too long and too full of posturing though the Dauricus are always entertaining."

Making a noncommittal noise, Ettoni held off on saying anything of note. Trapinze continued on, his gaze and mind obviously elsewhere as he continued. "You Aves backed the Doge." He sounded surprised by this.

Ettoni was new to the council, so he had no real way of knowing how Aves usually proceeded in these things. He'd been told to keep his eyes open and his mouth shut, and so he had. He'd seen no problem with backing the Doge on his idea to have the council look into the threat that Navolio posed. While it did bother him that the man seemed dismissive of the Diluvian connection, he thought it long past time for the Houses to pay attention to the preacher.

"It surprised me that you offered your own people for the project," Ettoni said before he could stop himself. He cursed silently, his curiosity getting the better of him. The Crows never sent their numbers on political missions, even when asked. It took a direct order from the Doge and plenty of favors or coin to get them to do something above board; Trapinze had volunteered his people this time. The Crows went on plenty of missions—they were the premiere assassins and were often hired by countries outside of Aerie to do their bloody work—but when they took assignments they did so for themselves.

Trapinze didn't answer the comment, not that Ettoni expected him to. He changed the subject with, "Have you had a chance to speak with your cousin?"

Ettoni's breath locked up in his chest. Was this a trick? Aves had declared Denevah an enemy and had tasked him with finding some way to control her; failing that, they would eliminate her. If he had any known contact with her, both of their lives were forfeit. Did Trapinze know that? Was he trying to get Ettoni compromised and killed? Or did he simply ask for his own ends? Ettoni had only visited Denevah once at House Corvus, but he knew the master of the house had been made aware of it.

He tried to discern Lord Trapinze's angle, and found his mind tangled with possibilities. The man waited for an answer. Putting on his best empty expression, Ettoni said, "She is dead to House Aves. I have no dealings with her."

The lord of assassins smirked, his light eyes glittering with humor. "Of course. I forgot that your House is less than pleased with her at present."

"She killed my master," Ettoni said stiffly.

"And what a horrendous loss to you that was, I'm sure," the Crow replied drily.

Ettoni gawped at him, then shut his mouth with an angry snap. "Good evening, my Lord Crow."

Trapinze chuckled and stopped Ettoni's going with a light touch on his arm. "I apologize," he said simply. "I merely wished to ask you a question about our mutual friend."

Ettoni stopped because he had no choice. It was suicide to be rude to the most deadly man in Aerie and he most definitely wanted to live. He needed to live. No one else could possibly effect a cure for Denevah. "Oh? What question is that?"

"Our friend's poisons." Ettoni's stomach plunged to his knees, the tightness in his chest growing by infinite degrees. He forced himself to nod. Trapinze continued. "I've noticed that she has packets of powder that she takes with her food. I'm assuming these do something to help her, else why would she take them so diligently?"

Ettoni stood there, saying nothing. Trapinze had not asked him a question of note yet. He didn't want to give anything away that he didn't have to.

"I simply wish to know what might happen to our friend if she were denied these, ah, supplements. Would she be unpleasantly affected?"

Ettoni ruthlessly controlled every expression as much as he could. He kept his breathing even, his mouth set in its usual line, his eyes focused on this man's face. Even though his heart sped up, racing like a ship under full sail, he kept his outward composure. If his face was flushed, he hoped Trapinze would blame it on the run and not on the nerves Ettoni did his best to hide.

"I really can't speak to the long term effects of her poisons," he said, voice even and detached. "That was my master's purview, not mine. Aves has ordered me to have nothing to do with her and I have other fields of study to pursue."

"And you always do what the elders tell you?" Trapinze said flatly, but Ettoni could hear the smirk in it, the subtle dig.

Ettoni frowned, brows pulling low over his eyes. Very little could be kept from House Corvus if they deemed it worth the effort to be interested; they were spies as well as assassins. He needed to appear as uninteresting as possible. If he attracted the continued attention of Denevah's patron, it would be next to impossible to continue his work in secret.

"When it means my life if I don't, yes," Ettoni answered smoothly, gaze unwavering. He saw the brief flash of surprise in the blue eyes of the Crow before he quickly shuttered it behind his façade of cool indifference. "Another lesson my former master taught me." Let Trapinze make of that what he would.

"I see." The assassin shrugged. "I will just have to pursue other lines of inquiry." He inclined his head in farewell. "Thank you for your time, Lord Ettoni."

"Good evening to you, Lord Trapinze," Ettoni replied, once again stepping around the older man. Relief filled him, like air filled a balloon, making him feel lighter now that the conversation was over. He moved past the Crow quickly, not waiting to delay his trip home any longer.

"Tread carefully, Ettoni," came Trapinze's voice as he cleared him. "The night is dark and there are many hidden eyes in it that might wish you harm. The canal is an easy place for a man to fall into and never resurface. Step with caution."

Ettoni mouth went dry with fear. Was this a warning or a threat? Both? He did not turn when he replied, "I'll bear that in mind, my Lord."

A rumble of laughter from deep in the Crow's chest followed him. "You do that."

Ettoni hurried away as fast as he could without being rude. He wasn't exactly running, but it was close. He did not look back. He did not want to see if Lord Trapinze watched him or not.

His mind raced with everything he'd heard. Ettoni hadn't told the other leaders of House Aves about Denevah's herbs. When news of Rodolfi's death reached their ears, they'd asked Ettoni if he knew a way to make her biddable, controllable. With someone like Denevah, the Ravens might be able to challenge the Crows in their preferred wheelhouse of assassination. She certainly would be a sizeable threat that the House could leverage at need. The knowledge that she needed "herbal" supplements in order to digest anything would give them a way, but Ettoni had kept that fact to himself. He didn't want Denevah controlled. He meant for her to be cured.

He'd provided her with pouches of the poisonous herb mixture she'd been fed since her infancy. They'd worked out a way to pass messages to each other so she could warn him when she was running low so he could send another pouch of herbs with an errand boy. Ettoni knew that the elders didn't entirely trust him, so he took great care in seeming above reproach.

He hadn't expected Lord Trapinze to notice something as small as what Denevah sprinkled on her food and in her drink. He should have known better. Trapinze had taken a steep risk in protecting Denevah from the Houses who clamored for her blood; he'd want some insurance against her deciding she didn't need his protection any longer. If he suspected he could control Denevah by regulating her herbs, and thus regulating her food intake, then he became impossibly more dangerous. Denevah was human and prone to starvation just as much as the next person. If she tried to eat anything that hadn't been treated with her herbs, she'd become violently sick, her body forcing her to expel it. She could appear to eat normal food and still starve to death without her supplements.

If Lord Trapinze gained proof of his theory, Denevah would be in even more danger. It was more pressing than ever that Ettoni discover a cure for her poisons. Everything else House Aves expected him to work on would have to be put on hold until he'd figured something out. He owed this to Denevah. She deserved his best work.

With a relieved sigh, Ettoni unlocked the palazzo's front door with his key and locked it tight behind him. It was late as he climbed the circular staircase, but he did not stop at the flight that held his bedroom. Instead he continued on to the top flight to his workroom. He had much to do and sand was already sliding through the hourglass.

He got to work.

CHAPTER THIRTEEN

When Savino finally arrived home in the early hours of morning, he'd left a note to the servants that he was not to be disturbed unless the palazzo was on fire, sinking into the canal, or both. He was exhausted from his nightly forays, but it had still taken him a long time to fall asleep once he'd returned to his room at his father's palazzo. He'd tossed in bed, his thoughts full of Navolio and the Shrikes and how they both fit together and what he might do with this information.

He didn't know much about the Shrikes, and that bothered him. Everyone knew of the Crows, but how did the Shrikes avoid the same notoriety? Were they simply the poor man's House Corvus? Savino had spent significant time in the less affluent quarters of Aerie trying to see exactly all the ways the Doge had broken the city and to think of ways to repair it, but he'd never caught even a mention of the Shrikes from those he spoke with. Then again, if they were really so secretive, he shouldn't have been surprised that no one would think to tell the noble's son about them.

He didn't remember finally falling asleep.

He woke the next morning to the muted sounds of canal traffic and diffuse sunlight filling his room. He groaned, hunkering back down among his pillows and pulling the covers close above his head. It was too early to be up.

Then his sleep-dulled brain caught up with what his senses were telling him. Savino flung the blankets off, his hands already scrabbling under his pillows for the dagger he kept there. His eyes were barely half-open, but he still knew someone was in the room with him.

The large windows that led onto his balcony overlooking the Capital Canal sat open, their draperies parted. They'd both been closed when he'd gone to bed.

Benedetto's dark face swung into view. Savino flailed with his dagger, scooting around on the bed until he fell off the side with a thump. He landed on the wooden floor in a tangle of sheets, dagger clutched tightly in his fist. Benedetto peered over the side of the bed at him, and offered a happy wave.

Extricating himself from his bedding, Savino climbed to his feet with a wince. His ribs were sore from the Night Watch's punches, making moving painful. As he looked around, he saw Denevah standing at the window, her back to the room and her gaze fixed firmly on the life teeming outside the walls.

"How—" he began, then stopped, unsure of which question to start with. "What a—" He stopped again. "Why—?"

Benedetto took pity on him. "You said we'd track down the Shrikes today," he answered, looking slightly manic with his wide, loopy grin.

"Did my father see you?" Savino's shoulders knotted with tension at the thought. The less his father knew about what Savino was doing and who he was doing it with, the happier everyone would be. Especially with Denevah involved. Poullo's anger had morphed into an obsession with revenge on House Aves and Denevah in particular. Her being here would go well for none of them.

Benedetto gave him a withering look. Dumping the sheets and blankets back on the bed, Savino sighed. "Stupid question. Then how did you get in? The roof?" He put his dagger in the drawer of his bedside table.

Denevah spoke, voice so soft Savino barely heard her over the noise carrying from the canals. "I still had a key." She didn't turn around.

Savino stilled, hands empty at his sides. "The gate to the canal?"

Most of the High Houses of the city had multiple entrances and exits from their palazzos, several of them hidden from prying eyes. Poullo's palazzo had an escape route through a pool at the base of the building via a gate that led out to the canals. It must have been how Denevah had gotten away after Cyngare—after her Match Night. Savino had never thought to ask for the key to the gate back. He'd assumed it lost like so much else that night.

Denevah nodded, shoulders hunched up around her ears, as if she expected a blow to land any moment. Benedetto stared at her, worry plain on his face. Savino shared a look with the Crow. What must it be like for Denevah to be back here?

"No one saw you?" he couldn't help but ask.

She shook her head. Savino relaxed infinitesimally. At least that was something. Servants talked, and if word got back to Poullo, Savino knew his father wouldn't respond well. He didn't want to risk the man turning his wrath on Savino's mother.

"I made sure we weren't seen," Benedetto assured him. "It was good practice for her." He slumped into a chair, kicking his feet up on an abalone inlaid table. "Where do we start looking?"

Savino couldn't stop the grin that spread across his face. "The Floating Market."

The Floating Market got its start as a few boats that gathered in the poorer quarters of the city to sell goods to people passing in the streets. Soon those craftsmen that couldn't afford their own shops on the expensive spits of land that peppered the lagoon the city was built on realized that rent didn't need to be paid on the water and they began setting up boats. Some were sandolos lashed together, others were massive rafts. As time went on, the Floating Market grew and became fixed; the boats and rafts that made up the hodge-podge of shops ending up roped to each other. Walkways sprang up between them to enable shoppers to get from one boat to the other more easily. It was still an adventure in balance and dexterity to make it from one end of the market to the other without having to grab a guideline at some point in your trek, a testament to the market's unique nature.

Haggling was encouraged—in most cases, downright required. Savino went to the market as often as his duties allowed. He'd always loved listening to the people talking, sometimes in different languages or dialects, and one of his favorite shopkeepers rented space on one of the rafts deep inside the Market. Savino had found a number of useful old parchments that the shop's owner, Ferrano, had unearthed in his scavengings.

Savino wore his oldest and most worn clothes whenever he visited the Floating Market, not wanting to attract attention. He did the same thing now. Denevah walked at his side, her clothes the usual Crow black. He thought the cut suited her. She looked androgynous with her hair tucked inside her hood and sharply angled features and lean frame. He doubted even her cousin would recognize her from a distance.

Benedetto trailed them some distance away; Savino could feel the man's sharp eyes on his back. Denevah still refused to speak to him directly or even look at him. Last night must have been a fluke. She'd barely spoken to him today.

"You can't pretend I don't exist forever, you know," he said, leaning down so he could be sure he wasn't overheard.

"I can try," she muttered.

"It's a pleasure to be working with you too." He turned his head to make sure Benedetto was close by. The Crow scanned the people in the crowd as they neared the edge of the market.

"I didn't ask to be given this assignment," Denevah snarled, her gaze finally settling on his face. "Your sarcasm is not necessary or appreciated."

"Neither is your avoidance," he said in rebuke.

She raised her head, frightened eyes dark in the pale moon of her face. Savino decided to be direct. They didn't have time for a long conversation, but he couldn't afford to wait until Denevah decided to discuss whatever bothered her with him. "I don't blame you."

She straightened, but kept her spot beside him. That was a promising sign. Savino continued. "For Cyngare. I thought I told you that. You didn't know what would happen and you didn't ask to be this way. Your father and his apprentice are responsible for my brother's death."

Her gaze shifted to take in the bright colors of the fluttering fabrics that demarcated different vendors in the Floating Market. "Maybe I blame myself."

Savino studied her profile, backlit by the bright sun filtering through thready clouds. She looked so different from the first time he'd seen her in the Temple Mark on the day of her Match Ceremony, and yet there was an echo of that girl still inside of her. "That's just stupid."

Her brows knit but she didn't look at him. When she stayed silent, Savino said softly, "You never struck me as someone who couldn't see reason."

"He was your brother," she shot back.

Savino kept staring at her, watching the play of emotions on her face. Anger, incredulity, and grief all crossed her features like clouds scudding across the sky. "Does your guilt bring him back?"

"I killed him!" she protested softly.

"Does the sword feel guilty for the lives it takes?" he asked.

"I'm not a sword," she growled, lengthening her stride to stalk away from him. "They don't feel anything at all."

He didn't contradict Denevah and he didn't keep her from leaving. But before she moved out of earshot, Savino did call after her. "I need your help, Denevah, and you can't avoid me forever."

Her footsteps stopped. Savino turned his head so he could see the dark shape of her, now some feet away from him. She waited, watching him over her shoulder. Meeting her eyes, he said, "Show me that you're more than a weapon then."

Her mouth opened, then snapped shut. She turned and continued forward without waiting for him.

Savino paused, rubbing his eyes with a tired hand. He needed Denevah on his side; she was useless to him if she saw Cyngare every time she looked at him. The pushing was necessary. They were going to need to rely on each other, and he couldn't have her doubting him or hesitating. Savino couldn't afford half measures.

"Diluvians," came Benedetto's voice from behind him. The Crow nudged Savino in his sore ribs, urging him to keep moving. "That was an impressive display of manipulation."

"I don't have time for niceties," Savino said, not in defense of his actions but in explanation.

"The blade may forget, Savino," Benedetto said, quoting an old Aeriean saying. "But the flesh remembers. Denevah is both."

Savino accepted the Crow's warning, but it didn't change his mind. "Let's go, Benedetto," as he took off after Denevah.

They made their way into the Floating Market, close enough to be able to signal to each other but far enough away so that they didn't get in each other's way. Savino wove his way through crowds, careful of his footing. Benedetto moved easily over the uneven terrain, keeping his balance effortlessly on the bobbing flat boats of the market. Denevah moved cautiously, but seemed to be keeping her balance as well.

He studied the people he passed, searching faces and bodies for any sign of a tattoo that indicated an affiliation with the Shrikes. Pausing at stalls to browse, Savino watched the throngs of folk perusing the wares on offer. The sun beat down, making him grateful to duck beneath a canvas covering of a cloth merchant to get out of the heat.

"Are you searching for something in particular?" an older woman asked him, a bright smile on her weathered walnut of a face. Her eyes were dark and lined with crow's feet.

"Just browsing," Savino told her with a smile.

As he gazed at her, he noticed a gap in the fabric of her tent. It afforded him a view of the street, and a young boy begging. The boy was missing both legs at the knee, but that wasn't what fascinated Savino. The boy sat on a small cart—low to the ground, with a padded seat and wheels. As he watched, he saw the boy shake his plate at a passerby, even as his other hand snaked out and plucked the purse from their pocket. The boy tucked his ill-gotten gains inside his shirt and began to push himself along the cobbled street with his hands. He wore fingerless leather gloves to protect his palms as he pressed them against the ground for leverage.

As the boy pushed off, the wrist of his threadbare jacket rode up higher on his arm, revealing a black mark. From where he stood, Savino couldn't be sure, but he'd bet it was a Shrike tattoo.

"Amazing," he murmured aloud.

"Sir?" asked the shopkeeper. She saw where he stared and grinned. "That's Mateneo," she said. "He's a devil, that one."

"And quite the accomplished pickpocket," Savino added, watching the smile fade from her face.

"He does what he needs to survive. As do we all." Her lip curled up slightly in derision, as if to ask what a pampered thing like him would know about survival in harsh conditions.

"You have some lovely fabrics. I look forward to returning to purchase some." Savino nodded his head in farewell and continued after the boy.

Mateneo moved along at a good clip despite the press of shoppers. Savino passed by Benedetto at a food vendor and signaled him with a nod before moving on. He saw Denevah ahead of him, sifting through a bunch of brightly beaded necklaces.

Mateneo set up on a new corner, turning his cart so that his back hugged the wall and he faced the canal. Savino paused, watching as the boy—he couldn't be more than eleven—pulled the plate from where it rested on his lap and went about his begging act once more. Glancing around for Benedetto and Denevah, Savino pulled out a silver sola from the inside pocket of his jacket and walked over to the boy.

"Here you go," he said, dropping the coin in the plate with a clank.

Shrewd brown eyes regarded him from a shock of dirt-matted pale hair. "Thank you, Lord," Mateneo answered in a reedy voice. His gaze slid down to the bright coin sitting in the middle of his plate.

"I was hoping we could have a chat," Savino said, keeping his distance so he didn't crowd the boy.

Those wary eyes flashed, sizing him up. Finally, he shrugged. "What do you want to know?" He sounded resigned.

"About your tattoo," Savino began, pointing to the spot on his own wrist where he'd seen Mateneo's. "That's a very interesting bird. What kind is it?"

Savino knew his questions would spook the boy; it was exactly the reaction he wanted. He didn't have time for subtlety.

He wasn't prepared for the boy to punch him in his crotch and roll away. Mateneo gave a high pitched whistle as Savino doubled over in pain. Out of the corner of his watering eye, he saw Denevah take off after the kid, but she followed on the rafts and not on the street itself. When he could finally straighten up again, he looked for any sign of Benedetto, but saw no sign of the Crow. Hoping he was already in pursuit, Savino pushed himself into a limping run after the boy.

Denevah shoved her way through the crowded paths of the market, moving parallel to Mateneo. Most passerby seemed to know to get out of his way; they scampered to the side of the narrow street to allow the boy room to pass. Occasionally Mateneo let out that shrill whistle, making Savino wonder just who he signaled.

He skidded around a corner, nearly losing his balance on the slick stones. Denevah came up beside him, finally managing to break out of the crowd. Shoppers and vendors were shouting and craning their heads to watch the chase as it passed them by.

"Have you seen Benedetto?" he asked her as they ran, dodging a man holding a large barrel of fish. Denevah shook her head, gaze intent on the retreating back of the boy. Savino decided to save his breath for running.

Mateneo slid around another corner, using a pole to fling himself around the turn without slowing. Savino surged forward, desperate to keep their one lead in sight. He'd just made the turn himself when he saw something out of the corner of his eye coming at his head. Savino flinched, unable to stop his momentum.

A fist crashed into his cheek, sending him sprawling. It would have hit him in the side of his head if not for his instinctive reaction, probably knocking him out. Savino twisted as a leg came toward his face, his hands out to catch the boot before it connected. He twisted it, jerking the foot up so the man it belonged to crashed to the ground beside him.

Denevah had problems of her own. Head swimming and face throbbing, Savino saw a young woman smash into Denevah, throwing her back onto the rafts of the Floating Market. The Crow went flying, landing heavily on a display of trinkets and smashing the table beneath it to splinters.

Savino climbed painfully to his feet. He worked his jaw to check for damage as he faced off against his attacker. Nothing was broken. He spat out blood—his teeth had cut the inside of his cheek. The man standing across from him was tall and broad, outweighing Savino by a significant amount. A shrike tattoo decorated the side of his neck.

He'd gotten someone's attention. He only wished it could have been a little less painful.

The man swore and swung again. His assailant wasn't carrying a weapon, so Savino kept his long daggers sheathed at the small of his back. Savino didn't want to alienate the Shrikes by killing off one of their men before he'd gotten the opportunity to speak with them. He jerked backwards, throwing his upper body out of reach, and then responded with a punch of his own. The man blocked it.

The Shrike waded in behind a series of hooks that would have rattled Savino's teeth loose if they'd connected. The Rook knew his arms would be bruised tomorrow as he protected his face from the blows. The Shrike changed tack when he couldn't land a punch to Savino's face, choosing instead to go for his ribs.

Savino blocked those as best he could, but a lucky one got through, blasting the breath from his body. He backpedaled, wincing as he put distance between them. Savino's ribs already ached from the fight with the guards—they were definitely his weak spot. He saw the man smile—now the Shrike knew it too.

Before his opponent could decide his next attack, Savino went on the offensive. He stepped back into reach, knee coming up and hip thrusting it forward into the man's chest. The Shrike staggered back a few paces, gasping for breath from the blow to the solar plexus. Savino followed up quickly, moving inside the man's guard to grab his neck. Forcing his head down with all of his strength, Savino smashed his knee up into the Shrike's face. He heard the crunch as the man's nose broke against his kneecap.

Savino fisted his hands together and brought them over his head. He slammed down on the back of the Shrike's head like a hammer, once, twice, thrice. The man went down and didn't get back up.

Savino's vision doubled and then returned to normal. He looked around to see what had happened to Denevah. She and the other Shrike were in the midst of trading blows, their fight ranging all over this end of the Floating Market. People tried to stay out of their way while at the same time wanting to get a good view of the action. Savino shook his aching head and ran towards them. He still saw no sign of Benedetto.

Denevah appeared to be getting the worst of it.

The Shrike was missing her left hand, but the lack didn't hamper her fighting style at all. Watching her was like seeing an acrobat or dancer fight. Savino remembered Benedetto's description of the young woman he fought on the roofs. He'd bet this was the same woman.

Denevah, meanwhile, looked to be doing her best to avoid a kick to the face. She backed away—or at least tried to—only to have the Shrike flip around and lash out with a kick that would have taken Denevah's head from her neck if the Crow hadn't dodged backwards. Savino pushed his way through the press of people to get to her, but the going was slow.

Denevah attacked with her fists, intending to strike where she could. The Shrike wove out of her way, moving in circular steps that seemed to have no discernable pattern. Denevah had nothing to hit. Then the Shrike was on the offensive again and Denevah could only attempt to block more strikes—elbows, knees, and a lot more feet.

The Shrike's boot connected with Denevah's stomach; even still some distance away, Savino heard the breath blast from the Crow's lungs. She flew backwards into the crowd of people that suddenly scattered in all directions. Denevah landed awkwardly on her shoulder, legs kicking out in a spasm of pain. Savino shoved through the crowd, finally managing to clear the knot of folk blocking him with their gawking. He hurried to Denevah's side.

She tried to sit up, one hand holding her shoulder. Blood leaked from a cut on her forehead and dribbled from the corner of her mouth. She wiped her face on the arm of her jacket, her breathing jerky and rasping.

"Anything broken?" he asked, extending a hand to help her up.

The Shrike turned and ran, seeming to melt into the press of bodies. "Damn it," Denevah muttered, using Savino's help to haul herself up. Savino dropped her hand and sprinted after the girl, Denevah on his heels.

He couldn't help but be amazed at the young woman's skill. Fast and agile, the shifting planks of the rafts and boats gave her no problem whatsoever. Several times Savino had to grab onto a guide line to steady himself or risk pitching over into a table of fruit or a rack of linens. He could hear Denevah crashing behind him, her steps clumsy with her pain and fatigue.

The Shrike turned, surprising Savino. She flung herself at him with a fury. A shin slammed into Savino's arm, driving it into his side, but at least he'd kept her leg from slamming into his ribs. Another impossible flip and twist from the Shrike sent him sprawling. He hit the wood hard, feeling the impact travel up his spine.

Denevah closed while the Shrike's focus turned to him. She attacked, but the woman avoided the Crow's strikes easily, leaping and bending out of their way. It really was amazing the way she moved—effortlessly gracefully and expending no energy at all. She stalked them in a constant circle, ducking and dodging between windmilling kicks that made it nearly impossible to hit her. Savino paired his strikes with Denevah's and still the woman fought.

Then the Shrike dove between Denevah's legs. Her foot came up, smacking Denevah in the face with the sole of her boot. Blood spurted. Denevah staggered backwards, immediately clapping her gloved hand to her nose.

Savino froze as Denevah's eyes went wide and dark. She ripped one of her gloves off with her teeth, spat it on the ground, and then wiped her bared hand across her bleeding nose.

Dread pooled in his guts. They needed a Shrike alive and able to talk and this girl was their best chance. "Denevah, don't!" he warned, already moving.

She lunged at the Shrike, bloodied hand outstretched.

A dark form dropped in front of the young woman just as Savino crashed into Denevah. His momentum slammed them both to the deck.

"Nobody do anything stupid!" Benedetto's voice echoed off of the buildings around them. People scattered in all directions.

Savino twisted in the air so that he landed on top of Denevah. She cried out as her injured shoulder hit the ground again. Her bloody hand slapped flat against the boards, the sticky red mixing with the dirt and mud that shoppers had tracked onto the decking. Savino sat up, boot pinning her wrist to the ground. She twisted onto her side, dazed from the collision and exhausted from the fight, her pinned arm caught beneath her as she coughed out blood.

Benedetto had his daggers crossed before the Shrike's neck, standing behind her. He glanced at Savino, lifting his chin. "You both all right?"

Savino nodded, almost too tired to speak. His head throbbed in time with his heartbeat. "I think so." He took a deep breath in, feeling the twinge in his ribs. "Nice timing. Where were you—did you stop to get something to eat?"

Benedetto grinned. "I've always believed that the proper entrance is worth waiting for."

Savino huffed out a tired laugh. He turned his attention back to Denevah, stirring weakly beneath his boot. "Denevah? You back with us now?"

She rolled over onto her back, using her free hand to pinch her nose closed to get the bleeding to stop. Ignoring the others for a moment, Savino leaned down, torn between elation, anger, and surprise. Denevah had gone after the girl with her blood. She'd tried to use her poisons to kill. Savino knew he shouldn't have been surprised—she was a member of House Corvus now—but she'd never struck him as someone who would want to kill another person. He realized that what he knew of Denevah was a very small part of who she actually was.

"Tilt your head forward—that will help the bleeding stop," he said softly. When she did so without comment, he asked, "If I let you up, promise not to try and kill anyone?"

She grunted in response. Savino frowned and said, "I'm going to need actual words, Denevah."

Her name pulled her out of the fog she'd fallen into. "My glove," she whispered to him. "Where's my other glove?"

Savino cast about, looking for the bit of leather. He found it lying a few feet away, trampled by the fleeing crowd. With a warning look at her, he stood, retrieved it, and handed it back to her. Denevah wrestled it back on with hands that shook, fingers clumsy. When she finished putting it back on, Savino reached out a hand and hauled her to her feet.

She swayed once, reeling as reaction hit her. He held her steady, his other hand grabbing Denevah under her elbow. He saw her throat bob up and down and wondered if she was going to be sick. She made a retching sound, but coughed and held herself together. She buried her mouth against the shoulder of her jacket.

"Denevah, I need you here," Savino whispered, dipping his head so his lips were next to her ear. "Can you do that?"

He squeezed her hand when she managed to nod. "Good." He took a moment to scuff away the blood drops that had fallen to the deck. "Benedetto?"

The Crow nodded, a wide grin on his face. Savino watched him press the edges of his daggers a touch harder against the sides of the Shrike's neck. "We'd like a meeting with the head of the Shrikes," the Crow said in a low voice. "And you're going to take us to them, little bird."

The girl bared her teeth at him as a ribbon of blood slid down her neck.

CHAPTER FOURTEEN

"What's your name?" Benedetto asked the girl as he led them away from Floating Market. She wasn't as tall as he was, but then again neither was anyone else. A mass of curls sat atop her head and framed a heart-shaped face. She had lighter skin than his—a warm brown rather than his own near ebony tones. Her eyes were wide, liquid, and an arresting greyish-golden brown.

He didn't look anywhere but her face. He imagined she got very tired of people staring at the stump at the end of her left arm. He wondered how she'd lost it—if she'd been born that way or if it had been cut off as punishment or in an accident.

She said nothing. She smelled of sunlight and something sweet, like sugared apples or berries. Benedetto wanted to lean closer for a better smell, but didn't want to appear strange. Or strange-er.

"What now?" Benedetto asked the Rook, putting away one of his blades, but keeping the point of the other pressed into her back in warning. "We can't just wander around with her."

"Well?" Savino asked, looking at the girl with a hard expression.

"This way," she answered, turning down a street that ran perpendicular to the Floating Market. Benedetto stayed close to her, his dagger tip touching her spine. One wrong move and he could paralyze her with a simple push of his wrist. He watched their surroundings, every nerve alight to signs of ambush. Every now and then he would check on Savino and Denevah.

The Rook walked with one hand pressed against his ribs, much as he had last night. A bruise already darkened the golden skin of his face. His hair was a wreck. He didn't look great, but he remained on his feet. Denevah concerned him more. The assassin noted how close the Rook kept to Denevah. She looked blasted, her eyes open but glazed, as if her mind was very far away. Savino all but steered her along.

It wasn't long before the telltale roll of wheels over the stone cobbles caught their attention. Benedetto pulled the Shrike around so she stood in front of him and watched as the boy in the strange wheeled cart approached Savino.

"Come with me," he said.

"Mateneo," the Shrike gasped, the first words out of her. Her voice was low, raspy, almost deep if a girl's voice could be said to be such. "No." Her words held an urgency that surprised Benedetto.

"The boss said to bring them," the boy told her, tossing his head back to clear shaggy hair from his eyes. His gaze shifted to Savino. "So I'll bring them."

Then Mateneo smiled at the Shrike. "It's all right, Vermillion."

Vermillion. So that was her name. An odd one, to be sure, but Benedetto liked the sound of it. Such a name fit this dangerous, talented, delightfully violent girl.

"Vermillion?" he whispered.

She turned her head enough to give him a withering look, then returned her gaze to Mateneo. Benedetto didn't think this was wise, following these two into Diluvians alone knew what kind of situation. He was brash and sometimes reckless, but he wasn't stupid. They would be walking into a trap and there were only three of them against who knew how many.

Savino knew this too. "We'll meet in a neutral place." He gave the boy a tight smile, the almost feral expression sliding across the Rook's face with ease. Benedetto had never glimpsed this side of Savino—and would not have expected it to be there beneath the layers of intelligence and refinement. "You'll forgive me for not trusting you."

The boy shrugged. Benedetto felt Vermillion's sharp intake of breath. She clearly didn't approve of this arrangement. Too bad. "Fine," Mateneo huffed with an eye roll.

Savino glanced at Benedetto, raising a cool eyebrow. It took the assassin a moment to figure out his meaning. When he did, he offered, "The House of Black Wings isn't too far from here."

He ignored Vermillion's snort, already regretting his suggestion. The House of Black Wings was another Dove Nest, though not nearly as high class as White Feathers. Black Wings catered to a considerably rougher clientele, though it still cost a pretty penny to roost there for any amount of time. It wasn't the business the house did that bothered him; it was the man he knew who worked there.

He hadn't seen Luc in over a year. Benedetto wondered how much he'd changed in the time since they'd last seen each other. They'd known each other since they were children, but their paths had diverged once Benedetto went to House Corvus. The Crow hoped that Luc's connections and Savino's money would be enough to grease the wheels and get them a secure room. It wouldn't be the kind of help Kinendra provided, but it would have to do.

Benedetto hoped he wouldn't regret calling on Luc.

Both Savino and Mateneo nodded. "One hour," the Rook instructed.

Mateneo reversed his cart and rolled away, but not without casting one last glance over his shoulder at Vermillion. Benedetto took the Shrike's arm and led her in the direction of pleasure house, feeling Denevah and Savino fall into line behind him on either side, like wings.

CHAPTER FIFTEEN

Denevah managed to hold herself together until they reached the House of Black Wings. Her blood still pounded through her veins, her heart still beat, her injuries still ached—especially her shoulder—but everything waited at a distance. Denevah knew she should be more present, that all their lives depended on her awareness and attention, but she needed the mental space. Otherwise, she feared she might fall into so many pieces there would be no putting her back together again.

She'd nearly killed someone with her poisons. Deliberately. Diluvians, what was she becoming? What was wrong with her? It hadn't been a fight for her life, like with the assassin in her bedroom. The girl hadn't been trying to kill her. Denevah knew that, just as she knew the girl could have if she'd wanted to. In response, Denevah had responded with lethal intent.

Diluvians, she wanted to be sick.

Benedetto gave a series of complicated knocks on the side door of a palazzo that still clung to an air of refinement with teeth and claws. The exterior needed a good cleaning, the steps needed sweeping, and a number of windows had cracks in the glass. A few shutters had gone to rot, barely hanging to the brick of the building. But the façade still held enough gilt to take in those who were easily awed. She imagined the wear didn't show in the darkness of the night when the Nest was open for business.

The door cracked open, revealing a pair of suspicious green eyes and a sliver of a body. "What?"

"Tell Lucian that Detto needs a favor," Benedetto said, wearing a pinched—almost nervous—expression. Denevah heard the Shrike gasp.

"Let him in," came another voice, this one belonging to a man.

The door spread wide, the woman on the other side urging them inside with flapping hands and muttered orders to hurry. Savino came last; Denevah felt his warm presence at her back and found it didn't bother her. She wrapped her arms around her torso and followed Benedetto and their captive deeper into the House of Black Wings.

They were led into a small, but surprisingly tastefully appointed parlor. It was dim, the curtains drawn, but candlelamps kept the room from being too dark to see. A tapestry of a beautiful woman cradling some kind of furry animal took up one wall. A table inlaid with bright shards of glass caught and splintered the light around the room. A young man, perhaps a few years older than Denevah sat draped across a low brocade couch, a slender cigar pinched between his fingers. His burnished golden hair fell across his forehead and shoulders, and he wore a gilded waistcoat that might not have been the height of fashion but still looked clean and crisply pressed.

He regarded their party with narrowed blue eyes. "You've been causing trouble for the wrong people," the man said, but he wore a fond smile when he looked at Benedetto.

"Eh," the assassin answered with a shrug and smile. "You know me, Luc. Word must travel awfully fast down here."

Luc's full lips spread into a true grin. He placed the burning cigar on a glass tray and straightened. "My little sparrows bring me all the news. A Crow and a noble throwing down with a Shrike in the middle of the Floating Market is juicy gossip indeed." He tilted his head up at them, a lock of blond hair falling across one eye. "You've always been one for spectacle, Detto. Even as a kid."

"I need a favor," the Crow said.

"I'd expect nothing less." The smile on Lucian's face grew strained and tight, not so friendly now. "You want to meet with the Shrikes." At Benedetto's guilty nod, he continued. "And you planned to use this place to do it."

"I had hoped." Benedetto pushed the Shrike toward a chair farthest from the door so that the three of them stood between her and it. The girl slumped into it with a glare.

"You have much more faith in me than you should. The mistress of the Black Wings may not prove agreeable." Benedetto scowled as Luc finished, brows pulled low over his eyes.

"We can pay," Savino offered. "For the disturbance and the use of her rooms."

"I should hope so," Lucian responded, his lapis gaze sweeping the Rook from head to foot. A slow smile spread across his lips like honey. "Nothing in Black Wings comes for free."

Denevah stilled as Lucian turned to her. She kept her eyes on the Shrike, but she felt the male Dove's assessing regard. She felt grateful when Benedetto pulled Lucian's focus back to him when he drawled, "I have infinite faith in your persuasive skills, Luc."

The Dove pushed himself to his feet with a sigh. "You are right. You can wait here while I speak to my mistress." On his way past Benedetto, he put his hand on the assassin's shoulder. "Don't stay away so long next time."

Denevah swore she saw the Crow flush. Benedetto cleared his throat nervously. "I guess we should make ourselves comfortable." He dropped onto the couch Lucian just vacated, gaze on the Shrike, who looked like she wanted to meld with the chair in order to avoid dealing with any of them.

Savino pulled Denevah's sleeve to get her attention, and gestured to a chair at the corner of the room. She went because she didn't want to protest, she was tired, and her heart felt like it would rattle apart as it beat inside of her body. He put his hand on her good shoulder, pushing her into the seat.

"How are you?" he asked her, squatting down in front of her chair.

Diluvians, she'd grown sick of always hearing that question. She shook her head, unable to put coherent thoughts together. Savino stared at her, his hazel eyes kind. Finally she swallowed hard and said, "I didn't mean to."

But she had meant to. There lay the problem. Denevah had never thought she'd want to kill anyone, or that she could be angry enough to respond with lethal intent. It was different than when she fought for her life—her fear of dying had always driven her to do whatever it took to survive. But today, she hadn't been afraid of dying. Savino had been beside her and Benedetto had been somewhere waiting to step in, so she hadn't been in a situation where her poisons were needed.

If not for Savino's intervention, she would have killed Vermillion.

Her stomach lurched violently. She ground her teeth together to keep from being sick.

"Denevah?" Savino prompted.

"I'm sorry," she whispered, throat burning with throttled emotions. "I don't know what happened."

He put a hand on her knee, a gentle, barely-there touch. She stilled, eyes on the long fingers, the bruised knuckles, the calluses from sword work. What might those hands feel like on her skin? Her gaze traced his fingernails, noting the dirt trapped beneath the nailbeds.

"Talk to me," he urged. "I want to help you."

Denevah placed her gloved hand over the top of his, lightly running her index finger along the back of his hand. "You should wash your hands." She tapped at one nail.

"Denevah," he started.

She spoke over him. "I can't right now." Denevah cut her eyes over to Vermillion. "Talk about it, what I did." She swallowed, her hand still covering Savino's where it rested on her knee. "It frightens me," she whispered. "What I'm turning into."

Savino's eyes widened. Before he could say anything, Lucian returned. He propped one shoulder against the doorframe, indolence in every line of him. Denevah wondered if Benedetto had learned his boneless grace from the Dove. She had to admit to a base curiosity of what might be between the two of them.

"You've got a deal," he announced, but his eyes were hard, cold. What had he needed to promise on their behalf to secure the acquiescence of Black Wings? Then he gave them a number that made Denevah's eyebrows rise.

Savino didn't even blink. He reached into his jacket, still moving gingerly with his ribs, and pulled out a pouch. Denevah heard the clink of coins as Savino tossed it to the Dove. Lucian snagged it neatly in midair and tucked the purse into his coat.

A strange voice caught Denevah's attention. It sounded raspy, like waves splashing over a stone beach. She glanced up to find Vermillion staring at all of them, her greyish brown eyes hard as moonstones. "When my master comes, I pray you get to live long enough to regret it."

CHAPTER SIXTEEN

Benedetto sat close to the Shrike—Vermillion, he reminded himself—doing his best not to stare. Now that he'd seen her in the light of day, he felt more than just attraction; she fascinated him. On the roof, she'd been shrouded in mystery, an idea more than a person. But seeing her on the canals, in the Floating Market— seeing her move and fight felt like he'd been granted some kind of Divine gift—it was more than he ever expected.

As Savino and Denevah moved to the opposite side of the room, the Crow scooted a bit closer to Vermillion. He'd expected her to be taller and slimmer. Her body was heavy with curves, but he knew better than to think she was soft. You couldn't move like she did and not have a ridiculous core of strength and muscle. She moved like a revelation.

Remembering the outcome of the fight, Benedetto glanced over at Denevah. She huddled into herself, arms wrapped around her middle as if she had a stomachache. Misery and terror were etched in lines on her face. Her dark blue eyes were wide and staring. He'd seen her take off her glove. He knew how close Vermillion had come to death, even if the Shrike didn't. Benedetto was grateful that Savino had been there to drive Denevah to the ground and keep her from doing something she'd regret.

Denevah was no assassin. She might pretend to one, but Benedetto knew that when it came down to it, she wouldn't be able to coldly kill a person at someone else's order. He hoped she realized it before she had to face a real test.

When he turned back to Vermillion, he saw her watching Savino and Denevah, head tilted in curiosity. The two of them spoke quietly, too low to hear from where Benedetto sat, but Savino had managed to pull her back from whatever dark place her thoughts and actions had taken her. He felt relieved she had someone to take care of her since he'd taken on the job of making sure Vermillion didn't wander off or kill anyone.

"She would not last two minutes with us," Vermillion said, confused. "Why is she with you?"

Benedetto blinked, banking the flare of his anger inside of him. Vermillion didn't know Denevah, nor did she realize how close she'd come to a horrible, painful death. He'd watched his friend Vitarro suffer one. He did not want to see something like that again. "You don't know what you're talking about." It came out harsher than he'd meant.

Vermillion shoulders jerked in surprise at his words. She twisted in her chair, gaze settling on Benedetto's face. "You're from the roof."

He dropped his hands between his knees as he nodded, exhaustion washing over him. "I am."

"You were good," she said grudgingly.

"I know."

"I was better."

He couldn't help his grin. "I know that too."

A small smile pricked at the corners of Vermillion's mouth. She ducked her head to hide it, but Benedetto caught it. "Where did you learn how to fight like that?"

Now her head come up sharply, a fearsome frown on her face. "Like what? You mean my arm?" She raised the one that ended in a stump, practically waving it in front of his face.

Benedetto leaned back, away from the flailing limb, brows pinched in confusion. He hadn't even brought up her missing hand. "What about your arm? I asked about your fighting style. I've never seen that way of fighting before."

A flush deepened the dusky glow of her cheeks. "Oh." She cleared her throat, picking at the ragged threads of her shirt. "I didn't understand."

Benedetto said nothing. Vermillion must have been tired of people constantly staring or asking after her missing hand, of constantly being underestimated or helped when she didn't need it. But he'd fought her, and he knew just how capable she was. After seeing her skills in daylight, he could only marvel at her ability. Her being short a hand didn't matter.

"So? Where did you learn it?"

"Why do you want to know?" she challenged.

"Maybe because I want to learn myself." He shrugged as if it didn't matter to him what she thought. "Is that so strange?"

Vermillion's gaze swept over him, as if deciding whether he was worthy of the information. He did his best to look serious, but it wasn't a natural state for him. He was fairly certain he just came off looking constipated. He should ask Denevah for lessons in moroseness since she seemed to be on a first name basis with all things serious and depressing.

Finally Vermillion spoke, her chin resting in her palm as she continued to survey him. "You are very odd."

When he opened his mouth to answer, she placed her wrist against his lips to quiet him. Benedetto held himself still, his gaze locking with hers. Had she been hoping to startle him by touching him so boldly with the limb missing a hand? Testing him?

"You will have to speak to my teacher yourself if you are truly interested," she told him, lowering her arm. She eyed him dubiously, like she didn't quite believe he was serious in his intent. "But first you'll have to survive this meeting."

"Why are you so sure your leader will want to kill us? We can be quite the charming bunch." He grinned, raising his eyebrows up and down.

Vermillion glanced away, but he saw her grey-brown eyes crinkle at the edges with the beginning of a smile. Her voice came out muffled, as if she had tucked her mouth in her shoulder, when she said, "Do you know how many people clamor for an audience with my master? Probably more than the Doge himself. Charm counts for very little with the leader of the Shrikes. They can also be quite charming."

"Mind telling me how you ended up working for them?" Benedetto wanted to glean as much information as he could from Vermillion. With Denevah and Savino occupied with her impending breakdown, it was up to him to collect what he could.

The sound of a throat clearing interrupted whatever Vermillion might have said. Benedetto scowled at the interruption, turning around to find his old friend standing near one end of the couch. Luc had returned from wherever he'd gone within the palazzo and now sat, close to Benedetto but not touching. Benedetto could feel him just on the edge of his senses—the heat of his body, the almost touch of their thighs, there but not quite brushing, the solid shoulder not pressed against his. Lucian's proximity was a study in wasn'ts. Benedetto didn't know whether to be relieved or irritated by it.

"I'm sorry I haven't come to see you more often," he offered, feeling like he should say something.

Lucian smirked. "No, you're not."

Grinning, Benedetto agreed. "You're right, I'm not. But it seemed the polite thing to say."

"Oh yes," the Dove said, laughter making his voice bright and easy. "Because you were always so concerned with politeness."

"To be fair, I have been pretty busy."

Luc gaze caught him squarely, his face no longer joking. Luc's seriousness hit him like a punch to the gut. "No excuses necessary, Detto. We were always friends before we were anything else. I knew we were never going to be more than a pleasant diversion. You had your Crows to keep you company."

Luc's words landed lightly, but they dug their hooks into Benedetto unexpectedly. Luc's words held accusation, but of what Benedetto didn't know. The Crows had taken him in when he was younger—they'd given him a place, a purpose, and a future. No one on the street where he came from got that much. Luc still had his family when Benedetto left the slums; he wouldn't have been a candidate for orphan tithe to the Crows anyway. Why did he feel guilty?

Leaning back, Benedetto took a moment to observe his childhood friend. Much had changed in the year since he'd last gotten an opportunity to visit with Luc—he looked better than he'd ever seen him. He dressed impeccably, and looked better fed and groomed than he had in years, even in his early days at Black Wings. Business must be good.

The Dove turned his head at Denevah's murmur from the corner of the room, and Benedetto caught a glint of metal. Lucian's straw-colored hair shifted enough to allow Benedetto to see the earring he wore. He hadn't had one the last time Benedetto had visited. He stared at it, noting the silver hoop with a delicate chain from which dangled an intricately worked silver bird. As he looked closer, he saw it wasn't a dove, like he'd expected.

It was a shrike.

Benedetto pulled a dagger from its sheath on his thigh, bringing it to rest just beneath Lucian's jaw. The Dove went still beneath his hand. "Detto, what ar—"

"Shut up."

Denevah called his name, Savino jumped to his feet, crossing the room in an instant, but Benedetto kept his gaze on Vermillion. She didn't look at all surprised. Not a gasp, an outcry, a flicker in her expression. She knew what Lucian was.

"It's a trap," the Crow said before anyone could do anything overtly stupid, beyond what had been done already. "He's a Shrike."

Savino didn't waste time on questions, something that Benedetto appreciated. He grabbed Vermillion, his own dagger out, and hauled her to her feet. "We need a way out of here," he said. The Rook stared pointedly at Lucian as Denevah came to his side.

"Well, Luc? You heard the man," Benedetto prompted, keeping the point of his knife steady. "Is there a hidden door we don't know about?"

Luc snorted, incredibly relaxed for a man with a dagger at his throat. "Like I'd give the option of a second exit. I'm not a complete moron, you know."

Benedetto wanted to laugh; he probably would have if the situation had not been so dire. He'd suggested Black Wings because he thought Luc trustworthy. He'd made a bad mistake. His only hope now was to get them all out of it alive. He walked Luc to the door, noticing as he did that Denevah had removed her gloves. She held a dagger in her bare hand. His heart thudded more painfully in his chest. "Den," he began.

"Just move, Benedetto," she said back, cutting him off with a hard glare.

He did as she bid, motioning for Luc to open the door. Two large men, obviously hired muscle for the Black Wings, immediately snapped to attention. Their eyes widened when they saw who held the knife.

"We just want out of here," Benedetto began, inching his way past them with Luc as his shield. "You let us leave and I'll happily give you back this one." He pricked Lucian's throat a bit harder with the point, making the skin beneath turn even paler from the pressure. "If you don't, his will be the first throat I cut."

"It's fine," Lucian told them when they exchanged a glance, obviously not buying anything Benedetto was selling. Did Luc think that Benedetto wouldn't kill him on account of their friendship? Lucian couldn't be that stupid. "You can let us through."

Or maybe he could.

The two guards nodded, stepping away to give Benedetto and his companions plenty of room to pass. He couldn't help putting a little spring in his step as they made their way down the front hall toward the main door of the palazzo. With Lucian as a hostage, they should have no trouble simply walking out of the House of Black Wings. Maybe this hadn't been such a horrible mistake after all.

A door to one of the front parlors opened, spilling out several more armed guards. These wore sleeveless tunics, their shrike tattoos displayed proudly. Benedetto pulled up short. He could practically feel Lucian's grin through the back of his head.

"I'll tell you what I told the others," Benedetto began, but the words died in his mouth when Denevah pushed by him.

She held a single blade, but she was a weapon made flesh all on her own. The sharp edge of the knife lay cupped in her palm, her other hand tight around the hilt. Her violet eyes were as cold as sapphires and just as hard. Jerking her head toward the door, she urged Benedetto to continue.

"I'm sure you've all heard the rumors of Bella Muerta. I'm no rumor. I don't want to kill anyone," she growled when one of the guards took a step towards them. "But that doesn't mean I won't."

Benedetto wasn't so certain of that, but he kept it to himself. Lucian struggled, doing his best to slow their progress to the front door. The Crow gritted his teeth, fisting his hand in the yellow hair to yank back Luc's head. "Stop being such a sore loser, you jackass," he muttered to his friend.

"Who says I've lost?" Lucian countered.

Before Benedetto could respond, a new, familiar voice spoke up. "Denevah, my dear, there is no need for such threats. Put your gloves back on and let's talk to each other like civilized folk."

"Kinendra," Savino said, his tone unsurprised.

Benedetto turned, sure that his mouth gaped open in shock. "Kinendra?"

Lucian pushed his way out of his hold once his grip slackened. He walked over to the dark skinned Dove, taking his place at her side. Benedetto blinked, the world tilting on its axis. What was going on? What was Kinendra doing here?

"Come inside," Kinendra offered with a graceful gesture of her arm. "I will explain everything."

CHAPTER SEVENTEEN

Denevah gawked. She couldn't help it. Kinendra was the last person she expected to see in the House of Black Wings or affiliated with the Shrikes. How long had she been one? How many lies had she told them to keep her secret?

Savino stepped inside the front parlor without hesitation. Vermillion followed, a smug smile playing about her full lips. Glancing back at Benedetto, still scuffling with Lucian, Denevah entered as well, certain that the Crow would join them whenever his pride didn't prick him quite so much. This parlor was much larger than the one they'd left, and arranged to seat a large number of guests. The sitting area must be where the Black Wings entertained their prospective clients before they went up to the private rooms on the upper floors of the palazzo.

She noticed that Savino had sheathed his dagger, so she did likewise. Tugging her gloves back on, Denevah stood at an angle that gave her a full view of the room. She'd had enough of sitting.

"So you're the Shrike?" Savino asked, settling himself in a wine-red armchair and crossing his legs.

Kinendra stood as coolly lovely as ever, her dark hair gathered into braids and then twisted into an intricate headpiece. The lovely sunny yellow of her dress contrasted beautifully with the dark ebon of her skin. She looked as out of place here as fins on a cow.

"I am not the Shrike," she clarified, putting heavy emphasis on the 'the'. "I am simply their ambassador in this endeavor and I have full authority to make the deals that I think will best suit our organization." Kinendra took a step forward as she said this, but Denevah stepped back to keep the distance even between them. She'd seen what Vermillion could do; Denevah wasn't in the mood for any other surprises.

Benedetto finally stepped inside, closely followed by Lucian. The Crow threw himself into a chair, slouching down in it with his arms crossed over his chest. He looked like a sulky child denied a sweet. If Denevah hadn't felt so out of her depth, she would have laughed at him.

"How long?" the Crow snarled, cutting his eyes at Kinendra.

She smoothed her hands down her long yellow dress before turning to address him. "I don't think that's the question you really wish to ask me."

"Yeah, well I highly doubt you're going to answer the one I want to ask," he snapped, straightening a bit in his chair now that there were eyes upon him.

Denevah took a moment to take stock of the room. Savino sat at ease, one side of his mouth quirked up in a half smile as he watched the scene play out before him. He hadn't seemed surprised—she couldn't wait to ask him if he'd always had a suspicion or if he was just really good at improvisation. Vermillion rested on one of the long couches, her arm without the hand draped across her forehead. She appeared the picture of unconcern. It made sense now, how little trouble she'd given them. She must have suspected Kinendra would be notified. Lucian stood at the door, cool and louche as ever.

Kinendra herself seemed much as she always did: composed, lovely, unflappable. She lowered herself into a chair with the same grace as a queen would sit on a throne. She gestured for Benedetto to go on.

He clasped his hands in front of his stomach. "Why didn't you tell me?" His question held a touch of petulance, and more than a little hurt. "I thought we were friends."

"We are friends," Kinendra assured him. "But you must realize that friendship and business have no place with each other. You're a Crow—you know it better than any. Survival is what matters most to anyone in Aerie. Those high up in the organization guard their identities zealously."

Denevah saw Kinendra glance at her when she said this. Guilt welled inside her as what she'd almost done to Vermillion came rushing back to her. She wanted to think her reaction had been about survival, but that was a lie. She knowingly taken off her glove in anger and wounded pride. Maybe she belonged with House Corvus after all. If she did, would it matter if Ettoni found a cure for her poisons? Was she just a killer—poison skin and blood or not?

Savino broke in before the conversation could be derailed any further. "The Shrikes are protecting the street preacher. Why?" He leaned forward, wrist resting on his knee.

Kinendra turned back to the Rook with a hard smile. "He pays handsomely."

Denevah caught Vermillion's frown before the girl quickly looked away to hide it from Kinendra. Interesting. At the mention of Navolio, the girl's whole demeanor changed. Did she not agree with the bargain made between them? Did other Shrikes feel the same way? Savino could use the rift surrounding an unpopular decision to his advantage.

"With what money? The guy looks like he hasn't two solas to rub together," Benedetto scoffed.

"We do not ask where the money comes from. Not everything can be bought with gold anyway."

"And if we could pay more?" Savino asked.

Kinendra settled deeper into her chair. "Let me tell you a story, won't you?" Savino inclined his head in acquiescence and the Dove began to speak, her voice soft, drawing her listeners in. Denevah stepped forward to hear her better.

"When I was a little girl, I had a difficult time walking. You see, one of my feet didn't form properly and so I walked with a limp. It wasn't a horrible thing—it didn't keep me from doing most of the things I enjoyed and my parents still doted on me as all loving parents should."

Denevah gritted her teeth. Her real parents had been murdered, and her adopted father had only doted on her insofar as it concerned his experiment. Doting had never entered into her childhood, as privileged as it might have been.

She glanced at Vermillion and saw the Shrike wearing a sour look of her own at Kinendra's words. Yet another piece to file away for a later time.

"It didn't become an issue until it came time for my parents to find me a Match. No one wanted a mate with such an apparent defect." Kinendra spoke matter-of-factly, as if none of this hurt her. Denevah doubted the woman had felt this way at the time though. Denevah had only noticed her limp once before, and even then it was minor. Kinendra moved with such grace that one simply couldn't look away from her. Her movements were captivating. When had the woman learned to mask it?

"My parents were killed in one of the earthquakes." Denevah heard the barest quiver in Kinendra's voice, noticed the hand on the arm of the chair clench. She was not as composed as she strove to appear. "I was truly alone for the first time in my life. I had no real skills, no family who could afford to take me in, nothing besides a pretty face and a limp." She smiled slightly, as if all of this was somehow amusing and not terribly sad. "So I tried to make my way on the streets of Aerie.

"I was not lucky enough to be orphan tithed into a House like Benedetto," Kinendra said with a nod at the Crow. Denevah had her answer to her unspoken question from earlier, but still didn't understand it.

"Wait," Denevah interrupted, holding up a hand. "What's an orphan tithe?" She looked between the Crow and Kinendra, her brows knitted in confusion. If Benedetto hadn't been born a Crow, then how had he become one?

"Most of the other Great Houses don't use it anymore," Savino said, his voice a rumble in the crowded parlor. "If they ever really did—I was never able to find records that the other Houses made use of it. Orphan tithe may have been something strictly unique to Corvus."

Benedetto's head came up, surprise plastered across his features. "How did you find out about that? Most nobles don't seem to know anything about it."

Savino shrugged, a brief rising of his shoulders. "I read," he offered in explanation.

Kinendra chuckled. "I'd love to get a look at your library. That bit of information was stricken from the records in all but the oldest documents." Her words made Denevah wonder how Kinendra had come to know about it.

Savino frowned, face closed off, expression a wall. "Nothing remains hidden if you search hard enough," he answered.

Benedetto raised an eyebrow at the Rook. Denevah frowned. Savino was too sharp by half. He drew knowledge to him like other people drew breath, and spoke like Lord Trapinze himself. She wondered how many stones the man had overturned to find this particular bit of information. What else might he have found in his searching?

She rapped her knuckles against the wall to get Benedetto's attention once more. "You still haven't told me what it is."

Benedetto leaned over Lucian so he could smirk at Denevah. "Ever wonder why we accepted you into our pillowy bosom so easily?"

She made a face. "Because I can kill people without even trying?" The joke fell flat. She saw Lucian's eyes grow wider in his pale face. "And please never use the term pillowy bosom again. I think you just gave me hives."

Vermillion's surprised cackle filled the room. Savino chuckled, a rich and mellow sound. Benedetto slumped back against the couch, hands cradling his head. "No, although that certainly is a reasonable argument and handy life skill," he answered, breezing over her words. "The leaders of House Corvus realized pretty early on that there was no way baby making supply could keep up with assassin demand," he drawled. "Crows lifespans tend to be cut short."

"Can't imagine why," Savino said drily from his spot against the wall.

"Yeah, it's almost like we're in a House where people kill each other for a living," Benedetto returned, just as drily.

"It would be delightful if you got to the point," Kinendra broke in.

Benedetto began to make a rude hand gesture, stopped, and then kept on with his story. "Anyway, with the rate of attrition climbing in House Corvus, the elders of all of the Houses came up with an ingenious way to both swell the ranks and take care of the orphan problem that plagued the city after the last round of swamp fever. That was, what, two centuries ago?" He looked at Savino for confirmation.

The Rook nodded and took up the narrative. "They collected those children who'd lost their parents—or had no one to speak for them—and offered them sanctuary in the House of Assassins." Savino's voice held the barest hint of admiration. "Very neat. No wonder the other Houses agreed to it. A simple solution to both problems."

Benedetto nodded. "The orphans couldn't claim full House membership in Corvus until they'd completed their first kill. Until that time, they were treated more like apprentices. But once in, they were treated as if they'd been born to the House until the day they died."

Denevah tilted her head. "I had no idea," she said, bracing her boot against the wall she leaned against. "I went to Corvus because I had nowhere else to go and I thought they'd appreciate my . . .," she swept her hand in front of her body.

"Unique fashion sense?" Benedetto guessed, sporting a cheeky grin. "Yes, we were all very impressed by your flair for pairing colors and patterns." He nodded to her all black ensemble.

Lucian cleared his throat, shooting Denevah an ugly glare. "Remove your boot from our wall, please. Were you raised in a cheap tavern?"

She dropped her foot to the floor, cheeks hot with embarrassment. "Sorry," she muttered before turning the conversation back to what she wanted to know. "So you were a part of the orphan tithe? What about your parents?" she asked him.

Benedetto huffed and dropped a hand into his lap. He said, "Don't know about my father. My mother was originally from somewhere in the Imperium. She didn't talk about how she ended up in Aerie."

"What happened to her?" Savino asked in his deep voice.

"She died of the wasting fever when I was seven springs old." Benedetto said it matter-of-factly.

"I'm sorry," Denevah offered, chewing at her lower lip. To be left alone that young—had he really had a choice when the Crows came for him?

After a brief moment, she glanced away. "How did you make it to the Crows after your mother's death?" she asked Benedetto.

"One of the other women—she smelled the body. Came in and found me." Benedetto's voice had a lost quality about it. Denevah had never heard him sound like that before.

Lucian added in a subdued voice, "He didn't leave her side for three days. Couldn't bear to leave her alone, I guess." He glanced at his old friend. Denevah saw something wordless pass between the two of them. "A Crow was a regular for the woman who found him. She passed word of Benedetto along to him."

"Benedetto, can anyone from any House make use of the orphan tithe?" Denevah asked, eyes alive and burning in her pale face.

"I think so. Ask one of them." He gestured at Kinendra and Savino airily. "They're the ones who seem to know the rule of law." He shifted on the couch so he could see her better. "Why do you ask?"

"Denevah?" Savino asked softly, his voice hanging in the perfumed air of the parlor.

"It's nothing. A silly question, nothing more," she said, giving him a not very convincing smile. "So does this mean I'm an orphan tithe?"

"Possibly the oldest one we've ever had," Benedetto answered.

Savino looked back at Kinendra. "I apologize. We seem to have gotten rather far afield. You were saying?"

Kinendra smiled, inclining her head to the Rook in graceful thanks. "Thank you, Lord Savino."

Denevah did her best not to roll her eyes. It was like watching a Match Night all over again. She slid down the wall to sit on the floor closest to the door.

"As I was saying, I was not tithed to any particular House and I was not doing very well on my own. My foot made it difficult for me to steal and run away. I had resorted to begging, but even that didn't go well. I was starving and desperate when the Shrikes found me."

She smiled at Vermillion, who sniffed, crossed her arms over her chest, and looked away. Denevah raised her eyebrows at the display, wondering what bound the two of them besides just being Shrikes. Savino's question interrupted her thoughts. "How did they know to even look for you?"

Kinendra's expression sobered quickly, like a blanket thrown over a fire to snuff out the flames. "What do Vermillion and I have in common? What do we have in common with Mateneo?"

Denevah thought about the question, staring at both women in the room and doing her best to recall Mateneo from the little she'd glimpsed of him. She saw nothing that connected them—their skin colors were all different, two were female but one was male, they weren't similar ages, they seemed to have vastly different skills. She couldn't think of what the answer might be.

Savino answered after several long moments of silence. "Vermillion lacks a hand, you say you have a limp, and Mateneo is missing his legs. Is that it?"

Kinendra nodded. "Astute, my Lord." She sounded pleased. "Tell me, what did you feel when you looked at Mateneo?"

Savino sat silent once more, his hazel eyes distant as he formulated his response to her question. When he took too long, Kinendra prompted, "He made you uncomfortable, didn't he?"

Denevah could see that Savino didn't like admitting it, but he answered honestly, despite his feelings. "Yes."

"Why?" Her gaze bored into him relentlessly.

The Rook took a deep breath, hands clasping the arms of his chair tightly. "Because looking at him reminds me of what I don't like to think about."

Silence. Denevah thought that even the very air had gone still with his admission. It made her skin prickle uncomfortably, like a thousand eyes were on her suddenly. She watched as Savino swallowed and held himself still.

Kinendra leaned forward, pressing her advantage. "What don't you want to think about?"

Savino did not lower his gaze from hers. He spoke clearly. "That there's something I could be doing to help him but I don't know how to start so it's easier not to."

"What makes you think he needs your help?" came Vermillion's sudden, whip crack response. She unwound from her tightly held position on the couch, looking moments away from attack. Her voice rose as she continued. "People like you always think there's something you have to do to make our lot better, like we can't help ourselves, like we need someone like you who only sees us as something to be pitied."

Vermillion sneered, shooting Denevah a hateful look. "I don't know which of you is worse."

"Enough, Vermillion!" Kinendra's mild tone sharpened, lashing out at the younger Shrike. When Vermillion opened her mouth to protest, Kinendra silenced her with a look. Lucian put a gentle hand on Vermillion's shoulder which she shrugged off.

When it looked like no further outbursts were forthcoming, Kinendra turned back to Savino. "How many times a day do you turn away from people like us?" Kinendra asked. "How many people do you think pass us by without seeing us simply because they don't want to?" She leaned both hands on her knee, peering up at all of them.

Denevah watched Savino carefully. He still looked into the middle distance, working out the problem in his head. He wouldn't come fully back until he'd figured out the answer. Slowly, he began to speak. "You rely on that." His words gained momentum as he became more certain of his theory. "That invisibility—that's what you count on."

"Not count on," she said, a slow smile breaking across her face like a wave on the shore. "Expect it. And people rarely, if ever, defy our expectations of them."

"So you have the perfect network of spies throughout the city," he said with grudging respect. "That's quite ingenious."

She inclined her head as if accepting a compliment from him. "And growing larger all the time. When a child is born with a disfigurement like a missing limb, the parents discard them like so much trash. They leave the poor thing outside to die from the elements or starve." She shifted with a creak of wood from the frame of the chair. "No one wants these children, these orphans."

"No one except you," Savino finished for her.

"No one except us," Kinendra agreed. "I'm glad you're able to keep up."

"I've always been a fast learner."

"What about Luc? He's not missing anything," Benedetto said, dropping his arm down onto his friend's shoulder. "That I know of anyway." He gave Lucian a smile that bordered on lewd.

"Anyone is welcome to the nest," Kinendra told him. "Lucian has proven to be a most valuable asset to our organization. You wouldn't believe the things people let slip when they are tired after a romp in the bedroom."

Denevah didn't want to think about romps or bedrooms. All she could remember was a beautifully appointed room covered in red as her Match coughed up blood in gouts that stained the white rugs. She shivered and wrapped her arms around her body as if that would keep her warm and safe.

"I still don't understand what the Shrikes get out of protecting this preacher," Savino said.

"Have you not heard what he promises?" This from Vermillion, who launched herself out of her seat. Her voice lowered in a remarkably good imitation of Navolio. "'The world is broken! The Houses don't care what happens to any of us, just so long as they get to keep on doing as they've always done. They do nothing as the earthquakes tear apart the city—so long as they remain safe, who cares what happens to anyone else?'" She shook her head, arm slashing down for emphasis, her face twisted in mockery. "A change is coming, something old made new again. And the people guzzle it up with a spoon!" She snorted in disgust.

"Vermillion!" Kinendra leapt to her feet, her usual grace gone in feral surprise. A spasm of pain crossed her face, there and then gone like a ripple in the water.

Savino rose too, much slower and more measured. He eyed Vermillion cautiously, as if wary of her outburst. "I understand your frustration and rage, and I sympathize with them. I do not presume to empathize with them since I cannot say I have ever gone through what you all have. But I must try to understand the city and its people if I wish to govern it," he said. His hazel eyes caught and held hers, his usual bland expression exchanged for something fiercer.

He spoke in a firm voice, resolute. "I know this city festers under the weight of the leadership we have now. I know we cannot go on as we have been. I want to put a stop to the ruin that undermines us all before we lose everything."

"Pretty words," Vermillion sneered. She didn't buy Navolio's sermons, but it seemed she didn't believe Savino either.

"If I become Doge, they will be more than just words. I promise you that."

Denevah bit back a gasp. That's what he had his sights on? He'd never struck her as a politico, but she knew little of him outside of what Cyngare had told her, which admittedly hadn't been much.

"The promise of a Rook?" Lucian scoffed. "We know, intimately, how much those are worth." Benedetto gave him a worried side-eyed glance.

"Is there something you want to tell me?" Benedetto asked him.

Lucian bristled, glaring at the Crow. "Besides 'you're an idiot?' Not really."

Kinendra rubbed her temples, looking like a woman in despair of ever having a serious conversation with the group in front of her.

Vermillion asked the assassin, "Is there anyone you haven't pissed off?"

Lucian snorted. "Probably not. But if it makes you feel better, the list of people he has *is* long and distinguished."

"Kind of like my—"

"Benedetto!" Denevah broke in, scandalized.

"I was going to say my sword," Benedetto said with a lopsided grin. "Diluvians, get your mind out of the trash."

"Perhaps we should continue this discussion just the two of us?" Savino suggested. "I think I can offer you something beyond anything the preacher has in his arsenal. Nothing else in the world can rival it"

Denevah saw him glance her way. She felt cold settle in her bones. Savino couldn't mean her, could he? He wouldn't parlay her poisonous touch for an alliance, would he? Not after some of the things he'd said to her, about being more than just her father's weapon.

"I think that is a practical idea." Kinendra looked at the four of them. "Run along and play, children. This won't take long."

"I'll be fine," Savino assured her when Denevah made no move to leave. "Go on."

Confusion and fear battled inside of her. Their mission was to keep Savino safe, but he had dismissed them. He wanted them out of the room to make a private deal, to broker something that Denevah feared might involve her. She wanted to stay, and yet at the same time she wanted to put her trust in someone. She wanted to believe in the words that Savino had given her.

Benedetto took her arm and led her out the door. She went with him easily, only glancing back once to see Savino giving her an encouraging smile. It was as the door closed behind her that Savino's comment about the city finally registered with her. He'd said he wished to govern Aerie.

Not rule.

Savino was a very strange Dauricus indeed.

CHAPTER EIGHTEEN

Ettoni couldn't sleep. It eluded him, like a maiden in the mist, just out of reach. He'd opened the window hoping that fresh air would help him rest. It only served to let in the teeming stench of the canals, made worse by the thick, oppressive heat that even darkness couldn't relieve. He'd closed it after a few minutes, unable to bear the smell.

He needed to rest. He knew that. The work on Denevah's cure tore at him, bit by bit. He caught sleep in fitful starts, he barely ate. He killed himself by inches, but if it meant she could survive, even thrive, then his suffering would all be worth it.

But he made mistakes. Earlier in the day, he'd slipped with the solution he'd distilled from some of the more virulent garden plants. He'd burned the skin from the back of his hand badly—the pain of it throbbed and gnawed at him from beneath the soothing ointments and bandages he'd wrapped it in. If he wasn't cautious, he might burn down the laboratory or inhale a mixture that would burn his lungs out from inside of his body. He couldn't afford a mistake when he was making such little headway.

He'd managed to partially negate the effects of Denevah's poisons, but still hadn't found a way to nullify them entirely. And he hadn't found a way to remove the toxins from her directly that wouldn't kill her in the process.

Flopping back on his bed, Ettoni flung his arm across his eyes. His body ached from standing for hours hunched over burners and alembics. His eyes hurt from deciphering his master's scrawling notes. His head throbbed from the swirl of ideas and thoughts that refused to settle down.

And his heart ached because it had been nearly a fortnight since he'd seen Denevah outside of House Corvus. He thought her absence would be an easy thing to bear, something he could put aside. It was not. He heard no word of or from her, not even a whisper, no chance of them running into each other on the street, no secret meetings to be held. His warnings had worked, but now his longing for her had no outlet but his work.

He rose from the bed with an angry curse. Ettoni wasn't going to be able to get any sleep this night—his mind refused to cooperate. He may as well do some research and hope that would be enough to allow him a few hours of rest.

Surveying his shelves, he found nothing he hadn't read. Everything in his workshop would be experiment related, and he didn't want to think about that right now. With a sigh, he made his way up the curling staircase to his former master's flight, pushing open the door to Rodolfi's bedroom. He hadn't been inside of it in moons. The last time had been in search of anything that might help Denevah, but then he'd shut it up tight. Ettoni could almost feel Rodolfi's breath against his neck, the man's hands clutching at his shoulders, dragging him down the same dark path Rodolfi had followed to his doom.

But tonight he needed whatever might be in there. Lighting the lamp on the side table from the candle he carried, Ettoni held it high so he could examine Rodolfi's bookshelves. There were slotted rows of cabinets that held parchment rolls below the shelves built into the wall of his sitting room. Setting the lamp down on a shelf, Ettoni knelt to get a better look at the scrolls. He put one hand on the top of the cabinet to steady himself when his legs ached as he sifted through the contents.

Most of the parchments were old drawings of plants or animals, dissected into parts that were beautifully and meticulously colored. The drawings had faded with time and some of the older scrolls crackled with age. Ettoni moved to another section of slots, his hand sliding along the top of the cabinet.

He froze. His thumb brushed over a raised piece of metal on the underside of the cabinet's lip. Pulling the lamp closer, Ettoni bent forward, twisting his neck to get a better look. Rodolfi had never mentioned a hidden drawer, although the things Rodolfi hadn't mentioned to Ettoni could have filled the palazzo. Using his fingers, he found the upraised piece, set nearly flush with the bottom of the cabinet's underside. With a deep breath, he pressed it in with his thumb.

A soft click, and then a piece of the cabinet's façade separated from the rest to reveal a small hidden drawer. Ettoni carefully pulled it out fully, revealing a hide-bound book of indeterminate age. He released his breath in a rush, unable to keep himself from glancing around as though he expected to be caught at any moment. No matter how many times Ettoni told himself he was now the master here, he knew it would never be enough. Rodolfi's presence lingered, filling every space, his fingerprints burned into the fabric of this place. Ettoni felt haunted by a ghost none but him could see.

He took the book from its place and shut the drawer. Ettoni had no idea what secrets might be held inside the tome, but they had to be important if Rodolfi had kept it hidden. Then again, with his luck, Ettoni would find nothing but gibberish scribbles, one last trick Rodolfi could play on his apprentice. Placing the book on the nearby desk, he flipped it open to the first breath and gasped, nearly shrinking back in his surprise.

A perfectly drawn picture of a Diluvian's eye stared back at him.

Heart hammering in his chest, Ettoni swallowed thickly. Sweat broke out on his brow and between his shoulder blades, sliding down his skin. The Diluvians terrified him, more so now than when they had just been an amorphous conglomeration of ideas inside of his head. To know they were real, and powerful, and obviously waiting, made it difficult to sleep with ease.

He closed the book, tucking it under his arm, and made his way back to his room.

Ettoni skimmed the first few pages, then skipped to the last entry. He recognized the strong heavy handwriting as Rodolfi's. What he read made him feel sick.

The earthquakes are increasing in frequency and growing in strength. The Diluvians continue to batter at the borders of their prison. The Doge has left it up to Aves to find a way to placate them. I fear that this time, it will not be possible. He suggested perhaps another cull, but that might weaken their magic to the point of the Seals being made useless. Aerie would drown anyway and there would be no help for it.

I fear what I might have unleashed, but at the same time I cannot deny that I am pleased. My daughter is my greatest achievement, the one shining example of my alchemy. If the world drowns for her, then she will have been worth it.

Ettoni felt ill. It was the last entry in Rodolfi's hand. He understood some of it—the references to Denevah were obvious. But the bit about the Diluvians and the barriers and something about a cull—none of that made sense. Whatever it was though made his stomach clench in fear. Something was very wrong in Aerie and it seemed his master had known about it.

It sounded like he didn't know how to stop it. Or hadn't wanted to.

Sitting up straighter in bed, Ettoni leaned over and turned up the flame on the lamp at his bedside. Avoiding the first page with the Diluvians eye, he started with the oldest entry, the script almost impossible to decipher.

He had a lot of reading to do.

Ettoni woke with a start, staring blearily about him, unsure of where he was. He rubbed at gummy, dry eyes, and raised his head. He lay sprawled across his bed sideways, the hidden book he'd been reading resting beside his head. Light streamed in from the windowpanes, filtering in through the sheer curtains to bathe the room in a milky light. From the direction of the sun, Ettoni guessed it to be late afternoon.

He sat up, groaning. He felt like he'd been bludgeoned with a hammer. His head ached, his eyes burned, and his brain felt like it had been turned into soup. Rubbing a hand over his face, Ettoni cracked his jaw on a yawn. The lamp beside his bed had burned out at some point while he slept.

Climbing painfully to his feet, Ettoni staggered to the bowl of water the servants had set out for him and splashed some over his face in an effort to come fully awake. The water was lukewarm, having sat there long enough to come to room temperature. His bedclothes clung to him, sodden with his sweat from the night's fruitless tossing and turning. He quickly bathed, and then dressed in a simple linen shirt and an old pair of pants. He had no desire to go up to his workroom today.

His mind worked, full of everything he'd read in that book. Ettoni had made it through each entry in the strange ledger—part journal and part observational record. Part of him wanted to burn it before anyone else found it, while the other part wanted to take it to the Doge and demand he find someone else to deal with this problem. With Rodolfi dead, House Aves did nothing to continue the research on the cause of the earthquakes. He feared the task would fall to him and he didn't have the slightest idea where to even begin.

Shaking his head to clear out the unwanted thoughts, Ettoni hunted around for his boots. He pulled those on, grabbed his jacket, and then headed out into the late afternoon bustle of the canals. The smell was nearly stifling in the heat; a bit like being slapped in the face with a wet fish. It took him a few moments to become accustomed to the stench before he went nose blind to it. He wandered the streets beside the canals, moving slowly through the crowds, with no particular destination in mind.

The heat subsided with the approach of sunset. Ettoni settled at the apex of a bridge that spanned the Capital Canal to watch dusk settle over the city. Boatmen poled sandolos and skiffs along the canal, hawkers yelled out for the last customers of the evening, and Ettoni felt something dark and heavy slip from his shoulders. Drawing in a deep breath, he found he didn't even mind the fetid smell of the canal water. He'd been cooped up inside of the palazzo for too long.

The sun sank below the horizon, settling into its watery bed for the night. Ettoni watched as the colors of burning flared up, and then pushed himself away from the stone railing of the bridge. He ambled away to walk deeper into the city, not ready to return to his workroom and everything that awaited him there.

He'd walked several blocks before he noticed the feeling of being watched. Ettoni turned his head, checking behind him. No one there on the street stuck out—just a few men and women going about their business at the end of the day. They were commoners—pigeons in the parlance of the great Houses. Ettoni shrugged off the odd sensation of observation. It was probably just being out in public after being sequestered in his laboratory for so long.

He walked on as twilight draped the city, staying to well-lit streets and squares, never straying too close to alleys or unlit areas. He'd learned his lesson after the evening following the street preacher's denizens. Ettoni tucked his hands in his pockets and walked, but he couldn't get away from his thoughts.

Everything he'd read came back to him with nauseating clarity. Stopping at a small square tucked between two large palazzos, Ettoni leaned against the rim of a fountain to calm his thoughts.

The spray from the water spilling out of the fountain-dragon's mouth felt refreshingly cool against his flushed skin. He rubbed a palm over his forehead and rested.

Someone settled next to him, not close enough to infringe on his space, but near enough that Ettoni felt the presence of a stranger. He glanced up, intending to give whomever had sat so close beside him a dirty look and leave, but froze at the wide-lipped smile that greeted him.

Navolio sat beside him.

Ettoni felt as though he were sitting beside one of those damn serpent lilies in Denevah's garden, waiting for it to strike without Denevah around to protect him. His shoulders hunched unconsciously, bracing for an attack. A few men, obviously loyal to the street preacher, milled close by. Ettoni wasn't going anywhere.

"Greetings, Raven," Navolio said, eyes alight with his mania.

Ettoni clenched his hands into fists inside of his pockets. "Good evening." He refused to look the man in the face.

"I've been waiting for you to return to one of my sermons. It's not often I get nobility at my speeches." He sounded amused.

Ettoni lifted one rounded shoulder. "It was an accident." His eyes searched the square for a way out.

"I don't believe in accidents," the preacher said, voice smug.

Ettoni said nothing, just shifted a little further away from Navolio in a way that he hoped wasn't obvious. The skinny man reeked, the sickly sweet smell of rot clinging to him like a shroud. Ettoni tried to breathe through his mouth and not gag.

Navolio leaned forward, his lined face pushing into Ettoni's space, as if he knew how much he bothered the young alchemist. His wild, greasy hair hung about his head in a nimbus, flaking scalp visible through the clumped strands. Ettoni did his best not to recoil.

"You were sent to me." The preacher dropped his voice; a soft growl. "They sent you to me."

The sweat trickling down Ettoni's spine turned frigid. "They?"

Navolio smiled, revealing surprisingly even, white teeth. "The Diluvians. The masters who control whether we live or die." The man sounded excited about that possibility.

"The water dragons?" Ettoni tried to scoff, but his voice fell flat. "They're just myths and legends," he lied.

Navolio frowned, manic eyes growing dark and shuttered. "You know better than that, apprentice," he hissed, voice menacing.

Ettoni shuddered. Navolio's tone reminded him of the voices of the Diluvians echoing in his head. The preacher had sounded like that during the sermon Ettoni had mistakenly attended. That sibilant hiss, that watery rasp still haunted his dreams and waking. And now with what he'd just read so fresh in his mind . . .

"I don't know what you mean," Ettoni told him, rising to a stand.

Navolio's hand locked around his wrist, dragging him back to his seat with a painful grip. "Don't play at stupid, apprentice," the preacher snarled, fetid breath hot in Ettoni's ear. "You and I both know you've seen them. And we both know why."

Ettoni tried to pull away, horrified. How did this man know anything about him—or Denevah?

Navolio held on, his grip on Ettoni's wrist like a vise. "You think you're the only one they see? Who speaks to them?" The preacher laughed deep in his throat, a low, guttural sound. He pulled aside the front of his robe, revealing an almost concave chest, pale and bird-light.

Gasping at the reveal, Ettoni stared, horrified. What looked like scales covered half of the man's chest, the skin around it red and seeping. Unable to help himself, the alchemist moved closer, lowering his head for a better look. He wished he had more light to see by.

Because what he saw was fascinating in a particularly horrible way. The scales were an oily, iridescent green, and they were pushing up through the man's skin, tearing his flesh open as they grew in. Pus oozed out around the edges of the scales. Angry red lines spread out in spider web tendrils, mapping out over the unmarked flesh like fractures in a mirror. Heat poured off of him like he burned from the inside out.

"What did this to you?" Ettoni whispered, a blend of awe and horror.

"Those same creatures that helped your master create his own beautiful monster," Navolio replied. "We are one and the same, she and I."

Ettoni recoiled, biting back on the urge to retch. Denevah was nothing like this corrupted flesh before him, this imperfect, flawed experiment of the Diluvians. The man was mad. This disease—whatever it might be—had eaten his mind.

"How do you know about her?" Ettoni could barely force the words out of his mouth. His throat felt tight, but not as tight as his chest.

Navolio's smile widened, splitting his lips in an almost obscene gape. "I have dreamed about her. The dragons—they whisper in my ears as I sleep. They are waiting for her. She will unleash them. And I will help her."

The words of the hidden journal came back to Ettoni. The Diluvians had been bound to the very fabric of Aerie by ancient magics and a pact between the four Great Houses that strengthened the seals keeping them prisoner. Each Great Seal had been bound inextricably to the life force of a member of said House. Lord Rodolfi had been the seal for House Aves. His death had weakened the magical bindings placed on the water dragons. The Diluvians fighting against the remaining bonds that held them captive caused the increase in quakes in and around the city. When all of the seals were sundered, the Diluvians would be free.

Navolio's preachings were true. The Diluvians were behind it all.

"How?" Ettoni asked, unsure of what he even wanted to know. How had a simple preacher found out about the Diluvians, how did he come to be marked, how did he plan to help Denevah? All of these questions and more roiled around in his brain.

"She tries to escape our reach, to deny what she is," Navolio said, ignoring Ettoni's query. "She must accept."

Ettoni drew back further, alarmed by the sudden urgency in the man's voice. Fear clawed at his insides at the echo of the Diluvians' drowned rasps in the preacher's voice. He glanced around, desperate for a way out. Navolio gripped his arm, tighter than before. Ettoni winced at the pressure; he'd have bruises in the morning. The preacher's weak-looking body belied a terrifying strength.

Jerking his arm free, Ettoni rose to his feet. He'd left his workshop to clear his head and now all he had were more questions. "I don't have any dealings with her anymore."

Navolio chuckled. "You are a poor liar." He stared into Ettoni's eyes, as if reading every secret the apprentice kept. "She will come to me. You both will eventually."

Ettoni didn't answer, just shoved his trembling hands back in his pockets and hurried from the square.

He couldn't shake the impression that Navolio had let him go.

CHAPTER NINETEEN

It was two days before Savino got a chance to speak with Denevah without Benedetto there. Evening settled over the city, and he and Denevah were in the library at the House of White Feathers, waiting for Benedetto's return. The glass doors that led to the balcony were open to allow the Crow entrance from the roof. A light breeze cooled the room as the city began its slow slide into night.

Kinendra had offered them the continued use of White Feathers while she waited for word from the head Shrike about Savino's proposition. She had told them that Navolio hadn't endeared himself to the Shrikes any more than the Doge had, especially not with his penchant for offering human sacrifices after each earthquake that seemed to have little to no effect on their frequency.

Savino had offered more than just his support should he become Doge. He offered knowledge—knowledge that only Rodolfi and his apprentice knew. Everyone wanted to control Denevah, including the Shrikes it turned out. Savino wasn't willing to use her as a bargaining piece but he had no trouble offering up the apprentice himself. For while Savino might not blame Denevah for what had happened to Cyngare, he could and did blame Ettoni. What the Shrikes did with Ettoni and the secrets he held was their business. Savino found he wasn't unduly upset at the thought.

He looked up from the book of poetry he scanned to see Denevah immersed in her own book. His eyes traced the line of her neck, the strands of pale hair that escaped the braid snaking down her back, the heavy fall of her lashes over her downcast eyes. She looked lovely, even sitting there in her stark black Crow clothes. He pulled his gaze away from her face to stare at her gloved hands.

She must have felt his gaze on her for she looked up. It took a moment for her eyes to focus on him, but when they did, her fair brows knit together. "What?"

He closed his book and stood, the question he'd been dying to ask pressing against his lips. "Why did you keep it?"

Her violet eyes clouded with confusion. "Keep what?"

"The key. To the gate at my father's palazzo."

Her face paled. He saw her hands tremble on the book she held. Denevah shrugged, eyes downcast, examining her knees. She dug the toe of her boot into the rug, worrying at the strands.

"You had to have a reason," he pressed.

"Some things don't mean anything. I just forgot about it."

He didn't believe her. "Denevah. Look at me, please."

Slowly she raised her eyes until she stared into his. "What do you want me to say?" she asked, voice breaking on the question.

"The truth?"

Her breath came out on a shuddering sob, but her eyes remained dry. Tears were a dangerous thing, just as poisonous as the rest of her. "The truth is that I don't know why I kept it. Except that it reminded me of him."

Savino blinked, a strange tightness circling his chest. He didn't know what to name it—all he knew was that the feeling made him uncomfortable. To hear her speak so about his dead half-brother, to hear the sadness and loss and regret in her voice did something painful to his insides. When he'd asked Denevah if she'd loved his brother those many weeks ago in House Corvus, she'd said she did not, but that she could have had she been given the time.

It hadn't bothered him then. Why did it affect him so now?

She held out her gloved hand. A heavy iron key rested on her palm, stark and ancient looking where it sat against the fine black leather.

"Here," she whispered, dark blue eyes so full of sadness that Savino felt guilty seeing it. This kind of grief wasn't meant to be shared. It wasn't just for his brother. It was for everything she could never have. "I have no right to this. I never did. You should have it back."

Standing in front of Denevah, Savino remembered the girl from the Match ceremony at Temple Mark. She'd been so alive, so bright with hope that she glowed with it. Where had that girl gone? Was she lost forever? Or had she grown into something else, something sharper and harder, built now to weather the storms the world threw at her?

Closing the distance between them, Savino reached out, engulfing her hand with both of his. "You keep it," he murmured, carefully closing her gloved fingers over the key. "It belongs with you now."

Her breath caught in her throat as she stared at their joined hands—his bare, hers gloved—eyes wide. "You trust me with this?"

"I trust you with my life," he whispered. Her hands trembled in his. Gently he released her.

She dropped her hands to her sides, a pained expression on her face. As he watched, she raised one hand to her shoulder, digging the fingers into the muscle there. Savino watched her silently for a few moments before making his decision.

"Sit over there," he ordered, gesturing at a large pillow on the floor.

Denevah looked up at him, pale brows furrowed in confusion. "I'm fine," she told him. When he just kept on pointing, she sighed and got up.

Savino watched as she settled herself on the pillow, a kind of easy grace to her movements. He found he liked watching her. In public he thought she looked stiff and uncomfortable, unused to the eyes of so many being trained on her. He couldn't blame her for it; Savino often felt the same under public scrutiny. But seeing her in private showed him her natural grace, the way she moved when she was herself. He imagined it something few people were lucky enough to witness.

He pulled on his silk gloves with a tug, and then knelt behind her, knees on the edge of the cushion. Denevah turned her head quickly, eyes narrowed. "What are you doing?"

"You're tense." He settled his gloved hands on her, near the join between her neck and shoulders, and pressed into the muscle running beneath his thumbs.

Denevah froze beneath his hands, eyes blown wide with fear. "What are you doing?" she repeated, voice low and rough.

Savino paused. He couldn't say what he wanted, not really. He didn't touch people—he didn't enjoy physical contact. He had to force himself to return his mother's hugs. But Denevah possessed something, something that called to him. He'd felt it the night they danced, that lightning spark of recognition, of like finally meeting like. The click of a dagger sliding home in a sheath. It was a strange feeling, and one he'd never had before. With Denevah, it seemed, he wanted to touch.

Savino felt no physical stirring, it wasn't that. He remained wary enough of what she was to be careful. But he would be lying if he denied the pull he felt to her, like she was the one person who would see him, who would know him in whatever form he took. Who would have him in whatever way she could. Just as he would have her.

She shuddered beneath the light touch of his hands. Gentling his hold, Savino ran his hands along the slope of her shoulders, the silk of his gloves catching on the rougher material of her linen shirt. She'd discarded the heavy jacket after dinner, the constricting laces making it hard to get truly comfortable.

"Is this all right?" he whispered, his gaze drinking in the side of her face, the pointed hinge of her jaw, the shell-like swirl of her ear.

"You shouldn't touch me," she murmured, sounding choked. But she did not shrug out from under his hands. "Nobody touches me."

Savino's hands stilled. His fingers stayed on her shirt where it rested over her collarbones. He could feel the jut of them through the fabric and his gloves. "Has no one ever offered you even this?" he asked, feeling the gulf of their disparate lives between them. He who never wanted touch had it at every opportunity, and she, who craved touch, forever denied it.

Denevah shook her head, unable or unwilling to speak. "May I?" he asked in a whisper.

He saw her eyelids flutter closed, a tear trembling, caught between her lashes. "Please," she whispered, the sound breaking as it left her lips.

Savino hummed his approval, a low thrum from the back of his throat. He wasn't sure what he was doing anymore, he who was always so certain of everything. All that mattered was that Denevah stayed with him, and if he could help her in even some small way, he would.

He ran his hands across her shoulders, following the sloping line down her upper arms to her elbows and past them until he reached her wrists. Then he slowly slid his hands back up until he reached the back of her neck. Moving his hands down her back, he lightly dug his fingers into the knobs of her spine until his palms were flat against the small of her back. Then he retraced his path until the tips of his fingers fanned against the base of her skull.

Denevah's breathing had quickened, small, hitched exhalations escaping her parted lips. Savino kept his touch light, barely a press against her shirt-covered skin. He watched her face as best he could for signs of distress. Tremors still shook her, but she did not tell him to stop, so he continued. He couldn't imagine what it must have been like for her to go her entire life without a kind touch, a hug, a reassuring brush of hands.

"Did your father . . .," he began before trailing off at the sight of a tear running down her cheek. Unconsciously he began to rub her shoulders soothingly, the way his mother had comforted him as a child when he'd gotten upset by something Poullo had said or done to hurt him.

"Rodolfi was not a man given to displays of affection," she answered softly. "Even with gloves, he rarely touched me." She smiled then, a fond expression on her face. "But I wasn't completely bereft."

"Oh?" The muscles beneath his hands quivered. Savino felt the tension held in them, the knots of stress. He began to knead them lightly, trying to work out some of the tightness he found there.

Her lips parted in a sigh and she sagged the slightest bit. It wasn't her usual hunch—this was a hard-won bit of relaxation and Savino felt proud to be the one to see it. He kept up with his massage.

"My cousin, Ettoni. He was my father's apprentice, but he would walk with me, play games with me. We sometimes held hands—gloved, of course—when we walked the garden. And when I was sad, he would sometimes hold me until I felt better."

Savino went still at the mention of the apprentice's name. He took a moment to collect himself, to make sure his voice sounded even when he spoke. Denevah didn't need to know how even the man's name filled him with rage. He waited until he'd mastered the swell of emotion. Then he began to knead her muscles once more.

"But it wasn't a common occurrence," he guessed. Denevah's breath shivered out of her. He felt her shudder beneath his hands and then stop, locking down on her reactions with a swiftness that surprised him.

Savino remembered his own childhood, bright with touch. His mother's hand on his shoulders, a pat on the head, the odd roughhousing with Cyngare before Poullo had them separated. He remembered seeing the physical affection bestowed on his brother by his father, noting the differences in treatment. Savino hadn't missed the loving hugs, the careless pats of approval—he hadn't wanted them, even then. But it had made him curious—why did Cyngare warrant them when Savino did not? What was so different about him?

"You could say that," Denevah said wryly. She rolled her shoulders beneath his hands experimentally and sighed again. "I found out later that everyone in the palazzo—not that we had many servants—were warned not to touch me for their own safety. I wasn't around any other people, so I thought it normal."

"You missed it though." Savino continued with his massage, digging deeper into the muscles of her back. Denevah's head fell forward. Her body leaned into him, eager for more.

"I'm not sure what I missed. I just knew I needed desperately for something to change." She took a deep breath as he dug into one very persistent knot beneath her shoulder blade. "I wasn't allowed out in the street, but I could watch the canals from my window. I could see what went on outside."

"Breathe," he admonished, pressing the heel of his hand into the spot. When Denevah let out an explosive breath, he continued. "My father showered Cyngare with affection. He would have been good for you." Sadness filled him, both for the loss of his brother and for the loss of Denevah's happiness. Cyngare would have made her very happy with his easy way with affection.

Denevah held her breath, but this time for a different reason. "Your father did not do the same to you?"

Savino felt the mirthless smile twist on his lips. "My father barely tolerated me," he said, voice deep and even. He had long ago made peace with Poullo's disdain. Nothing he did would ever win the man's approval.

"I do not understand," Denevah said, turning her head and then her body so that they faced each other. "He's your father."

Savino did not remove his hands; he just kept them resting on her shoulders. He shrugged, as if it meant nothing.

"You mentioned, when we danced," here she blushed and looked away briefly, "about you and Cyngare. What happened between you?"

Savino moved his hands until they rested on either side of her neck, his thumbs sitting against her jawline. He felt her swallow. She could look nowhere but at his face. "I loved my brother, make no mistake about that." He smiled sadly. "And I think he loved me. When we were younger we got on easier. My father ignored me, but Cyngare always had time for me. At least until Lord Poullo decided he wanted the honor of fathering the next Doge."

Denevah's gloved hands wrapped around his wrists. "Why would that change how Cyngare felt about you? You were brothers."

Savino smiled, a brief flash of teeth. "Lord Poullo does not love my mother. After the death of his first wife, he married for power. My mother is the daughter of a highly placed Hawk. She is not beautiful—not like Poullo's first wife—but she is kind. But my father, well, he does not see the virtue in that. He is angry at being denied what he wanted most."

Denevah's violet eyes darkened with her anger. Savino watched the series of expressions that crossed her face: disbelief, disgust, confusion, rage. "He, at least, had her for a little while. One can't stop death. Believe me, if you could, my father would have discovered it."

"In a way, he did," Savino countered. "He discovered you."

Closing her eyes, Denevah shook her head. Savino could feel her pulse jump beneath the fine cloth of his gloves. "He didn't stop death. He just found a new way of dealing it."

"You're more than the poisons in your skin, Denevah."

Her grip on his wrists tightened. "Then you are the only one who thinks so." Her eyes were sad. "You and Benedetto." She pulled his hands from her, but kept them clasped in hers. "What happened with Cyngare?"

Now Savino shook his head. "It all changed when Poullo started grooming him to be Doge. He wanted Father's approval, his regard. He spent more and more time away from the palazzo, away from me. After a time, I think Cyngare believed what our father said of me. Poullo liked to think of things as contests, as prizes to be won. And Cyngare wanted to win, even though there was never any competition between us."

"Did you hate him? Ever?" Denevah's eyes were bright, but whether from candlelight or tears, he couldn't say.

"No," Savino whispered, feeling the tightness in his throat. He'd never hated Cyngare. He'd been angry with him, and confused and sad when his brother no longer acknowledged him with anything but a sneer, but he had never hated him. "I didn't want to be Doge then. I always envisioned something quieter, with much less fuss. Cyngare could have had it with my blessing. I would have liked to have told him that, even if he wouldn't have believed me." He gave Denevah's hands a light squeeze.

"And do you hate your father?" Her words held an edge, dagger sharp and glistening. Her tone called for blood.

"I do not feel anything for my father, except perhaps pity."

"Pity?"

Savino looked down at their joined hands, their faces close. The room was dark, lit only by an incense brazier and a few candles. "Yes, pity. He's now burdened with watching the son he never wanted become the most powerful man in all of Aerie. I can only imagine how ill that sits inside of him." He glanced at Denevah and laughed quietly.

She joined in after a moment, the sound chiming in the dimness of the room.

"I hope I'm interrupting something," came Benedetto's drawl from inside the open door leading to the balcony.

Denevah snatched her hands from Savino's like she'd been burned by a flame. Savino moved slower, turning his head to survey the Crow lounging against the door frame, a lazy smile on his dark-skinned face. Benedetto watched them with glittering dark eyes, wearing an amused expression.

"Since you're here, I can go." Denevah leapt to her feet in an instant, heading for the door and her room. "I'll see you in the morning."

Savino sat back on the cushion, palms flat against the stone floor to support his upper body. Benedetto stopped at the table to pour them each a glass of wine from the pitcher still on the tray. Savino accepted the cup gratefully, and then said, "Out with it."

"Out with what?" Benedetto answered, draping himself on the lounging couch with the ease and grace of a leopard, holding his glass loosely by the rim.

"Out with whatever is going on in that head of yours. You're thinking loud enough to wake the dead." Savino took a swig from his own glass.

Benedetto slanted his gaze so he could watch Savino from the corners of his eyes. "I just didn't think you were attracted to women." He took a sip of his wine.

Savino dropped his head back to stare at the ceiling, feeling his conversation with Denevah weigh on him. "I'm not."

"Men then?"

Savino glanced at Benedetto, noting his curious stare. "No." Shifting, he faced the Crow. "Why are you so interested in who I'm attracted to?"

"Because you say you don't like anyone and you don't want to be touched and then I come in to find that." He waved his hand toward the cushion where Savino and Denevah had been sitting.

"Are you jealous?" Savino asked mildly.

"Of you?" Benedetto shook his head.

"Or of Denevah," Savino added with a shrug.

Benedetto's gaze slid to the canal glimmering in the moonlight. "You think because of Luc—"

"I think I don't care," Savino answered, cutting off the Crow before he could get far down that line of thought.

Benedetto looked puzzled. "You don't?"

Savino leaned back so he stared at the ceiling. "No." He turned his head so he could grin at the assassin. "You like women and men, Denevah likes men—I think—and I like neither. I'm certainly in no position to judge anyone else."

Benedetto cocked his head, confusion on his face. "But then why were you touching her?"

Savino closed his eyes, feeling the unsettled churn in his gut. He didn't know why, just that it made him happy to do so. He didn't think it was pity for Denevah. "Don't know. I can't explain it," he told the Crow. "I just don't mind touching her. But I don't feel anything, you know—stir—when I do."

He waited a moment as Benedetto pondered his words. Then the Crow nodded, accepting what Savino told him. "That's fair. Weird, but fair," Benedetto said, shaking his head. His usual rueful smile reappeared.

"Oh, you're one to talk," Savino joked back, glad that they were back on comfortable ground.

Benedetto's face turned serious. "Be careful of her."

Draining his glass, Savino replied, "I know how dangerous she is."

"I don't think you do." The Crow leaned over and refilled Savino's goblet. "And I'm not just talking about her skin."

Savino watched Benedetto carefully, gaze tracing the lean lines of his face. His expression held concern, and something else that he couldn't identify. "Speak plainly, please. I'm too tired to translate ominous vaguaries into common speech."

"I don't want Denevah getting hurt," Benedetto said, setting his half-full glass on the floor and leaning over to loom over Savino. "Or you either."

"I feel the same," Savino assured him. He pushed away from the floor, staggering a bit on feet gone nearly to sleep. He shook the pins and needles from his right one as he shed his gloves and began to strip out of his fine shirt in preparation for the evening's hunt. "We should leave shortly."

"You like her," Benedetto accused.

Savino twisted his body until he could see the Crow. "So do you." He tilted his head to the side, studying the assassin. "Are you warning me to stop?"

Benedetto ran a hand over his close cropped hair. "No. Nothing like that." He huffed out a frustrated breath. "I don't know what I'm saying anymore. Ignore me."

Savino paused, arms full of the white cloth of his shirt. "I would never say this to her," he admitted quietly, "but her father was a genius. She was made to draw people to her."

"She's easy to love," the Crow admitted, not looking at him. "But that has nothing to do with her father."

Savino nodded once, before pulling on the rough homespun linen of his disguise. His fingers twitched; he could still feel the slide of Denevah's skin beneath his palms.

CHAPTER TWENTY

Denevah crept along the edge of the roof, trying to keep Navolio in her line of sight without alerting him to her presence. This was the closest they'd come to finding out where he went after his "sermons" and she'd be damned if she'd mess up the chance to discover where he went to ground. She wished Benedetto was with her, but he looked after Savino this night as he tried to follow him from the ground. With the Shrikes still acting as the preacher's lookouts, it was more important than ever to follow their first directive: protect the Rook.

She neared the end of the block of roofs—she would need to find a way to keep following from a height. Denevah doubted she could make the jump to the next roof over. Perhaps a boat, keeping track of him from the water? She might lose him in the time it took to steal a sandolo.

Risking a glance down, Denevah noticed that the preacher had stopped. He stood like a statue in the middle of the empty street, surrounded by his attendants. Navolio had his head cocked, almost as if he were listening to voices only he could hear. As she watched, the preacher turned his face up in her direction.

A chill ripped through her, freezing her in place. A slow smile slid across Navolio's face like ink across water. His eyes locked with hers.

"We see you," he whispered and there was no way she should have been able to hear him, but she did, as if he stood right next to her. "We've been waiting for you." His smile grew wider and in it she swore she saw a dragon's smile.

Denevah's throat closed up in fear.

Navolio turned back to his attendants. He gestured for them to keep moving, walking ahead of them in his ragged clothes but with the demeanor of a king. Denevah tried to get her feet to move to follow them, but her body felt heavy and strange and unresponsive. Tears gathered in her eyes; she blinked them away.

A clatter of glass exploding against the roof tiles right beside her jolted Denevah from her stupor. A thick, acrid cloud of smoke enveloped her, cutting off her sight. It burned her lungs as she sucked in a startled breath. She coughed, tears running down her face as the horrible burning smoke clung to her. She couldn't get enough air.

Stumbling, Denevah fell to her knees. Gasping and choking, she clawed at her throat with gloved hands. Her vision dimmed, strobing in and out of focus. She heard footsteps approaching, but all Denevah could do was crawl forward on knees and elbows, hacking and drooling and weeping.

"We have her," said a voice she didn't recognize.

Then something hard struck the back of her head and Denevah knew nothing more for a long time.

Denevah came to consciousness slowly, head throbbing atrociously with the chilly sickness of disorientation. Keeping her eyes closed, she waited for the tumult of nausea to settle, taking the time to acquaint herself with her surroundings. The air felt clammy and damp. The air held a humidity that reminded her of the Diluvians' ruined palazzo. She suspected she was somewhere below the waterline of the canals.

Her hands were pressed on a cold, flat surface. A table perhaps. Stone certainly. She felt restraints binding her tightly at wrists and ankles, and again at elbows and knees. Another strap went across her neck, holding her head down. Terror made her want to thrash, but she managed to keep herself still.

The smell was harder to pin down. The air carried the scent of wet wood and stone and rot. It held a mineral quality she couldn't place. It reinforced her belief that she'd been taken underground. There was a stagnant smell to the room, like it wasn't used often, if ever.

Taste was out—she wasn't going to lick anything. Sounds though. She heard the shuffle of footsteps nearby, maybe more than one set. Her ears picked up the slow slide of metal on stone. Perhaps a blade being honed against a whetstone? She heard a faint drip of liquid coming from somewhere—she remembered the sound from enough time spent in her father's laboratory. Water hitting the floor or a potion being distilled? She didn't know.

Now for sight. Slowly she cracked open her eyes, seeing what she could glimpse from beneath her lids and lashes. She lay on her back on a table. Ropes held her wrists bound to iron rings set into the stone. They were at her sides, the rope barely pricking her with its rough fibers. She could see her ankles were bound similarly. Her gloves had been removed.

Her gaze roved, taking in the circular chamber and the lamps which illuminated it. She rested on a table in the center of the room. Shelves seemed to line the walls of the room but there were few books that she could see. Lots of bottles holding powders and liquids and preserved creatures of all shapes. Someone's laboratory—it reminded her of her father's workroom in a strange way. She couldn't see behind her, but from the sound of it, someone was already back there. Working. Fiddling.

Denevah took a tentative breath in, choking on the feel of humidity in her lungs. Her throat and chest ached; she suspected it was an aftereffect of the gas she'd inhaled. Cold gnawed at the depths of her bones—it felt like she might never be warm again. She wanted to reach her hand up and feel the back of her head where she remembered being struck, but knew that her bindings prevented it. She swallowed, throat dry with fear.

Savino and Benedetto had no idea what had happened to her. Denevah suspected that by the time they came looking, it would be too late for her. She bit her lip to keep the whimper locked in her throat.

She tried to get her rattled brain to think, but her thoughts ran sluggish. Denevah took deep breaths through her nose to calm the sick feeling crawling up her throat. She needed to buy herself time so she could think of a way out.

"I can tell you're awake," came a voice she recognized. It belonged to the woman who'd been talking to Ettoni in her father's old workroom. "Your breathing has shifted."

Lady Grimauldi of House Aves.

The woman crossed into her field of view. Denevah blinked to clear her blurred vision, desperate to focus. The roiling nausea in her stomach and the pain in her head were distractions she couldn't afford.

Lady Grimauldi was a handsome woman in her middle years. She wore the black working tunic of all Aves alchemists and magicians. Her dark eyes were distant, like twin stars, and just as cold when they looked down at her. Denevah felt like a bug being readied for study.

"What am I do—" Denevah began.

A gag came over her head. Lady Grimauldi forced it between her teeth before Denevah really knew what was happening. The woman wore long, heavy leather gloves, so even if Denevah could have bitten her, she wouldn't have broken skin. House Aves knew how virulent she was; they were taking no chances.

"I'm not going to waste my time listening to your pleading or your prattle. I have work to do," Lady Grimauldi said briskly. She stepped away from the table, gathering up supplies and implements on trays that she carried back to an adjacent worktable. As she set them out, she continued. "You are an experiment, one that has gone horribly wrong. But that doesn't mean we can't still gather useful information from our mistakes."

Denevah struggled against the bonds holding her flat but felt no slack in the ropes and straps. She could only watch and listen as Grimauldi bustled about the workroom. "There are still a number of things we can learn from you, in the hopes that we can improve upon our next attempt." The woman smiled down at her.

Next attempt? Denevah's eyes went wide, and she made a noise of protest behind the gag. Did Aves plan to try Rodolfi's experiment on some other poor child?

The woman continued to speak, obviously enjoying the sound of her own voice. "You are something of a failure," she said, disdain in her voice. "And your father did not keep the kind of notes that would do us any good in future. So it seems we're going to have to start testing from scratch before we get to any of the terribly interesting things." Denevah heard the squeaking of metal, and then Grimauldi walked around the side of the table, holding something small and furry in her gloved hands.

It was a rabbit, skinny and brown with frightened black eyes. As soon as Denevah saw it, she froze, breath going shallow around the gag in her mouth. Grimauldi scruffed the rabbit in one hand, then grabbed Denevah's bare hand, roped to the table. Denevah thrashed, but the grip on her forearm tightened painfully as the Aves slid the rabbit beneath her clenched fingers.

Grinding her teeth into the gag, Denevah glared at the Lady Grimauldi, hate rolling through her. She wanted to scream, but held herself still and silent. She breathed heavily through her nose, gaze never straying from Grimauldi's face. How had she managed to capture her? Who had helped her? She couldn't believe that Ettoni would do something like this, nor Savino. Benedetto only did as Trapinze bid, and she still held value to the Crows. At least she thought she did. But even though the potion that had felled her came from Aves, only House Corvus had a use for such things.

The rabbit began to twitch and convulse beneath her curled fingers. Lady Grimauldi watched the entire time, gaze avid upon the dying rabbit. Denevah wanted to be sick. She swallowed hard, and leaned her head back against the table. She didn't want to kill anything, but here she was again, not being given the choice. There was no point in trying to deny what she was. No one wanted her to be anything else.

The rabbit's fur felt soft against her skin. Without thinking, Denevah unclenched her hand, fingers gently stroking the shivering body. Grimauldi's hold on her arm had not relaxed; she knew the woman could feel her muscles working beneath her hand. Denevah didn't care. She kept up the petting, wishing she could do more, wishing she hadn't done this, until the poor animal's body shuddered one last time then went still. Still she slid her fingers through the soft fur, tracing the shape of the tiny head, the silken ears.

She didn't realize that Grimauldi had released her until a small flask pressed against the ridge of her cheekbone. The Aves angled it to collect the tears that spilled from her eyes. Denevah hadn't been aware she'd been crying.

"We don't want to waste any part of you," the alchemist whispered beside her head. "There's a great many things to collect before we're done."

Denevah closed her eyes so she wouldn't have to look at Grimauldi anymore.

She waited in darkness, but not alone. Denevah felt their presence like heat all along her skin. They felt far away, and yet there with her at the exact same time.

The Diluvians.

"**You have not come to us**," said one of the voices, multiplied by a thousand hissing echoes.

"**You seek to run**," said another.

"**It is not far enough**," the first voice said.

"**Never far enough**," said the third.

"**You are ours, child. We will wait for only so long**," the second voice warned.

"**Your place is here**," came the first voice once more.

The third voice said, "**Our venom works in you, even now**."

Denevah peered into the darkness, but saw nothing. Then she felt something squeeze her wrist; glancing down she saw a blue and white tail wrapping around her wrist like a shackle. An orange and black tail held the other. Thrashing, Denevah tried to tear loose only to have the restraints grow tighter.

"I'm not yours!" she shouted into the murk. "I never agreed to this—any of it!"

"**To the first bite, no, that is true**," answered the first voice. "**But the second . . .**"

"**And soon the third . . .**"

She felt a cold void open up at her feet at those words. She vaguely remembered a night when she was so sick, a night when she nearly died from the poisons inside of her body. She remembered a voice asking her a question. She remember saying yes, not knowing what the yes meant, only knowing she didn't want to die.

"**Come back to us soon, little one, before we come looking for you**." The voice faded as Denevah fell down into the void beneath her feet. . .

Heart hammering in her chest, Denevah jerked awake. She still lay strapped to the table so all she managed to do was rub her raw skin against her bindings. Another dream. She knew they meant something, but Denevah didn't know what. They frightened her more than nearly anything else, including what Lady Grimauldi had planned for her.

Her eyes were gummy with sleep—or unconsciousness, she didn't think that what she was doing could be called sleeping—and bleary. She couldn't eat. Lady Grimauldi wouldn't take her gag out long enough for that, and even if she did, Denevah didn't have her herbs that made eating possible. Grimauldi trickled water onto the gag for her to suck on, but that was it. She didn't know how long she'd been in this experimentation room. She hoped the Aves woman would kill her soon.

Denevah knew it did no good to hope she would release her.

Grimauldi had taken her blood, some of her fingernails, pieces of skin, hanks of her hair. She'd made Denevah touch countless animals of various sizes and types. She'd collected Denevah's saliva and her tears, had made Denevah cry more when she'd run out and needed additional samples.

Denevah stayed strapped to the table, bound and gagged. Her restraints were tightened every time Grimauldi cut her so she couldn't thrash and fling blood at her. The Aves alchemist was most careful, damn her. She'd thought of everything.

The sound of a key grating in a lock, then a door opening filtered to her ears. Denevah hadn't realized she'd been alone in the room. She didn't bother turning her head to look; she'd see what Grimauldi had in store for her soon enough. She didn't need a preview.

A baby's wail split the air. Denevah stiffened, eyes flying wider. She couldn't mean to . . .

She couldn't even complete the thought.

Grimauldi stepped around the side of the table, already gloved. The woman tightened the ropes brutally, the roughness abrading Denevah's skin as she struggled. She arched her back, working for slack in her bonds and found none, nearly choking herself against the leather strap around her neck. Blood ran down her wrists. She shook her head violently, hoping to dislodge the gag. Nothing.

The Aves stepped away, infant in her arms. The alchemist made a few notes in the journal where she'd been keeping the results of her experiments on Denevah. Then Grimauldi gathered a series of timeglasses of various heights and set them up on a nearby bench. The glass of each end had been marked with a series of striations that accounted for a measure of time. Sand filled the opposite end; when flipped the sand would pour through and fill the other end.

Denevah's gaze kept going back to the baby tucked in Grimauldi's arm. She couldn't tell gender. It wasn't newborn, and it wasn't able to walk, but other than that Denevah had no idea of the infant's age. It had the robust complexion of good health, appeared well-fed, and seemed in excellent condition. She pulled at the ropes that bound her arms to the table, tearing open more skin in the process.

A heavy knock on the door made Denevah's heart leap inside of her chest. She had no hope for rescue for herself, but perhaps whoever stood on the other side would see the infant and take it away. She closed her eyes and prayed to the Diluvians for this boon.

Grimauldi moved to answer it, placing the baby in a blanket lined basket before stepping out of Denevah's line of sight. She heard the clicks as locks were unbolted, and the slight creak as the door swung open. She heard the low murmur of several voices, but could see nothing.

"Lady Grimauldi. You sent for me?"

Denevah gasped around the gag, closing her eyes against the tears that welled in them. She knew that voice. Ettoni. She felt like she had been flung over a high cliff.

"Come in, my Lord. I have found something that will be of great interest to you." Lady Grimauldi sounded so smug that Denevah growled from behind the gag. She strained against the ropes holding her, not caring if she ripped all of the skin from her bones if it meant that she got to smear blood all over that woman and watch her writhe in agony.

"Where are you on replicating Rodolfi's work?" The older alchemist's voice held a note of mania. To Denevah's ears, she sounded demented.

"Not close enough for another experiment to be successful," Ettoni told her. His voice grew closer.

"I found something that will be of great help to your research then."

"What might that be?" Ettoni's voice sounded cool, detached. Denevah felt hope flare inside of her at the sound of his voice.

She heard footsteps as he entered the room, the door closing behind him. Denevah kept quiet, not wanting to risk Ettoni's surprised reaction if she were to cry out. Her body lay taut as a bowstring at full tension.

"Your missing piece of the puzzle," Lady Grimauldi said as the two Ravens walked into view.

Ettoni's eyes went wide with shock. His mouth dropped open, but he managed to stop his outcry. Instead he turned his shocked expression into one of disgust, lip pulled up as if he'd just smelled the canals in high summer. "Where did you find her?"

"She had to leave House Corvus eventually, and my spies inside tipped my men handily." Lady Grimauldi laid a hand—gloved, of course—on Denevah's chopped hair, and Denevah fought not to cringe in revulsion at the woman's touch.

"You infiltrated the Crows?" Ettoni sounded impressed. How much of what he was doing was an act?

"It's amazing what the right amount of leverage can accomplish," the woman answered with a particularly self-satisfied smile.

Denevah stared up into Ettoni's cold mask of a face imploringly. He had to help her—there had to be a way! Even if he could just loosen one of her wrist restraints, Denevah was sure she could get out of this mess. Her gaze skipped to Lady Grimauldi and the thin-bladed knife suddenly in her hand.

Denevah realized then that this was a test as much for her as for Ettoni.

She turned her head as best she could, unable to look at her cousin any longer. Denevah would be damned if she gave him away—damned if she would be the reason for his death. She waited a beat, and then lunged forward, yanking and fighting against her bindings. She gnashed her teeth against the gag, glaring up at him.

"She doesn't care for you much, does she?" Grimauldi sounded amused. Denevah shifted her glare to include the woman.

"It's to be expected," Ettoni answered, his voice cold, clinical.

Denevah couldn't stop the tremor that ripped through her at the sound of her cousin's voice. She'd never heard him sound so much like her father before. When he continued with, "I'm just as much her creator as my master," she shuddered.

She thrashed once again to give credence to his words. Ettoni couldn't be serious—he couldn't possibly think that way, could he? This was all just a show for Grimauldi. Rodolfi held the lion's share of the blame for the way she was.

Unless. . .

She shook her head. No. This was Ettoni. He would never hurt her deliberately. He'd been under a spell—he'd made a pact with her father that prevented him from helping her. He'd told her that.

But a small voice in the back of her mind whispered a poisonous thought: But what if he wasn't?

"I collected samples," Grimauldi told Ettoni.

Her cousin turned away from the woman so that his back was between her and Denevah. "I am going to get help," he mouthed when he was sure the other Aves couldn't see.

Denevah shook her head as best she could. It wasn't worth the risk—she wasn't worth it. Better to let Grimauldi kill her and be done with this whole mess. As long as she lived, she would be a danger, a threat. But there was someone else Ettoni needed to save. Glaring at her cousin, she cut her eyes in the direction of the basket where the baby lay sleeping.

Raising his eyebrows, Ettoni turned to look. She saw him go pale, his brown eyes growing impossibly wide. He stepped away from the table, toward the basket. As Denevah watched, Ettoni bent down, an elegant hand reaching out to pull back the blanket.

"You've found my next test subject, I see," Lady Grimauldi said, kneeling on the opposite side of the makeshift bassinet from Ettoni. "I worked out that Rodolfi must have started his regimen with the girl in childhood for the virulence to be so pronounced and widespread."

Denevah really wanted to be sick then. She'd never be clean again, and she certainly would never get those words out of her memory. Knowing what Rodolfi had done to her was bad enough; hearing someone else say it in relation to copying what he'd done was an entirely new level of awful.

Ettoni's expression didn't even flicker. "How exactly had you planned to proceed?"

Grimauldi smiled wolfishly. "I was going to consult you. Of course."

Denevah didn't believe her for a moment. She struggled again, drawing the woman's attention. Grimauldi sent her a scowl. "Your usefulness draws to an end, Denevah. Don't vex me."

"It won't work." Ettoni's voice was skin-searingly cold.

Grimauldi's head swiveled in his direction, nostrils flared in irritation. "What do you mean?" she nearly snarled, taking a step closer to him.

Denevah watched Ettoni pull himself to his full height, so that he topped Grimauldi by several inches. He looked dark and imposing in his black Aves jacket and leather gloves—he could have passed for a Crow with the stern expression he wore.

"Human alchemical experimentation wasn't the only rule Lord Rodolfi broke when he created Denevah. Did you never think to wonder how Denevah's toxicity didn't turn on her?" He almost sounded mocking when he spoke.

"I assumed the slow exposure had something to do with it. She had to build up an immunity to her poisons," Grimauldi said haughtily.

"You assumed incorrectly." At her angry scowl, Ettoni smiled without mirth. "He made a deal."

"With who?"

"The Diluvians. For their magic."

Denevah swallowed, lips dry around the gag in her mouth. Lady Grimauldi went still, eyes round as solas coins.

"He wouldn't."

Ettoni nodded. "Oh, but he did."

Grimauldi turned to stare at Denevah consideringly, gaze dark with secrets. "You found this in his notes."

"And witnessed it myself."

Denevah would have gasped if she'd been able. The risk Ettoni took was enormous. Aves could have him killed for meddling with the water dragons.

"You were just a child yourself when Rodolfi would have brought her to them," Grimauldi scoffed, clearly disinclined to believe him. It gave Denevah hope until her cousin spoke again.

"The first time, yes. But I was with him when he visited them a second time. I saw everything."

Lady Grimauldi gaped, words lost as she tried to make sense of what Ettoni revealed. "He tried to make another like her?"

Ettoni shook his head. Denevah struggled once more in a futile effort to get his attention. Grimauldi swatted absently at her. Denevah wished she were free to bite the woman.

"No. Lord Rodolfi decided Denevah's poisons did not act quickly enough and increased the amount he was feeding her." His voice sounded detached and empty when he described what happened next.

"She began to hemorrhage. What she caused in others was happening to her as her own poisons turned against her."

Denevah closed her eyes. She vaguely recalled the feelings of intense pain and disorientation as her own body turned against her.

She remembered winged serpents twining around her as she'd slipped away. She remembered the bite.

"If she died, all of his work would have been for nothing. Seventeen years wasted." Denevah flinched at Ettoni's cold words. "So he took her back to the Diluvians for their help."

"You saw them?" For the first time Grimauldi sounded awed, subdued.

Ettoni nodded once. Denevah saw the clench of his jaw, the deeply indrawn breaths, and knew how her cousin struggled with the memories. She was glad she didn't remember more of that night.

"My master pleaded with them to help her, to save her."

"Obviously they did or we wouldn't be here," the Aves said, snideness creeping back into her tone.

"Did it ever occur to you to wonder why the Diluvians might even be interested in making such a deal, my Lady?" Ettoni's words were short, dagger-sharp. "Did you ever think that perhaps such a thing is not in Aerie's best interests?"

Grimauldi swung around, wearing an honest expression of surprise. "You found something out."

Ettoni slowly shook his head. "I have theories—and concerns—but nothing concrete. Yet. Lord Rodolfi did not care for the future of Aerie so long as he got his revenge, and in his blindness he may have set something in motion that we will be hard-pressed to stop."

Denevah's stomach dropped. Her cousin might not know exactly what the danger was, but he certainly suspected, and that worried her. Toni did not overreact. If he was concerned, he would have a good reason. What remained to be seen was what Grimauldi would do with this information.

"You think it an unsound idea to try and replicate what Rodolfi wrought," Grimauldi surmised, a slight frown pulling at the corners of her lips.

"Tremendously," Ettoni stated, just as implacable.

Lady Grimauldi sniffed, emitting a faint sound of disappointment. Denevah felt the hard knot of fear unknot from her belly and spine at the woman's surrender, and she relaxed infinitesimally. The baby, at least, was safe.

Then she tensed once more when the woman spoke. "I would see what you've unearthed that confirms your suspicions. Bring it to me. If you suspect such a threat, we should take it before the Doge." When Ettoni didn't answer her immediately, she smiled sweetly, eyes full of venom. "You can't expect me to trust something like this, my Lord, without the appropriate proof."

Ettoni's face held no expression when he met Lady Grimauldi's predator's gaze. "I expect nothing less. You have always been a discerning woman."

If Denevah hadn't been gagged, she would have retched at the admiration Ettoni managed to slip into his voice. She knew it was a ruse, but even so, the ease with which he lied made her wonder. He said he'd had no choice in keeping Rodolfi's experiment from her because of the magical chains placed upon him, but what if that too was a lie? He'd lied to her so often before; what would stop him from doing so again?

"I will fetch Lord Rodolfi's notes and return," he said, turning away from Denevah to take his leave. "I would advise you to do nothing until I return." He spoke to Grimauldi, but Denevah suspected his words were for her.

What could she do? Grimauldi had her bound and gagged on a table. He left her with the woman who'd already ripped out fingernails, cut her open to collect her blood, and took samples of her skin and hair. If Denevah gained the opportunity, there was no way she was going to do nothing, despite Ettoni's warning.

He swept past Grimauldi who watched his departure with a restrained sort of glee. When he'd gone, she summoned the two men guarding the door. Denevah could only watch as the woman ordered, "Follow him. If he gives you any problems, kill him and anyone with him."

Denevah struggled uselessly as the men left to follow her cousin. She should have known the woman wouldn't risk trusting another Aves. This was Aerie, after all. Now that Denevah wasn't confined to Rodolfi's palazzo, she was learning just how devious the rest of Aerie was.

When they were alone once more, Lady Grimauldi walked to the basket that held the baby. It still slept in its blanket as she lifted it up into her arms. She moved closer to Denevah, an unpleasant look in her eyes. Denevah attempted to scramble away despite her bindings, boot heels marking the table with black streaks as she jerked and thrashed to get loose. The ropes held fast.

A frustrated shriek built inside of her, breaking around the gag. She'd dreamed of motherhood, of family, of raising children. Denevah's hands clenched into tight fists. She'd wanted to be a mother, had wanted to share it with Cyngare. Now she just wanted to get as far from that baby as possible, before she did something unthinkable.

"Just because I can't use this child in the way I planned, doesn't mean our testing is over." Grimauldi unwound the blanket from the baby as she moved to the row of timing glasses and began to reset them.

Denevah screamed through her gag for help that never came.

CHAPTER TWENTY-ONE

Savino paced, his worry over Denevah's absence wearing its way through the rug. She'd missed their rendezvous point, and hadn't returned to the House of White Feathers. No one had seen her, not even the Shrikes. Benedetto checked House Corvus to report in to Lord Trapinze and there had been no sign of her there either. She had sent no word of either her lateness or her whereabouts. If he'd learned one thing in his time with her, it was that Denevah took her responsibilities very seriously. She would not just disappear without notice.

Still, he had to be cautious. Denevah had three Houses hunting for her; he didn't want to make things worse by alerting them to her absence. He thought it likely that one or all of them already knew. One might even be responsible for it. Savino pushed that thought aside. He wouldn't give up hope on her just yet.

Savino turned at the sound of the door to the library opening. He'd holed up in the room in which he felt most comfortable—small though it was—now that things were going badly. He should have anticipated something like this; he'd planned for so many other eventualities, but had never thought to plan for this one, for the loss of someone he liked.

In stalked the assassin, followed by a man whom Savino never expected to see. He stiffened, taking a deep breath through his nose, head reared back in surprise. Anger burned slow and low in his belly, and he fought for the control not to take out one of his daggers and bury it in the man's guts.

Ettoni.

Rodolfi may have gone beyond Savino's reach, but Ettoni stood right in front of him. Cyngare and he hadn't had a good relationship in a long time, but Savino had always hoped they'd have the opportunity to repair it. But that option had been stolen from him. By this man.

"What's he doing here?" Savino snapped, cutting his eyes from Benedetto to the Aves newest Master Alchemist.

"I need your help," Ettoni said, eyes darting around the room as if expecting someone to leap out at him from the shadows in the corners.

Savino pursed his lips, gaze resting on Benedetto. The Crow said, "He knows where Denevah is." He jerked his head at Ettoni as he spoke.

"How?" Savino asked, staring at the Raven with suspicion. As concerned as he was for Denevah's safety, he didn't trust the alchemist.

Ettoni answered, words escaping him in a rush. "Lady Grimauldi summoned me to her laboratory—it's in a separate building from her palazzo. When I got there, she had Denevah. She's trying to recreate Lord Rodolfi's experiment with a baby! I think I talked her out of it, but she still plans to vivisect Denevah to see what makes her work." He paused, staring breathlessly at them. "Well? What are you waiting for? We have to go!"

"You believe him?" Savino glanced at Ettoni, who glowered at the Rook.

"Yeah, I do." Benedetto looked more serious than Savino had ever seen him.

"We need to hurry," Ettoni urged, his voice too sharp, too high, almost panicked. "Lady Grimauldi is expecting me back soon. I don't want to leave Denevah alone with her for too long."

"Yet here you are," Savino drawled. He didn't bother to hide the dislike in his voice as he spoke. He reserved politeness for those who deserved it.

"What was I supposed to do?" Ettoni snarled back, his face flushing red. "She has guards and I'm just one person!"

"If you'd freed Denevah, you'd be more than even," Savino pointed out as he stalked out the door.

"You didn't see her," Ettoni said accusingly.

Savino swung around, rage spiking inside of him. Benedetto put a hand against his chest and pushed him back. "Not helping, Savino. Yell at him later. We need to get to Denevah now."

"Fine," Savino growled, biting back his burn of frustration. "Let's go, apprentice." He flung the word like an insult, refusing to give the man his true title.

Savino turned on his heel, biting back on his anger by chewing on the inside of his cheek. He stormed down the stairs, grinding his boot heels into the floor, imagining it was Ettoni's face he stomped on. Benedetto padded behind him, Ettoni bringing up the rear.

They slipped out the front door of White Feathers. "Where to?" Benedetto asked, turning toward the Raven. As they walked where Ettoni indicated, Savino did his best to act as though the alchemist wasn't even there.

Benedetto was not so measured. The Crow slid behind the Aves and pressed a short dagger that he'd conjured from somewhere on his person to the base of his spine. "I just need to drive this in and twist and you'll need someone to clean up your piss for the rest of your Diluvian-forsaken life." He patted the Raven's shoulder companionably, as if he hadn't just threatened the young man. His dagger disappeared just as quickly and mysteriously as it appeared.

The Aves swallowed audibly. Savino would have felt bad for him if he didn't despise him so much. "This way."

Ettoni led them deeper into the heart of the city. He moved as quickly as he could without actually running. Savino felt the urgency of their errand pound through him, radiating out from his heart and into his feet in a furious rhythm.

The Aves led them unerringly, barely checking his surroundings for landmarks as he went. Savino raced behind him, Benedetto at his side. Their heels beat out a staccato tempo against the cobbles, and it matched the thoughts running through Savino's head: Hang on, Denevah. We're coming.

Out of the corner of his eye, Savino saw a dark shape lurking at the mouth of street to his left. He cried out a warning as he caught the glint of steel in a fist. He needn't have bothered. Benedetto had already slid near the attacker, long daggers out—one to block and the other to strike. The man folded over Benedetto's arm, a choked sound escaping his shocked mouth.

Savino covered Ettoni, stilettos in hand, his gaze sweeping the streets. Benedetto dealt with the second man just as easily as the first. The assassin spun, freeing his blade from the first man's body even as he used him as a shield from the second man's overhand attack. Dropping low, Benedetto punched up beneath the man's guard, the blade diving between cloth and flesh like a pole cleaving the canal water.

Ettoni cried out, his eyes wide and startled. Savino pushed him along, growling, "Keep moving."

"Those are Lady Grimauldi's guards," the alchemist stuttered out, shocked.

Savino scowled, brows low over his eyes. He held the point of his stiletto to the quivering Aves's throat. "Friends of yours?" Ettoni had seemed surprised by them as much as he'd been, but the alchemist could just be a very convincing actor.

Ettoni flinched, then held himself very still as the point of the stiletto pricked his skin. His brown eyes were huge, and a droplet of sweat rolled down his temple. "She must have sent them after me to make sure I wasn't lying."

Savino glanced at Benedetto who shrugged and wiped his blades on the dead man's jacket. "She didn't trust you," Savino said, an unnecessarily harsh reminder that the Raven probably didn't need or want.

Benedetto caught up to them quickly, sliding his blades back into their sheaths with a pleased grin on his face. "I don't think there are any others," he told them.

"Keep an eye out anyway," Savino warned, still watching the streets. "There may be more." He caught sight of Benedetto's fox-like grin, and resisted the urge to smile back. The Crow's seemingly limitless well of confidence was infectious.

There were no further incidents as they made their way to a street where several older palazzos huddled close together, like a bunch of old women leaning in to gossip. "Down here," Ettoni said, directing them to a narrow space between two houses. At a nod from Savino, Benedetto went first, pulling one dagger free. Savino brought up the rear, the Aves wedged between them. He pulled a stiletto as well.

A door. Ettoni sketched a ward in the air and the door opened on silent hinges. Benedetto slid forward on quiet feet, dark eyes flickering from the small entryway to the stairs that yawned like a mouth before him. Savino bustled through the door, herding Ettoni inside as well, and closed the door behind them.

"We go down?" Benedetto asked. At Ettoni's nod, the Crow proceeded down the narrow winding stairs. The walls wept water and the air felt humid and dank. Witchlight flickered off the stone walls.

At the bottom stood a large, iron-bound door. Ettoni gestured for the two of them to step back as he faced the door. The Aves raised his fist and knocked, the sound echoing around them. He raised a finger to his lips in warning.

"Lady Grimauldi," he called, loud enough to be heard through the wood of the door, "I've come back with the proof you requested."

Savino slanted a glance at Benedetto. The assassin held both of his knives in his hands, lanky limbs easy and confident. Savino unsheathed his second stiletto, and stood in a ready position. Ettoni hadn't mentioned additional guards, but that didn't mean she hadn't called for others in his absence.

They stood for a few moments in tense silence, the anxiety and uncertainty a palpable thing in the air between them. They heard the footsteps on the other side of the door. One set. Then the sound of the lock on the other side of the door being thrown.

Benedetto moved like lightning, slamming open the door with his shoulder. He surged forward. He led with his blades, and Savino heard the startled cry of a woman. He stepped through the doorway and into the room. Lady Grimauldi stood still, mouth open in a silent scream, the edge of Benedetto's dagger pressed hard against her throat. Confident that the woman was restrained, Savino stepped further inside, feeling the presence of Ettoni at his back.

He could see a large room, one half of which held tables and shelves that housed all manner of books and artifacts. The tables were covered in more books and glassware and other items Savino couldn't name.

The other half held Denevah.

She lay supine on an old, scarred wooden table. Her arms were lashed down, as were her legs. A leather strap held her neck to the table. Blood leaked from her wrists where the ropes had bit deep into her skin. The sleeves of Denevah's shirt and jacket had been cut away, the legs of her pants had been removed from the knees down. Her flesh was covered in bruises, abrasions, and cuts, only some of them from her struggles. She'd been gagged. Her eyes were closed, her breathing shallow. Her skin had a grey cast to it. As Savino watched, one of her hands twitched and he saw that three of her fingernails had been ripped out on that hand. Two were missing from the other.

Small animals were set in trays on another table, a few in the midst of dissection. Savino gripped the hilts of his stilettos tightly.

His gaze skipped to Benedetto and he saw the rage simmering in the young man's eyes, just waiting for a spark to strike tinder and then he would explode.

Savino passed them, on his way to untie Denevah. Ettoni raced to the table, already working on the strap around her neck.

Benedetto moved deeper into the room with Grimauldi, the woman's arm jerked high behind her back. She let out a high-pitched whine. From the look on the Crow's face, Savino wouldn't be surprised if he dislocated Grimauldi's shoulder. Good. Savino turned his attention back to the girl on the table. She still hadn't stirred.

"Denevah," Savino murmured, working his stiletto through the tight ropes on one side that bound her feet and lower legs to the table. Her eyes were open now, but unseeing; she didn't react to his voice at all. "Denevah, can you hear me?"

No response. Fear turned his guts to ice. He began to work on the ropes binding her chest to the table.

"What did you do?" he shouted at the elder Raven. Benedetto pressed the point of the knife into the edge of the woman's jaw until a trickle of blood ran down her throat.

The woman's mouth worked, but no sound came out. Ettoni joined Savino to work on the ropes holding Denevah's forearms and wrists. As Savino sawed at the bindings, he kept calling her name, trying to elicit some kind of response from her. Denevah blinked slowly once, but that was the only reaction he got.

"I need to know what she did," Savino whispered to Ettoni. The ropes parted and he went to work on Denevah's upper arm.

Ettoni's head jerked up, like a dog scenting prey. "Wait. Where's the baby?" His voice sounded shrill.

"What baby?" Savino growled. He glared at Grimauldi, fingers fumbling at the bindings as the import of what he'd asked hit home. "What's he talking about?" he demanded.

"There was a baby. She wanted to recreate the experiment that made Denevah," Ettoni whispered. "It was in the basket." He jerked his head at the now-empty container. Benedetto made a noise between a groan and a gasp, his gaze landing on it.

"You don't think . . .," Savino began, dread hollowing his voice.

The younger alchemist shook his head, gaze locked on the ropes his blade slowly sawed through. Each strand seemed to separate in slow motion. Ettoni did not hurry. The rope was buried in Denevah's wrist—she would need to clean her arm before it became infected from the fibers that had dug deeply into the wounds.

"The baby's not here," Ettoni began.

Several things happened in rapid succession. The ropes holding Denevah came free with a snap. Her eyes filled with a sudden clarity at Ettoni's words, and she threw herself from the table at Lady Grimauldi. The Aves tripped over her own feet as she scrambled in retreat, causing Benedetto to release his hold on the woman's neck lest he skewer her by accident. The Crow caught Grimauldi by the arm before she got far.

Denevah flung herself at the Aves alchemist like a mad thing before Savino could think to stop her. She slammed her shoulder into the woman's midsection, driving all three of them to the floor. Benedetto's knife clattered from his hand, skidding across the stone tiles. Savino swooped, snatching it up before Lady Grimauldi could get it. He straightened, then stared in shock at the scene unfolding before him.

Lady Grimauldi wrestled with Denevah, which was difficult since she didn't want to touch her. Denevah straddled the Raven, pinning the woman to the floor. Benedetto lay trapped beneath the both of them. His attempts to wriggle free proved futile, especially when Denevah shoved her bleeding wrist at the Aves' mouth.

"You wanted to know so badly," Denevah growled, eyes fiercely focused and feral. She pressed down harder, forcing Grimauldi to part her lips. Savino could hear her choking. "Now's your chance."

The woman's eyes widened in terror, visible beneath Denevah's shredded and bloody forearm. Savino glanced sideways at Ettoni, who watched with a horrified fascination as he clung to the table. Grimauldi tried to fling Denevah away, but she would not be moved. Her thighs trembled with the force of their grip around the woman's waist. Denevah finally removed her arm from Grimauldi's face, leaving behind smears of blood. The lower half of the alchemist's jaw and chin looked like it had been dipped in gore.

It wasn't until she began to writhe in pain that Denevah loosened her hold on the woman. Benedetto slid out from under them as Denevah climbed off, staggering up to stand beside Savino. Denevah leaned over Grimauldi as she began to cough, the sound ripping out of the woman's chest as if she were being torn apart from the inside. Denevah's eyes were narrow slits, her face a mask of fury. In all of the time that they'd spent in each other's company, Savino had never seen that kind of hatred on her face. Not even the few times she'd mentioned her father.

The Aves' next cough sprayed blood. Savino and Benedetto stepped backwards. Ettoni jerked even though he stood out of range. Denevah's face was splattered with red, but she didn't appear to mind. Her sharp grin flashed white in the nightmare of her face.

"Can you imagine what it must have been like?" she asked, sounding almost conversational. "For that child you rested in my arms?"

Grimauldi's eyes rolled back, but Denevah reached out with mangled hands to grab the sides of the Raven's head. She slammed it into the floor and awareness flooded back into the woman's eyes. She kept her hold on the Aves, gaze locked with hers. Grimauldi moaned from red-frothed lips.

"You don't get to pass out," Denevah hissed. "Not until you've felt everything that baby felt."

Savino felt sick. Had the woman really experimented with a child? An infant? He hadn't had time to process Ettoni's words, but seeing Denevah like this, he found he could believe it. Something truly terrible had pushed her past the edge of reason; he wanted to draw her back before she lost herself entirely. This rage wasn't her.

"For . . .give—" Lady Grimauldi's words cut out with a pained gurgle.

"The blade forgets," Denevah said, quoting the ancient Aeriean saying. "The flesh remembers."

Savino took a tentative step forward, gloved hand outstretched to grasp her shoulder. "Denev—," he started to say.

She twisted to face him, lips flat against her bared teeth, red drenching her skin. "Stay out of this!" she snapped, voice tight with fury. She stared at each of them in turn. "All of you!"

Benedetto held up his hands, a placating gesture. When Denevah turned her attention back to Grimauldi, he caught Savino's gaze. The Crow looked out of his depth, gutted by uncertainty. Savino passed him back his dagger. The both stood there, at a loss for what to do, but neither intervened. The Aves had this coming to her.

Grimauldi panted and coughed continuously, unable to draw enough air into her lungs. Denevah hovered over her, strangely chopped hair making her face appear even more skull-like. Her knuckles had turned white from the strength of her grip on the woman's head. Blood covered the front of Grimauldi's robes. She shivered almost constantly. Denevah's gaze devoured every tremor that shook the woman's body.

"You made me a monster," Denevah whispered, voice hoarse with emotion. "Worse than I ever was before."

Savino saw Denevah's arms tremble. Her legs gave out and she sprawled to the side of Grimauldi, her hands braced on the woman's chest to keep her body upright. "I didn't ask for this," Denevah said into the quiet as the Aves' struggles grew less and less. "I never wanted it." Denevah's head sagged forward on her neck. Her shoulders heaved with her silent sobs.

Savino unlaced the cuffs of his jacket and slid it off of his shoulders. Moving forward, one slow step at a time, he approached Denevah. Gently, he laid it over her, urging her arms through the sleeves. The undone laces trailed down to the floor. Carefully, he lifted her to her feet, fastening the front of the jacket as best he could to cover her ripped shirt.

She stumbled, leaning her weight against him. Ordinarily, Savino disliked touch of any kind, but he didn't mind it with her. It didn't bother him that she leaned on him for the briefest of moments before finding her footing.

"Let's get out of here," he murmured, lips close—but not touching—her ear.

She nodded. Her chest heaved with her hurt, but she stayed quiet. Savino kept his hand beneath her elbow, guiding her toward the doorway. Benedetto fell into step beside them, brows furrowed with worry.

Savino glanced behind him at the alchemist. Ettoni stared at Grimauldi's body, expression unreadable. He wondered if the man felt sorry for Grimauldi, or if there was something more behind it. Ettoni looked up and caught Savino watching him. The Raven quickly looked away.

Savino ushered Denevah out of the room, not waiting to see if Ettoni followed. Denevah moved like Savino's mother did when her joints were bothering her. She didn't pay attention to her surroundings, instead huddling into his jacket as if she wanted to wrap it around herself and disappear from view. He gripped her elbow tighter when she seemed to sag, his gaze meeting Benedetto's over Denevah's head.

The Crow's frown deepened when he noticed that Ettoni trailed after them. At Savino's pointed look, he dropped back to walk with him. Savino didn't want Ettoni unattended at Denevah's back. He may have helped them find Denevah, but Savino still wondered how Denevah had been taken in the first place. Had Ettoni been a part of it before having second thoughts? Savino did not intend on being surprised again.

He didn't attempt to speak to Denevah until they were safely back at the House of Black Wings. It was closer than White Feathers. Savino ordered food and drink from the first servant he saw outside their rooms, the order to hurry made more urgent by the gold coins he pressed into the young man's hands. While they waited for the refreshments to arrive, he coaxed Denevah into the bathing area for a bath. When Ettoni tried to protest that he should be the one taking care of her, Benedetto gestured—rather forcefully—for the Raven to sit down.

Savino helped her shrug off his jacket, setting it aside to burn. He didn't care, he had dozens more; Denevah matter more. He turned around to give her privacy as she stripped and slid into the deep tub. When he heard her pained hiss, he risked a glance behind him.

Denevah huddled neck deep beneath the water, her hands and wrists draped over the edge of the tub. Savino knew that much exposed skin was dangerous so he stayed where he was. He respected the power in Denevah, but he wasn't afraid of her. He'd seen her after Cyngare's death, and even knowing the subterfuge that came second-nature to nobles of the Great Houses, he didn't doubt that she hadn't meant to kill his brother. Everything he'd seen and heard from her since then just confirmed his belief.

"Denevah," he said, keeping his voice low. He still startled her; she jerked as if she'd forgotten he waited in the room with her.

She glanced over her shoulder at him, heavy lashes veiling her eyes. Grabbing a cloth and a bottle of soap, Denevah moved as far away from him as she could get in the tub. The set of her shoulders told him of the tension she carried.

"I can leave if you would prefer to be alone," he offered, only wanting to make her comfortable.

She swiveled around so fast she made the water wave and lap over the sides. "No!' she said quickly, before biting her lip and continuing. "I don't want—I mean," she ducked her head, "you can stay."

Savino imagined it would be difficult to be alone after her ordeal. He settled himself on a bench, leaning his back against the cool tiled wall. Weariness tugged at him. He wasn't certain of the time but he could feel it was closer to morning than evening. He dropped his head back to rest against the tiles, feeling their chill through his thick hair.

"We're going to need to clean those." He gestured to the raw, weeping wounds around her wrists.

She nodded absently. With a sigh, Savino pushed himself to his feet, collecting the items Benedetto had dropped just inside the door for him: tweezers, healing salve, honey, and linen wraps. He walked to the edge of tub and sat on a wooden stool, adjusting his leather gloves.

Denevah slowly moved closer to him, eyes wide and unfocused in a face far too pale. She lifted her hands and rested her forearms on the edge of the tub. Without a word, Savino got to work.

It was slow going. The steam from the hot water wreathed his face as he leaned over Denevah's wrists. She held herself still as he worked rope fibers out of the wounds, only jerking when he applied the disinfectant. Once he'd slathered everything with the salve and wrapped her wrists in bandages, Savino sat back to survey his work. Denevah rested her forehead against one knee, eyes closed.

"Can you tell me what happened? With Grimauldi?"

She flinched, eyes opening in startlement. Denevah didn't answer right away, instead ducking her head under the water to wet her hair. She emerged, water cascading down her face and neck to drip down smooth, tightly wound shoulders and arms. Savino watched a droplet curl around her bicep before dropping back into the water. He rubbed at his eyes with the back of his hand. He was tired.

"I don't wish to speak of it," she answered after a moment spent soaping her hair.

Her voice had a haughty edge to it. Savino noticed it got that way when she felt unsure or out of her depth. Like imperiousness could be used as a shield. When Denevah tried it, she sounded like a child playing at being a grown up, dressing herself up in clothes that didn't fit.

"Very well," he returned. He stood and returned to his bench against the wall, closing his eyes to the sight of her bathing.

The sound of the water lapping at the edges of the bathing tub relaxed him, sent his thoughts wandering in no particular direction. It felt good to just drift, anchored to his body, but somehow floating above it. His breathing grew deep and heavy as he dropped into a doze.

He nearly missed Denevah's words when she spoke. "I used to dream of having children of my own one day." Her voice was a whisper's whisper. "A family of my own to love." A pause. "I would never hurt a child."

Jerking back to full awareness, Savino opened his eyes to find Denevah watching him. He thought she might have preferred it if he'd stayed asleep—maybe even counted on it—but she didn't appear startled when he opened his eyes and stared at her.

"I know," he told her.

Her throat worked on a swallow, as though holding back some powerful emotion. Only her shoulders, neck, and head were visible above the waterline. Savino got up, back popping, and got a couple of drying sheets for her. He set them atop the stool beside the tub before returning to his seat.

"I just didn't want you to think that I could ever—"

"It never even crossed my mind," Savino said, locking his gaze with hers. "Never."

She lowered her eyes, cheeks flushed from the heat of the water. White teeth dug into the pink flesh of her lower lip. "Thank you," she mumbled, not looking up.

Savino pushed himself away from the wall, temper fraying. He couldn't stand it anymore. "Stop it."

Now she did look up at him, eyes startled. "Stop what?"

He stood, beginning to pace. The fine white shirt he wore billowed around him every time he turned. "Stop thanking me for treating you like a human being."

Denevah drew back, surprised. Savino jerked to a stop in front of the bathing tub, arms crossed in front of his chest. "You're not a monster. So stop expecting to be treated like one."

She blinked, staring at him with her jaw slack. "How can you even say that to me? You? After what I did?"

"Because I know you, damn it!" Savino's voice rose with his frustration. "You are more than just your skin! No one who knows you could ever think you're a monster."

She leaned forward, grabbing one of the drying sheets to wrap around her body. "I need to be dressed for this conversation," she said, sounding off-balance.

He backed away, intending to check on the status of their refreshments. When he stuck his head out of the bathroom door, he saw Benedetto hunkered over an enormous tray of food, stuffing his face until his cheeks were round like a puffer fish. Ettoni looked on in quiet horror.

"Save some for the rest of us. We'll be right out," he admonished the Crow while he shed his filthy gloves. Striding past the Aves who sat on a nearby divan, Savino gathered up an old pair of breeches and a shirt. He pulled on a spare pair of gloves.

"No promises," Benedetto said around a mouthful of food.

"You should go," Savino said to Ettoni as he reached the door to the bath, not bothering to turn around. "You've done quite enough."

"Not until I see her." The alchemist's voice grew stronger, more determined than Savino had ever heard it. Savino frowned and entered the bath, unwilling to waste time on arguing with the man.

Denevah had the sheet wrapped around her body, using the other to dry her hair when he returned to the bathroom. "These will do until we can get your own things," he said as he passed her the clothes. He turned around to give her privacy to dress.

"Thank you," she said, her words nearly lost in the rustle of cloth. "Or am I not allowed politeness now either?"

Savino grinned. "Politeness is acceptable." He clasped his hands behind his back, rocking forward on his feet. "But I meant what I said before, Denevah. You're a good person."

"I don't understand how you can say that—after what I've done." She paused. "You can turn around now."

She stood before him, wearing his clothes. The pants were somewhat baggy and pooled a bit at her feet, and the white linen shirt hung off her slender frame, slipping off one slim shoulder. Savino stared for a long moment, stunned at Denevah's simple loveliness. Her expression clouded with confusion as he continued to stand there, words locked up behind his lips.

"Savino?"

He pulled himself out of his thoughts with effort. He didn't understand what was happening with him—he'd never felt attraction to anyone before, not like this. Savino cleared his throat, heat filling his face. "What exactly is it that you've done?"

She pursed her lips. "How can you ask me that?"

He took a step closer to her. "You keep expecting me to hold what happened against you. I don't. It wasn't your fault."

Her eyes flashed up to his face, hurt and fear reflected in their violet depths. She took an inadvertent step back, a pale hand coming up to rest at her throat. Savino followed her, keeping the distance between them even.

"I'm going to keep telling you that until you finally believe it," he promised in a low voice, feeling the tension between them like a fission of heat in his blood. "You didn't know."

"And tonight? I knew what I was doing to Grimauldi. I knew what would happen." Denevah's voice came out bitter and hard, cutting like diamond shards.

Savino took another step forward, closing the distance between them. Denevah would end up back in the tub if she took another two steps backward. She stilled, staring up at him in challenge.

"From what I heard and saw, she had it coming." He smiled softly. "You keep hoping I'll run away. But I'm not going anywhere, so you may as well stop all that nonsense." He reached out with a gloved hand to touch her wrist. "You don't scare me."

She went completely still beneath his touch. He could feel her faint trembling, even through the leather of his gloves. "I should," came her faint reply.

He shook his head. "You'd never hurt me. I trust in that."

She laughed suddenly, a dark and mirthless sound. "I wonder what Cyngare would say if he could hear you speak."

"Nothing good, I'm sure, since he loathed me," Savino admitted, keeping the anger from his voice. "But Cyngare's not here. It's just us." He tilted his head, observing her where she stood. "You use him to keep me at arm's reach," he finally said, eyes narrowed.

"No one in their right mind should want to be in arm's reach of me," she scoffed.

He pulled at her hand so that he could entwine his gloved fingers in hers. The spark between them was there, no longer threatening to burst into conflagration; now it was something smaller, cozier. Something warm. "One, I'm not in my right mind. I suspect I haven't been for some time." Savino smiled. "And two, there's no place that I would rather be." He paused, mouth pulling down in a frown. "Three, I'm tired of talking about my brother."

He pulled away from Denevah slowly, letting her stop him if she wanted to, knowing he may have pushed too far this time. He needed to give her some space. "Let's eat."

CHAPTER TWENTY-TWO

He couldn't stop staring at Denevah. She sat by herself, both Savino and Benedetto giving her space. Ettoni watched as she picked at her food listlessly, uninterested in the morsels she pushed around on her plate. She'd dosed her meal with the packet of herbs he'd set before her, but she showed no signs of actually eating. Instead she hunched in on herself, looking both haunted and hunted.

Ettoni would give anything to take the horror of what she'd been through away from her. Savino had bandaged her fingers and had tended to her other injuries—the thought of the Rook caring for her made jealous anger flare in his chest—but he hadn't done anything about the uneven mess of Denevah's hair or the dark circles beneath her eyes. When she moved, she walked as if her bones were made of spun sugar, like she'd crack and break at any second.

"You should eat," he urged, getting up from his chair to cross the room to her.

"I'm not hungry," came Denevah's defeated whisper.

He stopped a few steps away from her chair. "It was two days. Your body needs fuel in order to recover." When she still did nothing, he said, "Denevah, you have to eat!"

She shuddered, her head dropping low on her neck and her shoulders rising as though ready to endure a blow. Her fork clattered to the plate, the sound ringing in the stillness of the room. Denevah's fingers knotted together, but he saw them tremble. She wouldn't look at him.

Benedetto stood, anger turning his usual easygoing expression into a hard scowl. "Back off and stop browbeating her," the assassin warned in a low grumble.

Ettoni glanced at the Rook, expecting him to join with Benedetto, but Savino slid past Ettoni as if he didn't exist to join Denevah. He gathered her hands in his gloved ones and spoke to her in a low voice. Ettoni couldn't make out what he said, but the jealousy flared and changed to hurt, burning him from the inside out. When had she stopped trusting him?

"I'm not browbeating her!" Ettoni spun around to face the assassin. "I'm trying to help her!"

"Like you did when Grimauldi had her?" Benedetto's icy gaze swept him, dismissing Ettoni as a threat. "How long was she with that woman before you did anything?"

Spine slamming straight, Ettoni sucked in an angry breath. Is that what Denevah thought? That he'd known she'd been captured, that he'd let Grimauldi torture and torment her? No, he didn't believe it. She couldn't possibly think he was that cruel. What had he ever done…

Everything, as Rodolfi's apprentice.

The realization nearly made him stagger. A whirlpool of sorrow and guilt and regret spiraled open inside of him. No matter what he did in the future, he would always be damned for that one thing. The fragile trust Denevah had in him would always come up short against his past actions—ones he hadn't been able to help. His insides ached at the thought that he would forever be in the shadow of his master's deeds, that his own motives would always be suspect. Even by her. Especially by her.

Benedetto hadn't let up on his diatribe. "What would you have done if you hadn't run into me, huh? Just let Grimauldi keep carving off pieces of her?" He ran a hand across his head, muscles taut with his anger and frustration. "Diluvians, Ettoni, the woman brought in a baby—"

"Stop it!" Denevah pushed herself to her feet, eyes rimmed with red, jaw clenched tight. "It's not Ettoni's fault!"

Ettoni watched Savino gently tuck a hand beneath her elbow, steadying her. She glared at Benedetto, eyes bright with tears she refused to shed. "Just leave him alone, Detto."

The assassin flung his arm at Ettoni, gesture violent and unforgiving. "He's done nothing but lie to you! How can you defend him?" The Crow's voice sounded choked, as though he were swallowing down more words that he wanted to say and they were sticking in his throat. "Why would you even want to after what he did?"

She shook her head, the uneven strands falling about her face. Grimauldi had hacked off sections indiscriminately, making Denevah look like a child had cut her hair. She shoved what she could behind her ears so she could stare at the Crow. Her gaze was steady as she answered him in a low voice.

"He didn't do this to me, Detto."

"You keep making excuses for him," Benedetto began again, only to be cut off, this time by Savino.

"Benedetto, let it go," the Rook advised, his gaze resting on Denevah's pale, strained face.

The door to their room opened and Lucian stuck his head in. "What are you idiots arguing about now? I can hear you down the stairs!"

Ettoni saw Benedetto's mouth snap shut, his nostrils flaring in fury. He grabbed his goblet of wine and stormed out of the room, bumping Lucian out of his way as he passed by.

"What's his problem?" the young man asked, gaze following after the irate assassin.

"It's nothing," Savino told him. "Thanks for the warning, Lucian. We'll keep the noise down."

"Please check on him," Denevah asked Lucian in a thready voice. She'd sat back down in her chair, an unsteady hand over her eyes.

Ettoni didn't miss the look of concern that crossed the young man's face. It flitted across it like a cloud in a bright blue sky, there and gone in a blink. His typical roguish smile replaced it. "Of course, my Lady," he answered with a slight bow, and then moved to pull the door shut.

"Wait," Ettoni said, the awkward currents in the room making it impossible for him to stay. He needed time alone to think. "I'm on my way out. I'll walk down with you."

Ettoni lashed his skiff to the post and stepped onto what remained of the street in front of the dilapidated palazzo, adjusting the bag on his shoulder as he did so. The ragged banner of House Aves still hung from the upper balcony, its colors faded by the elements, the fabric slowly rotting away. The alchemist shivered, unable to keep from drawing a parallel between his House specifically and the city as a whole.

They were drowning, rotting from the inside out. Ettoni wondered for a brief moment if they weren't all just poison; Denevah was only more obvious about it.

He straightened, facing the façade of the palazzo with a deep breath before stepping inside. The darkness took him by surprise— it always did. No light filtered in from the outside. The palazzo seemed wreathed in endless night, no matter how brightly the sun shone in the skies above Aerie. Ettoni thought it due to the wards placed around the place that helped keep the Diluvians contained to this plane, but that knowledge had been lost ages ago so he could only speculate.

The witchlight lamps flared to life at his approach. Ettoni descended though the ruined hallways, barely noticing the mildewing walls and peeling frescoes, the cracked marble floors of ballrooms, and solars long abandoned. He took the winding staircase down to the deeper levels of the palazzo, well below the canals of the flooded city. Water towered over him on every side, held in stasis by the powerful spells of the magicians of House Aves. He passed through quickly, mindful of the trap of the colored tiles on the floor, until he pushed through the door that led to the chamber of summoning.

Here he would call the Diluvians.

Ettoni had done everything he could with Rodolfi's notes on how he'd created Denevah's poisons. He'd tried reversing the process with healing plants and herbs, with alchemical potions and distillations. Nothing was strong enough to permanently overcome the virulence particular to her. He'd gotten close, but had always come up short in the end. He could proceed no further, not without assistance anyway. After what had happened with Lady Grimauldi, he knew he couldn't wait any longer.

Denevah's life was in danger. So long as the poisons ran through her, she would be hunted down by those who wanted the threat she posed eliminated or by those who wanted to use her as a weapon. She needed a cure if she ever hoped to live out her life in peace.

He could not afford to delay.

He knew Rodolfi had sought out the Diluvians, not once but twice, to help work the changes in Denevah. Ettoni had tried everything else. Now he could only seek a boon from the ancient water dragons. He tried to calm his racing heartbeat as he walked toward the altar at the water's edge.

The room was large, but it held a pool even larger than the walls could possibly contain. The feeling of magic prickled against him, a bit like the tightness he felt on his skin when he stayed out in the sun too long. The clammy humidity seeped inside him, making him sweat. Or maybe that was just his nerves. He'd never tried to call forth the Diluvians by himself before; he'd always had someone with him.

He lit the cake of incense in one shallow depression in the altar and poured oil into the matching one on the other side. In the center, he placed an empty glass alembic. With one last deep breath to calm his rattled nerves, Ettoni launched into the chant his master had taught him.

The sibilant syllables rolled over the water, the hisses of the words seeming to stretch out and fill the dark room. Tongues of mist began to appear above the pool, licking at the calm surface. Ettoni closed his eyes to focus on the intent of his call.

Denevah's serious face appeared in his mind's eye, nearly stopping his breath. It was how she'd looked a few weeks ago. He'd seen her with Benedetto—the sun had set and they were hurrying somewhere. Ettoni had been taking an evening stroll and he'd hung back, watching as she chatted with Benedetto, captivated by her sudden smile as the Crow said something that made her laugh. He hadn't seen her smile like that in a very long time.

The sibilant whispers grew louder, a counterpoint to his chant. Ettoni opened his eyes and almost screamed. His eyes nearly crossed as he focused on the head of the blue and white Diluvian that hovered in front of his face.

Ettoni scrambled away from the altar before he could stop himself. The sounds of hissing laughter filled the air as the other two Diluvians joined the first. Ettoni tried not to bristle as the water dragons continued to laugh at him for a few more moments.

They'd never come this quickly before. It was almost like they'd been expecting his call, which unnerved him. He'd only been to this temple twice before and both times it had taken much longer for them to show themselves. He remembered the last time he'd been here, with Denevah a broken mess beside him. They'd told him they'd see him again soon. Had they known even then what the outcome of his research would be? Had Navolio warned them?

The thought gave him pause. Too much about the Diluvians didn't make sense, and what he knew of them wouldn't fill the smallest vial in his laboratory. His former master had studied the water dragons for years before he'd made his deal with them, but Rodolfi had shared little of his knowledge with his apprentice. Ettoni wished he'd had the opportunity for more study, but Denevah didn't have the time. The time it took for her poisons to act grew shorter and shorter; he'd done the calculations and the experiments with what samples Rodolfi had left. Her touch would only continue to grow more devastating; soon even her breath would be able to kill someone in only a matter of minutes. If left unchecked, the touch of her hand might eventually kill in an instant.

He doubted Rodolfi had counted on that when he unwisely mixed magic beyond his understanding with plant alchemy to experiment on his adopted daughter.

The dragons' laughter died away into watery echoes. Ettoni hadn't known they could laugh—hadn't expected them to have that capacity. It unnerved him to think of them trapped in whatever half-life they had in this prison, amusing themselves endlessly.

"He has returned," said the orange and black Diluvian.

"Tell us what you sssseek, little Avesssss," the purple and green one hissed.

"What do you offer us today?" asked the blue and white one.

The three Diluvians had pulled back, leaving space at the altar. The bottom of their bodies twined around each other, their tails lost in the mist that now covered the water. Ettoni shivered and took a step forward.

"I seek your help." His voice came out weak, trembling. He cleared his throat and began again, stronger this time. "It's not for me, but for the girl I brought here with me some time ago. Do you remember her?"

The blue and white head nodded. The purple and green bared its teeth as if offended by Ettoni's question. His body jerked in an aborted step back. The alchemist wanted nothing more than to run away, but he knew he didn't dare show such weakness. He held his ground, digging his fingers into the flesh of his palm to ground himself.

"Lord Rodolfi's daughter," he continued haltingly, choosing his words carefully. "He made a deal with you to make her poisonous."

"**We remember,**" spoke the blue and white Diluvian inside his head.

Ettoni didn't know how he knew which one spoke, but somehow he did. He tried not to think about it too much. "I want you to undo it."

The orange and black Diluvian roared, the sound shattering the heavy stillness. Ettoni felt his hair blow backwards from the force of it. He squinted against the breeze, desperate to keep an eye on the three dragons, certain that he would end up dead at any moment.

"**We refused her once,**" came the hiss from the purple and green dragon. "**Why should we agree when you ask?**"

"Because I've come to deal." He blew out the breath he'd been anxiously holding. "Anything you want."

The orange and black Diluvian made as if to roar once more, but the blue and white one hissed him? her? it? to silence. The three water dragons began to commune in a language made up mostly of growls, trills, hisses, and snapping teeth. Ettoni stood there, never feeling more out of place. He waited, water seeping through the soles of his boots, hoping for a favorable outcome.

The orange and black dragon snapped at the blue and white one's snout. In retaliation, blue and white wrapped its sinuous body around the orange and black and began to squeeze. Ettoni could hear the rub of scales on scales, the noise setting his teeth on edge. He fought back the urge to clap his hands over his ears. Purple and green growled at the two of them, twining around them both.

Abruptly, blue and white let go. The orange and black Diluvian shook itself, spraying droplets of water everywhere. Ettoni held back a flinch when they struck him, wiping the wetness from his face with the sleeve of his jacket. As he watched, the dragon let out another roar, this one sounding less angry than the first.

Ettoni thought the blue and white Diluvian's eyes glittered with malicious laughter. Its jaws stretched wide in a toothy grin as it stared at him. The purple and green one hissed out its approval with amusement. Ettoni didn't understand what was going on, but it seemed as though they had all reached some kind of agreement. He could only hope it wasn't to snap his head off his neck with those vicious teeth. The way they were watching him made him uneasy.

"**You wish an antidote for the girl?**" the blue and white Diluvian asked, lowering its head terrifyingly close to Ettoni's.

"Yes," he answered in a very small voice.

"**And you will give us anything that is in your power to give?**"

Ettoni nodded.

"**We accept the deal.**"

Ettoni stared at the Diluvian, mouth hanging slack. His brain refused to work. He'd come there, knowing on some deeper level that he was doomed to failure, that the Diluvians would never agree to his request. They had turned Denevah down cold and they seemed to prefer her. And if what Navolio raved about held even a grain of truth, then the Diluvians wanted her just as she was.

He hadn't really expected them to accept.

Sweeping all of his fear and confusion away for the time being, Ettoni raised his head and locked gazes with the blue and white water dragon hovering in front of him. He bit the inside of his cheek to anchor his focus; looking into the Diluvian's eyes was like staring into an infinite sea where black waves crashed against an even darker shore.

He finally managed to choke out in a hoarse voice, "And the price?"

The purple and green dragon wound around his legs. Ettoni couldn't hold back the shudder that rippled through him at the cool rasp of its scales against his clothes. He managed to keep his place, even though everything inside of him howled at him to move, to run and to never look back. He waited.

"Your life," whispered the blue and white Diluvian. Ettoni heard the whispers of the other two inside his head, an uncanny mental echo.

He didn't know what expression he wore at those words, but it amused the three water dragons. Their hissing laughter broke the stillness, shattering it like ripples on the surface of calm water. The blue and white Diluvian undulated closer, until they were nearly snout to nose. Ettoni felt the blood drain from his face as he caught an up close glimpse of the creature's teeth. It looked like a mouth full of white bone spear points. His heart pounded fiercely against the wall of his chest.

"Not all of it, little mortal," it said, its heavy head scant paces away from his. "You must trade some of the time you have left on this plane—life for death."

Ettoni opened his mouth to speak, but found his words failing him. The water dragon prompted him with a drawn out hiss of a "Yessss?"

"How much--?" he trailed off, unable to complete his thought.

"You will have the time to effect a cure for your Denevah. Whether she is able to accept it or not is not for us to decide."

"Of course she'll accept it!" Ettoni countered, indignant. This is what Denevah wanted most all. Wasn't it? Did they know something he did not?

"Then you have nothing to fear," the purple and green one finished.

"Do we have a bargain?" asked the blue and white Diluvian, gaze unwavering.

Ettoni felt like he stood on the edge of a high cliff, waiting to jump. Except he didn't know if there was water or rocks below him, or if he would fall or fly. He hesitated, fear and uncertainty rising up inside of him. What if . . .?

He crushed that thought before it had a chance to take root. A cure was what Denevah wanted, what she needed, if she wished to have a normal life. Ettoni would do anything to make sure she got it. He owed her that much.

"We do," he said firmly.

He cried out as everything around him went dark and chilling knowledge dropped directly into his brain.

CHAPTER TWENTY-THREE

"Any sign of him?" Savino asked Denevah. The girl shook her head, dodging through the crowded streets.

The Rook clenched his teeth so hard his jaw ached. He and Denevah were searching the streets for signs of the preacher, working out in a circle from the epicenter of the latest quake. Benedetto did a search of his own. Savino hoped the assassin had better luck than they were.

He pulled Denevah off to the side, leading her onto a bridge spanning the narrow canal. Leaning his arms against the stone lip of the arch, Savino scanned the throngs of people trying to rebuild their lives, digging through the rubble of the half-sunken square and demolished buildings. His heart plummeted as he watched them work. There was no sign of aid arriving nor of the Doge's men. These people were on their own.

A slow but steady stream of folk moving down a side street caught his eye. "Denevah," he muttered, nudging her in the side. He jerked his head in their direction. She glanced over, eyes going wide.

"You don't think—" she said.

Savino grinned. "Only one way to find out."

They set off, doing their best to go unnoticed. He saw Denevah's gaze slide to the rooftops, the windows, and the balconies above them, never staying still for very long. "Anything?" he asked her after a few minutes.

"I thought I saw someone on the roof about a block ahead," she whispered. "Could have been a Shrike." She shrugged. "Or could just be a thief. They were too far away to tell."

"Keep looking," he urged as they crossed another bridge. They were heading deeper into the poorer section of the city, the part bordering the Floating Market. The crowd slowed. "I think we might be getting close."

The street narrowed. People jostled them, and Savino reached out to steady Denevah as she was shoved against him. His hand rested briefly on the small of her back. She turned her head, a flush painting her cheeks pink, then looked away. Savino's hand tingled with the warmth of her. They pushed on without speaking.

The crowd spilled into another square, this one more dilapidated than any he'd seen before. Denevah leaned close, breath fanning his cheek. "This is similar to the place where I saw his first sacrifice."

Savino craned his neck, hoping to catch a glimpse. "I don't see him," he told her.

"He's over there," Benedetto said, materializing at their side as if by magic. Denevah jerked away, surprised, but Savino managed to smother his shock and hold his position. Benedetto tilted his head in the direction he wanted them to look.

"When did you get here?" Denevah muttered, words an angry lash at being surprised.

"A few minutes ago. I was going to verify Navolio was here and then send an urchin to find you." His teeth flashed in a white grin. "But you managed to work it out for yourselves."

"How did you find him?" Savino asked, returning the smile.

"I asked Luc to keep an ear out with his Shrike friends for Navolio's next public appearance." When Savino kept staring at him, the assassin crossed his arms over his chest and set his jaw mulishly. "What?" he snapped.

Biting back a wide grin, Savino answered, "Nothing at all." He pushed at the two Crows. "Let's get a better spot so we can see."

Benedetto strode through the crowd like an arrow heading for a target. He used his height and Crow clothes to get people to move out of his way, with Savino and Denevah trailing after him like flotsam in his wake. He led them to an area near the outskirts of the gathering crowd, close to the preacher's right side.

"Is this what you had in mind?" the Crow asked, leaning his shoulder against a wall.

"Perfect." Savino watched as Navolio climbed up on a crate so that he stood head and shoulders above his makeshift congregation.

The Rook risked a glance at Denevah. She appeared tense, trembling with expectation. Her expression was vicious, driven, lethal. She was a naked blade, desperate to be put to use. Savino placed a hand on her shoulder, bringing her attention back to him.

"Take it easy," he told her, squeezing his fingers into the taut muscles.

"I don't see anyone with him. Maybe he's not going to sacrifice today." Her voice didn't sound hopeful though.

"We won't let him do anything," Savino assured her. Denevah gave him a look of incredulous disbelief and he realized just how stupid his statement was. They were in a crowd of people that only grew as word spread of Navolio's presence. They wouldn't be able to stop him from doing anything.

"My friends," Navolio began, his hands out in a placating gesture to the crowd milling at his feet. "Your struggle has gone unnoticed by those in power, but it has not gone unnoticed by me or those I serve." The noise of the mob slowly bled away as people began to pay attention to the preacher's words.

"With every quake, we see how the Doge and the Great Houses ignore our plight. We see how little they regard us and our contributions to this city!"

Benedetto snorted. He leaned it to whisper in Savino's ear. "His only contribution has been running his mouth." A few of the people closest to them gave them dirty looks.

Navolio rolled on with his speech. The crowd began to shout back to him, yelling examples of the Doge's indifference and cruelty. Savino glanced with apprehension at Benedetto and Denevah in the black jackets with the Corvus sigil picked out in glittering threads.

"Who suffers for the Doge's failings?" The crowd shouted back. "Who starves in the streets?" Another roar. "Who ends up homeless when the buildings fall?"

Flinching from the angry shouts of the mob, Savino eyed those closest to him warily. The undercurrent of violent protest crested. People began to push and shove, striving to get closer to the preacher as he whipped them up into a frenzy. This went beyond simple preaching. Navolio advocated rebellion.

He was recruiting an army.

"We have special guests with us today," Navolio said, his voice rich and deep, like a fine claret. Savino twitched, pulled in by the man's words. It took some time, but the crowd stilled. This was a deviation from his usual sermon. He could feel Benedetto go tense beside him; when Savino glanced down at Denevah, he saw her hands clenched into fists, her face chalky white.

Savino watched with dread as Navolio turned his body to face the three of them. "We should probably be running," Benedetto whispered.

"Too late," Denevah said, eyes wide and horrified as Navolio's thin lips split into a serpent's smile.

"It seems I may have been mistaken! Two of the Great Houses have taken an interest in our little enterprise!" The preacher gestured their way. The entire crowd began to turn their heads, looking at them. Savino's chest grew tight, sweat rolling down his spine.

"Welcome Lord Rook and Lord Crow!" Navolio greeted them jovially.

"We are so deeply screwed," Benedetto whispered, holding himself still.

"Shut up and let me think," Savino snapped. His heart galloped in his chest.

"Think faster," Denevah urged.

"Not helping."

"And you've brought a gift for us." Navolio's gaze sharpened, locking onto Denevah. Savino felt her stiffen beside him, quivering with tension, taut as a strung bow. "The very woman we've all been waiting for, the one thing we need to see all of our sins washed clean."

Navolio smiled wide. "Bella Muerta."

Denevah flinched, a full body shudder. Savino lightly touched the space between her shoulder blades, pressing his palm flat against the back of her jacket. He could feel her shaking beneath him. Her eyes were lit with anger, the dark violet-blue incandescent with fury, and her lips curled back from her teeth in a snarl.

The congregation went still for a moment, a hush descending over them. A few craned their necks to look at the trio, but most waited, like a dog with ears perked for the voice of its master. The moment stretched out, filling the square with expectation.

Savino moved in front of Denevah; he saw Benedetto doing the same. The Crow's gaze searched the buildings adjacent to them, probably formulating some kind of escape plan. Savino kept his attention on the people in front of him, and the preacher who would determine their next move.

An indrawn breath and then:

"Bring the girl to me."

The crowd erupted into shouts and violence, all of them scrambling to get to Denevah. Savino was pushed back by the wave of people, but he kept his body in front of hers. Hands pulled at his clothes, ripped at his hair, tried to drag him down and crush him beneath their feet. Pulling out his dagger, he slashed at the clutching fingers. Savino didn't want to hurt anyone, but he refused to allow himself or his friends to be trampled underfoot.

Across the sea of people, he saw Navolio smile, eyes only for Denevah.

Benedetto had one hand buried in the collar of Denevah's jacket, the other wrapped around the hilt of his long dagger. The Crow yanked her backwards, making for the wall of the building directly behind them. Savino covered them as best he could, buffeted by body blows. Fingernails scored his cheek, coming perilously close to his eye.

"Up here!" a familiar voice called.

Savino spared a glance to the roof above him. Vermillion's dark face appeared at the edge. She waved, and then a rope snaked down.

"Denevah, Benedetto, GO!" he ordered as the mob swarmed him.

Benedetto practically hoisted Denevah up the rope, but instead of following her, he jerked Savino backwards. "You first," he snapped, shoving the Rook toward the rope.

Savino didn't argue—there wasn't time. He scrambled up the rope as best he could, adrenaline surging through his body, as Benedetto wielded both his blades to carve out a pocket of space. It wouldn't last long.

Vermillion's dark eyes glittered as she leaned over the edge of the roof to help Denevah up. Savino scrambled up after. "Come on, Detto!" Savino yelled once he climbed to safety.

The assassin didn't need to be told twice. He sheathed his blades in an easy movement before he flung himself at the rope. He flowed up it like water, his movements so quick and graceful Savino could only gape in amazement. He'd never seen anyone move that way before.

Vermillion had stepped to the edge as Benedetto climbed, flinging her strange metal spikes into the edges of the crowd closest to the rope. It kept most of the crowd back, but a few made a grab for the rope. Two young men began to haul themselves up.

Then Benedetto slithered over the side, barely out of breath. He whipped around, unsheathed a blade and cut the rope. The two climbers tumbled to the ground, only a few bruises to show for their trouble.

"This way," Vermillion ordered, and took off at a run.

The three of them followed her without comment or complaint, too shaken to do anything else. Savino looked back at Denevah a few times as Vermillion led them across the roofs. She appeared to be coping and kept up well, which was all the Rook could hope for at the moment. Benedetto followed behind her and he looked none the worse for wear. Savino, on the other hand, felt like he'd been put through a clothes wringer.

"I knew you couldn't stay away," Benedetto called to the Shrike.

Savino's lips twitched. He almost felt sorry for Vermillion. Almost.

The young woman cut her eyes at the assassin, her lip curled up in a faint expression of disgust. "Oh yes," she said, voice flat, "you are irresistible. I couldn't help myself. Stop before I swoon."

Savino heard Denevah's decidedly unladylike snort of laughter behind him. Benedetto lapsed into hurt silence.

"Thank you for the timely rescue," the Rook said to Vermillion when she slowed their pace enough so he could speak without gasping.

She shrugged one narrow shoulder, the gesture fluid, graceful. She shoved open a battered wooden door at the next roof and led them down a series of rickety stairs. Strapped to the walls and in the rooms they passed were poles and oars; sandolos, the frames of barcariols, and wooden planks were stacked up in out of the way rooms and corridors. A thick layer of dust covered everything. Spider webs hung from the corners of the walls and Savino thought he heard the faint skitter of rat feet on the wood floors. They were in an abandoned boat maker's warehouse.

"Not to appear rude, but why would you do something like that?" Savino asked as they turned down another flight. "I thought the Shrikes were for Navolio."

Vermillion glanced over her shoulder at Benedetto, and Savino thought he saw the faintest blush color the girl's cheeks. But her next words stopped the smile that threatened to bloom on his face.

"Did you mean it? What you said back at Black Wings?" She asked in a voice like a stone rasp, a blade sharpened on a strap.

"I said a great deal of things at Black Wings. You'll need to be specific." Savino saw that both Benedetto and Denevah were listening intently.

"About wanting to make the city better. Did you mean it?" She bit her lip, gaze darting from Savino's face to her feet.

Savino nodded, stifling his surprise at her question. "Yes, I meant every word. I don't think it's fair that some suffer while those in power turn a blind eye. I think there's something I can do to help and I'm willing to try." He kept his words simple, uncomplicated. It was what he believed, why he felt so strongly about fighting his father. Poullo wanted fame and renown for Dauricus. Savino wanted to do the right thing for the people that he shared the city with.

They arrived at the last landing. Vermillion remained quiet, mulling over what he said. Savino wished he had a perfect speech planned, a way to make her understand the things that drove him. His mother's kindness and willingness to help. His brother's strength. Savino's own need to prove himself as more than just the spoiled second son.

Vermillion paused before the door that would take them back to the streets. Savino had no idea where they were, but he suspected Benedetto could find them a way back to White Feathers with ease. He moved to open the door, but Vermillion's hand on his chest stopped him.

She stared up at him with her eyes of jasper, weighing her words. "I think you believe it," she said after a few tense moments. When he nodded, she sighed.

Savino caught sight of her arm that ended in stump rather than a hand. "I do believe it. Everyone deserves a fair chance, not just the rare few."

"Things around here need to change. We're dying by inches." Her eyes dropped to his hands where they rested easy at his sides. She didn't frighten him.

"I can only promise to do my best, Vermillion, if I'm given the chance."

She nodded once. Pushing open the door, she stuck her head out to check the streets. Popping her head back into the warehouse, she told them, "No sign of Navolio's followers, but I wouldn't dawdle. You need to get somewhere safe until you know exactly how to deal with the preacher."

"I have an idea," Savino said, a plan already beginning to form in his mind.

Vermillion ducked her head. "Kinendra is stalling," she said finally. "I'll talk to The Shrike and get you a meeting. I'll send word through Lucian."

Savino stuck out his hand. "Thank you, Vermillion. I know this is not offered lightly. I'll try to be worthy of it."

The girl glanced at his hand as though it were a pit viper rearing back to attack her. Meeting his gaze, she warned, "You'd better be." Then she slipped out the door and was gone.

CHAPTER TWENTY-FOUR

Denevah drummed her fingers on her knees, wishing that she could get the boat pilot to pole faster. Ettoni had sent word that she needed to come to his workroom as soon as possible—that he might have a cure. It had been difficult to get time away from Benedetto and Savino and she didn't want to waste it stuck in a boat. At least they were occupied: Savino had requested a meeting with the Doge to go over his findings on Navolio, and Benedetto had accompanied him as his bodyguard. Denevah had been told to wait at White Feathers since she'd been branded an enemy of three of the four Great Houses and would probably be clapped in irons if she dared approach the Doge.

She stared into the murky green water of the canal, running Ettoni's brief message over in her mind. He'd written that he needed her to give him samples to test. Her hands sweated in the thin leather gloves she wore, her heart pounding so fast that she thought it would shoot up her throat and out of her body. She had to force herself to relax and breathe. She wondered how close he was to a cure. Why else would he need samples?

The sandolo's progress ground to a halt as several boats ahead of them tangled with each other in a common canal jam. Denevah ground her teeth together, feeling her jaw creak with the strain of keeping her temper. She wanted to rip the pole from boatman's hands and get them there quicker, but she managed to sit on the bench without clubbing the man over the head with the length of wood and paddling at top speed to Ettoni.

The pilots eventually freed their crafts from the logjam and the canal reopened. Denevah breathed an audible sigh of relief as they got underway once more. Flinging the coins at her boatman as soon as they stopped at the palazzo, Denevah hopped out. She debated about going in through the front door, but she'd never really done that before. Instead, she went around to the back of the house and let herself into the kitchens. Cook had left the service entrance unlatched for her, as she always did, in the faint hope she'd come home for good.

The palazzo was quiet. Ettoni would likely have released the few servants he kept early to make sure word of their meeting didn't get out to the rest of House Aves. Denevah made quick work of the circular stairs leading up the attic and workroom at the top. She passed the flight that led to her bedroom without a second glance.

Knocking once at the heavy oaken door, Denevah didn't wait for a greeting before throwing open the door.

"Toni?"

Ettoni swept her into a hug, careful to keep his face away from her hair and skin. He wore his alchemist robes and the light black gloves he usually did when dealing with the less toxic plants and potions.

"You look better," he whispered, holding her tightly.

"I came as soon as I could get away. Benedetto and Savino haven't let me out of their sight." She felt awkward in his arms, wrong somehow, in a way she never had before. As much as she loved her cousin, this was not her place anymore. He tried to hold onto her as she pulled away.

"Did you have any trouble?" he asked, keeping his hands on her upper arms. He gazed at her, relearning her features. Then he frowned, brows lowering as he frowned. "Your hair."

Denevah smiled, feeling the stretch of it in her cheeks. She ran her hand through the short locks. She'd decided to chop the length off when she'd discovered what a mess Grimauldi had made of her hair. She found she much preferred the short style that hit just below her chin. There were still shorter pieces, but now they weren't so noticeable. "Leaving it long when it looked like that was silly."

Ettoni continued to stare. Denevah fidgeted under his regard, moving out of his grip. "It will grow back," he assured her, as if she were at all bothered by the change. Her smile dropped from her face. Denevah enjoyed the freedom of shorter hair, and didn't know if she wanted long hair again.

"It will just take me some time to get used to it," Ettoni said. His gloved hand hovered over her hair.

Denevah took a step away, masking her discomfort by making a point of looking at the contents of his worktable. "You've been busy," she said to change the subject. She flipped a book cover open, careful not to upset the stack upon which it precariously balanced. Parchment littered the table, sheaves spread out like leaves among all the used glassware dotted with residue.

"I found it, Den," he told her, voice simmering with barely-contained excitement. "I think I have a cure."

She froze, outstretched hand stilled above a flask. Denevah blinked as the handwritten parchment in front of her wavered in her vision. She blinked back the tears that threatened to fall, swallowing thickly. Could this really be happening? She wasn't sure she believed it. "What?"

Ettoni stood beside her, his body pressed close. Suddenly the room seemed too warm, the closeness oppressive. She walked to the casement and threw open the window, letting in the evening breeze. The smell of the garden wafted up on the air, and Denevah stuck her head out to take a deep, cleansing breath.

"I've got a cure—or nearly so," he repeated, thankfully staying where he was. "Just a few more tests with your blood and then, I think, we can try it on you." He glanced at her, expression suddenly unsure. "That is if you still want a cure?"

Denevah gripped the sill tightly in her hands, feeling her bones creak with the strength of her grasp. She thought of Savino, of his hands lightly sliding over her back, of his voice in her ear. She remembered Benedetto, wearing one of his rare serious looks as he told her she shouldn't change for anyone, that she needed to accept who and what she was before looking for someone to change her.

But to finally touch someone, to feel bare skin against bare skin without the fear of pain and death? What might that be like? She'd dreamed of it for so long now that she felt frozen by the possibility of it, shocked into stasis.

"You do still want it?" Ettoni's voice sounded tentative, hesitant.

She forced herself to turn around and face him. "Yes," she said, staring into his eyes. She watched relief spark in them, and hope, and a deep joy with no second thoughts, no hesitation. "I do."

She wished she felt the same way.

CHAPTER TWENTY-FIVE

"I don't think I've ever seen you nervous before," Benedetto said to him as they climbed the steps that led to the massive doors of the Doge's palace.

Savino swiveled his head to look at the Crow in surprise. He thought he'd been hiding his anxiousness rather well. "It's obvious?"

The assassin shook his head. "Not to someone who doesn't know what to look for. Who doesn't know you," he added in almost a whisper.

"That's something at least," Savino said, giving a Benedetto a low chuckle. "None of these people know me." He felt the tension in his spine unknot a bit.

Few in Aerie knew the real him—a few allies in Accipitus, his mother, and now Benedetto and Denevah. Most had heard only the things Poullo and Cyngare had said of Savino in public. For once, Savino felt glad of it; such a reputation would insure he would be underestimated, at least in this first gambit. He doubted that his father would ever underestimate him again, so Savino had to make it count. He had to announce his intentions and skills with a flourish, not a whimper. A seat on the Doge's council would be a grand start.

"You sure this is wise?" Benedetto asked as they waited in a parlor for one of the Doge's myriad functionaries to announce them.

"Doing my job? Yes." Savino raised his eyebrows at the Crow. He knew there was more to Benedetto's question, but the Rook wasn't in the mood to parse it out. His mind was busy with other things.

The assassin shook his dark head, his body taut with tension. "You've got a target on your back already," he warned. "You sure you want to make it bigger?"

Savino was spared having to answer when the Doge's personal assistant entered the room. He gestured for Savino and Benedetto to follow him to the Doge's formal audience chamber. Savino ignored the painted frescoes on the walls, the delicately spun glass sculptures, and all of the other trappings of wealth that lined the hallways. The ostentation rubbed him raw inside as he recalled Vermillion's earnest dark gaze, Lucien's wry humor, and Kinendra's quiet pride. Each of them fought in their own way to survive, each day made more difficult by the quakes that the Doge did nothing to solve. The smoldering embers of Savino's disappointment flared into anger.

Savino had taken on the task of finding Navolio because he knew that something rotten ate away at the core of Aerie. The quakes were a symptom of it, not the cause. While the Great Houses turned a blind eye to it and pushed for foreign expansion, for wars, and the poor cast about for a mystical reason why such horrible events occurred, Savino searched for a more mundane reason behind it.

He didn't understand why the Doge had waited so long to look into Navolio. Savino didn't flatter himself to think he had more or better resources than the ruler of Aerie had at his disposal. The Night Watch had been searching for the street preacher for moons with little luck, and Savino wondered if they'd been given orders not to find him. But to what end?

"Your associate will have to remain outside," the assistant told Savino as they paused in front of an intricately carved wooden door.

Savino glanced at Benedetto, who shrugged. Benedetto eyed the guards stationed on either side of the door. "You're good?" Savino asked the Crow.

"I'm excellent," Benedetto reassured him. "But if you need me, just scream in terror." The look he threw the guards told Savino that the assassin didn't think they were worth his time.

"I'll do my best," Savino promised before gesturing for the assistant to let him in. He tugged lightly at the sleeves of his jacket before stepping inside.

The Doge's private audience chamber was a large room anchored by a massive desk against the back wall. It afforded a clear view of the door. Savino would lay coin that the bookcase behind it was not just a bookcase either; he'd bet it covered a hidden door, allowing the Doge to enter and exit without alerting the staff. It would function as a convenient emergency exit in case of assassination or attack.

The man sat behind the desk, his gaze hooded and dark as he watched Savino enter. Savino bowed from the waist in greeting. "Your Grace."

"Lord Savino." The Doge gestured to one of the chairs that sat in front of the desk. "You look well."

"As do you, Your Eminence." Savino took the seat offered, feeling strangely off-balance. He nodded his thanks. "I have some news to report on Navolio."

"Do you now?" Waving his hand, the Doge indicated Savino should continue. "This should be interesting."

Savino swallowed, but pressed on anyway, despite his misgivings. There was something off about the man in front of him; Savino couldn't put his finger on what it was that bothered him so much, but he listened to it, deciding to tread carefully.

"Your Grace," he began, leaning forward so that his wrist rested on the edge of the desk, "the preacher is not working alone. He has contracted with the Shrikes for protection. Without them, it would be a simple thing to capture and detain him for questioning."

"And?" the Doge asked, sitting back in his chair. He steepled his fingers in front of his full lips, dark eyes bright with a kind of malevolent interest.

Savino reared back, unable to keep the surprise from his features. "Your Grace? You asked for word of Navolio's location."

"Let's talk about what this is really about, yes?" The man smiled as though he'd won a war. Savino watched him, wary for traps. "I grow weary of games."

"I assure you, there is nothing of a game in this." Savino glanced around the room, expecting guards to pour in from hidden entrances at any moment.

The Doge made a scoffing noise. "Don't be coy, Lord Savino. You're playing in the greatest game there is. We all want power. Some of us are just more obvious about it than others."

Savino's narrowed his eyes, several things becoming clear. "You've spoken with my father."

"He doesn't like you much," the Doge agreed. "It makes one wonder exactly how a father could come to hate his son so much."

"The son wonders as well," Savino admitted, locking down his expressions. His voice sounded shockingly steady to his ears. "But that's not what you really want to know."

The Doge cocked an eyebrow. "Your father painted you as an inept dabbler, a child desperate for attention. But you are none of those things, are you?"

Savino didn't see the point in dissembling any longer. "No. I'm not."

"You want to be Doge." The man sounded vaguely amused.

"I do."

The Doge made a faint humming noise. "You aligned yourself with Accipitus because you thought it prudent."

Savino said nothing. That wasn't why he'd allied with Accipitus—or rather, not the only reason. Most of Dauricus rested firmly in his father's pocket, and House Corvus held no pull. That left him with Aves and Accipitus. He had more pull with the Hawks since his mother hailed from that House, so he'd started there. The Hawks were also the most vocal in their assessments of the Doge's inaction.

Continuing, the Doge rested his elbows on his desk, leaning forward. "And what would happen should you fail in this endeavor? How do you think your friends in Accipitus will respond?"

Biting the inside of his cheek to keep silent, Savino ignored the Doge's question, instead choosing to direct the conversation back to the more important matter. "Your Grace, I came to speak to you about Navolio."

"I'm well aware of the man and his benighted preachings. He's only marginally more delusional than those priests at Temple Mark. Water dragons are going to rise and destroy the city? Superstition and idiocy. We have moved beyond that kind of nonsense."

"The people are listening to that nonsense," Savino warned, lacing his fingers together and resting his hands upon his knee. "And they believe what he is telling them."

"What do they matter?" The Doge's lip curled in disgust. "We are a global power, Savino. Our navy is the most powerful in the world. The Ostvians are sending a prince to negotiate a trade treaty with us. Some unwashed imbeciles who would prefer to squat in the dark than walk upright in the light are not my concern."

"They are more than a few, Your Grace," Savino reminded him. "I've been to a number of his sermons. His audience grows larger with each one." Could the man really be so blind?

"And they will be dealt with," the Doge said with a finality that chilled Savino down to the marrow of his bones. "As will the preacher." He tilted his head and surveyed Savino. "You will bring him to me."

Savino sat up straighter, heart slamming into his ribs. "I don't understand, Your Grace."

"You wish to be Doge one day?" the man purred dangerously. "Let's see if you can accomplish this one task. Bring me the preacher so that I may speak with him myself. I would see this man with my own eyes and determine if he is so dangerous. You say you have discovered who protects him—show me you are more than your father claims you to be."

"And if I fail to deliver him to you?" Savino asked, dread arcing through him.

"Then your Accipitus allies will be greatly disappointed." The Doge smiled coldly. "You know how the game is played, Savino. Stupidity does not become you."

Savino bit back a laugh. It was a very neat gambit. If Savino didn't bring in Navolio, he would lose face and position, and so would Accipitus since that House backed him. Their complaints would be taken less seriously, and their political currency would take a hit. Savino's hopes at being nominated for Doge would be dashed. Savino would be made the scapegoat for everything wrong in Aerie, of that he had no doubt.

If he did bring in the preacher, the Doge still won. He would have finally neutralized the threat of a city-wide rebellion. Savino would get a seat on the council, but the bulk of the accolades would go to the Doge. He would look stronger and Accipitus would have less reason for griping.

Savino couldn't tell which outcome was preferable.

The Doge stood, giving him a bright smile. "But you know where and how to find the street preacher. It shouldn't be too hard to bring him to me."

Savino stood as well, knowing a dismissal when he heard one. "Yes, Your Grace."

"You have until Prince Abhishek's presentation to bring Navolio to me. Do you understand?" The Doge watched Savino through narrowed eyes.

"Perfectly, Your Eminence" Savino said, a wry smile curling up the corner of his mouth as he made his way to the door.

CHAPTER TWENTY-SIX

"I have a favor to ask of you."

Looking up from cleaning his daggers, Benedetto raised his eyebrows at Denevah. "I don't lend money."

"What are you talking about? Why would you think I need money?" He saw her brows scrunched in confusion and distaste.

He grinned. "That's good because I don't have any. Can I borrow some?"

She slapped at the back of his head gently. "You are impossible."

"Flattery will get you everywhere." Benedetto wagged his eyebrows up and down, hoping to cajole a smile from her.

Denevah heaved a sigh, plopping down in the chair beside him. "I need tomorrow evening free. Can you guard Savino without me?"

Benedetto set down his dagger and reached over to grab a handful of grapes from the bowl on the table. He threw one up in the air, catching it in his mouth with ease. "Shouldn't be a problem. Where will you be?" he asked, chewing and then popping up another grape.

Her eyes shifted, violet gaze darting around the room as though she were searching for intruders. Benedetto turned his head to check if she'd seen something he hadn't, but no, the room sat empty except for the two of them. He flicked another grape into his mouth, chewing absently as he waited her out. She dragged her gloved hands down her thighs, bracing them on her knees.

When she finally spoke, her voice snapped tight with tension. Softly, she said, "There's a cure."

Benedetto stared at her dumbly. "For what?"

She bit her lip, gaze straying to the door, the window, the balcony. When she met his eyes, he saw the hope that shimmered in hers. "For me." She swept her hand over her body. Denevah stared at him hopefully.

Finishing off the last of his grapes, Benedetto wiped his mouth with the back of his hand. "Who?" he asked.

Denevah glanced away. Her fingers interlocked around one knee, held together so tight that her wrists and forearms went taut with strain. "Ettoni."

Benedetto snorted, rising to his feet in a fluid motion. He planted his hands on the table and leaned forward on his fists, putting his face close to Denevah's. "You're joking." When she shook her head, short hair brushing her long neck, he added, "Then you're mad to trust him."

Ettoni had always been a cagey one as far as Benedetto knew him. He had been a student of possibly the greatest alchemist Aerie had ever known. He'd learned at the man's knee, watched as Rodolfi fed Denevah his poisons. Just as he'd watched Denevah the night she'd killed her father.

And now he was a powerful player in House Aves. Benedetto wasn't naïve enough to think it a coincidence.

"He's been trying to find a way to fix me since my father d— since I killed Lord Rodolfi," Denevah explained, urgency weighting her words.

Shaking his head, Benedetto pushed away from the table. "And you think he finally succeeded? What took your father seventeen years to create took him less than seven moons to undo?" he scoffed. "Denevah, he's lying to you." Ettoni wasn't good for Denevah, not if he kept filling her head with hope every chance he got.

"To what end?" she whispered, pushing herself back to her feet to square off with him. "He's trying to help me."

"Help himself, more like." His hands pulled into tight fists. Benedetto wanted desperately to punch something. Preferably Ettoni. Too bad the Raven wasn't there.

Denevah shook her head, clearly in denial about what kind of man her cousin was. Benedetto had seen his stripe before. He looked innocuous enough at first, drawing people in, gaining their trust, and then he struck. He'd take their money, their lives, or their dignity—sometimes all three. Ettoni didn't carry a blade, but the Crow knew the Aves could cut just as deep.

"I know you don't trust him," she began, stopping abruptly at the scoffing noise he let slip. "But don't you trust me?"

Benedetto turned his back to her, hiding his face from Denevah. He didn't want her picking up on all of the unasked questions he had. Lord Trapinze had asked him to watch her for instability along with the man's known agenda of keeping her safe. Benedetto already felt like he had betrayed their friendship by spying on her. His loyalty though was to House Corvus. It had to be. If not for the orphan tithe, he would have died on the streets. He owed the Crows.

"I trust you," he told her, not turning around. His voice held steady enough to hide his lie. "I just can't see why you'd put yourself through this. What if it doesn't work? What if it kills you? Or what if Aves finds out what you're both doing?" He twisted his neck to glance at her over his shoulder. "Grimauldi did and look where that got you."

He didn't add that Ettoni hadn't helped her, not really, though the words sat heavy in his mouth.

Anger flashed in her violet eyes, there and then gone as she mercilessly snuffed it out. The lines of her face hardened. It always amazed Benedetto how Denevah could ratchet down her expressions so ruthlessly. She hadn't been trained to hide them like most in House Corvus; it was more like she realized she let her emotions show on her face or in her eyes and throttled it as quickly as she could. He wondered when she'd learned that skill. Had her bastard of an adopted father taught it to her deliberately, or had she learned it unconsciously as a survival mechanism?

"A chance is enough for me. I don't want to live like this anymore," she whispered, gloved hands held out before her. "Isn't that a good enough reason?" Her words were bitten off, shards of her rage parceled out into manageable pieces.

Benedetto blinked. He thought Ettoni had sold her a scam, feeding on her hope. He was the worst kind of trickster, a charlatan who broke your heart like it meant nothing. Just because they'd grown up together didn't mean Ettoni had Denevah's interests at heart. After everything she'd been through, Denevah still made excuses for him. It infuriated Benedetto.

Rodolfi was the only one who truly understood just what changes had been wrought in Denevah. Ettoni was merely a substitute—highly skilled to be sure, but a substitute nonetheless. Benedetto didn't want to see her go through the kind of hurt she opened herself up to every time she listened to her cousin. She was a friend. Diluvians knew he had few enough of those as it was.

But no matter how misguided he might think her endeavor, wasn't it still her choice? Wouldn't she be the one who lived with the consequences, even if it meant dying?

Ettoni didn't deserve her.

His shoulders slumped. She wouldn't listen to him, not when there might be a glimmer of hope that a cure might be effective. She would have to learn disappointment the hard way.

He rubbed a tired hand across his face. "For you, Bella Muerta, anything."

She flinched when he said it, as he knew she would. Denevah hated that name. He knew that too. "Thank you," she said. Benedetto watched her back as she left the room.

Benedetto dropped into his chair with a sigh that seemed to come from his boots. Planting his elbow on the table, he rubbed at his temple, feeling the taut pull of his shoulder and neck muscles. He would do as she asked, he would give her the night away from guarding Savino. But he was not willing to simply give her up to Ettoni. She might think the Raven harmless or working for her best interest, but Benedetto did not.

His obligation tore at him. Denevah was his friend, but Corvus was his life. Without the House, he had nowhere to go, no one to be. The orphan tithe had brought him there, had given him a home and offered him a purpose. Benedetto owed Lord Trapinze everything. What was friendship compared to that?

He wondered briefly what Savino would do, but shied away from the answer. He knew what the Rook would do—he had witnessed the way the man's mind worked. He wouldn't betray Denevah. He'd think of a way out.

Benedetto wasn't Savino, and he didn't have that luxury.

Lord Trapinze glanced up from the stack of missives that claimed his attention as Benedetto entered his office. The man's lips pursed in an annoyed bow as his sharp blue gaze settled on him. Benedetto's spine turned to ice beneath that predatory look. Even seated behind a massive desk, the Lord of Corvus was still more dangerous than a troop of armed soldiers.

"It has been some time since I've seen you," Trapinze said when Benedetto didn't immediately speak.

Benedetto nodded, accepting the rebuke. "I did send word about Denevah's capture and rescue," he offered in apology.

Lord Crow sniffed, setting aside the parchment pages. He laced his fingers together atop his desk and leaned back in his chair, eyeing Benedetto thoughtfully. The assassin wished he knew what the man thought, but his face gave nothing away.

"Did you discover the men who worked with Grimauldi to capture Denevah?" Benedetto asked.

"Without a description from the girl, chances are slim that I would be able to narrow such a thing down so quickly. It will take time," Trapinze growled.

When Benedetto had reported what had happened to Denevah, Trapinze had been enraged at the thought that he might have more disloyalty in his ranks. He was still in the process of cleaning house from the first betrayal. Benedetto had left him to it.

"Denevah has no recollection of the men who took her."

"Then you'll have to wait on my methods to bear fruit." Trapinze arched a golden brow at him. "Is that all you came for?"

A rhetorical question. Benedetto knew better than to waste his master's time by telling him how to do his job. He hadn't suddenly become suicidal.

Benedetto took a deep breath in and let it out slowly. "You asked me to tell you if Denevah was experiencing any difficulties."

Trapinze nodded, gaze suddenly needle-sharp as he stared at his assassin. Benedetto swallowed, his guts tied in knots, feeling strangely vulnerable and unsure. He'd never been this way, never uncertain. Corvus had rules. His master had given him orders. It was as simple as that.

"Her cousin has offered her a cure for her poisons. She thinks he can deliver."

Trapinze's lips twitched up in amusement. "You don't believe him?"

"I find it strange that he can undo so easily something that even master alchemists failed to achieve." Benedetto smiled bitterly. "I don't think Denevah is thinking clearly."

He watched Lord Trapinze frown. It wasn't as fearsome as those not of Corvus suspected, but it unsettled him when paired with the calculating look in his eyes. "When is she to meet with her cousin?"

"Tomorrow night."

The man's lapis gaze bored into Benedetto, as if he could see every lie, every fabrication the Crow had ever said, done, or thought of. The assassin didn't dare look away. Trapinze said mildly, "Then I shall pay him a visit to impress upon him the concerns I have."

Benedetto nodded, a bird caught before a snake. His mouth felt dry. He wanted to get up and leave, but his legs weren't obeying him. He stood at the edge of a cliff, just waiting for someone to push him over.

"You're coming with me."

"My Lord?" Benedetto's voice nearly cracked. His muscles locked up, his guts churned. He knew what Trapinze expected of him, the knowledge pounded deep into his bones. He should have expected something like this. He'd been wrong to betray Denevah's trust.

This had been a mistake; he'd made a terrible mistake. "What about Lord Savino? There will be no one to guard him."

"I think he can do without us for one night. The young man seems imminently capable."

Benedetto nodded, mind already working on how to get out of this mess.

CHAPTER TWENTY-SEVEN

Ettoni had left the door to his workroom open, expecting Denevah. He felt alive with excitement, his skin electric with his hopes. He'd done it! It had taken months, but he'd managed an antidote, a serum that could reverse the ravages of a lifetime of poisonous supplements and magic. Thanks to the Diluvians, he had finally figured out the final process needed to heal her. The water dragons had been the key; now Ettoni understood why Lord Rodolfi had needed to visit them and make his bargain to save Denevah's life.

He'd made a bargain of his own to reverse what Rodolfi had done. He could live with the cost, if it meant Denevah got the chance to be happy, to find someone to love her, to have children with, to grow old. He dared to hope it might be with him, but even if it wasn't, he wanted her to have this peace. She deserved that, after what had been stolen from her. It was his small way of making amends for his unwilling silence over the years.

The vial of antidote gleamed in the metal holder. The liquid inside of it shimmered a deep blue, thick and viscous. He'd brewed it and tested it earlier in the day before sending the final confirmation to Denevah. Tonight, he would make amends.

Ettoni shivered, suddenly aware that he wasn't alone in the room. He turned, greeting on his lips. "You're early, but that's to b—," his words died in his throat.

It wasn't Denevah who stood just inside of his doorway.

It was Lord Trapinze, the head of House Corvus. Lord Crow. Beside him stood Benedetto.

Ettoni gawked, grateful he'd set down the alembic because he was fairly certain it would have slipped to the floor and shattered in his surprise. The older man stood tall and broad, muscles imposing. He may have been older than Ettoni, but was still frighteningly fit. His eyes were those of an executioner, a dead blue-grey in a craggy face.

Ettoni recovered, dipping into a cursory bow of respect. "Lord Trapinze." He nodded at the other assassin. "Benedetto." Moving across the room, he put space and furniture between them. "What brings you to my study unannounced?" he asked in mild rebuke. Had Denevah sent them instead of coming herself? Had something happened to her?

Trapinze made a clucking noise, tongue knocking against his teeth, dismissive. He gestured for Benedetto to stand at the door. "What is the nature of your relationship with Denevah?" he asked after a few silent moments.

Ettoni stifled a flinch at her name on Trapinze's lips. He did not know exactly why Lord Crow had shown up in his laboratory, but a visit from House Corvus was not something one ever wished for. "I am unsure what you mean by that question, my Lord. You know she is my adopted cousin."

Trapinze's mouth pulled down in a frown, only visible because of the silvery scruff at his neck and chin. "You know exactly what I mean by my question. Don't play the fool with me, boy."

"I fail to see how that is your business." Ettoni kept his voice carefully mild and respectful.

"She's orphan tithed to Corvus," the assassin said with a faint shrug. "Everything about her is my business so long as she's under my banner and accepting my hospitality. I'm afraid you're going to have to do better than that."

"I am her cousin," Ettoni repeated, unsure of what the man meant by orphan tithe. "We visit."

"Even with the price that Aves and Accipitus have on her head?" Trapinze grinned slyly. "You must be close indeed."

Ettoni bristled at the assassin lord's tone. "I would never betray her." He thought he saw Benedetto's shoulders jerk, as if he'd been struck.

Trapinze stepped fully inside the room. "Is that it?" he said, looking at the vial on the table.

"Is that what?" Ettoni's stomach dropped. The man needed to stop looking at the antidote. Immediately.

"The cure."

"Why have you come?" Ettoni's voice trembled when he spoke. He didn't know how the head of House Corvus had found out about his antidote to Denevah's poisons, but somehow he had. There was no point in denying it. He had a feeling that lying would be what he normally classified as an Exceedingly Bad Idea. He stepped in front of the table, his body shielding the vial.

Trapinze stopped. His mouth twisted up on one side in a smile—at least it would have been on a normal person. But Ettoni saw the expression held no real feeling. The man wore a mask to cover a yawning void of emptiness.

"You're going to want to move out of the way," the bigger man growled.

Ettoni froze. He didn't want to die. But he couldn't stop now, even if Trapinze meant to kill him. He had no choice. "You'll have to forgive me if I don't."

Trapinze's false smile spread wider, like oil across water. "Why would you risk your life for her? She's adequate the way she is. There's no reason she needs a cure."

"Except that she wants one," Ettoni answered tartly, immediately regretting it. One did not speak sharply to a man who could probably kill them twenty-five ways with an ink pot.

"Has she told you this? Herself?"

Ettoni shifted, suddenly uncertain. "Has she said something different?" He glanced at Benedetto, but the other Crow's back was a blank line to him, impossible to read anything in his posture.

"She's a girl, a child really. She can't be expected to make a decision as important as this one on her own." Trapinze shook his head in mock concern. "Denevah doesn't see the bigger picture—she's too blinded by immediate concerns."

"Such as not being able to touch a living being for the rest of her life?" Ettoni answered, fury swallowing up his fear. "She's becoming more poisonous—did you know that? The longer she lives, the more virulent she becomes! No one can live like that—no one should have to!"

Ettoni saw Benedetto's head turn, a horrified look on his face.

Trapinze shrugged one heavily muscled shoulder. "It is not a surprise." He leaned forward, though he was still too far away to strike. Ettoni stepped back anyway, his spine hitting the edge of the table.

"You would have her trade away all of her power, and for what?" Trapinze sneered. "A chance at a Match? To bear children until one of them kills her or she's too worn out to care?"

He paced the length of the table, and then turned to face Ettoni. "She has the chance to change the face of our world. And you want to take that from her and make her ordinary?" Disgust coated his voice like tar, thick and dripping. Ettoni thought he'd drown in it.

"She'll never be ordinary," he breathed. Then he lifted his chin, rallying. "And if she wants ordinary—so what? Shouldn't she determine what is best for her? Shouldn't what she wants be what's most important?"

Trapinze made a scoffing noise, his fingers moving to the dagger sheathed at his hip. Ettoni tensed, his own fingers groping for the neck of a heavy alembic. He waited for the assassin's answer.

"You're a fool."

As verbal ripostes went it was simple and direct, and probably true. Ettoni couldn't think of anything to say, and then the chance passed. Trapinze lashed out, drawing the dagger and striking in one motion. Ettoni ducked clumsily, swinging the alembic at him in a wild throw. Trapinze twisted his body and the glass bottle sailed past him to crash into the wall.

Ettoni grabbed up one of Rodolfi's large sketchbooks, holding it up as a shield. The dagger's point slammed into it. Trapinze jerked his arm back, ripping the book from Ettoni's hands. Trapinze flung the book, dagger still embedded in it, aside, and advanced on the alchemist.

He pulled another dagger from its sheath at the small of his back. Ettoni began to lob anything he could find to hand: glassware, baskets of herbs, books, a stool—all of which Trapinze either dodged or knocked away with barely an effort. Each step the Crow took brought him closer and closer to stabbing that knife into Ettoni's body.

Ettoni didn't think he was wrong to not want that.

"Why are you so afraid of letting Denevah make her own choice?" he rasped, breathing hard. He'd nearly reached the window; soon his back would be against the wall and there would be nowhere else for him to go.

"I don't believe in wasting the gifts we've been given," Trapinze said in a voice with a pull like the tides.

"It's not a gift," Ettoni insisted, taking another step back and wishing he had a better weapon than his words, or that he'd learned how to fight. He dodged to the right, trying to get around Trapinze's body, but a slash of the dagger brought him up short. "You might feel differently if you were the one with such a gift as you call it."

He heard low voices at the threshold. Denevah stood there, arguing with Benedetto. The younger Crow had a hand wrapped around Denevah's upper arm preventing her from entering the room, and he spoke rapidly in her ear.

"Such fuss," Lord Trapinze said, reaching out his hand to take the alembic filled with the poison's antidote, "over something so unimportant."

"I don't think it's unimportant at all." Ettoni said those words with all of the surety inside himself. Nothing to do with Denevah would ever be unimportant.

Trapinze didn't touch the vial of antidote, his hand hovering close but never reaching the slim neck. "And you're the only one who knows how to distill this potion?"

Ettoni nodded firmly, unashamed. "Without me, there will never be another." The Diluvians had made their deal with him and had given him just enough of their venomous magic to distill a cure.

Denevah shoved past Benedetto finally, forcing her way inside the laboratory. "Stop it!" she cried, face furious, her hand going to the long dagger strapped at her side.

Trapinze turned his head to look at her. Seeing his chance, Ettoni shouldered past the assassin, intent on getting to Denevah. He had just cleared the man when he felt Trapinze's calloused hand fall heavily on his slim shoulder.

"Den, the vial," Ettoni began, pointing at his worktable.

Pain sliced through him, a wickedly hot burning that left him open mouthed and panting with shock. He fell forward, legs dead weight. He saw Denevah's face go pale. Her scream echoed in the cavernous space of his skull. The dagger plunged into him again, higher this time. Ettoni gagged in agony.

Denevah's arms came around him, turning his fall into a controlled slide to the floor. He felt blood pour down his back, until it reached a certain point, and then he couldn't feel anything at all. He thought he should be worried about that, but he couldn't draw in air to breathe.

He opened his eyes, not even realizing he'd closed them. Denevah's gloved hands held his head, her thumbs resting against his cheekbones. Violet eyes bright with unshed tears, she called him. "Toni? Can you hear me?"

He managed a weak nod. He couldn't get enough air in to speak. Ettoni gazed up at Denevah's face, Benedetto a looming dark presence behind her. The Crow looked angry and confused. Ettoni found he liked looking at Denevah more.

Suddenly, he wanted to laugh at the unfairness of it all. They'd been so close! But Ettoni knew that Lord Trapinze would never allow Denevah to swallow his potion. The Diluvians were cunning creatures, far more dangerous than even he'd imagined. The deal he'd made with them spun out in his memory: a life for a life. He'd given up a span of his own lifetime for the opportunity to give Denevah hers.

But the water dragons had never promised she'd be able to take the antidote.

He was such an idiot. The Diluvians had never intended for her to be cured.

A tear splashed onto his cheek. Denevah's tears were finally falling, spilling over her lower lashes like water over a fall. She gasped as the tear hit his skin, brushing it away clumsily in her haste. Ettoni reached up to take her hand. There was no need to worry now. Her tears couldn't hurt him.

Not anymore.

CHAPTER TWENTY-EIGHT

Tugging off her gloves, Denevah gazed down at her bared hands—
a sight rarely seen. Always covered, always shuttered away. She
hadn't known it wasn't normal to go gloved everywhere until
recently. Turning her hands over in her lap, she noted the changes
to them: she had calluses now from holding weapons, not garden
tools; one fingernail was black with a bruise, and a mixture of old
and new knicks and cuts marred the once pristine skin. Denevah
appreciated the differences.

Her body too had transformed. Gone was the girlish softness of
idleness. She had defined muscles in her arms and calves, on her
abdomen and across her back. She was—perhaps not strong, but
growing stronger. For the first time in her short life, she felt
capable of doing more than picking flowers and gathering honey.
This too, she appreciated.

Thought the price she'd paid for it felt far too high.

She began to dress in her garb for the evening's activities: black
pants, black jacket, and a black hood to cover her nearly white hair.
Knives tucked away in boots, in arm sheaths, at her waist and back.
A purse, heavy with coin tucked into the interior folds of her

jacket. She hadn't spoken with Ettoni about her plans yet, but she knew she couldn't stay in Aerie after her cure. There would be nothing keeping her here and a number of good reasons to go. Her plan was to take ship to the Ostvian Imperium and make her way into the interior of the country. She wanted to get lost and never be found.

Once equipped, Denevah set aside the few books she had. Her father's journal and his notes on the Diluvians had already been returned to Ettoni for his own research. She'd found nothing in it besides a mention of the fourth Diluvian, Am, and a great betrayal. She could find nothing else that piqued her interest like that one question, but she was no closer to finding an answer.

Dusk came and went, then night. Denevah slipped out her window and climbed to the roof before making her way to her father's old palazzo. She saw a few Shrikes on other rooftops, but Denevah ignored them. The rooftops were the assassin's highway in Aerie, allowing them to move about the city without needing a boat or leaving a trail. Most people failed to look up, Benedetto had told her, and Denevah had realized it was true the more time she spent outside of her father's house. With the fall of night, Crows could move virtually unseen and unheard throughout the city.

It made avoiding the Aves eyes that hunted for signs of her that much easier.

Denevah found her usual foot and handholds in the façade of Rodolfi's—now Ettoni's—palazzo as she climbed down, and slid through the unlocked cellar door. She smiled as she entered the kitchen. Cook had left out a plate for her again. She must do that every night, just in case Denevah came by to see Ettoni. Denevah wondered how many mornings Cook walked in to find a disappointingly full plate.

With that in mind, Denevah picked up a piece of thick brown bread and drizzled some of the apiary's honey over it. Wolfing the snack down, she took a piece of cheese, dusted with the herbs she needed to eat it, and swallowed that too. She hoped that this small thing would make Cook happy come morning.

As she climbed up the winding stairs, past flights that led to rooms she knew as well as the lines on her palm, Denevah heard the sound of voices drifting down from the workroom at the top of the palazzo. Ettoni, certainly, but she couldn't make out the others. She hurried up the rest of the curving staircase.

She drew up short when she crested the final rise. "Benedetto?" she asked, confused to see the Crow standing guard in front of the workroom door. Her heart sank like a stone. "What are you doing here?"

He looked torn, like he didn't know what he should do. She peered around him to see inside the room. "Is that Lord Trapinze?" Cold prickles broke out along her flesh. What was the master of assassins doing here?

Denevah moved past him, but Benedetto caught her arm, pulling her back. "You can't go in there," he said, a dusky flush of guilt deepening the color in his cheeks.

She stepped back, arching an eyebrow. She had to remain calm. "Oh, really." Her words came out flat, unamused. Denevah looked at Benedetto's hand, still on her arm, and then back up at him. He hastily removed it. "Last time I checked, I was more welcome here than you."

"Why are you so afraid of letting Denevah make her own choice?" came Ettoni's voice from inside the laboratory she still thought of as her father's.

"You told him?" Denevah accused, betrayal making her chest tight with hurt.

She heard Trapinze's response to her cousin's question. "I don't believe in wasting the gifts we've been given."

"I had to," Benedetto whispered. His dark eyes pleaded with her to understand.

"You had to." Denevah met his gaze with a furious glare. "You *had* to." She heard Ettoni say something else to Lord Trapinze, but she didn't hear exactly what. She just stared at Benedetto. "What about being my friend? Or was that all a lie too?"

That shocked a reaction out of the Crow. "It wasn't a lie!" Then, more quietly, he continued. "He's my master."

"And now I know who has your loyalty." Denevah pushed the hot burn of hurt deep down, packing in beneath layers of icy fury. Why had she trusted him, trusted anyone? Hadn't Ettoni proved that no one could ever be trusted completely? She should have learned her lesson with her father—someone who should have loved and protected her. And yet she kept trying, kept waiting to see if this time it would be any different.

"I didn't know that we," his gaze found hers again, but he looked away quickly, "that he was going to—"

"You're not that stupid, Benedetto. And neither am I." She could hear the sounds of struggle. "I'm going in there." She pulled off one of her gloves. "You really don't want to get in my way."

Denevah did her best not to feel disappointment at the fear that flooded Benedetto's eyes at the sight of her bare skin. She brushed past him. He did not stop her.

That hurt too.

She didn't have time to dwell on that though. Trapinze stood with his back to her as he herded Ettoni against the wall. His dagger was out. The master assassin hadn't struck yet, which meant there might still be time to diffuse the situation. If Trapinze had truly wanted Ettoni dead, the alchemist wouldn't have seen him coming.

Trapinze stretched out his hand, reaching for something. Her gaze went to the vial and she nearly gasped. That must be her antidote. Had Toni really managed it? Could she really be this close to a normal life?

"Stop it!" she shouted. Both men's heads swiveled in her direction.

"Den, the vial," Ettoni yelled as he shouldered past Lord Trapinze. He only had eyes for her so he didn't see the Crow's arm draw back, knife poised to strike.

But Denevah did. "TONI!" she screamed as the blade slammed into his back. Her cousin made a surprised grunt and pitched forward.

Trapinze twisted the dagger's handle once before pulling it out and stabbing again. Blood flew as the blade flashed up and then down. Toni stumbled. Denevah caught him in her arms. His mouth gaped wide in a silent scream.

Red obscured her vision as she lowered him to the floor. Her heart beat so fast she thought it would crash its way through her chest. Blood poured out of him from the two stab wounds, one close to the small of his back, the other near a lung. Ettoni gasped for breath as she settled his head onto her lap.

"Toni? Can you hear me?" His face blurred as her eyes filled with tears. She clutched at him with fingers gone clumsy in desperation.

He nodded weakly. One of her tears fell on his naked cheek. She scrambled to wipe it away with her gloved hand, but Ettoni stopped her. He held her bare hand in his, gaze abstract with pain.

"I can't feel my legs."

His words smashed into her like an arrow from a crossbow. She didn't think she could hurt any more than she did, and yet she kept on being surprised. Pressing her hands to one of the wounds in his back to slow the bleeding, she strangled out, "Toni."

"It's all right, Den." His voice was low, but full of such love for her that it made everything inside of her clench in pain and longing. "It was worth it."

She bowed her head over his face, feeling the heavy weight of tears at the back of her throat. "How can you say that?" she whispered. Denevah felt a presence at her back, but ignored it. Benedetto.

Ettoni gave her the sweetest smile she'd ever seen on a human face. "Because it was for you."

Denevah's shoulders shook with her silent sobs, tears slipping out between closed eyelids. Ettoni didn't deserve to pay for her mistakes. It should be her on the floor, leaking her life's blood out in crimson pulses. Not Ettoni. Never Ettoni.

A gentle hand caressed her cheek. Denevah opened her eyes, shocked. Ettoni gazed up at her in wonder, a smile still on his lips. "What are you . . .?" she murmured.

"I love you, Denevah." He took a deep, rattling breath. "I always have." He swallowed thickly. Pain shuddered through him, his upper body shaking while his lower half remained disturbingly still.

"I only wish I'd told you sooner." His words were coming slower, haltingly, as he fought to breathe. "I wish I could have kissed you."

"I knew," she whispered, because what else could she say? Before Cyngare, before her father, and the Crows, there had always been Ettoni.

Carefully Denevah lowered her head to his. She saw his eyes widen briefly before slipping closed just before her mouth met his in a gentle kiss.

His mouth was warm. He tasted of blood and fear and pain. Denevah slanted her lips over his, feeling him sigh against her. She pressed and held there for a long moment before pulling away. Ettoni's eyes remained closed, but he smiled still.

Benedetto's hand rested on her shoulder, offering comfort she didn't want, but she didn't shake him off. Denevah sat with Ettoni cradled in her arms, bloody hands stroking through the dark waves of his hair. Her tears had dried on her cheeks. She sat with her oldest friend, with the boy she might have loved first, with the only family she had left, and she waited.

A shuffle of sound jerked her head up. Denevah's eyes narrowed as she fixed her gaze on Lord Trapinze, standing beside the worktable, the vial of antidote in his hand. Her muscles locked up with her need to launch herself at him, but she managed to stay still.

"Such fuss over so small a thing," he said, raising the vial to his eye so he could peer at it.

"Put it down," Denevah rasped. She felt Benedetto squeeze her shoulder in warning, but she didn't care.

"Certainly." Lord Trapinze upended the vial and spilled the contents on the floor.

A growling snarl filled the room and it came from her. She thought she'd known hatred before—she'd hated Rodolfi when she'd found out what he'd made her—but what she'd felt then had been nothing in comparison to the feeling that pounded through her like a wave hitting the beach. At least her father had a reason for what he'd done, however misguided and wrongheaded.

That was Ettoni's life's blood Trapinze had spilled. Twice.

It would not stand.

Denevah didn't care that her hopes for a normal life had just been splashed on the floor like so much waste. Rage filled her at how disdainfully Trapinze had dismantled the work of Ettoni's life. How he'd dismissed him, as though he meant nothing.

Gently, she slid her knees out from under Ettoni. He had lapsed into unconsciousness, though his breath still sawed in and out of him painfully in shallow gasps. She set him back down on the floor, wishing she had something to make his last minutes more comfortable, that she could do more for him.

But Denevah's skills had never been in healing. She'd always been meant for death. And she was going to deal it now.

Tonight, Denevah would earn the name Bella Muerta.

"Denevah," Benedetto began, a warning in his voice.

She cut him off. "Watch over my cousin. It's the very least you can do."

The assassin ducked his head in shame before he knelt down beside the prostrate alchemist. Denevah blew out a breath. At least she didn't have to worry about him.

Pulling the other glove from her hand, she faced Trapinze. He was better than her—this she knew. She couldn't hope to beat him in a fair fight. Good. Denevah had no intention of actually fighting fair. She pushed up her sleeves, revealing the pale flesh of her forearms. She just had to stay alive long enough to touch him. And the more he hit her with his dagger, the more her blood would flow. All she had to do was stay out of his way until he dropped.

"You think you can take me?" Trapinze's voice sounded detached, clinical. His eyes were cold, chips of ice inside a body carved of the stuff. He had no feeling left in him.

Denevah took a small throwing knife from the holster of them she wore across her back. Never taking her eyes from his, she dragged the blade over the skin of her arm. Ribbons of scarlet streaked her pale flesh. She was ready.

She flung the knife at Trapinze's head. He dodged, and then bounded forward, his own blade slashing on the diagonal across her chest. Denevah leapt backwards, hand already reached behind her to grab another set of throwing knives. As she did so, she swept her other arm out, sending out spatters of blood in an arc.

That caused him to pull his attack up short and back away. Denevah fired off her knives, one-two-three, as fast as she could. She'd never fought Trapinze, not in earnest, but she knew he was far better than she could ever hope to be.

He smacked one out of the air and dodged the other two, but it gave Denevah time to close on him. She didn't need to stab him, just touch him or hit him with her blood. She spun, flinging out her bleeding arms. More blood flew. She saw a few drops land on his clothes but she'd missed his face, the only part of him that wasn't covered.

Trapinze recovered quickly. He went low, leg kicking out as he spun around to sweep Denevah's feet out from under her. She crashed to the floor, flipping into a roll to get back up. Trapinze moved after her, dagger slamming down toward her chest. Denevah raised her arm in a block, catching his forearm against hers. Her teeth clacked together from the force of stopping his blow.

This close she could see the grim determination in his eyes. He felt no remorse for what he'd done. As with everything he did, killing Ettoni had been a calculated strike. To expect him to be sorry for it was akin to asking a bird to be sorry for flying. It was in his nature.

This close, Denevah could strike back.

She spit in his face.

"Give my father my fondest regards when you see him," she hissed.

He roared in disgust. Disengaging with a smirk, Denevah shoved him up and slipped away as he wiped spittle from his cheeks and nose. She felt a thrill of triumph—she'd gotten him. Now she just had to wait for the effects of her poisons to finish him. It shouldn't take long, especially if she could keep exposing him to her blood.

Trapinze spun, his fist cracking into her cheek on a vicious backswing. Denevah slammed into the worktable, rocking it. Staggering back, she realized her mistake almost immediately. The Lord of Assassins hadn't truly been fighting to kill her before; he'd only wanted to disable or incapacitate her. Now that she'd struck the killing blow, he unleashed all of his skill.

He reversed his grip on the dagger and came at her, a whirlwind of punches and kicks and knife slashes. Denevah skipped and dodged and ducked out of the way as best she could, blocking what she couldn't. More blood flew from slashes on her arms that she hadn't made, each of Trapinze's strikes opening up new wounds. The top of her thigh burned from one long gash, her forearms open and bleeding in half a dozen places.

Her breath rasped in and out, great gasps leaving her as she tried to recover. Trapinze didn't let her. He pressed closer, the blade in his hand the stuff of nightmares. Denevah's lessons with Benedetto came back to her and she began to chuck whatever she could find at him: papers, books, glass vials. Glittering shards and torn pages soon littered the floor. She kicked a stool over as Trapinze lunged, hoping to tangle his legs, but he evaded.

Then Denevah stumbled. Her boot heel hit a box of alembics that hadn't been stowed completely beneath a table. Off-balance, her arms pinwheeled as she tried to keep her feet. Time seemed to slow down: Trapinze pushed forward, arm up, the dagger's point dragging down towards her unprotected chest. His eyes were a blazing blue, feral light shining in them as he came in for the kill. Denevah couldn't hope to get her own blade up in time.

The shocking sound of steel locking with steel drove the breath from her lungs in a surprised gasp. Benedetto stood in front of her, his two daggers crossed in a block, holding Lord Trapinze's blade at bay. The Lord of the Crows stared at his favored assassin in shock, a shock mirrored on Benedetto's own face, as though he had surprised even himself with his intervention.

Denevah recovered her balance in the split second of time Benedetto's interference had bought her. From over his shoulder, she caught Trapinze's snarl of disapproval.

"Step aside, Benedetto," he growled, eyes gone cold and narrow.

"Afraid I can't do that, my Lord." Benedetto spoke matter-of-factly, his voice that familiar drawl, as if he betrayed his master every day.

"Are you forgetting who owns you? Who saved your life and took you in? Who gave you food and clothes and a place to sleep? Who trained you?" Trapinze's nostrils flared with his rage. Benedetto's defection seemed to affect him far more than Denevah's refusal to fall in line with his plans for Crow ascendency.

Denevah could see the strain in Benedetto's arm muscles as he struggled to hold back Trapinze's dagger. But his voice betrayed nothing of his effort. "You don't own me any more than you own Denevah. You mistake obligation for ownership."

"Where do you think you'd be without Corvus' orphan tithe?" Denevah could see the bunching of Trapinze's muscles as he tried to force Benedetto's block to yield.

"Probably dead." Benedetto met Trapinze's gaze. "But that doesn't mean you own my future any more than you own my past."

"You would throw it all away for her? What, you think she'll have you after you betrayed her? You think she's worth it?"

Benedetto said simply, "She's my friend."

Denevah's breath caught in her throat. A friend. Memories of the three of them--she and Benedetto and Savino—all huddled together in the House of White Feathers, gathering in Savino's apartments in his palazzo, the three of them watching each other's backs in unfriendly territory.

Friends. She had friends for the first time in her life.

Trapinze disengaged with a twist of metal. He drew his second dagger and faced off against both of them. "Then you can die with her."

Denevah drew two more throwing knives, holding them in her off hand. She had no idea how to fight two-on-one; she feared she'd get in the way. But Trapinze didn't give her much time to think, instead launching his own double-pronged attack at them. He seemed to have no problem splitting his focus.

Until a cough shook him, causing him to miss a strike at Benedetto's throat. The dark assassin looked startled, his gaze sliding to Denevah. She nodded, a grim smile stretching her lips.

Realizing that Denevah's poisons were working fast on him, Trapinze redoubled his attacks while he still had the strength. Benedetto's upper arm bled from a deep gash, and blood dribbled from Denevah's cheek from barely parried strikes. Even with the two of them they could barely fight Trapinze to a standstill.

A kick to Denevah's wrist sent her dagger flying from now-numbed fingers. Trapinze followed the slash with a brutal knee to her midsection. She folded around the point of pain, unable to do more than gasp for air. A hand grabbed hers, yanking her out of the way of Trapinze's knife that would have plunged into the back of her neck.

She stumbled into Benedetto, her bare hand locked with his. She sucked in a heaving breath, eyes watering. "Detto?" she whispered, staring at their joined hands.

CHAPTER TWENTY-NINE

He'd reacted before he could even think of the consequences. It was automatic. Benedetto reached out and grabbed Denevah's hand, and yanked her out of the path of Trapinze's knife. It was only when bare skin touched bare skin that he realized exactly what he'd done.

Denevah gaped at their joined hands, both bare. "Detto?" Her voice quavered with uncertainty, almost like she couldn't believe their Diluvian-cursed luck.

"Eh," he answered with a shrug, but he knew Denevah could see the terror in his eyes that belied his casual words. "We all gotta go sometime."

Lord Trapinze began to laugh, an ugly sound broken by hacking coughs. "Try to save her and she kills you." Blood bubbled and burst on his lips, turning his toothy smile into a crimson mess. Benedetto bared his own teeth in response.

The master assassin lashed out once more, determination overriding his body's weakness. Benedetto met him with his daggers, moving to block him from getting to Denevah. They fought, blades turning to slashing blurs. Benedetto felt Trapinze's knife open several more cuts in his arms, but he didn't care. The man grew slower as Denevah's poisons did their bloody work.

An unlucky strike, and one of Benedetto's daggers went flying from his hands. Trapinze followed up, his speed still a fearsome thing, and Benedetto knew he wouldn't be able to block this strike with only one knife.

A small blade flew past his face, scoring his cheek. He'd forgotten that Denevah still held one of her throwing knives. As Trapinze doubled over in a coughing fit, her knife sheathed itself in the side of his neck. He gave an aborted gurgle as he clawed at the blade's hilt, falling to his knees.

"Nice throw," Benedetto gasped, putting a hand up to his grazed cheek.

"That wasn't where I aimed," she replied, her breathing shaky. She glanced at the ever widening pool of blood beneath the lord of House Corvus, and then looked away quickly, swallowing hard.

Benedetto didn't pay Trapinze any further mind. The man wasn't getting up from a knife to the throat. "In the future, never admit it," he said, slumping against the table. He felt scraped thin. There was too much in his head to process.

He caught Denevah's eye. She stood covered in blood, most of it her own "How long do I have?" he asked, unable to hide the fear that made his voice shake.

"I'm not sure." She bent down to check on Ettoni. Then she sat beside his body, her head bowed in grief.

Benedetto swallowed, unable to parse everything he felt. He hadn't meant to hurt Denevah, and he certainly never meant for Ettoni to end up dead, but he'd be lying to himself if he said he hadn't suspected what Lord Trapinze would do to the young alchemist. His gaze fell to the blue antidote soaking into the wooden floor. This mess was his fault. If there was a way he could have avoided it, he didn't see it right now. He'd made his choices and this was the outcome.

Maybe dying was his payment for those choices. His penance.

Or maybe it was just his terrible luck. Either way, it amounted to the same thing.

He didn't want to die.

His gaze traveled around the room, lighting on a short sword that hung on the wall among a few other House Aves trinkets. Benedetto raced to it and took the sword from its fastenings, a desperate idea forming in his head.

"I need a belt. Or something I can make a tourniquet with," he ordered, hoping to snap Denevah out of her grieving. Benedetto stepped over Lord Trapinze's body without a second glance. The man who'd taken him in, who'd given him purpose—who'd made him a killer—was dead. He would mourn later. If he got a later.

Her head jerked up at his words. "What are you doing?" she asked, even as she scanned the room.

"How does your poison work?" He rummaged through drawers and shelves as he spoke. "Does it travel through the body slowly? Can we maybe head it off?"

"I have no idea." She watched as he pulled out a length of rope and a metal rod from Ettoni's laboratory supplies. She climbed slowly to her feet. "I don't understand."

He dumped everything he had on the table. "I don't want to die and I'm pretty sure you don't want to be the one to kill me." At least he hoped that was the case. Benedetto looked at the drying antidote. There wasn't enough left for either of them, but even if there had been, Denevah had prior and better claim to it. He took a deep breath before plunging on with his idea. "I'm going to need you to cut off my arm."

"What?!" She stared at him, jaw slack in her blood spattered face. "Are you insane? I am not cutting off your arm!"

"Denevah, I don't have time to argue. I don't know if this will work, but it's the best solution I can think of. If I don't do it, I'm dead for sure, and neither of us want that. I know I sure as Diluvians don't. I'd rather risk it."

"You're asking me to cut off a piece of you! And you could still die." Denevah took a step back from him, shaking her head.

"I trust you." He stared into her face, taking the measure of what he saw there. "Do you trust me?"

Denevah stilled, hands outstretched as if to push him away. Her violet gaze met his dark one, her expression full of the horror of what he was asking her to do. He wished there was someone else to ask, but it was just the two of them. He needed her to try.

Her gaze slid to Ettoni's still form. Benedetto saw her jaw clench, the muscle jumping beneath her smooth skin. Slowly she nodded her head. "Yes."

Benedetto smiled, the swell of feeling at her words like a gift to him. "Then do this for me."

Denevah took a deep, steadying breath and let it out slowly. "Okay. What do I do?"

He instructed her on how to tie the ropes and use the rod to tighten them when the cut was done. Once that he finished, Benedetto handed her the sword and shoved everything that still remained on the worktable onto the floor. Then he set his arm down on it and looked at Denevah.

"Here," she said, handing him a leather belt she'd found. "You're going to want to bite down on this." Denevah waited while he settled himself, and then asked, "Are you sure?"

A single nod was all the answer he could give to her. Benedetto pointed at where she should cut. He didn't know if this would save his life, but it was better than coughing up his lungs while his insides liquefied like Trapinze's were doing right now. Benedetto had watched Vitarro die, had witnessed Grimauldi's painful demise. Now his master had succumbed. He did not want to die like that. Either way, this was better.

Denevah unsheathed the sword, testing the blade. It was sharp, even Benedetto could see that. She glanced at him, eyes full of sadness. The leather strap clenched between his teeth kept him from speaking, from reassuring her that this was the only way. He wished he could do it himself, but he knew he was going to pass out from shock and he wouldn't be able to get proper leverage.

At least it was his off-hand.

She took a final steadying breath. "On three."

Benedetto nodded again, watching as she raised the sword above her head. He forced himself to keep his eyes open.

"One," she began in a soft voice that only shook a little. Benedetto swallowed around the fear that clotted in his throat like blood. "Two."

The sword swept down and agony followed in its wake.

CHAPTER THIRTY

Vermillion was as good as her word. She sent a meeting time and place with Lucian. Savino was a bit worried without Benedetto or Denevah behind him, but they were both engaged that evening and the Rook wasn't willing to pass up such an opportunity. He was so close to catching the street preacher and finding out what all of his nonsensical prattling meant, he could nearly taste it.

He made his way through the sparsely traveled early evening streets. The heat of the day lingered, making his shirt stick unpleasantly to his back. Savino was familiar with the location of the meet—a simple public house near the Floating Market. He'd never been inside of it, but had seen it during his forays. It was always busy, and the people frequenting it were more day laborers and weary husbands than mercenaries or criminals. Savino left a note detailing his whereabouts with Kinendra just in case something happened to him. She would pass it along to Benedetto when the Crow returned from whatever errand he had to run.

A sharp point dug into his back, pressing into his jacket above his kidney. "Don't make a fuss," a deep voice said next to his ear.

"I hadn't planned on it," Savino said, noticing another man behind the first. Both were large, well-muscled, and better armed than he was. One was bearded, the other clean shaven, and their clothes were of hardy materials like most tradesmen wore. Nothing seemed strange or out of the ordinary about them.

"What do you want?" he asked as the one with the knife pressed it closer to get him to move forward.

"There's someone who wants to meet you," the bearded man answered, while the one with the knife gave him another poke to keep him moving.

"We shouldn't keep them waiting," Savino said mildly. He'd expected something like this, considering the secretive nature of The Shrike. He went along quietly and without fuss, as he wanted this meeting.

The men led him to a dilapidated palazzo. The brickwork façade crumbled in spots, the steps had been swallowed by the canal. Inside, the place smelled of damp and rot. It had once been a fine home, but looters and the elements had all taken their toll. Wallpaper peeled from the wall, dark with mold.

He followed them up a winding stairway that listed heavily to one side. It was a miracle that a quake hadn't taken down this palazzo. Savino's foot nearly went through a rotten board, causing him to stagger. The bearded guard hauled him up by his arm, setting him on the solid ground of the landing.

"In there," he said, shoving Savino towards a closed door on that flight.

Straightening his coat, the Rook opened the door and stepped inside, accompanied by the two guards. His words of greeting died on his lips.

The street preacher stood in the center of the room, that unsettling serpent's smile on his face.

Savino studied Navolio, noting his body language. The man's manner was relaxed, his posture easy and comfortable. The preacher controlled the situation and he knew it. He stood in front of a chair, its wooden frame warped and its fabric rotted away in places. From his arrogance, Savino would have thought it was a throne.

Savino glanced at the two men flanking him, but knew that the bigger threat stood before him. Sweat beaded his palms, trapped as they were in the leather gloves he wore.

"This is most unexpected," Savino said, forcing his voice steady. Benedetto and Denevah were each busy with their own affairs and wouldn't be coming. He wondered how long Navolio had waited for this opportunity to get him alone. And how he had known his usual security detail would be unavailable?

Savino didn't want to think it could have been Benedetto, and especially not Denevah, who'd betrayed him. He'd grown used to the two of them having his back, grown used to their presence in his life, grown used to relying on their protection. He was alone now and no help was coming. He'd have to deal with the preacher himself.

He had to bite back a smile. He'd always wanted this. Would he be enough on his own?

Navolio chuckled, bony fingers tapping his upper arm. "I doubt that," the preacher replied.

"Am I to assume you're The Shrike?"

Navolio chuckled. "No, I don't hold that title. Although one of his little birds told me that you offered a deal to him."

Savino felt the blood drain from his face. Had it been Lucian? Or Vermillion? He kept silent, waiting for whatever Navolio had to say next. Doing his best to remain still, Savino ran through the Ostvian alphabet backwards to serve as a distraction from the fear and excitement growing inside of him. It pulled at his guts, winding them tighter and tighter until he felt certain something inside of him would rip in two.

Nodding, Savino said, "You sent your men to intercept me."

"I did." Navolio sauntered over to the chair and sat, draping himself over it like a blanket. "I thought it long past time for us to have a friendly chat."

Savino frowned. "What do you want?"

Navolio made a humming noise—it almost sounded like approval—in the back of his throat, and he spread out his arms on the back of the chair. His shirt gaped open a bit, allowing a glimpse at the scaled and angry red skin of his chest. Savino narrowed his eyes, trying to get a better look. What had happened to him?

"You wish to see this?" He gestured toward his chest.

Savino kept his mouth shut. The manic gleam in Navolio's eyes faded somewhat. He pursed his lips. "Cat claimed your tongue?"

"You still haven't answered my question," Savino answered evenly.

"But I have." The man pushed away from the chair and stepped closer. Savino held himself still as the man grew nearer. His presence smothered him, a dense blackness that Savino had never felt before. It was like being in a room with a suffocating cloud. The heat of fever rolled off of Navolio in waves. "You made an offer of the secret to Rodolfi's daughter to the Shrikes." He shook his head. "I'm afraid that is not for you to give."

Savino met the preacher's gaze, his own hard and cold. "I merely offered the alchemist. What they plan to do with him was not my affair."

Navolio threw back his head and laughed. "My masters have a prior claim on him, I fear," the man said when his laughter died down.

Savino frowned. "Your masters?" Just who did this man serve?

The preacher's expression turned wolfish, threatening. "Do not act the fool, Lord Rook. You who have spent time with the masters' favored child."

Savino crossed his arms. Favored child? He couldn't be talking about... "Denevah?"

Navolio's dark eyes snapped with cunning. He nodded. "There is none as perfect as she."

"And you think the Diluvians are somehow responsible for her?" Savino glanced back at the patch of corrupted skin he could still see beneath the other man's shirt. Tilting his head, the Rook asked him, "What are you to them?"

He couldn't believe he entertained this man's delusions. The Diluvians were a myth, a call back to an older, more superstitious time. They weren't actually real, and they certainly didn't speak through this strange, misbegotten man.

"I speak of their coming and I pave the way. But it is Bella Muerta who will call them forth."

Savino recoiled. Benedetto called Denevah Bella Muerta. So this was all there was to Navolio? Just more of the same insane prattle from his sermons, except that now he thought to tie Denevah into his madness? Savino believed not a whit of it. The man was crazed, probably driven mad by whatever had gone wrong with his body.

"What does Denevah have to do with any of this?" Savino snarled, not liking the shine in Navolio's eyes when the preacher spoke of her.

"Everything."

Fury blew through him at the thought of this man having anything to do with Denevah. "She's just a girl, not some fodder for your misguided obsession!"

Navolio spun, the sparse, wild tufts of hair flaring out around his head. "You know nothing!" the man snapped, showing all of his teeth in a snarl. "You think that you are the one who can save this city?"

The preacher's throaty chuckle echoed in Savino's ears. "You can't even save yourself."

The blood in Savino's body turned to ice. He stood, frozen to the spot, feeling a growing unease in his heart. The two men guarding him had stepped away, leaving just him and Navolio in the center of the room. Savino glared at the man, not caring what happened to him anymore. This man was dangerous. If the Doge wasn't interested in doing more than watch until Navolio plunged the city into chaos, then it was up to Savino to stop him.

"Watch me," Savino growled, muscles tightening in preparation for a fight. He didn't care about the man's guards—if he could get a clear shot at the preacher, he'd take it.

"The one thing you had to offer the Shrikes is dead—or as good as." Navolio's smile was so wide and unappealing that Savino prayed he'd never have to see it again. "You have nothing left to bargain with. Not that there will be any Shrikes left to care."

As if to give credence to his words, a faint rumbling sounded beneath them.

Savino flexed his knees, gauging the distance he'd need to cover in order to bury the knife he carried into the preacher's throat. He began to turn his head when he felt the presence of someone at his back.

"I did warn you," a voice whispered in his ear. "We aren't called the butcher birds for nothing, my Lord."

Kinendra.

He should have known.

Pain, so swift and intense that it stole his breath, exploded in his body. Savino looked down in time to see a dagger slide deep into the side of his abdomen. He folded over the blade, eyes wide and stunned. His mouth opened, but all that came out were pained gasps.

He saw Kinendra walk over to Navolio, a pleased smile pulling at her full lips. The preacher set his hand on her wrist, his eyes burning pits as he stared at her handiwork. "As always, simply marvelous timing," Navolio said.

Savino staggered, staring around the room dully. A loud groaning filled his ears. The floor rippled beneath his feet, throwing him to the ground. He bit his lip to keep from screaming, tasting the blood in his mouth. The searing pain in his side was nearly unbearable, and every shift in the floor made him shake with need to gasp and howl.

"Quake!" he heard Kinendra cry out.

He heard running footsteps and the sound of something heavy crashing into the flight above him. The building shuddered. Savino pushed himself to his hands and knees, panting with the pain of movement. He didn't remember going down. A piece of the ceiling landed a mere hands breadth from his head, plaster pieces flying and embedding in his skin. He began to crawl towards the stairs, slowly, painfully. He had to get out of there—the old palazzo was too unstable to withstand the quake. It was going to come down on top of him if he didn't move.

Bracing one hand on the closest wall, Savino dragged himself up. His other hand clutched at the dagger in his side, trying to keep it still. Another quake sent Savino crashing down as the floor beneath him began to buckle.

"Savino!"

He forced his head up, vision swimming. He groaned, and hauled himself to his feet once more. Someone stood over the bodies of the men who had guarded him. His brain couldn't make sense of it. He sagged. Sweat slid down his face, the pain in his side making him sick. All he wanted to do was lie down.

"Savino! Damn it, you need to move!" The voice was closer now.

Another tremor sent Savino's shoulder slamming into the wall. He cried out, the jarring to his body sending bolts of pain slicing through him. Then someone stood beside him, getting a shoulder under his arm and propping him up. He looked down blearily, tears blurring his vision.

"Vermillion?"

"Come on," the young woman growled. "Luc is waiting downstairs with a boat."

"H-how—"

He felt Vermillion hauling him forward. He stumbled, balance gone, sight fading in and out. He pulled himself along, gasping with every step. His side felt hot and slick with his own blood.

"Benedetto asked me to watch out for you since he was busy. I followed you when you were taken before you met with the Shrike's men. Good thing I did." She grunted as she shouldered more of his weight. "Just a few steps more," she urged.

They began their slow way down the curving stairs. Vermillion's voice was a steady stream of breathless sound in his ear. He tried to focus on that, on anything that wasn't the burning in his side or the weakness in his body.

Another quake rumbled through the Aerie. The structure heaved and shook. Savino felt his feet go out from under him as the staircase lurched drunkenly to the side, pulling free of the wall. The sound of tortured masonry and falling wood filled his ears. Vermillion screamed, her support suddenly gone, and then he fell into nothing.

CHAPTER THIRTY-ONE

Denevah sat on a stool in the parlor of White Feathers, head in her hands. The smell of blood sat heavy in her nostrils. She couldn't seem to get rid of it. The silence pressed down on her shoulders like heavy hands. She wanted to sleep forever, but she feared what dreams might come to her in the darkness. She'd had too many waking nightmares already.

Benedetto fought for his life in one of the rooms above, surrounded by Doves and a physik. Kinendra couldn't be found, but other girls had stepped in to serve as nurses. Denevah hoped they would be able to help him. She shuddered at the memory of the sound of the sword cleaving through the flesh of his arm, and the strangled scream he'd made. It had taken a second cut to smash through the bone. Benedetto's eyes had been wild, sweat streaming down his face as she'd worked as quickly as she could to do as he'd asked her.

Cut off my arm, he'd said.

So she'd done it.

Then she'd managed to get him to a boat, pole them back to White Feathers, and call for help, hoping that chopping off his arm had been enough to stop the spread of her poisons. If not, she'd find out soon enough. The thought filled her with bitter laughter. Denevah swallowed it down.

She wondered when House Corvus would realize that Lord Trapinze was dead. Denevah could only hope that they hadn't missed him yet. That bought her a stretch of space to think. The quakes that had followed would have the city in chaos. That bought her a bit more.

She stared out the window of the parlor. The sun rose over the lagoon. The grey of dawn melted away beneath the burning candleflame of sunlight as day broke over the watery horizon. Denevah had opened the windows to help clear her head. Pale yellow beams spilled across the casement, gently touching the ornate carpet, her scuffed boots.

Her gaze rested on a leather bound book on the table at her elbow. She tapped her fingers on it lightly, noticing the drying flakes of blood pressed into her nail beds and caught beneath her fingernails. The journal held Ettoni's notes.

She'd gone back to collect what she could from the laboratory and to say a private, final goodbye to her cousin. The antidote was gone—soaked into the wooden floorboards and mixed with congealing blood. The vial contained only a drop or two. Denevah had upended it above her tongue, unwilling to think that all of Ettoni's work had been in vain. His death had to mean something.

Dropping her head to the table, she let out a bitter chuckle. He'd gone to the Diluvians, the great idiot, and he'd made a deal. For her. He'd given up his future so that she'd have one. It was so like him that if he were still here with her, she'd have strangled him after hugging him breathless. But he wasn't, and he never would be again.

It was her fault. Why did she hurt everyone she cared about?

She put her face in her hands, unable to dredge up any more tears. She'd cried rivers, oceans. Perhaps there was nothing left inside of her; maybe she was just a vast, empty desert, a sandy wasteland.

The palazzo shook. Denevah sat up straight, gaze going to the window. The rumble of another aftershock shook the windows in their panes. She stood, crossing to the window, being careful not to trip because of another tremor passing through the palazzo. It rippled the water in the canals below her, sending waves to break against the streets. It was still early enough that few people were out; most would be involved in the clean up effort.

Denevah rubbed a tired hand down her face. Her skin was tacky with dried blood. Leaning against the sill, she wondered if Navolio would use this minor quake as reason for another pointless sacrifice. She wondered where Savino was, if he'd found somewhere safe from the quake. She hoped so.

He wasn't her concern anymore. Denevah wasn't a Crow. She wasn't a Dauricus or an Aves either. She would never be Accipitus. She was a menace, a poisonous cancer that ate away at anything that came near it. Savino would be far safer without her. She put her hand on the journal. She hadn't read all of it—just enough to know of the deal Ettoni had made for her. She didn't want to take it with her where she was going. She couldn't bear to destroy it though; that would be like killing Ettoni all over again.

Savino would appreciate it. He'd know and respect the knowledge she left in his care. Let him be the one to decide whether to burn the journal or keep it for future generations. Let it be his choice. Denevah was done with all of it.

Crossing to the bookshelves at the rear wall of the parlor, Denevah took down a tome large enough to comfortably hold the journal. She made sure the title was something that promised to be as dry and desolate as a wind-scoured cliff face, a title no one would ever want to read. She pulled out a dagger—one she'd lifted from Trapinze's body, the one he'd used to stab Ettoni—the hilt stamped with the Corvus sigil, and then turned her attention back to the book. Spreading it open, Denevah cut out rectangular section of pages, making a hollow nest inside of it large enough to hold Ettoni's journal. Placing it inside of the other book, she closed the cover and placed it back on the shelf. That would have to do until she could get word to Savino about its placement. She threw the pages out of the balcony, watching as the ink bled and the paper washed away to drown in the canal.

Denevah was tired. She was done running. There was nowhere left for her to go anyway. Turning the Corvus dagger over in her hands, she tried to think of what she should do next and came up empty. There was no cure for her. If what Toni wrote was true, she was only going to become more deadly with time. Unless she wanted to keep killing people—and she knew now that she did not—there was no life for her in Aerie or anywhere else. Someone would always want to use what she was.

The blade forgets. The flesh remembers. How was she supposed to cope when she was both?

The Doge's guards were surprised at Denevah's appearance in their midst, offering herself up for his judgment. It wasn't every day that a blood spattered girl in Crow colors walked into the palace carrying the preferred weapon of the master of assassins. She warned them of her poisons, holding out her wrists for the restraints. She did not struggle.

They clapped her in irons and chains, leading her to the cells below the palace. She stood in the center of the narrow room—only wide enough for a pallet of straw—and waited. The stone walls wept water and the air was damp. The door to her cell was heavy, iron-banded oak, with a small barred window set in it for the jailers to check on the occupant. Witchlight flickered in the hall outside of her cell, but inside it was almost completely dark.

She wondered endlessly if Benedetto had survived, if the amputation had been enough to save him from her poisons. Denevah hoped so. She wondered too, what Savino would think when he heard what happened. The thought concerned her more than it should.

She didn't know how long she stood in that place, her chains weighing heavy upon her. Her body ached, her skin itched. Dried blood flaked off every time she shifted. Denevah wished for water to ease the thirst of her parched throat. She debated about calling for a guard when she heard footsteps. They rang hollow against the stone walls that made up her confinement in these cells deep beneath the Doge's palace.

The door opened with a grinding of keys in the metal lock and a creak of unused hinges. In the doorway, backlit by torches, stood the Doge. Denevah blinked at the sudden light, and did her best to sketch a bow at the ruler of all Aerie.

"I must confess my surprise," came the laconic drawl she remembered from her Match night to Cyngare, "when I was told of your surrender, Lady Denevah. And the circumstances behind it." He held the Corvus dagger in his palm. "It's a difficult thing to give credence to."

"Do you want a demonstration?" she countered, her voice cracking from disuse.

One of the guards that flanked the Doge bristled. Denevah kept her eyes downcast "Your reputation precedes you, Lady Denevah. If even half of what they say about you is true, you are a young woman to be reckoned with." His voice had lost its friendly tone. "What do you want here?"

Denevah closed her eyes, feeling the weight of the chains and her exhaustion pull on her. She was ready to be done. Done with Houses, with Diluvians, with politics and poisons and position. There was nothing left for her and no hope for a reprieve from a lonely, touchless life. "I came to confess."

So she did.

The story poured out of her: her father's garden, the Diluvians, the names of the dead. At one point, the Doge ordered a chair to be brought for him as he continued to listen to Denevah's tale of the events that brought her to this cell, this moment. When she finished, she stood in her irons, awaiting the Doge's censure.

"You have made an enemy of every house," he said after a few tense moments, "and in such a short time, too." He tilted his head, staring up at her where she stood, nearly swaying with exhaustion. "What is it you expect of me, my Lady?"

Denevah considered his question carefully. She knew what she expected, and what she wanted. "I expect you'd have me killed, Your Grace."

He smiled, a show of teeth and nothing more. Abruptly he stood, gesturing for one of the guards to take his chair. On his way out, the Doge tossed a parting remark over his shoulder. "I find it odd that someone with such a strong will would simply give it all up to my hands. Are you certain my judgment is what you wish?"

Guilt swallowed her whole. Why did she keep living when everyone she cared for was dead? How was that fair? Where was the justice? She'd tried to have a normal life, then she'd tried to use her poisons as they were meant to be used. Neither had been the right thing to do. It didn't matter what she tried—it was others who always died for her mistakes.

"Whatever you deem a fitting punishment, Your Grace," she answered, happy to be locked away in the dark once more.

She slept. Even the chains and shackles weren't enough to stave off her exhaustion forever. Denevah had just meant to sit down on the straw pallet and rest her shaking legs for a few moments; it was only when she heard the creak of the hinges of her cell door that she realized she'd fallen into a deep sleep. Denevah sat up with a series of clanks and wiped the grit from her eyes.

"Your Grace?" she greeted, unable to see who stood in her cell with the torches behind him. The Doge was the only one who knew she was here.

"Not quite," came Lord Poullo's voice from the cell's doorway.

Denevah shrank against the wall, chains jangling harshly with every move she made. "I . . ."

"Be. Silent." Poullo stepped into the cell, looming over Denevah. His florid face looked carved from stone. He stared down at her for long time. She watched him, waiting for whatever he intended to do.

The Doge must have told Poullo of her surrender. They were both Dauricus and Poullo was Cyngare's father; she supposed it made sense that he would be given the power to determine her punishment.

"I've wondered what it would be like to see you like this," Poullo began. He tried to pace, but the dimensions of the cell brought him up short. Instead he rocked back and forth on his heels, arms crossed behind his back.

Denevah stood in silence. There was so much she wanted to say to him, and so little at the same time. What good would an apology do? I didn't mean to kill your son, I didn't know I was poison, sounded less than sincere even though it was the truth.

"I wanted you dead—you and your bastard of a father." His brown eyes narrowed into a hateful glare. "I suppose you think I should thank you for dispatching him for me."

Now she did speak, unable to remain silent in the face of that comment. "No, I don't want your thanks. I didn't do it for you," she murmured. Rodolfi's death had been her revenge, not Poullo's.

His gloved fist collided with her cheek. Chains clattered as she lost her balance and hit the pallet with her shoulder, too slow to catch herself. As she pushed herself back into a sitting position, Denevah swallowed blood; she'd cut the inside of her mouth on her teeth from the blow. She glanced up at Cyngare's father and saw the disgust on his face. Whether it was because she'd spoken or because he'd had to touch her, she didn't know. It didn't matter.

Abruptly everything struck her as funny, hilarious really. Here she sat again, at the mercy of some man she barely knew. He held her life in his hands, and she found she honestly didn't care about it. Just let it be over. As long as she lived, someone would want to leverage her talents for their own use. Benedetto was right. She'd never be free. Sitting in this cell was at least honest—no matter where she went, she'd always find herself in some kind of cage.

Her laughter pealed out of her, bright as the bells at Temple Mark. She couldn't stop it, didn't even want to. Everything was just so . . . pointless. What did it all mean and why should she care? None of it mattered to her.

Lord Poullo stared at her, mouth agape. She imagined he thought she'd gone mad. Denevah tried to get her laughter under control, feeling the bubbles of hilarity bursting in her stomach. It took a few minutes, but eventually she wiped at streaming eyes and met his gaze with a heavy-lidded one of her own. She didn't bother getting up.

"Apologies," she rasped, still somewhat out of breath. Her stomach hurt, which almost set off another round of chuckles. "You were ranting?"

"You're mad," Poullo whispered. He backed up a step.

"Unfortunately, no. Madness might actually be a welcome change," she answered, trying to get comfortable on the cold stone. Ignoring the rattling clank of her chains, Denevah prompted, "You were saying something about wanting me dead?"

Poullo surveyed her with a calculating look that reminded her very much of Savino. She briefly wondered where he was. Had he heard of what had happened to Benedetto? Had he seen him yet? Knowing better than to ask these questions, she kept her thoughts to herself.

"You want to die?" His tone sounded strange, an almost scheming lilt to his words.

Denevah shrugged. "I've made my peace with it. I'm too dangerous to keep around. House Aves and Accipitus are howling for my blood—although you certainly have your own claim to stake—so I won't live long regardless, especially once Corvus throws in with them." Leaning her head back against the seeping stone wall, she finished, "I imagine the Doge will garner quite a bit of good will with my execution."

"You're not going to die."

Denevah raised her eyebrows in surprise. "Really?" At his nod, she closed her eyes. "Not interested."

"You're familiar with my second son, Savino, yes?" Poullo's voice had taken on an oily tone.

She felt her mouth pinch together in a thin line and forced it to relax. Denevah said nothing.

"He actually managed to outwit me." His voice held a grudging respect for his son. "I was not expecting that. He has the ear of some powerful people. They are watching him."

Denevah said nothing, although every muscle in her body twitched "What are you asking me to do? Protect him?"

He smiled, slow and lethal. Denevah felt a chill slide through her, like a knife sliding home in a sheath or a body. Poullo took a single step closer, and she fought the urge to scuttle away from the malevolence on his face.

"Not at all, you stupid thing. I want you to kill him."

Denevah felt the blood drain from her face. This was Savino's father. He couldn't possibly want his son dead, not after losing one already. Even if what Savino said was true and Poullo hated him, it still didn't make sense. Wouldn't Poullo want his family name to be honored by Savino's accomplishments?

"I don't understand," she said, hoping she hadn't heard him properly the first time.

"My son trusts you. It will make it easier for you when the time is right and I give the order." Poullo grimaced. "Just think of him like you did Cyngare."

Denevah flinched at the name. Her stomach heaved, and she clenched her jaw on the sick feeling in the back of her throat. She would not show this man her heart. He was not worth it.

Denevah sat for a moment, letting her mind work. Poullo knew that Savino was being protected. He knew that Savino trusted her, though how he found out about their friendship remained a mystery. If she did not agree to his terms, she knew Poullo would simply find someone else to kill Savino. If she told him she'd do the job, Poullo wouldn't trust her, but it would get her free long enough to warn Savino. They might even be able to figure out a way to smuggle him out of the city before her deadline.

It wasn't ideal. But then, none of this was. But Savino. She'd promised to protect him, to make up for Cyngare's death. She had to try.

"And if I say I'm happy to die in this cell?"

Poullo's laugh twisted around her in the dark, loud and mocking. "Nobody who fights as hard as you to stay alive truly wants to die. You're like a cockroach. I could cut off your head and you'd still find a way to live." The last word was said with such disgust, Denevah expected him to spit at her.

His eyes gleamed as he watched her, arms crossed over his barrel of a chest. "The Doge told me you might be obstinate. If you decide not to accept my offer, you won't die. Oh no, that would be far too simple for one such as you."

His grin filled Denevah's veins with ice. "No, you'll be our new executioner. Kept alive, but barely. We'll harvest your blood, your spit, your tears. Every part of you. You'll be made to kill and kill and kill before you're given your own release." The smile dropped from his face. "It's all you're good for, after all."

Her panicked heartbeats thundered in her ears. It was like Grimauldi's all over again. The sound of her gasping breaths filled the small cell. Poullo gazed down at her like she was something he'd found on the bottom of his boot. Chillbumps covered her flesh. She huddled into herself, feeling her body shiver and quake at his words.

Kneeling in front of her, Poullo grabbed her chin in his gloved hand, forcing her head up. He glared into her eyes, hatred etched into the lines of his face. "And in case you get any ideas," here he reached into his pocket and held something up so she could see it, "I'll be keeping this safe."

Denevah's gaze shifted to the pouch in his hands. She swallowed, dread nearly choking her. He held the pouch of the herbs that Ettoni usually provided for her so she would be able to digest food. Without them, she'd starve.

"Do we have a deal?"

Denevah closed her eyes as the witchlight swam in her vision. She didn't want to see Poullo's smile of triumph.

"We do."

End Book Two

ABOUT THE AUTHOR

Jeanette Battista is the award winning and Amazon best selling young adult author of The Moon Series, Long Black Veil, and The Demon's Gate series. She received her MA in English literature with a concentration in medieval studies. She loves words, weapons, and epic fantasy. She believes Tolkien's Lord of the Rings should be classified as a gateway drug. She was a technical writer and project manager before leaving the private sector to write what the voices in her head tell her fulltime. She believes raisins are the devil's mischief and that brownies should never have nuts in them. She lives and works in North Carolina.

9 780997 319736